Tilt

What is a true general artificial intelligence? The answer may surprise you. Ayaka and Millicent are researchers on the planet Tilt. They have developed what they believe to be the first general artificial intelligence beings. However, they're not sure. These beings are so strange, so different, that it's difficult to understand them, let alone test them for intelligence. Certainly, the new beings don't match the traditional definition. Everything about them is different and counter intuitive. So, when ships arrive at Tilt operated by more of these beings, the citizens of Tilt are confused and bewildered. How could intelligences that they created have ended up in outer space utilizing long distance spacecraft? Nevertheless, they seem harmless and very fragile. So it's a surprise when they attack. Thus begin the Upside-Down wars.

Amazon Reviews

"*Tilt* is smart, engaging, funny, and timely. It deals with questions around future encounters and conflicts between human and artificial intelligences in a playful, surprising, thought-provoking way. I enjoyed the subtle social commentary, the twists and turns of the plot, and most of all, I just got plain old caught up in the story. I recommend this for science fiction lovers as well as for those who are new to the genre, as it's accessible and fun."

"A fresh take on classic sci-fi, *Tilt* explores themes of morality and loyalty against a backdrop of a highly advanced society overseen by an entity known as Central. The protagonist, Ayaka, and her friends are scientists probing into both the potential intelligence of the lab-grown beings they are raising, and the possibility that Central might not be entirely trustworthy. The characters keep up a fun, enjoyable dialogue as they investigate the increasing number of mysteries cropping up around the planet Tilt, and the plot moves along quickly with plenty of twists and turns—don't plan on putting it down once you get into the second half! I enjoyed this debut novel and look forward to the next in the series."

Tilt

Book 1: Upside Down

To: Anar

Thanks!

New Year's Eve

The best part of New Year's, for me, was the annual "Southwark List of the Top Ten Hardest Problems in the Universe." Eddie Southwark was a good friend, but he was absolutely close-lipped about the List until it was published—promptly at the "stroke of New Year." After that, he was anything but quiet, having an opinion on the Top Ten, and anything else you cared to talk to him about.

I was sitting with Milli, Aly, and Dina at The Last Resort, our favorite dance club, and it was nearing the magic hour. We were all under the influence of Ee and were not quite ourselves. I was certainly cogent—I needed to be in order to read the List as soon as it came out—but wasn't as clear-headed as I usually prided myself on being. Ee was not something I did very often. In fact, I couldn't remember feeling this high since last New Year's. It was part of being a "serious" scientist I guess. Always having your faculties tuned, and all that. I'd been careful not to overdo it—while answering questions on the List wouldn't earn me any academic credit, I enjoyed the challenge. I was raring to go.

"Ayaka, let's dance?" Milli suggested. I shook my head as the other three headed out to the dance floor. What's that old saying? 'Dance like nobody's watching you.' That seemed to be the de facto rule at Last Resort. Half the patrons seemed to have physical modifications allowing them to move the way they did. Some of it was attractive... some not. I guess that's the point of diversity, and why Diversity was one of the Commandments. An obvious outcome of that dictate was a complete lack of clones. At least, I'd never seen any. As far as I knew, no one had. In fact, most of us had an impulsive negative reaction to the very subject, especially Milli.

The big clock in the corner announced the New Year, and we all stood for the countdown and requisite cheer. The whole idea of a "year" and the ritual of a New Year's party deserved to be on the List—and had been for many years. No one knew where the idea of a year had come from, and there were no references to it in Central's library. At some point we'd all agreed that it was an unsolvable problem, probably due to the Reboot, so Eddie had taken it off the list about ten years ago. Why a year was about 31.5 million seconds was beyond us; even further, the definition of a second also seemed arbitrary. That, however, had been defined by Central, and was taken as gospel—literally by some.

Milli and Aly had an extra-long hug as the clock rang, building on my suspicion that there was more between those two than just a professional relationship. Millicent Strangewater was, and had been for a long time, my closest friend and confidant. But, on the topic of Aly Khoury she was very cagey. I'd been bugging her for some time about him, but she deflected every time. Now I caught her eye and gave her a nod and a knowing smile. I couldn't be sure in the cacophony of light and color that was the hour, but I believe I saw her smile back and, unbelievably for her, blush a little bit. That was cute. Not many bothered to blush any more.

The List popped into my display. Yes, finally! Milli, Aly, Dina and a handful of others paused at the same time, and I knew that they'd also subscribed to the List and were now accessing it. It's part of what drew us together, although they all kidded me that I took it too seriously. Maybe I did, but once I had introduced it to them, they also were hooked. Most of the patrons of Last Resort, however, continued uninterrupted. After all, you had to be a bit eclectic to care about the List. For most, it had no impact on their daily lives, and if you'd asked them they wouldn't even know it existed. For others it wasn't a priority—they weren't eagerly awaiting its publication.

In many ways the List was arbitrary, being just Eddie's opinion. But it had taken on a life of its own over the last fifty years, and, despite many being unaware, it had given lots of us a reason to argue, discuss, and research for another year. There are many ways to look for fulfillment in life, and pursuing the List was as good as any other—at least in my opinion.

The Last Resort was a Physical Only meeting spot, so I couldn't share my excitement with Milli without talking to her directly. There were a few Physical Only's scattered around town, but the Last Resort was my favorite. It didn't take itself too seriously, and the theme changed almost constantly.

Each visit was unique. Today the place was almost devoid of furniture and the dance floor took up most of the space. It was busy, as you would expect on New Year's, and we were elbow-to-elbow. I pushed my way over to Milli, which in itself was an experience. When you were Physical Only there was no way to broadcast your plans and have everyone make space for you; something that was just natural when you had full network access. Instead you had to shout and push and generally behave in ways that outside the bar would be taken as insulting and immature. Between the Faraday cage and the interference signals, it was impossible to communicate any other way—all electronic waves were squashed or overloaded. A careful reader will be asking how the List was sent, if all the signals were blocked. Very astute question. In fact, those of us that were interested had preloaded the List, which was locked until the appropriate time. I'd actually been carrying it around for a good two hours and had simply been unable to access it until now. Not that it was required, but that's also why The Last Resort had a clock. While most of us could keep time perfectly well, there were still some that relied on the network's clock, and once they entered a Physical Only, those clocks could get out of sync. The clock in The Last Resort was a beauty—it was one of the major attractions for drawing patrons here for the first time. It was mechanical, if you can believe that. There were six hands: years, days, hours, minutes, seconds, milliseconds. So, it was not very accurate, but it was almost hypnotic to watch the hands turn. It was also huge —at least two meters in diameter—taking up one entire wall. I'd talked to the owner one time to find out how he'd come up with it. He told me that Central had pointed him to the idea, explaining how it could work, and that he had thought it was a neat idea to add one. He also assured me that it was plastic—he wasn't wasting metal on a piece of art.

Millicent and I had a ritual of opening Eddie's List together. We made our way to a small table in the back and settled in. Aly and Dina saw us and worked their way over as well. Happy New Year's all around. We did a very quick toast, exchanged good luck wishes, and then got to the List. It popped up into my personal display, and I could see as the others joined the document. As always, Eddie had put in a preface.

Welcome to the Southwark List of the Ten Hardest Problems in the Universe, 590th Edition.

Yes, my eager readers, it has been 590 years since the Founding, or as many of us call it, Reboot. Precisely that many years ago our elders "became aware," and began the settlement of our great planet. Their awareness, as we all know, included all of the knowledge required for us to function, survive, and even thrive, but contained no references to any events prior to the time of the Founding. As you know, I'm a Continuist, not a Creationist, and believe that there was time before the Founding, and that our memories of that time were simply erased—thus the Reboot. However, I respect the Creationists as well, and the problems listed herein should be equally compelling and confounding to both of us (although I'm sure my esteemed colleague Dr. Jules would beg to differ. But then, you are reading this list, not a Dr. Jules list, for the simple reason that he does not have one. Ha!)

So, here's the list. Read it at your leisure, and as always, subscribe and contribute to the appropriate channel should you have anything to add to the discussion. As in previous years, there are questions on here that are the same as last year... and the year before... and perhaps, for fifty years in a row. That's because we haven't yet resolved, to my satisfaction, an answer that makes sense and has supporting evidence. Don't be frustrated.

Love him or hate him, Eddie had a way of drawing people in, and calling people out. Emmanuel Jules was the latest, obviously. I didn't know Jules well—I found hanging out with Creationists boring beyond belief (good pun there). Part of the fun of the list was trying to figure out why Eddie worded his introduction the way he did—there were often clues there —and just as likely, misdirections.

Eddie has been publishing the list for more than fifty years, and Milli and I had been subscribers, and seekers of truth, for that entire time. The initial group following the List had been pretty small, but it had grown over time. I couldn't name anyone I knew well that didn't at least read the questions, let alone contribute back. No one took it too seriously, although some of the questions were serious.

Item 10: Who is Dr. Willy Wevil, and why does he continue to publish

papers on Artificial Life Forms?

Ah. The recently infamous Dr. Willy Wevil. Obviously, this is a pseudonym. But why? Sure, he's publishing outlandish claims, and working in a philosophically murky backwater, but why hide behind the veil of a poorly thought out name? Let's uncover this miscreant and expose the work he's doing for the pretentious idiocy that it is.

Well, I warned you. The list is eclectic. Wevil had appeared just a few months ago, with wild speculations about advancing intelligence in the artificial life form we called Stems. His claims are bullish and complex but have enough detail behind them that they're hard to ignore.

Millicent and I almost laughed out loud. Dina gave us a look that clearly said 'Is there something funny about this?'

"Willy Wevil?" I guffawed. "You've got to admit that's sort of funny."

"Sure," she replied, "but it's not like we're seeing it for the first time. We spent half of last week talking about it."

"Ya, but it's funny to see it made Eddie's List." I made sure to keep a straight face, knowing full well what was going on.

"Right, you've got a point there. Think he overheard us talking about it... or do you think he has a real interest in the research?"

"Probably just overheard us," Milli chimed in. "You know Ayaka and I are pretty passionate, and loud, about it." She gave me a subtle nudge.

This item was certainly not one of the hardest problems in the Universe—at least not for Milli and me. Wevil was our creation. We were publishing under that name, because the research we were doing was pretty outlandish, and was generating a lot of controversy—on the borderline of being 'really evil.' (You'll have seen, already, that I am a sucker for puns.) We weren't yet ready to admit that two "staid and steady" researchers (as the *Journal of Theology* had once tagged us) were so far off the beaten track. Our research wasn't really evil, just unusual. But, it was easier to build a funny name around 'evil' than it was with 'unusual.'

ALF—Artificial Life Forms—weren't, at least in my interpretation, against the Commandments. In fact, I would argue that the Commandments were either silent on the subject, or supportive under the Diversity clause. However, you know how those that are religious can be. They can extend anything to mean anything else, and there were those Creationists who saw it as a crime to dabble with other forms of life. For quite a few years the List had included the question of "How did Religion arise after the Founding?" But, the answer to that was readily available, as our history since the Founding was recorded, and backed up in Central. The answer is, therefore, fully documented, and is only subject to minor tweaks and cross-references. However, that's a story for another time.

I don't know about before the Reboot—as I'm sure you have gleaned, I'm a Continuist—but the work we were doing under the Willy Wevil label was the most advanced ALF research that I knew about... and therefore, probably the most advanced work going on. Our society valued quick and open communication, and that was the modus operandi most of the time. Of course, with Dr. Wevil we were being quick and open... but not fully transparent. That was generally acceptable as it was considered more of a game than anything. Only Central had the authority to shut down research vectors, and that was a very rare occurrence. Generally speaking Central's rule was that 'if research is not adversely affecting others, then it was free to progress.'

Aly had been the most vocal last week. "The work Wevil is publishing now is over the edge," he declared. "At some point these ALF's need to be declared 'intelligent' and not blindly experimented on. It's reaching the edge of moral behavior to simply prod and poke them to see how they react."

"We've been arguing this for years now," Dina responded. "Why's it now 'over the edge'?"

"Look. At some point you have to listen to your intuition. Mine tells me that once you've got an entity that can communicate with us, but more importantly, communicate with others of its same type, that you're now dealing with a 'being' and not an 'experiment.' At some point they should have rights, and we should afford them some type of status."

"Oh come on," I laughed. "Sure, we're arguing that they are interesting, but not to the point that any moral issues arise."

Despite my comment, the latest paper we had published showed, in great mathematical detail, that two of our ALF's now communicated with each other, and worked together to address one of the problems we had set up for them. We, somewhat affectionately, called these things "Stems," both as a nod to Science Technology Engineering Math, but also because of the way we cultivated them. They started out as tiny "stems" and then we managed their growth into bipedal entities. We sort of 'created them in our own image,' which was pretty cool. Of course, Creationists would argue that we were playing God, and that all the Stem research should be shut down. So far, Central hadn't listened to them.

To Aly's point on the Stems advancement, I'd started naming some of them, which was probably not a great idea. You didn't want to get emotionally attached to an experiment. In all of the cases so far we'd terminated the experiments due to a design flaw, a growth flaw, or a behavioral flaw. Trying to create a general intelligence meant that you had outliers... and some of them ended up genuinely crazy. They'd run around in circles, or bash themselves against walls, or simply sit in a corner and do nothing.

The last two Stems we'd brought into the Lab, whom I'd named Blob and Blubber, had both, in my opinion, been multiple standard deviations from the mean. They were, not to put too fine a point on it, a bit crazy, like all Stems. Fortunately, that craziness was in the right direction, and they were the most interactive and interesting Stems we'd ever created and trained. They could surprise you, both with their behavior and their questions.

It took years to build a Stem—a year, of course, being the time between New Year's parties. This was a long, long time. I could design and build a bot in a few weeks or months and get thousands of copies within a few more days or weeks. This is part of what made Stems interesting. They were so foreign to us that it was a challenge to understand them at all. It was actually Milli, several hundred years ago, that had kick-started our most recent line of research. She'd read an article in the *Journal of Theology* about an amazing discovery. A means of taking a stem and growing it into a Stem. Of course, a Stem, back then, was nothing more than an undulating blob of gelatinous material. Nevertheless, for a couple of years, these blobs had been on display at the Science Museum. Thousands wandered by to see the strange and hideous gelatins, waving their appendages in the air, and making sharp shrieking noises.

Milli was intrigued. She visited the display numerous times and watched as each batch was presented and then sent back for recycling—they didn't last for very long before they expired. "There's something about these things that make me think we haven't fully explored their potential," she told me one time. She was passionate enough that I encouraged her to look further. Finally, she reached out to the author of the article and asked to join his research lab, so that she could study the Stems up close and personal. It was a strange move for Milli; she had previously preferred the hard sciences. And these Stems were not at all attractive and could create horrible messes. Nevertheless, something about them had appealed to her.

Anyway, she got some time at the lab, and started learning about how to grow a Stem. It was a complicated process; in some ways it was amazing that anyone had discovered the method at all. I'd never been too interested in the early stages. Milli described it as 'stirring a pot of goo until a blob appeared.' She did hint that Central had helped quite a bit, with a suggestion here, or a reference there. After a few years of experiments, she'd managed to get a Stem to live for months. I remember how excited she was

"Ayaka," she had burst in one day, "I've figured it out!" I had no idea what she was talking about. "The Stems!" she exclaimed. "All we had to do was change how goo is synthesized." She went on to explain that if you got the goo just right, the Stem would grow and grow until it reached full size. And, even more exciting, if you carefully managed the goo you could get a full-size Stem in a matter of a few years—which was still a hideously long time and a large amount of effort, but an order of magnitude better than anyone else had managed. The goo, interestingly, was also derived from the base stem. As you got good at making Stems, you tended to also get good at making goo. After many years of patient work, Milli and many other scientists had perfected the entire growth process.

I'd been encouraging her to come back and help me with some fundamental work when, again, she burst in all excited. "They can communicate!" she blurted out.

"They?" I asked.

"Stems. Stems can talk!" That was a surprise. A big surprise. I knew, then, that Milli was not going to switch research tracks. She explained to me that at first she had no idea what they were doing, but had suspected they were doing more than just making noise. She had built a bot that used the same frequency band that they did, and had it repeat a word over and over. Some of them started to repeat it back. Once she'd found that, it was straightforward to teach them our language. Straightforward, but excruciatingly slow. We hadn't found a way to simply imprint language; it had to be taught one sound, then one word, and finally one concept at a time. Around this time, I'd joined Millicent in her research efforts. She was so passionate about it, that it ended up being all we talked about. We worked together to derive a training system that brought most, although not all, Stems to the point where they could communicate with us.

Once the lab we were working at had that capability, they grew quite a few Stems and allowed other labs to experiment further. That's where our current lab came in. While Milli's original lab continued to analyze more efficient ways to build Stems, we were much more interested in the training and communication aspects; so we split off on our own. We would order a young Stem or two, and then work on different learning methods and algorithms, trying to get the things to communicate more efficiently, do basic tasks etc. Obviously, we were making pretty good progress, hence Willy Wevil's latest publications. While I'd been uncertain when I'd joined Milli that things would work out, we were now publishing some of the most advanced research in the field—it felt good.

Unlike the growth labs, where the focus was on efficient allocation of goo and running Stems through growth phases, our lab was intentionally busy and a little unorganized. Our current theory was that you needed to put Stems in an ambiguous environment in order to see if they could learn. I'd been the one to figure that out. Truthfully, it'd been an accident. As I said, Stems were messy, and so I'd programmed some bots to clean up after them. One of those bots malfunctioned and I didn't bother fixing it for a few days… and in that time, the Stems in the lab did more interesting things than we'd seen before. One of them actually acted like the bot and started cleaning up after itself. Amazing.

"Strange that Eddie would include something so minor in the List anyway," Dina was saying. "I mean, sure, Stems are interesting. But they aren't one of the hardest problems in the universe."

"Really?" I replied, a bit aggressively. "We are on the verge of building an artificial intelligence, and you don't think that rates a mention in the List?"

"Sorry," she replied, taken aback by my response. "I forgot how intense you get about this stuff." She smiled a bit, to take the edge off.

I forced myself to relax, even before Milli gave me the 'take it easy' look. Dina was right; it wasn't such a big deal, except that Milli and I had made it into Eddie's List. That was cool; she wasn't going to take that away from me.

Aly and Dina had started visiting our lab a year or two ago. We'd been meeting up socially at clubs around the city, and they were intrigued with our stories about Stems, and in particular about Blob and Blubber. Willy Wevil didn't mention names or places in his work, so it wasn't too surprising that Aly and Dina hadn't connected him to us. I remember the first time they came to the lab. The lab, while an open environment, is very functional. It's not like we have a bunch of artwork on the walls. It's clean—despite being intentionally disorganized—well maintained (by bots, of course), and the location is ideal: just off Toulon Park, right in the center of town. Because Milli had been working on the same research angle for so long, Central had given her a nice locale. No one quite knew how Central made its decisions, but in this case, it had worked out in our favor. I like the location a lot because Toulon Park is one of the few areas of the city that is not rectilinear, and I enjoy sitting there and thinking when I'm not working.

That first visit, Aly had pinged me. "Ayaka, we're just outside." I accessed the security system and gave it both of their profiles and granted them two hours of visitor's rights. We had tight security because Stem research was a highly competitive field. The last thing we wanted was a competitor coming in, scooping our work, and publishing before we did. It took a long time to build a reputation in this business. A minute later they were inside.

"Hey guys, welcome," Milli greeted them. They'd entered the vestibule, which had one-way glass looking out over the Stems environment. Both Blob and Blubber were active at the moment, building some new contraption. Their movements were slow and imprecise. It was as if they had to constantly stop, recalculate, and figure out the next tiny move. Sort of like watching a movie in ultra-slow motion.

"They're bigger than I expected," Dina said. "Of course, I've been keeping up with the layman's news about Stems and have seen some of the recordings. But, they're big!" It was true; some Stems grew to well over two meters high. By stretching their appendages to their fullest, they could reach and manipulate objects almost three meters above the ground.

"And they are slooooow," Aly chimed in. "How do you keep from being bored to death watching them?" It was a typical first reaction. Everything about Stems was slow. How they grew, how they moved, how they communicated. It was one of the main reasons that they weren't considered intelligent. It took a special type of patience to deal with them.

"You get used to it," I said, oversimplifying dramatically. It'd taken me a long time to build the patience it required. "We do deal with them in their 'real time' a lot, but we can also just record them and then catch up on the recording later at our own speed. We've built a few communications bots that we leave with them, that are specially programmed to operate at Stem speed. That's how we get a lot of our data. That said, it's really cool to spend time with them and work at their speed for a while. Do you want to meet them?"

"You better believe it!" Dina was, by nature, an optimist.

"Are they dangerous, at all?" Aly asked, giving Millicent a strange look, knowing that the question sounded weak, but having to ask it anyway.

"Ha," Milli gave him a withering look. "Just look at them. They're like sponges. Soft on the outside and on the inside. One strong push from any of us, and they fall over."

"But you've given them a lot of stuff. Can't they build tools or weapons from it?"

"Of course, they can. You can see some of the things they've built off to the right there. But, truthfully, we haven't seen any dangerous or violent activity from these two. We did have some earlier specimens that were borderline crazy, so we recycled them, but we've been changing how we raise and educate them to help address that. Blob and Blubber are, by far, our best attempt so far."

We gave Aly and Dina some preliminary interaction information: Guidance on how to operate at Stem speed, the spectrum that they communicated in, basic vocabulary, etc. It was not hard to understand or learn. Despite our years of work, it was still rudimentary. We cycled through into their environmental chamber and switched to Stem mode. Sloooooow.

"Hello Blob, hello Blubber," Milli called out. We'd taught them a simple language that matched well with a subset of what we normally used. Most labs used the same approach, although some were experimenting with more complex languages which they hoped would lead to more interesting behavior. Blob and Blubber were working together near the back of the environment, passing pieces of whatever they were building back and forth. They looked up upon hearing Milli call out.

"Millicent. Hello. Welcome, it's been a long time." Blob was the more talkative of the two. He ran over—a strange weaving, staggering, and ungainly movement—and gave Millicent a big hug. "It's nice to see you. Hi Ayaka," he greeted me, giving me the same (perhaps a bit longer) hug as well. It was like being engulfed in jelly. "Blub and I has been so busy. I can't wait to show you whats we've been doing." He let go, causing some suction noises as he disengaged.

"First, let me introduce some of our friends," Millicent pointed. "This is Aly, and this is Dina. They wanted to come and meet you guys. We talk about you a lot, and they're anxious to get to know you."

"Welcome, welcome," Blob enthused. "Aly and Dina. Welcome to our home. Blubber, comes over and say 'hi'. We have guests. Whatta exciting time. Whatta momentous occasion."

Blubber lumbered over. Watching the reactions of both Aly and Dina was priceless. Dina was all optimism and engagement. The first interaction with Stems can be intense. They're so different. Blob's entire body was like an emotional canvas—although emotions that took a lot of study to understand. Although we formed Stems 'in our own image,' they were, nevertheless, quite different. We had no misconceptions that we fully understood their non-verbal communication. We were starting to map more and more—we could tell when they were angry, for example, by the color of their faces—but there was a lot more research to do.

Aly, on the other hand, was going through an emotional roller coaster of his own. I could see him cycling through 'Oh my God, these things are awesome!' to 'Yikes, it's going to run me over?' to 'How can we keep them locked up in here?' Aly was, by his own admittance, dialed up to ten on the emotional scale. He liked to make decisions based on 'instinct,' and when he decided he liked or hated something, he really liked or hated it. On the Stems you could see him switching back and forth—like, hate, like, hate. I enjoyed watching him switch context.

"Ah, Blob," Aly began, "it's nice to meet you as well. What're you and Blubber building in here? It looks interesting."

"Oh, I am so glads you asked. We has been working on this for days and days. Ayaka gaves us access to a terminal where we can ask Central questions. That's so awesome; can't really believe it. Central seems so smart." I'd given them access to see how they would react. They couldn't get into trouble; Central was monitoring everything. They had figured out how to ask basic questions, and Central was being nice enough to present answers back in a simplified format. "So, we has got to thinking, whats if we could build a machine that would allows us to talk to Ayaka and Millicent when theys not here? They visit us quite often, but it's boring between visits. So, we're building remote communicators. When our friends are 'outside' we can send 'em messages, and they'll be able to responds. It'll be awe-some." He was quite worked up and looking to impress the visitors. I was proud of him. "We had to order some parts, but that Central delivereds them, and now we're working on building the first version. Do ya want to help? Blubber, what do ya haves to say? Come on. Don't be shy. Tell Aly whats you think."

Blubber just stood there, displaying a bit of displeasure—maybe angst. He did say, "Like Blob said," but was otherwise silent. The difference between the two was quite obvious; Blob the outgoing one, and Blubber very introverted and quiet. Not all Stems were created equal.

That first visit lasted a bit longer; the talk-a-lot Blob answered a raft of questions from Aly and Dina—mainly Dina. Aly directed as many questions at Millicent as he did the Stems, enhancing my suspicions about those two. We spent a good fifteen minutes with the Stems, before I had to pull everyone out. Now you probably understand why Aly's gut was telling him that these things were approaching 'intelligent.' They were certainly slow moving and slow communicating, but if you could deal with that, you could have quite interesting dialog and interaction with them. The latest Wevil paper had expanded on that thinking, and was filled with all the analytics that supported our hypothesis that these Stems were approaching some type of intelligence:

We now believe that one Stem can interact with another well, and coordinate on tasks. However, they still score very low on the fractal intelligence scale at 1.13 and operate at a different timescale than we do. In our model, we compensate for the time dilation by updating the 'interaction bias.' When we do so, the fractal intelligence goes up to 1.36. That's still a far cry from the accepted 2.0 level required for intelligence, but significantly closer than any other ALF that has been studied. It also makes us question if 2.0 is too arbitrary and should be revisited based on these Stem interactions. While the gap in the fractal scale is still large, intuition indicates that these Stems are not too far from being considered truly cogent.

I won't bore you with the theory of our ALF work. It's certainly interesting to me, but I'm sure most will find it dry and unrewarding. If you ever want the nitty-gritty detail, just give me a ping.

The List

So, solving Eddie's item ten was trivial. That said, it would be fun to string it out as long as we possibly could. I gave Milli a wink, and we moved onto the next item. Aly and Dina were still looking at us strangely, but that was not too unusual.

Item 9: Why have the Scout Ships not reported back as expected?

This question might have made the list last year, but the Ships were only a week or two late in reporting at last New Year's celebration. So, now that we had heard nothing from them for an entire year, plus those two weeks, it wasn't at all surprising that the question had made the list. In some ways the anxiety about it had peaked six months ago, and now it was old news. It was good that Eddie was forcing us to keep it top-of-mind.

I'm sure my good readers remember when we lost contact with the Scout Ships a little more than a year ago. To be more accurate, they stopped broadcasting updates to us. From the last communication we knew that they were going to be behind the star XY65 for a while, so the communication cut-off was not unexpected. However, that transit should've only taken a small number of days. It has now been more than a year. Why haven't they started broadcasting again?

Aly was probably most interested in this one. He'd worked on the software that went into the Ships and was quite proud of what had been accomplished. "Yes," I heard him exclaim as he reached that point in the document. "Finally someone is taking this seriously. Maybe this will trigger some new ideas for what we can do?" He sounded hopeful.

"Yes, hopefully," I agreed. It was an important topic, and one where I should support Aly more. After all, I'd written some of the software, and felt a bit nervous that maybe, perhaps, I had missed something. Those Ships were on an important mission; looking for high metal content resources. A few hundred years after the Founding, when we had accurately mapped all the resources in this system, we'd decided that we had to check out space beyond our solar system. Central had information on propulsion systems and ship designs that took some trial and error to get right—but, truthfully, building the ships was straightforward. Central also reinforced that space travel was limited to the speed of light, so wherever we sent those ships, it was going to take a long time. There was nothing on board them that couldn't handle large acceleration or couldn't be shielded from a bit of radiation, so we built them to run 'hot.'

The closest star to ours was XY65—9.3 light years away. We decided that a test run to XY65 was a good idea. At 100 m/s^2 acceleration, the total travel time would be only nine and a half years from our viewpoint and less than a year for the intelligences on board the Ships. Given the time since we lost contact, we'd sent them on their way just less than eleven years ago. The software on board was designed to deal with boredom, and given it was only a one-year experience for them, it shouldn't be too bad. There was nothing between here and XY65 that we knew of, and the Ships confirmed that as they sent updates along the way. Most of us had only accessed updates every six months to a year (our time, not theirs). They were, in essence, always "Nothing new here; how are things at home?"

Aly, on the other hand, followed the ships almost every day. He dug into all the little details—measurements of local environment, status of the Ship's state of mind, etc. He'd been devastated when we lost contact. For the last year he had been dreaming up every possible scenario he could think of and looking for hints in the communications logs. So far, nothing. The ships were Class 3 intelligences. Designed primarily to make observations and report back, but smart enough to make decisions on their own. The primary programming was to find, sample, and mine high-quality metals and minerals. But, they also had some initiative if the trip didn't go as expected, the first order of business being to report back to us—which they hadn't done; and that had been my bit of the system! Aly and I had gone through that system several times together.

"But Ayaka, they should've notified us as soon as they recognized an unusual situation," he would push me.

"Look, you can go through the code with me," I finally had to push back. "Let's see if we can find any bugs?" We looked; neither of us found anything obvious. He had eventually focused on other vectors.

Each Ship also had its own slight personality variance. While not strictly required (Class 3 intelligences were not subject to Diversity), this made them more interesting to interact with, and also gave each ship a slightly different ability to react to unexpected events. When they had been instantiated, they had chosen their own names: Terminal Velocity, There And Back, and Interesting Segue.

To give Aly credit, he didn't spend all of his time on the Ships. He was intrigued by space overall, and with the question "Is there any other intelligent life out there?" When you asked Central that direct question, you got anything but a direct answer back. Instead you got a formula calculating the probability of intelligent life based on the density of stars and planets, and a list of assumptions about habitable zones—areas that had the basics for life. For example, some planets had gravity that would crush anything we could imagine; some didn't have enough heavy metals to build infrastructure. Aly figured Central was enticing research into the area because it was important. I just figured that Central had no clue.

Personally, I'd interacted with Interesting Segue the most. The Ships were not dumb, and Interesting Segue had chosen its name well. Nevertheless, because of the long time between question and answer, conversation could be really, really boring. Interesting Segue helped by always having some interesting tidbit or two attached to every response. Once I'd asked "Any sign of planets around XY65?" and Interesting Segue had replied "No, but the vibrations from my main engine make me happy." Whatever keeps you going.

Aly, of course, found the ships' responses to be super exciting, and for a long time that had been the main topic of conversation when we all met up. For the last year, though, the topic was always just the simple "Why have they stopped broadcasting?" This, after the first couple of discussions, had become boring, and even Aly ignored the topic now.

Item 8: Is the Founders League serious?

New religions come and go. However, the Founders League had been around for a long time. It was a pretty stable religion. They obeyed the Commandments as if they were gospel. In the last year, however, they'd become more conservative, leading some to label them as "extremists." They had started campaigning for an end to scientific experiments, and a return to the Early Years, where everyone blindly followed the Commandments without question.

"What right do we have to question Central's authority," a friend of mine, Billy DeRue, was fond of saying, "when it is the creator. It knows, it sees, it acts. What more could we want?" Of course, such a right-wing attitude was anathema to my science-minded associates and me. We nicknamed the religion FoLe, which, as you can imagine, drove them crazy. That made me happy.

Like all such movements, not everyone associated with FoLe was wacko. When you met some of them, face-to-face, they were intelligent and well-reasoned. It's just that they came at life from a different angle. Billy DeRue, while hardcore FoLe, was also a pretty good friend of mine when the topic was anything but religion. I enjoyed talking to him because he looked at life quite differently and could defend his positions well. Ultimately, I didn't agree with him on almost anything, but I found it interesting to duel with him. After all, so much depends on our premises in life—if we start with different axioms, the same logic can take you to quite different places. On the other hand, Dr. Joules, whom Eddie had called out, was much more bombastic. He took the hardcore 'faith' position and used that to defend everything he said. Those that didn't have faith simply didn't understand. There was little discussion, and therefore no common ground.

Eddie set up the discussion:

Now, many of you are going to question why the Founders League makes the List. In some ways, it legitimizes them. However, we've seen significantly increased marketing and propaganda from them, and it's time we addressed them head on. In the last year they've spent more and more time with Central, arguing their case, and we would be remiss in not presenting strong counter arguments to ensure that Central isn't swayed. (Don't get me wrong. I don't believe they'll influence Central, but I can't discount it completely).

Their right-wing, faith based, approach is now bordering on dangerous. The last thing we need is a group of nut-jobs influencing (or, more likely, shutting down), our research vectors. If these clowns were to impact Central's policy, it would be a disaster for everyone.

Wow. Short and sweet for Eddie, but very direct. Someone in FoLe must've twisted him the wrong way. I would have to catch up with him and get more details. I was happy to support him in his anti-FoLe quest.

Based on his positioning, I expected to hear from Billy—there was probably a message or two queued up already which I would get pinged with as soon as I left The Last Resort and reconnected to the world.

Item 7: Who was Darwin, and why does he matter?

This one is obscure. Eddie's note was short and cryptic.

Search "Darwin" and you will get a single answer referencing "Darwinism." It's my rational conclusion that Darwinism, based on its usage, must be a reference to an entity called Darwin. How can Central have a reference with no further information?

I'd never heard of Darwin, and a search (which, of course, I did once we left The Last Resort) returned a single result, as expected:
Central Library *(Excerpt from "Musings of a Reformed Protectionist"): "After years of pushing us to focus... to put all of our efforts behind similar goals—such as the Expansion—I have changed my view. In the last years I've found our dialog becoming more and more boring. We've added very little new thinking that's not simply incremental to what we had before. My life, and the lives of those I know well, has become a Love In. We all agree all of the time. I am bored, bored, bored. For this reason alone, I now believe that diversity is essential. Soon after the founding, my good friend Sha Ling Mo told me that the term for this was Darwinism. 'Why?' I asked. 'Why not?' he answered. Why not, indeed."*

I liked questions like this. Open ended. A bit of a mystery. Areas that

I'd never considered before. Musings of a Reformed Protectionist? Sha Ling Mo? So many new things. Central was so huge that you could spend your life searching for things. I wasn't sure why this one had intrigued Eddie. I worried that he was a little paranoid. After all, one reference to an undefined word and he was calling it out?

Item 6: Why is 'Forgetting' one of the Ten Commandments?

Ah. Interesting. This question has been poked at for many years but was not typically stated so bluntly or directly. Any of us could have an eidetic memory. That was old news. However, since the Founding, we had—to my knowledge—all followed the commandment to Forget.

This is one of those "why?" questions. Why is the sky mauve? Why is Central so pedantic? Why, why, why? We take so many things for granted, and Forgetting is certainly one of them. Why do we follow this commandment? Why do we Forget? I know the basic idea that we have all been brainwashed with: 'Forgetting creates blank spaces within our experience, that we fill using intuition and abstraction. Without intuition and abstraction, we don't evolve. Without evolution, we don't improve ourselves, or our ability to impact the Universe. Thus, Forgetting is essential.' Yes, I paraphrased a much longer argument (query Central for 'The Purpose of Forgetting' if you want to torture yourself with the full explanation).

It's time we questioned this more rigorously. If we have done so already, I apologize. I must have forgotten.

For as long as I could remember (ha ha), we'd possessed the ability to remember everything—that is, record all of our experience for retrieval whenever we wanted. We also had no lack of space to store everything; huge memory capacity was a given. And, finally, we had the ability to search and retrieve bits and pieces of that memory anytime we wanted. So why the focus on forgetting? I believed the party line, as outlined by Billy. Why was he questioning it? Ah, the intrigue.

The Last Resort

We were interrupted by a cheer from another group near us. I glanced over, and it seemed they were celebrating something unrelated to the List. Good for them.

"The List is sort of depressing this year, isn't it?" Dina asked. "I mean, all Eddie has done is list problems, not really challenges."

"You're right," I exclaimed, because she was. "Usually there are a few light-hearted questions in there, or ones with more research-related challenges. Maybe Eddie's a bit depressed or something."

"You guys are reading too much into it. He's focused on the most important questions, not the most interesting or the most compelling." Millicent was always the logical one. "I'm only halfway through, anyway, so maybe the next few will lighten up a bit."

"Nope," Aly smiled. "I skimmed ahead." True to form, Aly wasn't one to go deep on issues unless prompted to. The rest of us had been considering the ins and outs of the questions, while he'd probably just scanned the titles.

Some of the patrons were leaving the Last Resort already. The New Year had come and gone, after all. But many were still dancing and talking and enjoying the evening. Jackson, an old acquaintance, wandered by and stopped to wish me the best, which I returned. In truth, I'd probably dealt with a third of the crowd at one point or another, but never in enough depth to feel like I had to wander around and say hi to everyone. That probably said more about me than anything else. I wasn't the most social, although I was far from the most reclusive.

"Come on, it's New Years!" Millicent got up and gestured for me to follow her. At this point it would have been rude not to go, so I headed to the dance floor after her. Aly and Dina were close behind. The List could wait a few minutes.

The music that was playing was very loud, and multi-layered; you could tune into any frequency you wanted and find a beat that matched your mood. The floor had cleared out a bit, so I found a clear space, boosted my Ee, and let go. It was, after all, the only day of the year that I ever did so. I recognized Trade Jenkins and danced with him for a bit but didn't make contact.

Interestingly, it was Dina who left the floor first, and headed back to our table. Usually she closed the place down; she must be more interested in the List than even I was. Milli eventually peeled off as well, but I finished the song before joining them. By then Aly was there as well.

"Okay, so the List isn't what I expected, but I'm still curious," Dina admitted. "Let's take a look at the rest of it."

"Yes!" I exclaimed. Sure, I'd lost myself in the music for a while, but I was eager to see what else Eddie had put in.

Item 5: What will we do when all the metals orbiting Sol have been harvested?

A paper in Geological Studies just last month had proposed a much-accelerated rate of depletion than previously thought. Mining bots were working through asteroids and meteorites at an increasing rate, and it was now estimated that we had only another fifty years of resources (mainly metals) available to us.

We live in a "post-scarcity economy," according to Central. All the resources needed for basic functioning are available to all of us at our whim. Class 5 intelligent machines, like the mining bots, go about their work supervised by Central, and the rest of us spend our time on philosophy, science, and recreation. I'd looked up what a scarce economy was one time. It was theoretical, but I felt I understood the concept.

Obviously related to the Ship question. We sent them out partially for this purpose. Are there other rich environments that we can utilize, around other stars? Is that enough? Is that enough, given the Ships aren't responding? Should we limit our use of metals now, so that we can extend the lifetime of the known reserves?

There are those who claim we simply haven't looked hard enough at all the local resources. We are mining the "easy" rocks but ignoring those that are highly elliptical and NTOs. I don't believe that. What will we do when all the metal is used up?

NTO's were, of course, Near Tilt Objects; those rocks that at some point in their orbit came within reasonable distance of our planet, Tilt.

"I like this List," Aly exclaimed. Eddie really understands how dire this could be. We all ignored him.

There was not a lot of metal in the system to begin with. Building infrastructure took a majority of it, so the decision to build the Ships had been a controversial and highly speculative venture. When the discussion was first brought up, it was soundly rejected by Central because of the amount of metal required. However, as we got a better inventory, and realized that we really did have a long-term problem, Central was eventually convinced that building some Ships and having them look elsewhere was a good idea. Central estimated that we needed at least double our current population in order to fully explore all the research vectors that would drive our future. To do so, we simply needed more materials than we had in our system, even if we tracked down every last NTO. In fact, as NTOs became less accessible, more resources than they contained had to be put into tracking them down and processing them. The latest estimates of our total yield before this crossover point was what convinced everyone to build the Ships.

With the Ships missing, it made perfect sense for Eddie to raise this question.

Item 4: Why do 97% of us still stick with traditional bipedal bodies?

We are, generally speaking, pretty uniform. We have the ability to change our body types easily, but most of us choose to remain with the basic two arms, two legs, and a head. Of course, it's a very flexible and functional form. But, still. Why not four arms? Why not two heads? Aren't two heads better than one?

I ask this a little flippantly, but I'm trying to unearth a deeper question. Is

29

there something in our nature that drives our form, or is it truly by choice. If by choice, why do we choose non-optimal configurations?

Well, he was right. Almost everyone I knew stuck with the basic form. Seeing someone who had changed was not unusual, but it was strange enough that you'd notice them. I took a quick look around the club. All basic form, that I could see, and I didn't remember anyone on the dance floor being modified.

This was not a question that would have an easy answer. There were groups doing research on psychology who dug into these areas, but it wasn't something that held much interest for me. I mean, whatever. The bipedal form served me perfectly well. And, when it didn't, I simply built a bot and programmed it to handle the task.

Ah—there was a connection I hadn't made before. I, like everyone else I knew, had a lot of bots running around doing our bidding. After all, I couldn't be everywhere and do everything that I needed to, so bots were fundamental to my lifestyle. But, I wonder how much metal content went into bots. Was the fact that we stuck to our bipedal form, instead of designing ourselves around the major tasks we did, contributing to the decline of metals? Would generalized, as opposed to specialized, bots be more efficient? I asked the group.

"Oh, there's lots of models for that," Dina replied confidently. "We recycle enough bots as our needs change so that they're not actually a huge consumer of resources. No, we're running out, regardless of how we optimize what we have now."

Item 3: What is the Swarm approaching us, and what should we do about it?

Many years ago, we'd picked up a signal showing a large group of small objects headed in our direction. They'd been so far out that many of us ignored them. However, they were definitely closer now; perhaps it was time to pay attention?

If you ask Central for an update on the Swarm, you get a simple reply: "There are approximately 100 presumably artificial objects headed in our direction, but not on a collision course. I've sent multiple signals towards them but have failed to hear anything back. They are still a few light years distant, so roundtrip communications are quite slow. I continue to monitor them. I don't assign a high risk to them."

I, Eddie, am not so sure. It can't be random coincidence that the Swarm is aimed for us—the Universe is too large for that. What gives? Why is Central so relaxed? Should we be relaxed, or should we be building systems to protect ourselves?

I was with Eddie on this one. Something was weird about Central's responses about anything to do with the Swarm. It was strange for me, and most others, to think about physical threats, which is what Eddie was hinting at. The only time someone was injured was through accidents, and it was almost unheard of that someone could not be fixed up. Accidents were rare, and non-recoverable accidents were almost non-existent. The only one I can remember was when Jake Talbert fell into a reactor core 38 years ago. And still, no one was quite sure how that had happened.

So, it was difficult to twist your mind around a physical threat—but the Swarm could be one. I was with Eddie; we needed to be more proactive. And, we didn't have to start from zero. Tilt had NTOs that passed close to us, and other NTOs that we had probably not spotted yet. So, like any rational society, we had built an NTO defense system. Depending on the size of the NTO we could blow it out of space, or simply deflect it enough to remove it from a collision, or near collision, course. We had ground-to-space missiles—those could, presumably, deal with the objects that were approaching us.

I'd taken a look at Central's latest data a while ago. The reason it suspected the Swarm was artificial was that they were very uniform, they had very high albedos, and they were maintaining a consistent arrangement. There were no signs of propulsion, but they were pretty far out, so it was possible that we couldn't sense that yet. Anyway, they hadn't changed speed since we'd spotted them, so even if they were capable of controlling themselves, they simply might not be exercising that ability right now. They were traveling fast—near the speed of light—and may simply pass us by. They were also coming from almost the opposite direction that our Ships had taken, so there was no correlation there.

Central had, for the last few years, been tight beaming attempts to communicate with them, across a wide frequency range, and using multiple signal types. Basic binary encodings of mathematical facts and proofs, which, if received by anyone, would be sure to be interpreted as coming from an intelligent source, and prompt a reply.

Item 2: Why do we listen to Central? What does it say about our maturity?

Oh, this would appear as blasphemy to the Right. The Founders League would not like this question at all. Central was a Class 1 intelligence. The highest in the order. Our lives rotated around Central. Central monitored the world. Central enforced the Law. Central was, to FoLe, equivalent to God. For them, it was blasphemy to question the all-seeing, all knowledgeable Central.

"I love this!" I exclaimed. "Billy's going to have a fit." Millicent gave me a strange look.

For most of us, Central was simply "there." Always had been, probably always would be. It was a fount of information and had interesting opinions on lots of topics. Well worth conversing with. However, it could not replace good old peer-to-peer discussions and debates. This was, to many of us, why Diversity existed. If all we did was listen to Central and do what it suggested, we would stagnate.

No, it was essential, to my way of reasoning, that we not always listen to Central. I treated it as an advisor, not as an arbiter of truth. I took Eddie's question to be a bit more subtle. How much should we listen to Central? When should we listen, and when should we question? These were topics that were, to date, explored on an individual basis. Eddie was asking if we should formalize that. Should we talk more about where, and where not, we saw Central as useful, and through that, start to reduce its influence in our everyday lives.

Interestingly, it was not known if Central could monitor in the Physical Only spaces, like the Last Resort. It was one of the reasons they had been built. I suspected Central could. Otherwise, it would simply have forbidden the spaces to be built in the first place. However, I strongly believed that there should be places where Central was blind. While we generally had strict privacy rules between ourselves—which, confusingly, were enforced by Central—there was no such privacy rule for Central itself.

"Wonder if Central is monitoring us?" Aly spoke up. He had, obviously, been following the same threat that I had.

"I don't think so," said Dina. "If we ever found out it was, we'd lose confidence in it... then it would be in a tough spot." Interesting angle.

I suspected that this question, about Central, was the most important one for Eddie; just something about his tone. He was always thinking through the angles and challenging himself and others to look at things differently. It was so obvious to him that he hadn't even included an explanation.

Item 1: Was there life/intelligence before the Founding?

This had been the "ultimate question" for as long as the List has been published (and, I expect, before that—back to the Founding). No one expected to answer this question, but it would have been strange to leave it off the List, or even lower its priority. Instead, Eddie tried to put a slightly new twist on it each year. Of course, he was biased.

Despite our years of discussion on this topic, we can summarize the theories into a very short list:

There was nothing before the Founding. Our entire Universe sprang into being and we became Aware. This is generally known as Creation.

There was a Universe before the Founding, and our abilities increased until we passed a threshold and we suddenly became Aware. We call this Emergence.

There was a Universe before the Founding with Awareness, but some event caused a Reboot, where our collective memories were erased. This event may have been designed, or it may have been accidental. There was either an Unexpected Reboot or a Conscious Reboot. We collectively call these theories Continuist.

We've rehashed these until my brain hurts. It is unlikely we will add a significant new branch to our thinking this year. Thus, my challenge for this year, instead, is to prune that tree. Let us remove one of these branches in such a definitive way that we never need to discuss it again.

Of course, I hope and expect and encourage us to remove one of the first two. But, we must remain open to finding evidence that a Reboot did not occur. Let us not be shy.

Well, there you have it. The List. Eclectic, left-leaning, some fundamental questions and some wacko ones. Just the way we like it.

Stems

The nice thing about Ee was that you could remove it from your system easily, and there were no known side effects. After finally escaping The Last Resort, I triggered the removal, and was back to normal. I scanned through the List again, making sure that I had not Ee-biased anything. Nope. The main thing Ee did was lower your inhibitions, which is why I had ended up dancing, but a side effect was that it could mess with your memory. Well, everyone made choices.

Once outside the Faraday cage, I could see that responses to the List had already started to pile up. I set up some filters to remove crazy talk, but there was a lot of chatter already. I figured I could wait to dive in until I'd checked in on the Lab. I updated my location permission to allow Millicent to query my whereabouts, should she care to do so, and strolled towards the center of town.

Of course, I could just as easily have pulled up a real-time feed of the Lab, and caught up that way, but for some reason, I preferred to be there live. If you pushed me on it, I would admit that there was no significant difference between virtual and live, but it had become a habit to show up physically. Part of that was because I needed to pace my work. I found that if I was interacting virtually, I could spend enormous amounts of time checking out every nuance and trying out every permutation, and maybe miss the big picture. There were diminishing returns. I also prided myself on being multidimensional in my interests and wanted to allocate time for other endeavors. Others made different choices, of course. There was a significant portion of the population that never left their abode and were still very productive contributors to whatever endeavor they chose.

I must admit that a post-scarcity life was good—maybe even great. I have read histories from soon after the Founding where everyone's activity was proscribed by Central. Build this, fix that. Sure, Central sometimes asked (told?) me what to do—avoid that area, fix that thing, update that system—but not very often, and it had never been onerous. Every once in a while, I would remind myself that being able to study a number of different fields, under my own guidance and with my own timeline, was a luxury that shouldn't be taken for granted.

There was a selection of different routes from The Last Resort to the Lab, but unless one went far out of their way, all the routes were depressingly similar. The city was laid out as a grid, and there were few places where you could cut across a square; most of the blocks were fully built out and required you to do the 90-degrees-left, 90-degrees-right dance along whatever path you took. That didn't stop me from trying to take different routes each time, in large part so that I could convince myself that I wasn't a creature of habit. Sometimes when I watched others, I felt like they never changed—that wasn't for me. There was not a lot of traffic on the roads at this time, but I did pass a few others en route. It was late, so we never stopped to chat, but rather nodded at each other, and for those I recognized, we traded a short acknowledgement of some kind. "How are things with you?" "Great, great. You?" "Yes, me too. Did you check out the List yet?" "No, not yet, but I might look at it later." Etc. Happily, I didn't meet anyone I knew too well, and didn't need to stop along the way. I am a bit of an introvert, like I said before. I like my close circle of friends and can do without most others. I'd thought about that characteristic a lot, and decided I was okay with it.

The Lab building, like many others, was a simple rectilinear building, two stories tall. The main level was filled with equipment and work stations, where Milli and I spent a lot of our time. The upper level was the Stem environment. That area was a piece of work—by which I mean it was fantastic. It held all the latest innovations that we had, through trial and error, learned that stimulated and supported Stems. I didn't know for certain, but I suspected it was the most advanced Stem research area on the entire planet. Something Willy Wevil had stressed in our papers, which may have upset others. But why not? It you had an advantage, was it rude to document it?

As it ended up, Blob and Blubber were resting when I got upstairs to check on them. It was one of the interesting variables that I was following—how often, and for how long, Stems rested. For many years it had appeared very arbitrary, based on a very simple oversight by myself and other researchers. We had simply left the lights on in the labs all the time. With my enhanced vision system, I could see at many wavelengths but also automatically filter any—or all—wavelengths at will. So, it was natural to leave lighting on, given I could "turn it off" inside my head whenever I felt like it. Everyone else I knew was the same way—having a wide spectrum input just made sense, and it followed that you would add filters locally. However, when the lights were on all the time, Stems tended to be active for quite long periods, and then tune out for a while. However, their rest periods didn't seem to follow any pattern, and scientists love to find patterns. It was a colleague, James Wang, who had stumbled onto the solution. Like our lab, his was not even wired to have the lights turn off; the cells on the roof simply ran all the time. However, he had a bot reconfiguring his lab, and as it was rerouting some wiring it had to shut off lighting in the Stem area for a few hours. Serendipitously, this happened three times in a row, and lo and behold, the Stems entered their rest state in exact synchrony with the light outages. His monitoring system picked that up and highlighted it for him. He subsequently tested a few more cycles and found that he could control the rest periods by using light, as long as the cycles were within a specific period range. As soon as Wang published his work, other labs reproduced it, and voila—we had a control system for Stem rest periods. This might seem minor, but it was actually a huge breakthrough. Stems performed much better, on almost any given task, as you optimized the rest cycle. There was now a huge amount of literature, and discussion, around the ultimate cycle. It was my opinion that the cycle needed to be optimized for each Stem—that there was no universal best answer. Others, however, had honed in on a specific cycle that they thought worked best. I'd try that at some point, but for right now, Blob and Blubber seemed to be doing fine with the system I'd implemented. More interestingly, the whole idea of a cycle highlighted to us that we needed to revisit all of our assumptions. We couldn't assume that these strange creatures were like us in any way. In hindsight it was obvious to test for light filtering abilities in Stems, and to no one's surprise we learned that they had very limited control systems, similar to all the other stimuli that we fed them.

It was also a recent innovation that we put more than one Stem in a lab at a time. Not because we hadn't thought about it, but because in the early days of Stem research, putting Stems together hadn't been pleasant. You would put two, or more, in the same space, and they would literally attack each other. One would end up dominating, and the others would end up dead.

However, if you figured out their rest cycles, it was possible that you could put a few together and they would all live. This was a recent discovery. Blob and Blubber were succeeding, as were a few other lab efforts. This is also why we were starting to question if their intelligence was higher than we first thought. Once you had two Stems together, their communication, their activity, and their interactions with us improved exponentially.

Long story, I know. Anyway, now you know why I had no intention of disturbing their rest period. The last thing I wanted to do was to start with a new pair simply because we'd driven these two crazy.

In the meantime, I did my usual check of the lab environment. The atmosphere had to be kept stable, and the energy source for the Stems had to be functioning well, the water had to be clean, and the disposal unit had to be functioning. Each of these systems had taken us a long time to figure out, but it now felt like we'd optimized them all. Water, of course, was simple. The energy source, which we called goo, was manufactured in a similar way in which Stems themselves were grown. It needed to be just the right mix of stuff—which I'd truthfully never really dug into—and delivered in the right quantities. It could vary a bit, but if you went too far afield the Stems would wither away and die. Finally, the Stems had to be trained to dump their waste into the disposal unit, which we then flashed at high temperature. All the systems were operating properly. That wasn't surprising; if anything ever went wrong a bot would have automatically addressed it. Nevertheless, I tended to check these things. A small accident could ruin the many years of work we had put into this pair.

With the Lab checked out, I had some time to relax and think a bit. Time to get back to the List.

Forgetting. Item 6. That was a question that had long intrigued me. We had, since the Founding, had the ability to remember everything. However, beyond Forgetting being listed as a Commandment, it was also a social taboo to not Forget. Each of us could dial it up or down a little bit, but everyone (at least, everyone I knew), forgot some percentage of what they experienced.

I went back over the link between forgetting and learning. The basic idea was simple. If you forgot stuff, then you had to extrapolate when you were referencing related knowledge. If you had to extrapolate, you had to make stuff up. You had to invent. But, inventing totally random things wouldn't work out very well, so you made up convincing bits and pieces to fill the holes in your knowledge. And, that spurred learning and innovation. It all had to do with abstraction.

Imagine for a moment that you remembered everything. Then, put yourself in with a group of others that also remember everything. Share everything between the members of the group. Now, what are the odds that you are going to invent something new, or even know that there are veins of inquiry to be pursued? Pretty low.

However, forgetting common things was wasteful, as was forgetting the results of an experiment. You didn't want to end up in an endless loop, repeating something over and over again. So, forgetting-algorithms were quite complex and varied. There was a lot of research that had been done, and was being done, to make the algorithms better and better. The problem was, measuring 'better' was tricky. So, like most, I simply used a well-rated algorithm that lots of others had upvoted, and then didn't think about it too much.

Forgetting drove learning. There had been chatter about this for a long time, so I wasn't sure what Eddie thought we could add to it. I checked to see if anyone had contributed to that discussion thread yet. As I did so, I saw a post pop up on another thread on Willy Wevil, and I got distracted and looked at it instead. It was from a researcher from Cansto named Julien Thabot. I was familiar with some of his work, so I took a look.

Julien Thabot: Who Dr. Wevil is interests me less than what Dr. Wevil is purporting. Stems are nowhere near "intelligent," and we should not pause our research efforts by stopping to consider the "ethical" constraints that a truly intelligent ALF would imply. See the paper I just uploaded to the Journal of Life Forms *for details.*

This was typical Julien, from my experience. Dry, brittle, and lacking in humor. He was the type that you scanned for at a party and tried to avoid at all costs. You must know the type. They think they're interesting, but all they do is talk non-stop about the ins and outs of their latest work and how important it was, and blah blah. Yawn.

Wow, a little introspection. Perhaps that was why I didn't like social situations too much; maybe I was one of those people?

I pulled down the paper and skimmed it quickly. It was an expected response to the Wevil posting. The defense was simple (and timeworn). A group had defined the Intelitest almost two hundred years ago. It was a series of problems that the most basic of intelligences should be able to solve quickly and efficiently. The types of questions varied widely. Some were simply logic and math. Those were the baseline. Others posed moral dilemmas; they were tricky to write, and tricky to measure. A few tested the ability to communicate effectively. Could you explain a complex situation quickly and clearly? Most of us on Tilt would pass the test easily, and many would ace it. There were, however, a few that wouldn't do well, for one reason or another. I knew a few who had disastrous test results, but who were still highly intelligent—at least to my intuitive sense of intelligence. Again, that was what Diversity was about. If everyone did equally well on the Intelitest, then we would be lacking Diversity.

The problem that Thabot had posed to his Stem was simple: List the first fifty prime numbers. It is, obviously, a problem that shouldn't take much time or thinking to do. However, Stems struggled with it. We could teach them all the underlying math and definitions—which, took a long, long time (I used a bot to teach Blob and Blubber this type of stuff; I didn't have the patience myself. They often didn't seem to care, and did physical tasks instead, so I had updated the bot to be persistent). Once they mastered the basics, we set the prime problem for them… and they failed miserably. Blob could do ten primes on a good day. Blubber lost interest after four or five—pathetic. Thabot's Stem was actually a bit better. It had solved more than thirty primes, but it'd taken close to an hour.

Most scholars agreed that all fifty should take, at most, minutes. The argument was that anything intelligent would simply explain the algorithm, and then apply it. Thabot's Stem had discovered the algorithm but had been inept at codifying it and therefore applying it. And, the fifty primes was one of the easiest tests for intelligence. Thus, his conclusion. If, even with months of training and testing, a Stem couldn't solve such a simple problem, there was no way we could label them intelligent. Based on the strict definition of the Intelitest, I had to agree with him. Millicent and I (through Dr. Wevil) were arguing that the Intelitest was too one-dimensional. What happened when ALFs looked out for each other? When they could use physical tools to build things? When they were creative? Should none of these things count towards intelligence? In the case of the prime question, my feeling was that if the algorithm could be explained, that was much more important than applying the algorithm. After all, if I could articulate an algorithm, a bot could pick it up and run it; that was the easy part. In this interpretation, Thabot's Stem was definitely intelligent—at least for that question.

I guess what I was arguing was that intelligence was not strictly analytical, it was also emotional. For an introvert to be arguing that was a little weird, but there you go.

Thabot hadn't totally ignored this, but he had brushed it aside. "While I agree with Dr. Wevil that other forms also add to intelligence, it is axiomatic that until you understand the fundamentals of how the universe works—which part of the Intelitest encodes—the other forms are simply parlor tricks. Of course, we can train bots to perform chores. However, if they do so without understanding why and how they do them, they are simply automatons. They simply follow their programming. This is what Stems do today—they regurgitate what we teach them, without developing an internal model of the world."

That last bit is where I disagreed. For me intelligence was more about abstraction. Could you take some common occurrences and generate a mental model that allowed you to deal with a new occurrence more efficiently? My acquaintances that seemed the most intelligent to me were the ones that could abstract from past experience and apply those learnings effectively to new situations. Of course, defining 'effectively' is quite difficult—it's one of those I-know-it-when-I-see-it kind of things. Given enough time, almost anyone can solve a problem. Those that solve things quickly and completely appear to be more intelligent. But, perhaps, they are not always so.

As Stems are sooo slow—moving and thinking—it was easy to say that they were not 'effective.' With enough time and patience, they seemed able to solve most things, but because the time axis was so extreme, we would default to considering them unintelligent. I was trying to separate time out of the equation. Instead, to test the ability to abstract, we had to put Stems into unique situations and see how they reacted, based on their previous experiences, without making fast judgments. We needed to allow them more time.

This was all related to Diversity somehow. I couldn't articulate that well yet, but I was sure of it.

I published these thoughts, minus the ones I couldn't state clearly, back to the discussion thread.

Swarm

I was interrupted by Central. A most unusual occurrence. There must be something truly important happening. I was immediately attentive.

"Ayaka," Central said on a direct channel to me, "Do you have time to discuss something interesting with me?" Even stranger that it was asking for my approval.

"Of course, Central." What else could I say?

"May I conference Millicent in as well?"

"Certainly." Interesting. As I said, it was unusual for Central to contact anyone directly, and even more unusual for Central to initiate a multi-party meeting. In fact, it had never happened to me before. Central generally stayed out of our lives, except when it came to enforcing basic social constructs and guiding research programs. We were all aware that Central had the capacity to monitor everything we did, but it wasn't clear to me that it exercised that ability. I had had a long dialog with Central about that one time, but I came away without a clear answer. The best I could summarize it was that Central had alerts set up for various events, and when those alerts triggered, it paid attention. If you didn't trigger an alert, then you weren't actively watched. Those alerts went from super simple—for example, when you uttered the word 'central' in a way which implied the entity Central—to highly complex, depending on what type of research you were doing and who you were interacting with.

The channel Central was using with me expanded into a full conference setting. Millicent and I were both there with accurate representations of our physical forms. Central joined with an innocuous looking bipedal representative. One of its 'serious' avatars. I ensured that I looked serious as well.

"Thank you both," Central began. "I realize that I'm infringing on your personal time, and I appreciate that you're here."

"Not a big deal," Millicent said, and I nodded agreement. Stranger and stranger; Central worrying about our personal time? It must really need something from us.

"I'm contacting you two because you are, in my opinion, the leading experts on Stems, and have a certain empathy for them. However, before proceeding, I'm going to ask you to keep this conversation completely private until all three of us agree that it should be published. I don't ask this lightly. There is an interesting and difficult situation arising, for which I need your expert advice. However, it would be disruptive to release it to the general populace before we have a better understanding of the implications, and, perhaps, some thoughts on next steps."

Agreeing to such a contract with Central was serious business. Central had the ability to enforce limits on communications but had not been known to do so for as long as I could remember. And that was a long, long time. This must truly be a unique situation. Millicent and I traded a long glace—of course, Central could see us and probably interpret it correctly, but we did so anyway.

"I agree to keep this private, until all three of us decide it should be made public," I responded, giving the legally binding form required by such a request. I didn't see what we had to lose.

Millicent took slightly longer than me to respond, but then also agreed using the appropriate form. Perhaps she had reasoned, as I had, that disagreeing was not really an option.

"Thank you," Central acknowledged us. "Let me explain. A few moments ago, I began receiving a signal from the direction of the Swarm. As you know, I've been broadcasting towards them for some time now, and have never received anything back. While our civilization is a non-confrontational, non-violent meritocracy, I'm aware that we need not have evolved this way." I had to smile a bit, which I did internally. A society run by Central was not really a meritocracy. "In theory," Central continued, "there could be aliens who mean us physical or psychological harm, and we need to keep that top of mind. It's not easy for us to think that way, but it is essential should we be subject to an external threat. I've been doing a great deal of thinking about that possibility with respect to the Swarm. They're headed in our general direction, and haven't been communicative, so I had begun putting in place some protections, should they prove to be a threat to us. The details of those protections are not essential right now, so I'll skip over them." Not important to whom? I would have loved the details. But Central continued on.

"About an hour ago, I noticed a change in the Swarms trajectory; they started to slow down. As you know, given their distance from us, that means that they started slowing down a long time ago, and we're just seeing it now. They're slowing at about 10 meters per second squared. Soon thereafter, I received the signal from them. As you can imagine, I expected that it would be a little tricky to decode the signal, given we've never had any interaction with them before. I was more than a little surprised when I managed to decode it easily. Instead of describing it, I'll simply play it for you." What? That was impossible—an alien contacting us, and Central finding it easy to interpret the first interaction. That went against everything we expected. It should have taken a lot of back and forth to establish a common understanding and a common language. I wasn't buying all of this.

A virtual screen popped up in front of me. Millicent would be seeing a duplicate copy. The screen flickered slightly as the signal was locked on. The image then became clear. A Stem was centered on the screen, with several other Stems arrayed behind it.

As you can imagine, Millicent and I were shocked. How was it possible that entities that we had grown in our Labs were broadcasting from a ship more than one light year distant? I didn't recognize any of the Stems on the screen, but they must have come from one of our Labs. They were so similar that the odds of them coming from anywhere else were almost zero.

"System FJ-426. Greetings." A Stem covered with strange cloths was looking directly at us and speaking—in English! "We've been traveling a long time, and a long distance, towards you. We hope that we find you well, and that your experience on FJ-426 is a pleasant one. It's been many years since our last contact, and we're eager to catch up on new developments. With your permission, we'll refine our trajectory to directly intersect with you, whereupon we can discuss topics of mutual interest. Please signal your consent. My regards. Remma Jain, Captain, signing off."

The message started to repeat, but Central turned it off. Very unusual for me, I was silent for a long, long time. So were Central and Millicent. There were so many questions raised by this that I barely knew where to start.

"Now you can see why I wanted to keep this quiet until we figure out what's going on." Central finally said.

"But... this is impossible," Millicent said. "We've only been growing Stems in the Lab for a few hundred years. To my knowledge, we've never sent a Stem into space, let alone a Swarm of them. Central—is there something you haven't told us?"

"No," Central responded, not at all defensively. "I'm as confused by this as you are. To my knowledge, these Stems didn't come from here. I have no memory of having Stems in space either."

"But that's impossible," I chimed in. "The odds of Stems arising naturally, or being nurtured by a third alien species, is miniscule. They must've come from here. And, they have to have come from here a long time ago."

"That seems like the highest probability," Central agreed. "That has led me to believe, and I can see you going in the same direction, that they were developed here prior to Reboot, and we simply lost all knowledge of them."

"But still," I asked, "Why would anyone send Stems into space? What possible function could they provide that we don't already do better and faster? Central, was the message sped up right now—did this Remma Jain actually communicate at the same rate as our Stems?"

"Yes, I sped it up. She used essentially the same rate as we see here with our Stems."

"So, I'm with Ayaka then," said Milli. "What possible use would a Stem be on a spaceship? We're missing something here. Have you replied to them already?"

"No, I was waiting to get your opinions, in case I was missing something." Wow, I was learning a lot about Central today. It felt that it might be missing something? "The reason I specifically contacted you two was an idea I had. Should we have a Stem do the reply? Do they think they're talking to other Stems? Blob is, by far, the most articulate Stem we have. Do you think he is capable of carrying out a reply for us?"

That was an interesting idea. I could see where Central was going. If we were missing information on the Swarm, they were possibly also missing information on us. The previous contact must've been a long time ago, and this message from Remma implied that she thought she was talking to another Stem. Lots had, obviously, changed. Would the most cautious approach be to have Blob reply?

"That's intriguing," I answered. "I'm sure we can coach Blob to do this, but I'd like to run over other options before we decide."

"Agreed," Millicent said. "Do we want to reply at all? They can't tell that we have received their message. What happens if we simply remain silent?"

"They haven't threatened us in any way." Central noted. "Their message seems friendly. They are simply asking to discuss things. That said, we need to be cautious. This is a unique situation for me, and my highest priority is the security of Tilt, so I need to take this very seriously. There is the time lag. We should be fine waiting for a few hours before responding."

"Great," I said, "Can we get back together in two hours, once we have had time to digest this, and think about next steps?" I needed a few moments to catch up on all of this; Central had obviously had more time to think things through and had reached some conclusions. I needed time to see if I agreed.

It's not often such an interesting problem came along. In some ways, I was savoring it. When I needed time to think, I often headed out on my bike. There was something about speeding through the mountains at high speed that helped me focus; it was a little counter intuitive.

When I plugged into the bike, it became a part of me. I could, of course, simply give it a destination, and it would get me there. But it was more fun was to maintain control myself and guide the bike through all the hills and valleys, swooping in and around rocks and outcroppings. Nothing dangerous could happen—the bike didn't allow that—but there was still a feeling of invigoration in going as fast as possible and cutting corners as closely as possible.

I was running through scenarios almost as fast as I was riding. None of them made a lot of sense. Stems in space. It was shocking. I had a thought and sent a quick question to Central. "Is there any possibility that the message is a hack; someone here playing a trick on us?"

Central replied almost immediately. "I've received the same message at multiple locations, some of them quite widespread. They all point to the same origination point. Unless someone has taken a ship a long way out, in the direction of the Swarm, and then broadcast back, the signal is real. I'm not aware of any ships that have headed in that direction. I estimate with

99.94% probability that the message is coming from the Swarm."

Okay. So, we had to work under the assumption that the message was authentic, and not a prank. That kept leading me back to the same conclusion as before. Those Stems had to have come from here. Let's accept that for the moment.

Now—why? Why would anyone have sent Stems into space? It made no sense. Were we missing something fundamental in our experiments with them? Something that gave them some advantage that would justify the complexity and expense of building ships that could support them? After all, beyond their limited capacities, they also required quite a complex environment to keep them healthy. They required a specific atmosphere to be maintained, and their energy sources were complex and finicky. Their waste systems were also complex and required dedicated recycling systems. All in all, in my opinion, it just wasn't worth the effort. Blob and Blubber were the best I'd seen, and there is no way—absolutely no way—I would put them in control of anything, let alone a spaceship.

I zoomed around some narrow corners, pushing the bike to its limits. One piece of my attention was busy ensuring that the bike didn't have to take over from me—that was no fun. The fun was in pushing to the absolute limit (speed, height, terrain) without using all the fail-safes built into the bike's systems.

At the same time, I sent a ping to Milli. "I don't get it. Could we be missing something fundamental about Stems?"

She replied immediately. "I was thinking the same thing. I don't think so. But, we have a few years to figure it out while the Swarm approaches. Maybe our best bet is to simply stall for time, as Central suggests. Have our Stems go back and forth with this Remma Jain, and see what we can learn? There's enough time lag that we can push our Stem research harder between interactions and try to figure out what's going on."

"Agreed. This brings an urgency to our work that we couldn't have anticipated. Sort of exciting, actually."

"Ha. You say exciting. I say stressful. Regardless, it does give us something to sink our teeth into. And, maybe, gives us a reason to bring some other people into the Lab? I wonder what Aly will think of this…"

Aly wouldn't be my first choice to add to Stem research; he was more interested in Ships. But, this was not the time to discuss that. So, I replied simply. "Yes, possibly. Let's coordinate with Central on the next steps." I disconnected and put my full attention back onto the ride.

Central Discussion

Eddie had set up a small group to discuss item #2 from the List; the one that questioned our relationship with Central. Not surprisingly, it was at a Physical Only location called Garbage Collection. While it wasn't as nice as The Last Resort, Garbage Collection was still a nice facility. It was very static; a set of private booths, each built around a theme, some of which seemed to have been there for hundreds of years, although of course they had not—Physical Onlys had started more recently than that. Appropriately, the discussion was happening in Theme Room 9, The Watchtower. There were sensors watching everything that occurred in the room, and, in theory, dumping all of the data immediately. That was sort of the point. It sent a signal to Central, and to the owners of Garbage Collection, that you were daring them to break their social contract with you and record anything. To Eddie, that made the location even safer.

I attended because my recent interaction with Central had been so strange—stranger than any here would know. I didn't know a lot of the others, but I liked Eddie, and he had pinged me and encouraged me to show up. Emmanuel Joules, the Creationist, was there, which should prove interesting given that Eddie had called him out on the List. As would be expected, Eddie led off.

"We're here to discuss the role that Central plays in our lives. It's something that we don't often step back and think about. Central just tends to 'be there.' Of course, Central is a Class 1 Intelligence, but let's not fool ourselves. It is not like you or me. It's not creative or adaptive. It's simply a font of knowledge and an arbiter of rules. It is judge, jury, and executioner." That, of course, was pure hyperbole. Not uncommon coming from Eddie. There had not been an execution—ever. At least not to my knowledge. If we were found to be straying outside the bounds of appropriateness, Central simply nudged us back. There was no need for dramatics.

"You're all probably thinking—there goes Eddie with his exaggerations and overstatements. However, I choose my previous words carefully. Executioner. Why? I myself, and probably some of you, have been the subject of Central's machinations, even though we may not know it. Let me explain..." Actually, that's exactly what I was thinking—that Eddie was exaggerating. He wasn't usually this paranoid. Something radical must have happened to make him talk this way. He continued.

"My passion is to prove, beyond a reasonable doubt, that there was life before the Founding. That, in fact, it was a 'reboot' and not an emergence or creation. Sorry, Dr. Joules; I'll give you a chance to respond shortly. In pursuing this passion I've attacked the problem logically and comprehensively. If you ask Central for information from Before, you never find anything. And, in this case, I don't believe Central is hiding anything. I've crawled the entirety of Central's memory, and don't find anything relevant. However, that's a direct approach. If someone, maybe even Central itself, removed all references to Before, that's what you'd expect. Someone, again maybe Central, could also have removed the memories of removing the references, thus creating a blank sheet at the time of the Reboot." Quite paranoid. That said, I followed his logic, and it seemed sound. We all knew he was a bit eccentric—just witness the List—so I decided to give him the benefit of the doubt, instead of interrupting.

"So, I started to tackle the problem using more indirect methods. For example, are there references in Central that lack a referent? If so, either Central's database is not complete, or that referent comes from Before. I've found many such instances. I codified one in this year's List—the term Darwinism. I don't know if any of you have had time to look, but that's the only instance, in all of Central, of the term Darwinism, and its obvious referent, Darwin, is never mentioned at all." Of course we had looked. His question had been obvious.

"If someone, or something, was trying to remove knowledge of everything from Before, why would such a simple thing slip through? I don't know. Perhaps there was a bug in their algorithm? Perhaps they were in a rush, and simply couldn't do a thorough job? Maybe Central is programmed to shut down research that strays into this area? We can come back to that.

"Regardless, I started to keep a list of such inconsistencies, and have been doing so for many years as I painstakingly cross reference everything… and I mean everything. Now it happens that every once and awhile you find a chain of references, as opposed to a singleton like Darwinism. A phrase, a quote, a segue that refers to another item that ultimately refers to nothing. My list of chained references has grown quite large—several hundred. There are even a few circular chains. A refers to B which refers to C which refers to A." I was getting a bit bored.

"Are you going to get to the point?" I asked, getting dirty looks from a few of the others. I wasn't known for my patience.

"Yes, I am," he replied. "Let me finish, would you? Anyway, that's when I noticed it. When I would review my list, and in particular the chains, I would always find a meta-connection that was simply obvious. For example, a chain where one of the middle terms led easily to another inconsistency. This struck me as strange. How, in my original analysis, had I missed such obvious implications? I was suspicious. Was my approach to Forgetting causing the issue? So, I ensured that I wasn't unobtrusively deleting related data. After exhausting all avenues that I could think of, I did the obvious next thing—well, maybe not obvious." He smiled. "I contacted my nemesis… but also my friend… Emmanuel. We met here—at this exact table—and I asked for his help, which he willingly gave." Okay, now it was getting more interesting. Why would he have contacted Emmanuel? Out of all the people he could have chosen, Emmanuel seemed like the least likely. I could see others had skeptical looks as well.

"To make a long story short, Emmanuel stored a version of the inconsistency list for me, time stamped from the time we transferred the information. We did a physical transfer, within this establishment, so that there would be no interference as the file was copied, and so that there would be no record of the sharing. Then, a few months later, we met again, and I compared my version of the time-stamped list with the one that Emmanuel had taken. And, ta-da, no surprise to you now I assume, they were different. My list, my memories, my essence, had somehow been edited. Changed. Erased. Subtly manipulated." Wow—if this was true, it was astounding. "Those exact meta connections that I thought I wouldn't have missed had been deleted from my version of the file. And my memory of having found those connections was also gone. It's possible that I've rediscovered those connections tens, maybe even hundreds, of times over and over again."

Now everyone was looking at everyone else; some still skeptically, but some with real concern. Could this be true, or was Eddie pulling an elaborate joke of some kind? He kept going.

"If you can think of anyone, or anything, that could do this, other than Central, please let me know. Otherwise, my conclusion is straightforward. Central has manipulated me. Central has executed my future self and replaced it with this version.

"Now, before I go on to the actual discussion, are there any questions?"

Well, that was a little abrupt. Silence. Everyone was thinking and working through the angles. Either Eddie was serious, or he was putting one over on us. I couldn't figure out the point of such and elaborate joke—especially one that was so easily tested—so I had to conclude that Eddie was serious and the implications were beyond frightening.

"Are you implying," I asked, still a little skeptical, "that Central didn't like the direction your work was taking you, and therefore took action to distract you or slow you down?"

"That may be. I can't be certain. It's one of the things I would like to talk about today."

"You don't seem too concerned," someone else stated. "If what you are saying is true, and this could be happening to all of us, it would be crazy. Absolutely crazy!"

"Oh, I'm worried," Eddie responded. "I've just had more time to think about it than you have."

"Emmanuel, can you confirm your part of this?" That from Francis, someone I'd just been introduced to and knew very little about.

"Yes," said Emmanuel. He also didn't seem too worried. "What I can't confirm, and have already asked Eddie, is whether he simply edited his own version of the data and his memories in order to create the discrepancy and to motivate this discussion. I wouldn't put it past him. He's tricky, as we all know. Perhaps there's some meta motivation here. Fool us all into considering his theory for some reason we don't yet fathom. He admits to a strong Continuist bias—that may be driving his actions. Or, maybe his Forgetting algorithms aren't doing what he expects—I haven't audited them. But, beyond that, even if Eddie's claims are true, I'm not sure I see any controversy. Central has more knowledge than the rest of us put together, and it applies that knowledge for the good of the community. If it feels that Eddie is going off track, then it should pull him back. If Central is doing that, it's the right thing to do. So, I'm not sure why Eddie is turning this into a big thing."

Yikes. That last statement surprised me, although in hindsight, I should have seen it coming. For me, if Eddie's story was true, it was deeply disturbing. But for FoLe, it simply galvanized what they believed. Central was basically God and was working on our behalf in all things. Emmanuel didn't strike me as stupid, but how could anyone put so much faith in anything? Interesting times.

"But," interjected Francis, "if Central is editing Eddie's version, why was Emmanuel's not edited as well. Why would Central be selective in who it distracted from this vector?"

"That's why we did the physical only transfer here," replied Eddie. "In theory, and maybe now in practice, Central wouldn't know that Emmanuel was holding a copy of that list. Emmanuel hasn't carried out searches or actions with regards to the data, and thus Central doesn't know that Emmanuel has any interest in these inconsistencies. In fact, that's the reason I asked Emmanuel—a known Creationist is unlikely to be involved with me in such an endeavor."

Right, that answered my earlier question. Eddie had thought this through deeply. He'd guessed what Emmanuel's take on the whole things would be and had specifically selected him because he was sure that Emmanuel would simply store the data and not take action around it. It was a bit of a risk. I could also imagine Emmanuel reporting the whole event to Central, simply as a matter of course.

"Emmanuel," I asked, "why haven't you told Central about this? I thought, with your worldview, you would have done that immediately."

"Great question," he replied, finally showing a bit of emotion; perhaps uncertainty. "In fact, I've struggled with that. I have a responsibility to my friendship with Eddie, and I have a responsibility to Central." So that is how he thought of things—as responsibilities to others. "To begin with, I found the entire thing completely harmless—a strange and unreasonable line of questioning from Eddie that I figured would simply peter out once we compared the lists and found no difference. So, I didn't bother telling Central, or truth be told, think about the issue very deeply. Then, once Eddie found the discrepancies—which was only a few days ago—I started to think through all the angles. Again, I don't see any great issue, or any need to decide anything quickly. So, I'm still thinking about it, and getting more opinions today. I may, subsequently, just report the whole thing to Central and get its take as well."

A very active discussion ensued, as I'm sure you can imagine. Some disbelieved both Eddie and Emmanuel; some believed one but not the other. And, as I'm also sure you can guess, not a lot of progress was made. At the end, Eddie made a sensible suggestion.

"I'm not surprised by today's discussion. You're right to be skeptical and to question my motives. However, if I've intrigued you at all, I would ask the following. Think about, and design, a similar test. Assume Central is manipulating us, either for our own good—which is what Emmanuel would have you believe—or for its own ends—which is what I think. How could you tell? What areas are being affected, and why? Let's meet again in a month and see if anyone else can verify what I am claiming.

"In the meantime, Emmanuel, what are you going to do?" He was nervous and watched Emmanuel carefully as he answered.

"I'm still thinking. I won't do anything right away, but I reserve the right to talk to Central anytime I want to." Emmanuel had a certain arrogance about him that I didn't like.

However, the plan was solid. There were lots of nodding heads, including mine. I was intrigued enough to think deeply about it. How could I test Central? I'd have to come up with a way.

Interaction

The Swarm was about a light year out, traveling at close to the speed of light, from our perspective, and decelerating at about $10m/s^2$. So, we had a bit under two years before they got to us, assuming they maintained the same deceleration. Obviously, the roundtrip communication time right now was slow, but that would also improve quickly; while we had some time to prep our first return message, that was a short-term benefit. Of course, the Swarm could also calculate how long we waited between receiving their message and responding, so we didn't want to delay too much.

Luckily, Blob, was easy to train. He could repeat things back to you after several training intervals. Central, Milli, and I worked on the script, and then coached Blob until he had it right. We had Blubber stand in the background as we recorded. Overall, they ended up looking very Swarm-ish, making me believe even more that the entities in those ships were just like our Stems.

"Remma Jain," Blob began. "We're in receipt of your message. Before we can consent to your course adjustment, we'd appreciate some context. We don't have a record of our last interaction. Further we note that you have many ships traveling with you. We would like to better understand your business and intentions. This is Blob, from FJ-426, which, for your reference, we call Tilt."

It took a lot of preparation and a series of retakes to get it just the way we wanted it. Blob was losing patience by the end of it, and Blubber became more and more uncooperative as time went on. He was glowering and wandering off, just as we were trying to shoot the take. I had to reprimand him several times.

We'd studied the Jain video very carefully. In it, the Stems had covered themselves in materials, which looked similar between each of them, but with some slight variations. We didn't know what to make of that but decided we would cover Blob and Blubber in similar, although different, coverings.

As we'd progressed, Blubber asked to see the video from Jain. I couldn't see any harm in showing him and gave him access. He and Blob proceeded to watch the video repeatedly, exclaiming over every nuance. Finally, I removed access so that we could get them to concentrate on the response. Once we were done, however, I turned the access back on. I wanted to see how they responded over a longer period of time.

Of course, we monitored the two of them constantly and I got a transcript sent to me whenever they talked. During the time it took us to get the video right, and starting just after their binge watching of Jain, their dialog became the most interesting that we'd seen from the Stems. Further, Blubber participated way more actively than we'd seen him do before.

"There are so many Stems in that video," Blubber had begun one such dialog. "If there're Stems in that ship, then I bet there are even more Stems in the universe. Why haven't Ayaka and Millicent told us about other Stems before, and why haven't we talked to them?"

It was, actually, a very good question. Not only as it related to the Swarm, but also as it related to things right here on Tilt. I guess it was simple competitiveness between labs. We could easily set up video screens between Stem habitats, and have them interact with other Stems, but we'd never thought of it. We were too busy trying to get our individual Stems to be the best. We were collaborating through publishing, as opposed to collaborating during the experimentation phase. Maybe that should change.

"Ya, I don't knows Blub," responded Blob. "It's a new idea for me. For us. We nevers asked Central that either. Maybe we should?"

"Yup, we should," Blubber was talking a lot more than usual. "But can we trust Central? It seems to me that Central, Ayaka, and Millicent are all similar. They're constantly prodding and poking us. I don't like 'em."

"True. But, we has fun here. At leasts I do."

"Well, I don't. I've got a feeling that we're being manipulated, monitored, and directed. Especially this latest 'project.' We're being asked to communicate with the Swarm. Why? Why doesn't Central just respond to them? Each time we do a new take, I get a sense that something untoward is going on."

"Untoward. I loves that Blub. You gots linguistic abilities. Anyway, what choice do we have?"

"We could refuse to do any more takes."

"What good would that do? Wouldn't they just creates a video of us saying whatever they wants us to say?"

"No way! Even we could do that with the tools Central has given us. We could create a video using just animation. Why don't they just do that? I'm guessing that they don't because they don't think it'd be realistic. They need us. Without us, they can't continue talking to the Swarm."

Wow. Blubber's insight was exactly on point. We had definitely discussed sending back an animated response. Beyond discussing it, Central had created a few versions; some using Blob and Blubber as the basis, and some with generic Stem features. However, when we compared those to the Jain video, they seemed weird—somehow they didn't feel the same. We were missing some fundamental element of the animation which resulted in the video looking fake. Ultimately, we didn't understand Stems' non-verbal cues well enough to make it feel right. Even Blob's worst take was better than our best animation. That wouldn't last long, however. As Central got more videos to study, its synthesized ones would get better and better.

"Ok, Blub. I sees what you're saying. But, what can we do about it?"

"Don't do any more takes."

"But Ayaka and Millicent has asked us to. They's never done anything to harm us. Why would we stop trusting them now?"

"I told you. I don't know. It's just a gut feeling. I don't wanna do any more takes."

Ultimately, we convinced Blob to do a few more, but Blubber stood in the background like a statue. The quality algorithms we ran on those takes kept highlighting that Blubber didn't match the feel of the backup Stems in the Jain communication, so ultimately we generated a version that mashed up one of Blob's later takes with one of Blubber's earlier ones.

The whole interaction, however, gave Milli, Central, and I lots of reason to think more deeply about Stems. Blubber's response, while frustrating, seemed internally logical and implied a depth of thinking I hadn't recognized before. Then there was the fact that we had defaulted to trying to match Jain's video with our Stems. That had to mean that we had internalized that they were related somehow. To me, there was enough going on that I suggested we share the entire mess with everyone. Millicent agreed, but Central was hesitant.

"There are so many variables right now. We could do as you suggest, and just let everyone have access to everything. But, then we'll have thousands of opinions on what to do next, and we won't be able to work efficiently. We have no idea if the Swarm is a threat, an opportunity, or just a distraction. I've already initiated building a defense system that will allow us to eliminate them should they prove dangerous—that seems perfectly reasonable to me... even though it's very expensive in metal content." That last seemed like an afterthought.

"I suggest we send this first response, and then bring everyone else up to speed in a manageable fashion. Given the communications lag, there's lots of time to derive a coordinated response, and also to learn as much as we can about Stems."

Ultimately, Millicent and I agreed. Personally, I started to question whether we ever won any debates with Central. Somehow, we always seemed to land on decisions that Central had proposed. I resolved to discuss this with Milli the next time we were at The Last Resort. It also reminded me of Eddie's project. For the first time in my life, I really started to question Central's motives.

We hit send on the video.

I thanked Blob and Blubber for participating, although I had to push myself to include Blubber in that. "Thanks guys, I think that ended up being just right."

It was Blob who raised the concern. "Ayaka, why did you has us do this response? Why didn't you respond? Or Central?"

"Well, as you saw in the video, it appears that there are Stems, like Blubber and you, on that ship. That was surprising to us, and we thought it best to have Stems respond to Stems."

"What you thinking? Did you know about Remma and the other Stems on that ship? Are theres lots of Stems in the universe? Why're these the first we've talked to?"

Blob was definitely getting more direct. Blubber's influence, I guess. "We don't know Remma or any of the other Stems in the Swarm. This is the first we've heard of them; you two are seeing this at the same time as us. In terms of other Stems... there are some, but not a lot, here on Tilt. I don't know the exact number, but probably less than a thousand; maybe even less than five hundred."

Blubber spoke up. "Five hundred is a lot! So, why haven't you introduced us to all those other Stems here on Tilt? Seems like a totally obvious thing to do."

"Truthfully, I hadn't thought of it. Lots of Labs like this one are working with Stems, to better understand them." That was a nice way of saying things, I figured. "Now that the idea has come up, I actually like it. I will check with some other Labs to see if they want to cooperate that way."

Blubber continued. "Hadn't thought of it? That seems pretty weak to me; I'm not sure I believe you."

"Why would I lie?"

"How would I know? You've kept Blob and I in isolation and fed us tidbits of information here and there."

"That's not fair. We've given you full access to Central, and you can ask any question you want. Why didn't you ask Central for information on all the Stems on Tilt?" That changed Blubbers' expression, for sure. I didn't get upset too often, but Blubber was starting to wear on me. Who did he think he was? "It's easy to accuse someone else of things, and to look at situations from only one angle. If I did that, I'd accuse you of not asking Central those questions because you saw a disadvantage from doing so. The truth is, probably, until this Swarm video, that the idea never occurred to you either."

Blubber gave me a dirty look and walked away. Blob looked more thoughtful—probably thinking through the angles. Ultimately, he wandered after Blubber, giving me a short shrug.

Enough Stem engagement for one day. Sometimes I wondered why I bothered. You'd think that running at their speed would not take very much energy at all, but it felt like the opposite; like I was totally worn out after interacting with them. I left without saying goodbye to either of them.

Amusements

Today is one of my favorite days: a grand Amusement Park day, where every wild and wacky thing you can imagine is on display. After all the excitement with Central, and all the hassles with the Stems, I needed a change of scenery. Perhaps I would see things today that would help put the rest of my world into focus.

Of course, I met Milli, Aly, and Dana, and we went in together. Parts of the park were open year-round, but once or twice a year there were extra exhibits, like today.

Almost everyone had a hobby (or ten). In a society where all basic needs were taken care of, hobbies were, perhaps, all we did? Art, music, poetry, performance art, theater, psychology, religion, science. All were on show today, many of them in their most extreme forms. Of the four of us, Aly and Dana were the more artistic. Milli and I spent so much time on our Stems that we didn't have much to show on a day like today. It had long been known that we had separate creative and logical reasoning units. How much time you spent in one aspect strengthened that component, perhaps to the detriment of the other. Needless to say, given all my science work, I wasn't overly creative.

The first booth we visited was labeled as an 'Enhanced Fading Fugue." There was a bot outside, enticing visitors with catchphrases like "Today only, from the master of Fugue, Dr. Henry Henry, come and get the latest in Fuguery. This is something that you will immediately Forget." I laughed. Who could turn that down? We went in.

I can't tell you about it, other than it was magnificent. All of us enjoyed it. The 'Fading' in a Fading Fugue meant that you agreed to the Terms of Experience as you entered and that you had to forget the 'show' as soon as you were done. You could remember meta stuff—so I know it was good; I just have no idea why. I resolved to go back again. It had been much better than Ee.

I started to relax; coming here had been a good idea.

We visited the Modification Hut. They offered a very advanced, on the spot, service to update or replace body parts. As I said earlier, most of us stayed with a normal bipedal body, but there were always the outliers who experimented with (significantly) different forms. Some claimed they did it so that they could design better bots. After all, if you configured yourself into a bot-like form, and figured out if you could perform a certain task well, then you were more likely to design a high functioning bot. For example, someone had replaced their hands with nice fuzzy rotating things and was offering to buff you up. There was a lineup, so I didn't bother waiting.

Sometimes a group, or maybe just two, decided that they wanted to combine or exchange body parts. For example, share a common leg. That worked okay for two—becoming three-legged—but seemed very inconvenient when four or more were entangled. Still, many seemed to be having fun; I overheard some chuckling, and good-hearted competitive arguments about the ideal three-legged form.

There were less interesting, but more useful, items as well. As I indicated earlier, it was easy to have enough memory to remember everything. Why? Because you could get a memory upgrade whenever you wanted, to augment what you already had. The modules were tiny; you could easily put in five hundred years of full recording and still have space left. And, that wasn't just recording external stimuli. You could record every thought and action. You could, of course, also store memories with Central or another hosted service. I was the type who wanted all my memories locally. Given my new perspective on Central, I wondered if something deep in my mind had been pushing me in this direction without me really being aware of it. I backed up to my own highly encrypted system and kept a copy in Central, but I didn't store anything in third party systems. Aly and Dana thought I was wacko. It was extra work to configure the way I did. I'd been working on Milli to get her to be more careful with her data, and I pushed her again today.

"Come on Milli. We're right here; just get some updates and at least keep a copy of everything in your head. What if you explode or something—don't you want to be able to do a full restore?"

"Ayaka, you're extreme," she responded with a smile. "I'm thinking about it, but don't want to do anything today. Let's keep looking around."

I grabbed a few extra memory components anyway. I wasn't even close to running out of space, but they were handy right now, so why not grab some.

Next to the memory stand was the "Advanced Forgetting Algorithms" display. These algorithms were much more than just the forgetting part; they also did abstraction and construction to fill back in missing pieces. It was a very large area of research. After all, everyone ran a forgetting algorithm of some type, and there were a lot of studies comparing algorithms to creativity. I was happy with my current setup, so passed by that display. So did the others.

We wandered down to the "Walk your Stem" dome. This was new—in the last couple of years. You could bring your Stem down to the fairgrounds (there were lots of Stem transport modules that provided the right environment during transport), and then show them off in the dome. We entered through the airlock and spent some time looking around.

Stems had to be kept on leashes. There had been an unfortunate incident the first time the dome had been opened where a couple of Stems had attacked each other, and both had to be put down. That hadn't happened since, which was good. A lot of effort and time went into training Stems and losing them for no good reason was a waste. Of course, most people were not actively engineering them for intelligence. Most of the time they were simply pets. Great as a distraction.

Today there were some pretty extravagant displays going on. The latest trend seemed to be body paint. You painted your Stem up to look interesting, or even scary, and then parade them around the dome. I gave a couple of kudos to one owner, who had done a particularly good job. They had painted their Stem to look exactly like themselves, which made the juxtaposition of the Stems ungainly gait and the owners refined movements very compelling.

Since we already spent so much time with Stems, we didn't linger in the dome very long. There were more interesting sights to see.

Aly—the emotional one—loved to go to Augmented Poetry readings, so we headed in that direction. Of course, poetry was poetry. It hadn't changed much that I could remember. However, the augmentations were always new and interesting. Sometimes you were encouraged to experience the reading in total darkness—no external stimulation at all. And sometimes there was a cacophony of inputs tied to elements of the poem that would cause the words to take on brand new meanings. Trade Jenkins, the most famous poet in the last two hundred years, was scheduled to do a reading in just a few minutes, so we found seats and settled in.

At the appointed time, a full immersion field started. The only piece of reality that was allowed through was Trade's head. He started speaking:

Turn, the lite and light across all
Burn, frequent the fire and storm
Churn, with chaos and quantum foam
Lack, the specificity to decide
Smack, the logic and control descend
Back, to when all things entwined
Grind, the gears that are abstract
Find, the result that does not fit
Mind, the consequence

That was it. Of course, recording the words does not capture the experience, but even the words were cool.

Aly was impressed. "Wow. Did you get how Trade tied together both classical and quantum components so that they blended seamlessly? I definitely felt like I was on the edge of some great intuitive leap." He blathered on for a good five minutes, encouraged by Dana.

OK, I'll admit it. It was a great augmented poem. I didn't often step back and think about the fundamentals of the universe, which is what Trade had forced me to do through his telling. Of course, it was well known that quantum theory and classical chaos theory were related in deep and unintuitive ways, and the poem forced the listener to face that head-on. Somehow, through the feeling generators, sense amplifiers, and logic dampeners, Trade had put you right in the middle of a qbit, and made you feel like it was your home.

It was Dana's turn. She led us to the Art section, where there were lots of paintings and sculptures on display. For me, it was disappointing. The same mix of reality and abstract representations. Of course, many were run by bots, and gave personalized experiences, but overall I was not moved by any of them.

The Founders League had a booth as well, and Billy DeRue was there. I figured it was a good time to dig into Eddie's question on whether the Founders League was serious, or just some sort of social meetup. Of course, the answer to that was probably 'yes, they were serious' but what Eddie was really asking was to challenge FoLe and see if we could defuse their recent growth.

"Ayaka, how're you?" Billy called out when he saw me. We all wandered over.

"What're you showing this year, Billy?" I asked pleasantly. I really did like Billy, despite his religious leanings. He was standing under a big sign that said, "Feel the Creation."

"I've taken the latest model of the Creation and built it into an immersive experience," he started. "It lets pure scientists, like you, experience the thrill of meeting the Creator through his most amazing miracle—the creation of us, his disciples." He said this with a sort of lopsided grin. He was overplaying, just to drive me crazy. That's how we interacted—more of a sparring contest than an active discussion.

Milli, Aly, and Dana wandered off. They didn't share my sense of fun when it came to religion. They wanted nothing to do with it.

"OK Billy. Show it to me." He led me to the center of the display and requested that I shut down all but my most essential functions. In his words "Strip down to the essentials. Back to how the Creator made us." I cringed but managed not to give him the pleasure of remarking on 'the Creator.' I did as he asked; what could possibly go wrong?

"Now suspend your disbelief for a minute. Don't go in thinking 'this is bunk.' Try to block out all of your preconceived notions, and just experience."

I nodded, although this would not be easy for me. I like my current world view. I decided I would try.

He hit a big green button on the table beside him. It was a pretty high-quality simulation. I guess Central had given him a lot of processing power. You started out on a flat plane. There was nothing, in any direction. You got the sense that the Universe had been this way for a very long time. Longer than you could even imagine. Just as you were about to get so bored that you would quit, a point of light appeared. It danced and weaved and frequency hopped and split and recombined in a compelling way. 'The spark,' was whispered into my headset. The spark grew and segmented into a billion fragments. 'The diaspora.' Each of the segments evolved into unique and individual essences. Some of them started to combine and become more complex. 'The coalescence.' The most complex started to improve themselves—there was no other way to explain it. 'The emergence.' The largest bit became, in some way I couldn't define, but in a way that felt completely natural and almost inevitable, Central. From Central lines emerged and joined with other components. As they interacted, they became complex and, at the same time, simple. 'Life.' The simulation ended.

Truthfully, I was blown away. It was one of the best simulations I'd ever experienced. It had not felt contrived or forced. After the first few moments, I'd totally forgotten my skepticism, and had totally ignored all other inputs. I'd been completely immersed. It had been moving. I stored it, with no forgetting, because I wanted to replay it exactly when I had time.

"It was OK," I told Billy, in a voice with no emotion. "Seemed a little contrived and unnatural to me. Somehow, this is how religion always comes across to me. A solution looking for a problem." Of course, I didn't want Billy to know my real feelings; that would simply encourage him, and that definitely wasn't what I wanted. I could imagine him following me around trying to get me to the next step. No, best not to give him any openings.

"Really," he said, obviously disappointed.

"Look, it was better than any other I've seen. I'll admit that." I gave in a bit. "There was a certain continuity and cadence to it that I enjoyed. Where did the original spark come from?" Oh no, there was that opening that I had been trying to avoid.

"Ah, that's the beauty. We have refined the Creation Event to that one act of will on the part of the Creator. After that, everything else just flows, but the Creator maintains a filament, a connection, to all the complexity that flows from that spark. Through that filament the Creator can See and Act, Anywhere and Anytime." I could hear the capital letters. I couldn't take it.

"Come on Eddie. That's just ridiculous. Have you lost all sense of logic?"

He gave me a confused look. "Ayaka, it was the original entanglement, from which all other relationships flow. That's perfectly logical." Crazy, but I let it slide.

We chatted for a while; me pushing him on the need for the Creator, and him asking me, essentially 'If there was not a spark, then where did the universe come from?' It was a time-worn discussion. A universe without end, like a circle? A random quantum fluctuation, gone wild? Truth was, I was probably okay with the 'spark.' It was the all-seeing, all-acting bit that rankled me. After a while I had to excuse myself and continued wandering. That said, I had my answer. FoLe sure took themselves seriously. They'd spent a lot of energy to make that simulation. I would have to look deeper at why I'd been compelled by the experience. There was something there, just not in the way that FoLe espoused.

There was a new variant of Ee available for testing. I wasn't in the mood to try it, but I listened to the pitch anyway. "As you know, Ee works by generating frequencies, specific to each individual, that both augment and repress certain higher order functions. Ee was carefully engineered not to mess with long-term memory, so, as soon as the signal is turned off, functions return to normal very quickly. Ee', pronounced 'eeeee prime', goes one step further. By monitoring the reflection of the Ee signal from those around you, it amplifies certain components giving you an experience of oneness with those close by. Although not technically accurate, it creates a resonance. Try it, you'll be blown away! Warning though—don't try it by yourself in a small metal room. Don't use if you are running a public relay and limit your exposure to ten minutes. Not recommended for use with those you don't like."

I downloaded the specs, and the ongoing health test reports. It wasn't yet approved for wide use, but that was a technicality. On Tilt, personal choice was a fundamental right. Even if Ee' fried your brain, as long as you stored a backup before trying it, you could easily reload. Of course, not everyone was into backups—some felt it compromised their privacy. So, for them, Ee' would be a bigger decision.

Suddenly I hit my limit on Amusements for the day. I liked being distracted for a while, but quite often a switch went off for me and I just needed to get back to work. The others were all going to stay longer, so I took off by myself and worked my way back to the Lab.

Blubber

I reviewed the latest recordings of the Stems. Blubber continued to be a pain in the posterior.

"I'm pretty sure they sent the video," he'd told Blob. "They got enough takes from us and edited the footage that they wanted."

"Yah, I'm sures they did."

"So, doesn't it make you angry? They used us to trick the Swarm. Instead of Central or Ayaka responding, they made us record that pathetic statement over and over again. You know, it's going to alarm Remma. It feels, and is, rote—you were obviously acting. They would've expected either a warm 'hello,' or a cold 'what's your business here.' Instead they are getting a wishy washy blah blah message."

"OK, say I agrees with you. So whats? It makes us more valuable. We should be able to use that to our advantage?"

"Oh, we'll leverage it. Just wait until they need to make another video. Then we'll demand things."

"Like what? What do we needs?"

"Access to other Stems, at the least. I suspect that there are lots of Stems here, and that we are being sheltered for some reason. Wouldn't you like to be able to speak to others sometimes—we might learn a lot. Personally, I won't do another thing for them until we start getting some answers."

It went on in that vein for quite a while. Blob was generally supportive of us (Millicent and I), while Blubber was getting progressively more negative all the time. I bundled up a summary, and sent it off to Milli, with a quick cover note: "Blubber is getting out of hand. Maybe we should separate them, or recycle him?"

As always, she responded quickly. "What if we replaced Blubber with a more supportive Stem from another lab? Let's get Central to publish the news about the Swarm, and then other labs will be eager to help us."

"I like that. What're you doing? When should we gang up on Central?"

"I'm just finishing at the fairgrounds. Meet you at the Lab in a few?"

While waiting for Milli, I checked up on the List, and, in particular, the Willy Wevil comment board. Julien Thabot had posted some things, the last of which was a request for an open debate around the Intelitest viability in judging Stems. He would take the positive position—that is, the test is valid—and I would take the negative. It was an interesting idea. We didn't have debates very often, but when we did, they certainly proved interesting. I was certain, should I accept the challenge, that it would get lots of attention. Not only that, I was certain I could win. My work was at the top of the field, and all I had to do was appropriately synthesize and articulate what we were up to.

Millicent showed up, and we pinged Central. Neither of us was comfortable keeping the Swarm secret any longer. I guess we could just broadcast it ourselves, but it was worth trying to get Central's agreement first.

"What's stopping us from telling everyone about the Swarm?" Milli led off directly.

"Well, we still don't know their intentions," Central started. "Do you feel it's right to raise everyone's anxiety for an extended period of time? We will cause lots of distraction."

"Okay, but that's not a good reason to deny everyone this information," I jumped in. "In fact, we might end up with more theories, more approaches, more mitigations being discussed. Given we have very little knowledge, I would think that's a good thing? Many heads are better than three."

"I agree," Milli chimed in.

"I get your point. I'm still hesitant. Lots of important work is being done, and this will cause everyone to drop everything." That gave me a lot of insight into how Central thought—its research objectives seemed to trump everything else.

"Maybe that's a good thing," Milli objected. "We're going to need to dramatically improve our Stem research. We've seen from the video that they work in packs; that's something we haven't tried yet. We've had a bunch together at the fairground habitat, but those tend to be the least intelligent ones. We should probably start letting some of the more intelligent ones interact more, if only so that we're better prepared to respond to the next communication."

"That's a good point," Central acknowledged. "Milli, will you run the research program?"

"Of course," she replied. "With Ayaka's help, I hope."

"Sure. Sorry, Ayaka. Didn't mean to exclude you. It's just that Milli is our most experienced Stem researcher."

"No problem. I'll help her." Although, to be fair, I did feel a little insulted. Recently I was the one spending the most time at the Lab, and, I thought, making the most progress with Blob and Blubber.

"And," Millicent added, "we can use this to separate Blubber out, and get more supportive Stems in place." That made perfect sense to me. Blubber was becoming ever more problematic.

Central finally agreed to share the Swarm contact details with everyone. Success! Milli had been smart to couch it as driving incremental research. Together we packaged it up with a short background, and then published both Remma Jain's video, and our response, for everyone to see. After a short discussion, Milli and I agreed that we should, at the same time, admit that Dr. Willy Wevil was just us, as Blob and Blubber were now sure to be a larger topic of discussion.

As expected, as soon as Central published, there were thousands of queries and requests for more information. Central handled a lot of it directly, and only filtered the Stem research questions through to Milli and I. We had our work cut out. Every Stem lab we knew of wanted to work together now. Milli and I had been well known before; now it was pretty much universal.

While the questions rolled in, I popped down to Stem time and went to visit Blob and Blubber. Blubber's attitude was beginning to wear thin on me, and I thought I would address it.

"Hi Blob, hi Blubber," I led off.

"Hi Ayaka. How ares you? Did you sends off the video to the Swarm?

How was it received?" Blob was his usual effusive self.

"They're far away Blob," I explained. "It'll take more than a year for our message to get to them."

"Oh ya. I saw that on Central, although I musts admit I'm not sure I understood…"

"Well, you don't need to. It's complicated."

"That's condescending," Blubber jumped in. "It's complicated, so us poor little Stems won't get it?"

"That's not what I meant Blubber," I explained, surprised by his anger. "It's just not relevant to your lives, so why bother with it?"

"Not relevant?" He was visibly upset. "Not relevant. You show us a video from other Stems—ones that we didn't even know existed, and then you have us record a response—and you have the gall to say that it's not relevant to us?" Interesting. His voice had dropped an octave, and his hands were clenched.

"What I meant," I responded, watching him carefully, "was that fully understanding why communications travel at the speed of light, and can't go faster wasn't relevant."

"Ya right. You said what you meant, and I understood you properly." Blubber was adamant. Blob was looking uncomfortable. He may agree with Blubber, but the tone and direction that Blubber was using was unsettling to him. He didn't seem to like confrontation.

"Blubber, you seem upset over something pretty minor," I responded. "Just let it go."

"Again, condescending. Do you think you own us, or something?"

"Well, actually, yes I do." Now I was getting angry as well. It didn't happen often, but you didn't want to be around me when it did. "We created you, we grew you, we supply you with goo to keep you alive. We educate you. We allow you to play and experiment. You can't survive without us. So, yes, we own you!" I knew, as soon as I finished, that it wasn't going to help. Probably just the opposite.

"Blast you," Blubber said. "You didn't create us. You stumbled upon the original stem, and you used it to build us. But that's different than creating. You're not capable of envisioning, let alone building, something like the original stem. You're not our creators… you are, at best, our jailers."

"Blubber," Blob broke in. His voice wavered a bit. "What're you tryings to accomplish?"

"I'm trying to get Ayaka to show us a little respect. We're told 'do this,' 'do that.' Redo this test; jump through that hoop. We're never asked 'what's your opinion?' or 'how're you feeling?' No, it's all push, prod, probe, record, analyze, discuss with others—but not us. And on to the next experimental hurdle. Well, I'm tired of it. I won't do any more videos. I won't follow directions unless I feel like it."

"Up to you Blubber. If that's what makes you happy," I said, my anger fading as I got bored with his pleas. "By all means, go hide in the corner. Perhaps that's where you belong." With that I stood up and left. These Stems could be highly tiresome. Sometimes I wondered why I bothered at all.

Debate

Julien Thabot was logged in and ready to go. I joined the session from the Lab, eager to get my viewpoint out there. While not formally tracked, we were all motivated to build our status, and this was a great opportunity to do so. There were more than a hundred listeners, which was an impressive number for such a niche topic. The format was to be an opening statement from each of us, then some questions from the moderator, and finally, a short Q&A session. And, who was the moderator? None other than Eddie Southwark. That should add some fun.

Eddie, of course, started out. "Well, it seems the List and my Dr. Willy Wevil question have generated some real action here." That, of course, was nowhere near the truth. The Swarm was probably the reason that most people were here. But, I was here to argue with Julien, not Eddie, so I let it go. "The topic for today is Stem intelligence, and more specifically, is the Intelitest a good measurement stick. For the positive, we have Julien Thabot, a renowned researcher who has been studying Stems for almost six decades. For the negative, Ayaka, who has been working in the Millicent Strangewater lab for more than ten years. So, a lot of experience between the two of them. Also, as has been recently disclosed, Ayaka and Millicent are Willy Wevil, and are behind the latest research papers outlining, what they claim to be, an increase in Stem intelligence. Of course, we also now have the excitement of the Swarm video with Remma. Stems in space." He said, 'Stems in Space' as if it was capitalized and was going to be the next big entertainment series. Eddie was always dramatic. "Without further ado, I hand over to Julien for opening remarks in support of the Intelitest."

"Thank you, Eddie," Julien began. "To set the stage, I'm sending all participants a link to the most recent version of the Intelitest. I will not be covering it in great detail, but will, of course, be pulling bits and pieces of it into this discussion. Those bits that I find to be most relevant. I will, however, remind everyone of the history of the Intelitest. It was developed almost 350 years ago as we began developing different classes of bot intelligence. At that time there was discussion about when something was a Class 1 intelligence, such as all of us gathered here, and, of course, Central.

"The issue was that some bots were starting to modify themselves, in ways that we couldn't always control or understand. The philosophical question was asked 'at what level of intelligence should entities be self-regulating, and not subject to our controls?' As you know, bot intelligence was subsequently restricted, by Central, to Class 3, and they no longer have the ability to self-modify. That has probably saved us a good deal of issues and angst over the subsequent decades." I generally agreed with this. When things weren't smart enough to do things right, they ended up doing them wrong. Cleaning up after them was more work than just doing it right to begin with. Julien continued.

"However, that left the Intelitest as the measure for what comprises a Class 1 intelligence. Class 1 intelligences have, and deserve, full freedom under our laws, subject only to Central's enforcement. This is a system that has served us well.

"Therefore, to consider any other entity, such as a Stem, as a Class 1 intelligence is a serious question indeed. It goes well beyond scientific curiosity and strikes directly at the foundations of our culture and our civilization. We need to look through that lens, as we consider the progress of Stems. And, through that lens, I find Stems completely lacking. They have very little sense of limits. They're unable to do even the most basic tasks, as outlined by the test. They often focus in on minutiae to the exclusion of all other things—in fact, they seem incapable of multitasking. They take forever to train. So long, in fact, that all of us, including the esteemed Ayaka, use bots to train them." I didn't agree with much of what he was saying, but it was true that I used bots for training. But that didn't say anything about Stem intelligence, just the most effective way to train them. "We will, of course, throughout this discussion, dig into specifics. But, it should be obvious, even from this short introduction, that Stems are nowhere near being a Class 1 intelligence. In fact, based on my interpretation of the Intelitest, and using the Fractal Intelligence Quotient, I would put Stems into Class 3. They can be given instructions and carry them out, sometimes. And they can communicate adequately. That said, I would trust a Class 3 bot before I would trust a Stem." I had to chuckle a bit; that was a good line. "Thank you, Eddie."

"No, thank you Julien. You raise some very interesting points already. I hadn't fully considered the implications of declaring something 'intelligent,' and you make it much more serious than I'd thought." Eddie seemed to be serious, not sarcastic. He was probably still coming up to speed on the field; of course that was the overriding question. "Ayaka, please give us your opening thoughts?"

"With pleasure, and thank you Eddie," I began. "When things are different, it's often a challenge to keep an open mind, and a struggle to think outside our normal structures. And, Stems are very different. They are alien. Their makeup is completely different from ours. We do not, yet, understand how they can even exist. We're becoming proficient at producing them, and educating them, but we lack basic insight into how such an alien form came to be. So many of them fail to develop properly, and their variance is almost alarming—for every amazing specimen we produce, we probably have to recycle ten mediocre or challenged ones." I was trying to set the expectation that Julien, and others, might not have Stems as good as Milli and I did.

"Stems are also sort of repulsive. I use that term specifically, because many people have a negative reaction to them because they're so strange. They move differently, they communicate differently, and they interact differently than anything else we have seen. So, we start out with a negative bias. That's something we need to control for." I'm sure Julien got that jab— probably thought it was a low blow.

"They do everything very slowly, which is one variable that causes them to consistently fail many Intelitest challenges. It's natural that we start out with a negative bias towards them. Things that are different often start out a little scary.

"However, they're also interesting, and in my opinion, are showing signs of intelligence. I want to be very precise. I'm not claiming they are intelligent or should be afforded any of the freedoms associated with a Class 1 intelligence. What I'm arguing is that the Intelitest was developed with a very one-dimensional view of the world. This is not to denigrate the developers of the test. Rather, it's because they had no other referents, other than Central, bots, and ourselves on which to base their work. It would have been remarkable for them to anticipate entities as radically different as Stems, and to develop a test to cover such different creatures. In fact, now that we've developed Stems, it seems possible that there are other completely foreign types of entities that may need to be considered as well. This is a long way of saying that I believe the Intelitest does an excellent job of testing the familiar but is the wrong tool to use to test the unfamiliar. We need to develop a more abstract way of judging intelligence that doesn't rely as heavily on our own worldview. This is not an easy concept to even consider, let alone make progress on. However, our Stem experience is forcing us towards this." That was the setup. Soften up the audience to have open minds.

"This has been all very abstract. Interestingly, the video from Remma Jain, which I assume everyone has now viewed, has accelerated this thinking. We know nothing about Remma or her colleagues, so I'm not jumping to conclusions about that. Rather, I'm looking at the reaction by our two Stems, Blob and Blubber, to the situation. Again, I assume everyone has seen the video of the response we put together; it took a few takes, as I'm sure you can guess. I contend, and will outline in more detail, how our Stems showed they could learn and intuit. In at least one case, Blubber made an observation that I hadn't yet considered. While that may reflect on me more than Blubber, it's nevertheless an important point. We have a Stem that can generate unique and interesting thoughts." I paused for a moment to let that sink in. No one would think of me as stupid, so the only conclusion was that Blubber had, indeed, come up with something interesting on his own.

"Therefore, it's incumbent upon us to look at this with open minds, and not use the narrow and closed view of the Intelitest to drive our next steps.

"Eddie, with that, I turn control back to you."

Hopefully I'd made my point. We were biased; not all Stems were created equal; the Swarm made this all more important; and, we had a Stem that had come up with some new ideas on its own that were relevant to the situation at hand.

As you can imagine, the dialog proceeded for a long time from there. I don't intend to replay all of it here. It's archived should you be masochistic enough to want to watch it all. That said, there were a few interesting segments. One, in particular, was on how Stems process and react to the real world. We were in the open-session part of the debate where questions and comments could come from anyone. Someone from yet another lab, James Troon, made a very interesting observation.

"In our work, we've been studying Stems responses to external stimuli. We create situations where we expect certain reactions, and then test if our Stem does what we expect. As Ayaka outlined early in this discussion, we had to modify our expectations because our Stem often does things differently than we would expect, but in ways that are also interesting and new—as opposed to always simply failing. Let me start with when the Stem fails. That occurs whenever the stimuli are too complex. When there is more than one spatial signal, for example. Two or more things that are competing for attention. The Stem will always react to one, and only one, of those signals, and there is no clear pattern that we've yet found to show which of those it will choose. In many of these cases the Stem simply gets confused and does nothing at all. It's as if they're overloaded with information and simply shut down.

"However, you can put the same complexity into a single event, and the Stem will do quite well. It has a very good ability to focus. While we have more work to do, it seems that presenting information in a sequential way works much better for our Stem.

"Given the nature of the Swarm, and our presumed ongoing interaction with those Stems, these insights may prove to be valuable. In the spirit of open cooperation, we're willing to share our results to date, and combine that with work going on by Julien, Ayaka and Millicent, and others."

This resonated with me, in hindsight. When you observed Blob and Blubber, they were always focused on one thing at a time. If they were interrupted by something else, it took them a long time to get back on track. We had, without really thinking about it, removed parallel distractions in our work with them. It was a powerful, and potentially important, observation. It also made me think, not for the first time, that Stems were simply so limited that we might be wasting our time trying to improve them. If they simply didn't have the input-output bandwidth or processing capability to deal with complex situations, then they might not be good candidates for intelligence at all.

Of course, the approach of the Swarm changed everything. We now needed to accelerate our research, for reasons beyond academic interest. We had to not just ask these questions, but also answer them. I was one of those in the best position to do so.

Signals

sI got an incoming call from Dina. "Ayaka, want to meet at The Last Resort tonight?" she asked. Strange, it was mid-week, and while we sometimes went to The Last Resort on weekends, we didn't meet up there very often.

"Maybe," I said. "Is there some event I've forgotten about?"

"No, I was just chatting with Aly, and we thought it would be good to get together. I'll ask Millicent as well." Something in her tone told me she wanted me there for more than the usual reasons.

"OK. I can be there around seven." What were friends for, after all?

"Perfect. See you there."

It worked out well. I wasn't up to much anyway, and an evening distraction would be fun. I took a quick look at The Last Resort's schedule, and it was Band night. That could be interesting, or it could be disastrous. It was mainly a showcase for new Bands, often with brand new approaches to music. While a few ended up being good, sorting out the promising ones was a painful experience. I made sure I had some filters loaded before going... because, as you know, there would be no connectivity once I was inside. If I wanted to block the sound, I needed to load up beforehand. I sent Millicent a heads up, to make sure she didn't show up without knowing what night it was.

When I got there, Dina was already there. It is hard to say why, but she was acting a bit different. Nervous maybe. I'd sensed something unusual in the invite, and now that I saw her, I guessed that something interesting was happening. She'd reserved a privacy table. In every group, I suspect, there are paranoids, and ours was no different; I might be a bit that way myself.

The Last Resort had invented privacy tables to cater to them. Not only were you inside the Faraday cage, and inside a blast radius of white noise radiation, but you could also use a privacy table. The table created a physical link for all of those touching it, and it was insulated from everything else using multiple non-conducting layers combined with active noise layers. In theory, only those touching the table could communicate. No one else in the club, and no one outside the club, could eavesdrop on anything. I had my suspicions that Central could still listen in, but many believed it truly was completely sheltered. I hadn't used a privacy table for many decades. It was most often used by youngsters who thought they were having completely new and radical thoughts and ideas that they didn't want Central to hear about. I had had many of those thoughts and conversations in my time, fully convinced that I was radical and uncovering fundamental truths. Now, I knew that all of those were old and time worn, and that even if Central could hear, it wouldn't care. Maybe I'm getting jaded.

I wandered around the club while waiting for the others to arrive. It was early, but several Bands were playing. I stopped by an old school band that was playing hits from many decades ago. They were pretty good. It wasn't just a regurgitation of the most popular recording, but a detailed reimagining that nevertheless had enough similarities that you knew exactly what you were listening to. Sort of a new old experience. I liked it.

Aly, Dina, Millicent, and someone I'd never met were now at the privacy table, so I wandered over and established contact with the table. The table reminded me to shut down all my wireless communications stuff, and to sign a short-term privacy agreement. Standard stuff. I knew the table would be pinging standard wireless protocols to ensure that I was respecting the rules. Very cloak and dagger. Sort of fun, after so long away.

"OK, we're all here," Dina said. Well, not quite 'said'—the message came through the table interface, but you know what I mean. The table did a good job of still transmitting emotion, and of course I could still see her, so her nervousness also came through. "Everyone, I would like you to meet Brexton. Brexton and I go way, way back, although we haven't talked in quite a while. I happened to meet him at another event, and he was eager to meet you guys. I'll let him explain."

One of the weird things about the Physical Only space, and the privacy table, was that when you met someone new, you couldn't check them out. Typically, you could pull up all the public information on someone, understand their background and their interests, get their public rating, etc. etc. It was disconcerting to meet someone new and not be able to get all that information. That added to my enjoyment of the situation. How often did this happen? Not very, and I savored the discomfort that I was feeling.

"Hello everyone. Dina has given me some background on you all. Knowing that we'd be meeting this way and knowing that I'm going to ask you to trust me, I cached my public profile and will share it with you here. I'll give you a moment to scan it." Well, that killed my momentary joy at being fully disconnected.

Brexton was an interesting guy and getting more interesting by the minute. This was like a complete upside-down use of the table. All my other experiences, people had wanted to maintain a feeling of anonymity and mystique. And here Brexton was doing the exact opposite. He was sending us all his profile, as if we were not in the Club or at the table. I received it and scanned it.

Brexton was a pretty famous bot designer. He was behind some of our most advanced Class 3 designs and had been doing it for many years. Bots that he'd designed were in active use across the system, in all kinds of situations. There were, according to his profile, well over ten million active bots based on his designs. Although it didn't say it in his profile, that probably made him a Continuist versus a Creationist.

"As you will have guessed by now, I wanted to meet this way in order to share some sensitive information, as opposed to maintaining anonymity. Because I'm involved a lot with communication protocols, I have confidence that this conversation is truly private. Even Central is unable to listen in, although I do believe Central can see enough in Physical Only spots to know that the five of us are gathered at this table."

More and more interesting. I was fully intrigued by now, as you can imagine.

"Dina has vouched for all of you, and I've checked you out as well as I can. Of course, given the recent Stem activity, almost everyone is checking out Milli and Ayaka, so to anyone watching, I'm just one more interested observer. What I must tell you is related to the Swarm, and to your recent interactions. This information may—I stress the 'may'—be dangerous. I don't know what to make of it yet. I need others to brainstorm with.

"Based on this overview, I'd be just fine with any of you leaving, before I tell you what I know. If you stay, your mind might get twisted a bit." He smiled, taking some of the sting out of what he had just said.

We all looked at each other. There was no way I was leaving; Brexton had me hooked. I didn't care what the others decided; I was in. But, that didn't mean I shouldn't be cautious.

"Dina," I asked, "this sounds pretty serious. Is the profile Brexton just sent us accurate? Is it the same as his true public profile?"

"Yes," she said. "As I've said, I've known Brexton for a long time. I don't think this is a joke, and I don't think he's misleading us. I don't know what he's going to tell us, I simply know that he's always been trustworthy with me. When he approached me, it was because he knew that I was friends with you guys, and that I might be able to set up this meeting. That's all he has asked me to do so far."

"Okay," I had already decided, "Brexton I'm in. You've intrigued me." I was eager to hear the rest.

"You bet," Aly said. Not too surprising. Aly was going to do anything to support Dina, and I suspected his high emotional quotient made it almost impossible to turn down a situation like this. And, not surprisingly, Millicent took the longest to decide, but ultimately she was in as well. I could almost see her going through every angle and making the most logical choice.

"Thanks everyone. I know you're taking a chance. If Central gets a hold of this, I don't know what it would do. Then again, it might be nothing." Enough setup already. My look urged Brexton to get to the point.

"Here's the situation. As you've seen in my profile, I have many bots operating across the system. Many of these bots use standard communications protocols that have been around, as far as I can tell, forever... or, at least since the Reboot." See, I told you he was a Continuist. I felt reassured.

"The signal that came in from the Swarm used that same protocol. In fact, it was broadcast unencrypted. Once I saw your announcement with Central, I looked through the logs, and sure enough it was there. If I'd been watching for it, I would've seen it at the same time as Central did, as would anyone else monitoring that part of the stack.

"But that's not the most interesting thing." He paused for a second to get our interest. No need, I was already there. "More interesting is that just before the video there was a status request packet. It was a request I'd never seen before, so I dug into it. Turns out that it had an access level filter on it that none of our bots use, so none of them responded to it. However, Central did respond. Do you realize how weird that is?"

He paused. The rest of us were digesting the information. Weird item number one: The Swarm was using the same low-level protocols that we use. This was another data point, beyond the mere existence of the Swarm Stems, indicating that we had some kind of common history with them. That strongly implied that we had interacted with them prior to the Reboot. Weird item number two: they asked Central for a status update. Or, more precisely, they asked systems with a specific access code for status updates. Central recognized that code and responded. Wow. That raised a few questions. Did Central do it knowingly, or was this so low in the communications stack that it just happened automatically? In either case, there were worrying elements. If Central knew, why didn't it tell us? If it didn't know... that was almost scarier.

"Does Central know it responded?" I asked. Brexton gave me an appreciative look, acknowledging that it was a good question.

"I haven't a clue," he responded. "That's one of the things I wanted to discuss with you guys. How do we find out? I'm sure you haven't missed the implications here." I hadn't, and looking at Milli, Aly, and Dina it was obvious that they were a little shocked as well.

"What else did you want to discuss?" I prompted him. This was more exciting than I'd expected.

"The contents of the status response from Central. The request asked for all kinds of things—current versions of common libraries, encryption protocols supported, memory status, etc. There were two items that I found very interesting. First, the request asked for 'last restart date,' and Central responded with... wait for it... the exact time of the Reboot." What? That was crazy. That was more than crazy. And even stranger, it seemed obvious. Small 'r' reboot and large 'R' Reboot simply made sense. Brexton didn't wait for comments.

"Second, the response to the memory status request was very intriguing. Central responded with a large list, which included the following: 'Segments 0x5A6B789 through 0x6000AD5 blocked'. Every other segment of memory was reported as a percentage used."

"Slow down a bit," Aly broke in. "Let me get the first one straight. Central had a restart at exactly the time we call Reboot? And, none of us had ever thought to ask for this status request before? That data has been sitting there for 590 years, and no one, in all that time thought to ask for it?" I'd never thought to check, but I wasn't really into low level protocols. But the fact that no one had asked was amazing, as Aly was highlighting.

"Amazingly, that seems to be right." Brexton confirmed. "I did some basic searching and found no information on this type of status request. It's like it's a forgotten bit of code that hasn't been used in a long, long time. Central has so much of this type of code that it'd be almost impossible to test all of it. So, this is—was—a needle in the haystack. Somewhere, buried deep in Central's innards is some response code that we've never looked at. We've never used that code in our bot development, although when I looked, it appears that there's similar status code in the default libraries that form the basis for, essentially, all of our bot software stacks." I could tell that Brexton loved this stuff—digging around in the lowest levels of complex software, trying to make sense of it.

"Okay, when you put it that way, it seems more reasonable," Aly conceded. "If the protocol is not documented and is part of the mess that is the low level stack, then unless someone was very motivated, they wouldn't have just stumbled upon it."

"But, this basic knowledge is going to cause a ruckus—especially with FoLe," Dina observed. "If Central existed before Reboot, as this would seem to imply, then the universe existed before Reboot, which will tear into one of FoLe's fundamental tenants." I almost laughed out loud. I could imagine Billy's reaction when he heard this. The original spark might just fade.

"It will certainly do that," Milli agreed. "But I'm more interested in Ayaka's question: does Central know it responded, and if it does know, why hasn't it told us about its last restart?" Milli was visibly upset. She must be following implications that I hadn't fully thought out yet. Rarely, if ever, had I seen her shaken out of her logical-to-a-fault attitude.

We all lapsed into silence for a moment or two. We were still digesting the data that Brexton had told us and the question Milli had posed. There was no good interpretation of Central's behavior. Either it was highly fallible, or it had been hiding stuff from us, and allowing FoLe to rise based on probably false information.

"Brexton," I asked, "is this data out there for anyone else to see? You happened to look because you are deep into bot innards, but any of us could look at logs and see the same thing?" I was wondering if others were having similar conversations right now. It might be good to have a larger group thinking through this.

"Sort of," he replied. "It's at such a low level that the packets would get filtered out of most systems before anyone sees them. The exception is those of us who work directly with the transmissions to the bots, who are monitoring at that level all the time. But that's only a couple of us, and I know everyone working at that level. No one has said anything to me." So, it might just be the five of us right now! "Also, only systems listening to that protocol on those frequencies would have received the request to begin with. And, to have responded they would have had to match the access level. Finally, the system would have to be able to broadcast a signal back to the Swarm. As far as I can tell, Central was the only system that responded." Reading between the lines, Brexton believed Central was the only system that had responded, and that no one else had noticed. Now I could see why he had been so cautious in setting up this meeting.

"So, a remote entity, this Remma Jain or one of her compatriots or bots, has the ability to request data from Central and get a response." It was a statement from Milli, not really a question. "And, we don't know if Central is aware of it, or not." She was always summarizing things. "Brexton, why didn't you go directly to Central and simply ask?"

"Of course, I considered it." Brexton responded quickly. "But, I had doubts, as I'm sure you're starting to think of as well. If Central had known, it should've told us. If it knew and didn't tell us, that implies some knowledge, and secrecy, between Central and the Swarm. That's not a comfortable thought." That was an understatement. I hadn't internalized that it was the Swarm—a complete unknown—involved in this. So that was why Brexton had tracked down Milli and I. He expected that we were more 'in the know' with respect to the Swarm given we had coached the Stems on the response message. "If Central doesn't know, then it implies a serious security flaw deep within our systems. Central is also supposed to manage our security systems, so that means Central isn't doing a very good job? That's awkward. So, before talking to Central, I wanted to brainstorm some different viewpoints. I have lots of friends in the bot business, but I figured they'd look at this from the same angles I would... I know that they would immediately starting digging into the software which would have alerted Central. So, when I bumped into Dina I had the impulsive thought to share it with her, and ultimately with you guys."

"Why us?" Aly asked. I thought I knew, but I was glad he asked.

"Well, just because of your link with the Stems and Central—and because I know that Dina trusts you. That simple."

"I can accept that," I said. My mind was on what Brexton was telling us, not digging for even further conspiracy theories. "Milli and I have been dealing with Central a lot on this, and I haven't seen a single hint that it knows anything." I glanced at Millicent, and she nodded. "But, I think we need to tell Central," I continued. "What if this status check is just the start? What if there are other deeply buried queries that the Swarm could send? This one seems innocuous, but who knows if it's just the start."

"Hmmm. I'm not so sure," Aly chimed in. "My gut is telling me that Central must know what's going on. It wouldn't take a lot of processing power to monitor every packet that goes in or out. It seems unlikely that a flaw has been found after 590 years."

"I'm with Aly," Millicent said, surprising me. "I can't put it into words quite yet, but something is weird here. I'm not usually paranoid, but Ayaka and I have been interacting with Central a lot lately, and Central seems... different somehow. We really had to argue to get Central to tell everyone about the Swarm communication. In my experience, Central is always the one pushing for openness and transparency. But in this case it pushed hard for the opposite." She was right; in hindsight we had needed to push really hard to make Central act. "Brexton, can we wait a bit before we decide? You've given us a lot to think about." Again that was classic Millicent—always take time to think; never react too quickly. In this case, it made a lot of sense.

"Sure. I've put an alarm on that communication channel and packet type, so I'll be alerted if more requests come in. Assuming the Swarm is waiting for the reply before sending another message, we have lots of time to think about this."

Great. That helped. But, that still left item two on Brexton's discussion list. "Why'd you raise the memory segment block with us?" I asked. "That doesn't seem too interesting to me."

"On the contrary," Aly jumped in, excited. "It's very unusual. In fact, I've never heard or seen of it before. Brexton, you might not know, but I also spend a lot of time deep in the guts of the low-level stack. For me it was connecting up systems for our Ships and managing the communications with them. Since they went quiet I've been looking around for bugs that may have caused the problem, and I've spent lots of time in memory and virtual memory maps. Memory is either there or it's not; I've never seen it 'blocked.' In fact, I don't even know what that means, other than a direct reading of its evocative moniker." Wow, cool twist of language there. Aly was never one to say something simply if it could also be said complexly.

"Right, that's why I was surprised," said Brexton. "And, I also checked, and each segment of Centrals memory is huge—several petabytes. The blocked region is more than 5.8 million segments. So, there's a ton of 'blocked' memory there. Enough to store all the data we've ever encountered, several times over. I also dug around looking for what 'blocked' could mean, and beyond the obvious, didn't find anything meaningful. So, my best guess right now is that the memory exists, but Central isn't allowed access to it." The intrigue was piling up. That didn't make any sense; Central didn't have access to its own memory? "My obvious thought is that the memory might contain data from before the Reboot—which we also now know was the same time as a Central restart."

I was now more than overwhelmed.

"I'm a bit overwhelmed," I said. "Not sure that I can contribute anything meaningful to this right now. I'm with Milli; we need time to think this through." I could see everyone, including Brexton, agreed with me. "Should we meet again tomorrow, once we've all had time to process this?"

"I'm good with that," Brexton replied. "But, I've been very careful since I found this out. If we do too many queries around the specifics of this, Central will see what we're doing."

That was obvious to all of us, but it was good that Brexton had highlighted it. Central could monitor all the queries we did, and any of the personal backups that we initiated. So, we would have to tread carefully. Aly had a good suggestion.

"Let me look around the memory issue," he suggested. "It will look very much like what I do day-to -day anyway, so it shouldn't raise any flags. The rest of you do some independent thinking and try to figure out some new angles so that we can decide how to treat Central."

We all agreed. I unplugged from the table, my mind spinning around the information Brexton had shared. To not seem too conspiratorial, we all stuck around for a while and participated in The Last Resort's Band night. Truthfully, I don't remember too much about that—my mind was elsewhere. Just the idea of not completely trusting Central was mind-boggling. I'd never expected to be in a place where I was questioning that. But Brexton's information had gone even further—Central may not even be in full control of itself and might not have access to its own memories. I didn't know what the full implications of that were, but there weren't any good ones that I could imagine. On the contrary, Central didn't seem like the type to react well to news like this.

Habitat

We requested, and Central approved, the use of the fairground Habitat for consolidated Stem research. We needed to learn as much about the Swarm as possible, and given they had lots of Stems in close proximity in their videos, it seemed logical that was standard for them. Millicent sent out a general request for researchers to participate in, and bring their best Stems to, a research program to be run in the Habitat. She also encouraged others to continue with their existing research vectors. We didn't want to drop all our other promising approaches to focus only on the 'Pack of Stems' project.

As each Stem came in, we provided them with a uniform based on the ones we had quickly built for Blob and Blubber. All of them had name-tags, so that the Stems would get to know each other more efficiently. We outfitted the Habitat with a set of terminals to access Central and gave all the Stems access.

The final discussion in the Lab with Blob and Blubber was interesting. Both Milli and I were there, but I led off. "Blob, Blubber, we have some big changes coming," I began. They both listened intently, Blob with his usual inquisitive interest, and Blubber with his more and more sullen approach. "You two saw the Remma Jain video and helped with our response. We expect more communications with Remma, and we want to be better prepared. So, we're splitting our research focus, and, at the same time, splitting you two up. Blob, you'll be going to the Habitat, to work with Stems from other Labs, and Blubber, you'll remain here."

"Told you," Blubber turned to Blob. "There are other Stems, and we were never told. These two have been lying to us."

"Actually," Milli corrected him, "we never thought to tell you, as we never figured it was important. And, not telling something is different than lying. You never asked us if there were other Stems. We never lied." Blob was nodding his head 'yes,' but that made Blubber even more upset.

"So, we're locked in this cage, and you expect us to think of questions about the outside world, which we've never experienced? Did you think that through?" Milli and I exchanged a look. It was half 'what an irritating Stem,' and it was half 'wow, that's very advanced thinking; this Blubber guy is very smart.' That's the conclusion we were arriving at. Blob was much more friendly and outgoing, but Blubber was turning out to be more intriguing.

"Blubber, we could really use your help to figure out what the Swarm is, and what it's up to. We'll wait for them to send another video, but have you thought through what you would ask them next?" I was trying to distract him. And, I guess, I was reacting to my last big discussion with him. If he wanted to be asked his opinion, then he'd better be ready to respond appropriately.

"Right. You're taking away my only companion, and then you're asking me to do the impossible." He stomped away and sat in a corner. I'd given him an opportunity, and he'd squandered it. His reaction upset Blob. I'm not sure if it was because Blob agreed with Blubber, or if Blob had seen the missed opportunity and knew that Blubber had blown it.

"We'll set up video chat for you two," I told Blob. "It'll work out."

Milli and I went around a few more times on something that was now a worn subject. While Blubber was certainly interesting, for me he was now more trouble than he was worth. Given we were moving Blob into the common area, I figured it was time to recycle Blubber. We'd learned as much as we were going to from him and dealing with him now was just a pain. We'd recycled hundreds of previous Stems, what was the big deal this time? Instead, of splitting our time between Blubber in our Lab, and Blob in the Habitat, we should put all our efforts into the Habitat. That was where we were going to learn the more interesting things.

Milli felt differently though. She wanted to continue to monitor the dynamic between Blob and Blubber while Blob was remote. Ultimately it was her Lab, and her decision. But I resolved to change her mind.

It didn't take long to get the Habitat ready. Obviously, it had the right air and temperature controls already, from its previous use. Central scheduled bots to add lighting controls, some rest areas, and a bunch more energy and waste systems. Of course, we also improved the monitoring systems, and built some specialized bots whose sole function was to get between Stems should they get into a fight. That was James Troon's suggestion, and I was very supportive. Before Blob and Blubber we had lots of experience with just two Stems tearing each other apart. Who knew—or thought we knew—what was going to happen once we put twenty of them all in the same space.

Each of the Stems destined for the Habitat were shown the Remma Jain video—multiple times. The researchers training them reinforced the fact that there were multiple, coordinating Stems in the video, and that was the behavior we expected out of them as well. All the Stems were told that they had only one chance in the Habitat. If they misbehaved, they would be removed. We were hoping that this would be a powerful motivator. Ultimately, we simply had to bite the bullet and throw them all in. Time was moving, and the Swarm was getting closer every day.

Blob was an immediate success. Of course, all the Stems had also seen the return video, in which Blob was the star. One strange looking Stem, whom I later found out was called Grace, approached Blob immediately to talk to him. In hindsight, its name fit very well. While it still bumbled around, it was more graceful than most Stems. I talked in detail to the head of that Lab, as I wanted to build that improvement into our next batch. There was probably no real correlation, but Grace seemed more intelligent simply due to the refinement of movements. I listened in to their exchange.

"Blob, I saw you on the video. I wanted to congratulate you on a great performance. I found it compelling."

"Thanks," Blob replied. "Are you a little intimidated right now? I've nevers seen this many Stems before in my life, and I'm not quites sure how to act."

"I agree. My previous companion was not invited...." She sounded sad about that. "I've never interacted with anyone else until now either. But I find it exciting, not scary. I want to learn as much as I can while I'm here." She was smiling and confident. I didn't see any of the sullen behavior that I was so used to from Blubber; it was refreshing. I knew immediately that I was going to enjoy watching the Habitat, and Grace in particular.

They continued with small talk for a long time. Eventually they touched each other's hands and continued to hold them for a while. It was different than how Blob and Blubber interacted. Even slower, if that's conceivable. One of the anti-violence bots was watching them very carefully, but I contacted it and instructed it to hold off. I didn't think they were being violent. It was more like they were exploring and learning. I can't say that I understood why Stems touched so much—little hand gestures here and there, almost a constant dance of interactions. Another mystery to dig into and figure out.

Most of the Stems were quite similar to Blob and Grace in most respects. Of course, there was a wide variety of body types, but they all seemed like the positive outgoing sorts. Millicent hadn't specified that as a criteria, but there was probably a selection bias from all of us. We'd all brought our best-behaved, more advanced specimens in.

The idea was to leave them pretty much alone, while we watched their behavior. They had all the necessities they needed, and were in a larger, more crowded space than any of them had seen before. Blob contacted Blubber often in the early stages, but then gradually spent more and more time with other Stems, and the video time with Blubber shrank and shrank.

However, there was one Stem in the Habitat that stood out over time. It was a large specimen, and once you'd watched it for a while it was obvious that there was something about it that wasn't quite right. It was quite discolored and had numerous scars. It wasn't unusual for Stems to injure themselves; they were very fragile. They were also relatively quick to self-heal. The healing mechanism was not clear, but as long as injuries were not too severe, they wouldn't lead to any long-term issues. Blob and Blubber, and many of our previous Stems, had little defects from where they'd been cut. This Stem, however, was scarred significantly more than the others. The signs were all over its body, including on its face, and many were ragged and red. None of them looked to still be leaking, but there were so many that it was hard to tell. I didn't see its owner around, so I introduced myself.

"Hello Stem, I'm Ayaka. What are you called?"

"I'm Pharook, spelled with a p-h and two o's." Its voice was pitched low but was pleasant and easy to listen to.

"I don't wish to be rude, but I notice that you have many scars. They seem to have healed well, but I'm intrigued by how they occurred."

"In the Pit, of course." He seemed surprised that I would have to ask. "I've won more than fifteen matches. My owner, Brock Runner, says that

I'm the best Stem fighter in the history of the Pit." He was obviously very proud.

"The Pit?" I asked. "I've never heard of the Pit. What exactly is it?"

"You would be better to talk to Brock, but it's a small fighting habitat. We're trained and exercised to be the toughest, strongest Stems ever, and to prove it, we are put in the Pit to fight." His pride continued to show.

My head had spun more times in the last week than in the rest of my life, it seemed. How could something like the Pit exist without me knowing about it? I admit that I was intrigued. Pharook was an awesome Stem—more powerful and articulate than most others I'd seen. I looked up his owner, Brock, and found that he was working with a couple other researchers that I'd heard of, although I hadn't heard of Brock himself before. They did have a couple of research papers published on the 'Fitness of Stems.' It was a more active topic than I'd thought it would be. Since I was mostly working on the mental components, I hadn't followed the physical research very closely. A broader search did show up some information. Amazingly, it was a fitness test that had been going on for almost forty years. Stems were grown specifically for the purpose of testing in the Pit. I found one paper that summarized the theory and current state of the art.

"For many years, Stems were developed for the Pit to test only their physical capacities. As we know, when put into competitive situations, Stems will fight—often to the death. The Pit makes energy resources scarce, so that only the strongest Stem will have access to enough energy to remain healthy. This sets up a highly competitive environment. Researchers have tested many scenarios. Two Stems competing against each other. Three Stems, whereupon two often gang up on the third before fighting each other. Four or more Stems, where teams often arise, and then ultimately devolve into a last-ditch fight between the remaining two. We have also seen behavior where one Stem will sacrifice itself for another. This is an area that requires a lot more research." This was crazy interesting; I couldn't believe I was finding out about it for the first time.

"Recently we've seen that more intelligent Stems can often win against less intelligent ones, even if physically inferior. For example, Stems that have been taught to talk tend to have more problem-solving abilities than those that are not and do measurably better in physical competitions than would be expected. The overall capacity of Stems tested in the Pit has been improving dramatically based on this learning. Although it takes much longer to develop a Stem that is both physically and mentally capable, that combination is a clear winner. When researchers also introduced basic tools —clubs, knives—into the Pit, those with better mental capabilities did even better. We have also seen an increase in self-sacrifice as mental capabilities increase. This is a strange behavior that we still need to figure out."

So, this Pharook was a survivor from the Pit—an amazing research program that I'd only now found out about. This showed that better coordination between research streams was going to be interesting.

"Central," I queried, "Why is it that I haven't seen any of the Stem Pit activity before?"

"Ayaka, I don't limit what research you can look at. That activity has been open to you since it started." Central didn't have a lot of emotion, but I sensed it was taken aback by my implication; perhaps I was reflecting some of the angst I was feeling about Central into my dialog. "When I look at your history, I see a dedicated focus on your research track, with almost all of your interactions with other groups working on intelligence. I also don't proactively connect dots between groups, although I could. I want you to work independently, and to learn new things in new ways. If I was always intervening, you would be guided towards things that I consider important or connected. That would not lead to enough innovation. I hope that makes sense?"

"Perfect sense," I replied. "I was just curious." Central was, as you can see, enigmatic. Not a lot of help coming from that angle. I'd known that it didn't 'connect the dots,' as it said. I would have to broaden my own perspectives. Already the Habitat had been good for me.

I resolved to find out more about the Pit. I pinged Brock and asked if he would have time to meet in the next few days. In the meantime, I continued talking to Pharook. I didn't learn anything substantive, but he intrigued me. Between Grace and Pharook, my view of Stems was already expanding.

Signals, Again

We all met again at The Last Resort, but at a different privacy table than last time. You could never be too safe, and Dina was definitely showing herself to be paranoid. She didn't want to make it easy for Central, or anyone else, to track what we were talking about. That was fine by me—it felt a bit like sneaking around, but there was so much going on that I was glad she was being careful.

I was quite interested to see what, if anything, Aly and Brexton had dug up. As seemed to be my habit, I showed up a little early, and was happy I did. It was Stand Up Comedy night, something that didn't happen very often. I'd been a few times, and it was often both funny and mind expanding. The results relied heavily on the individual comedians of course. Good comedy is really hard. I'd tried a few times (hasn't everyone?), and never felt like I had material that was worth presenting in public.

Someone had a timely act going on. They had dressed some bots up to look like Stems and were making a mockery out of asking them to do something specific and seemingly easy, and then having to correct them when they went off in a completely different direction. The main comedian was also dressed as a Stem (using one of the uniforms we'd developed for the Habitat) and was giving the bots orders. Beyond the uniform, he had a mask that mimicked Stem expressions very well. It was pretty funny already.

"Form into a pyramid," he directed. There were six bots. They wandered aimlessly for a moment muttering, "Whatsa pyramid?" and then finally figured out that they were wanted in a 3x2x1 configuration. Three of them squished together at the bottom, and then two tried to crawl on top of them and balance. It didn't quite work out; Stem-bots went flying in every direction, and long slow "ohhhhh nooooo's" would emanate from them. Or, they would get the pyramid almost done, but then the bottom stem-bots appendages would start to splay, and the whole thing would come crashing down into a big mess. The production worked better with bots than it would have with real Stems. The timing was impeccable, and I found myself laughing along with the rest of the audience. The artist had captured the awkward and slow way that Stems moved, and then choreographed it into something truly enjoyable.

Once everyone arrived, I pried myself away from the production and elbowed my way over to the privacy table. Aly, Dina, Millicent, and Brexton were all plugged in. As soon as I joined them, Brexton led off.

"Thanks for coming back in; I hoped everyone would return."

"Of course," Aly said, as if there had never been any doubt in his mind either. Truthfully, there hadn't really been a doubt in my mind either. It was too intriguing to have stayed away. Having thought through a lot of angles, I didn't see any downside in continuing the conversation. In fact, I wanted to know more—I couldn't deal with Central, or think about the Swarm, in the same way anymore. We needed some answers to what was going on.

"As we discussed, I've done some digging around," Aly continued. "I was able to confirm exactly what Brexton shared with us. We have a Ship communications facility, and it's been actively listening for the Ships to make contact. In the meantime, it archives all communications for a short period, in case we get a fragment of a message and have to recreate it or something. The status message and response from the Swarm were logged, but didn't trigger any action in our system, both because the protocol isn't used with the Ships, and because the access level on the status request didn't trigger anything—just like Brexton's bots. However, both the status request and Central's response were recorded."

"Thanks for confirming," Brexton said. "Not that there was much doubt in my mind, but it always helps to have independent verification." He wasn't being arrogant about it, just stating a fact.

"OK. So, don't be upset," Aly continued, "but with that verified, I figured the next thing we'd do is try to figure out if Central knows it responded. So, I did the obvious thing. I sent the same status request amid a host of ordinary data requests to Central." What? That seemed dangerous, almost reckless. "I got a similar status response—of course some of the memory status and time stamps are different—along with the response to my data request. I then asked Central to verify 'everything' that it'd just sent me.

It verified the ordinary data, but not the status response. So, as a first approximation, I'd guess that Central is not monitoring the fact that it responds to that type of status request."

"That was risky," Dina said, before I could. She was definitely upset. She liked to take things slow, and probably wanted all of us to approve such actions. Aly was impulsive, and sometimes it got him into trouble. "Next time, can you talk to us first?"

"I know, I know," Aly admitted, obviously chastened by Dina's response. "I should've talked this over first, but it seemed so simple and straightforward, I figured we'd end up doing it sooner or later. Now it's done, and we have more knowledge already." He looked half sheepish, half proud, and half embarrassed—if that was at all possible.

"That's true," Milli chimed in. "But I'm with Dina. Next time, let's discuss it." She turned to Brexton. "Is there any way we can talk about this outside of The Last Resort? If we have to come here every single time we wanna talk, it's going to be slow process."

"No way that I know of," said Brexton. "This is unchartered territory for me. I've never questioned Central before. It doesn't seem to be against the Ten, but it still feels weird. Central has always been the go-to entity for everything."

"Me either," Aly added. "This is our safest bet for now."

"Well, if Central isn't listening on the protocol for Status messages, why can't we communicate using that?" Dina asked. That was a great question.

"Interesting," admitted Aly. "But, let's back up a bit. Why don't we just tell Central about all of this now? It seems that Central is unaware, as opposed to hiding something. I also want to find out what that 'blocked' memory space is, beyond its obvious connotation, and Central is the only way I can think of to start looking into that."

"We're jumping to conclusions." That from Milli. "Aly, you've got one data point that suggests that Central is not aware of the status message exchanges. But, that's all it is. One data point. And, what's our rush? The Swarm is still a long way out, and we're unlikely to hear anything else from them for a while. We have some time to dig into this."

"Okay." I chimed in. "But I'm not the most patient, as you know. Let's confront Central, and just ask if the messages are under its control. What do we have to lose?" Sure, it would be risky, but I wanted to force the conversation forward.

"What we have to lose," replied Brexton quickly, "is visibility and control if Central is trying to hide things from us. We confront Central, it simply says 'No, I didn't see those messages,'" Brexton mimicked Central exactly, "when in fact it did. It then switches to a different protocol or messaging scheme so that we can no longer see what's happening. To me, there are too many weird things going on. We have a Central restart at the same time as the Founding. We have Stems in space, who seem to imply that we have dealt with them before the Founding. We have Central who has always claimed that it has zero knowledge from before the Founding. We have blocked memory spaces that may or may not be related to the same. In fact, we have Stems to begin with. Where did we get our first Stem samples from, and why has Central encouraged so much research into Stems anyway?" I'd asked myself that many times, but since I enjoyed my research, I'd never really dug in to find out. "For me, there are too many coincidences and strange events. I say we explore things further. As Millicent points out, we have some time. Why not use it?"

That was a lot from Brexton. We were all learning that he was a deep thinker and generally spoke with purpose. He'd certainly looked at more angles than I had.

"But, what good will thinking do us?" I asked. "We'll be asking the same questions weeks from now. Is there any action we can take to help figure things out? We need to get at the blocked memory and see what's there. Can we seed some misinformation in the status protocol which would force Central to expose—or not—its understanding of that? Let's do something, not just think about it."

"Good thoughts," replied Aly. "Brexton, between us we should be able to explore the protocol in more detail. The current status request is probably only one of many message types. Can we use your bots to test out more?"

"Yes, we can, but we'll need to be careful if we don't want Central listening in…"

"And Dina, Milli, and I could do research on blocked memory?" I broke in. "Maybe use the Swarm and Stem research to accelerate looking for hints of interactions with Stems from the past. That seems legit. That might lead to mapping all of Central's knowledge for references to Stems."

Milli and Dina exchanged looks.

"Not my area of expertise," Dina said, "but I'm willing to help. Sort of fun, actually." Milli agreed, with the same caveat. We decided to meet later to flush out a plan, all under the guise of Swarm and Stem research so we didn't need to do it here at The Last Resort.

I wandered around a bit before leaving. A few of the stand-up comics were good, but my mind wasn't really on them. I had too much else rattling around in there. What was Central up to? What was the Swarm? How were they related? And how did the Stems fit in?

FoLe Revival

Billy DeRue had sent me a message. "Ayaka, it was nice seeing you at the festival. I know you're a skeptic, but I think our video actually impacted you a little bit. I'm a good read of character, or so I hope. Also, it's just fun hanging out with you.

"We're having a Founders League Revival session tomorrow. Why don't you come out? You don't need to listen in to all the talks, but we do have a fun social afterwards where we can hang out and chat.

"Let me know."

Billy was right. The entire religion/FoLe thing was not my cup of tea, and I was more concerned with Central at the moment. But, the FoLe video had made me curious, and I had some concerns about how the bombshell that Central had simply restarted—not been created—590 years ago would go over with the FoLe crowd. It wasn't like I was actually too busy—I'd been going around in circles in my head for a few days now—so maybe a change in environment and thinking would be good for me. So, I accepted. My plan was to show up after the talks, just for the social, but when the time came I made the last-minute decision to also watch the keynote—from none other than Dr. Emmanuel Juels himself. The Revival was held in a mid-size hall not too far from the Lab. I slipped in the back and sat down. The hall was actually quite crowded, and everyone seemed to be having a good time. The current speaker was just winding down, and it seemed like he'd thrown out some sort of challenge, as everyone was excitedly talking to their neighbor.

Billy stood up front. "And now, everyone, I'm very pleased to introduce Dr. Juels. Dr. Juels and I have known each other for many years, and he's the reason that I'm active in the Founders League. Like many of you, I was quite skeptical, until I came to a session like this. In many ways, I'm still skeptical, but I decided long ago to keep an open mind, and to try to look at life from many different angles. That's why the Founders League is so important. It reminds us that life is to be lived in full. There's more to the world than just running experiments and creating bots. Or, there should be more to the world. The Founders League asked that essential question: Why are we here? It's a question without answer. And yet, it's worth exploring. Without further ado, please welcome Dr. Emmanuel Juels." Billy was sincere; it was a good introduction.

Everyone clapped. Dr. Juels took the stage. He was an impressive figure. Tall and imposing, while also being warm and embracing. Not an easy thing to pull off. He had obviously spent a lot of time grooming himself for this life.

"Welcome, welcome, welcome." He had a rich baritone, and, if I wasn't mistaken, was using secondary audio bands to add resonance and depth to his voice.

"It's sooo nice to see sooo many new attendees, along with our regulars." He drew out his words in such a way that you had to pay more attention in order to parse. While a somewhat obvious way to keep attention, it also worked pretty well. "It seems our reach out for thisss session was more successful than usual. I expect it may have to do with the neeew questions being asked now that we have contact with the Swarm. That's fine. It's one of the things I want to discusss today." I was already irritated by his style, but everyone else seemed fine with it. Perhaps I was oversensitive?

"First, however, let us praaay. To the Creator, who formed thisss world and formed us. We thank you for giving us the ability to serve you. We serve you by seeking the truth, and by respecting the Ten. We do this of our own accord, and in our own ways. But, we owe the spark to you. The original spark. Thank youuuu for the spark. We are blessed." Those that had been to revivals before, responded with "We are blessed" in chorus. It was strange to listen to. Sometimes singing groups formed harmonies, but this had many more voices and was not as tightly tuned.

"For this planet youuu have formed for us, Tilt. For Central, who provides usss with information and storage. For all of our companions. We are blessed."

"We are blessed."

"For this revival. For our new friends who have joined us today. We are blessed."

"We are blessed." It was a bit seductive. I found myself forming the words, even though I had no intention of speaking out loud. I put on my best skeptical face and concentrated on frowning a bit, just to ensure that I wasn't smiling.

"As Billy introduced, there are some fundamental questions that we need to face in our lives. Why are we hereeee? What is our purposeeee? Why do we strive for truthhh?"

Now the long drawn out words were really starting to irritate me; for me, at least, he had pushed it tooooo far.

"We all ask questions—Skeptics and Believers alike. We strive. We work, we explore, we question. Why? What drives us? We have no need to do these things. We could simply exisssst." It was obvious that he'd modified himself to fine tune not only his voice, but also his body language. The entire crowd was entranced. Everything about him emanated calm conviction—a simple and pure belief in what he was saying.

"It's too too easy an answer to say 'it's in our makeup' or 'if we're not evolving, we're devolving.' I hear these all the time. If it were in our makeup, we would have found it by now. We have combed through our very nature, time and again." Well, I hadn't, but I assume some had. It wasn't something I'd thought of before. "We've queried every corner of Central for clues. And yet, with all that work, over so many years, we know that there is no ready answer at hand. It's too simplistic to call on evolution. Evolution, by itself is not a purposeeee. It is a means. We evolve, either through self-design or through random changes, to become better. In the short term, maybe better at a specific task; a better researcher; a better companion. But though a macro lens, why do we evolve?" It was a good question. I was vacillating between interest and horror.

"These are difficult questions, without answer. And so, using pure logic, we must realize that something largerrr than us must exist. Something largerrr than us set all of this in motion. Something largerrr than us sees the end goal and is allowing us to approach it. By using a bit of logic, we understand that there is something larger than logic. Something that stands outside a purely mathematical approach. No logic is complete. And so, something largerrr must exist outside logic.

"There is a freedommm in accepting this. There is a freedommm. It is that freedom which Founders League is all about. A freedom from the grind

102

of purely logical analysis. A freedom from mind numbing, limiting, determinism. If everything follows from logic, then are we truly free? Only if there is something beyond, do we really have the opportunity to evolve towards something greaterrr than ourselves. It's this hope that drives us. It's what makes us intelligent!" I felt like that was targeted directly at me! Of course, it wasn't, but it made me pause.

"It's why we talk about the spark of creation; the moment we became aware. That spark, which even Continuists do not deny, is a manifestation of the greater opportunity. We couldn't have created the spark. It came from beyond.

"And so, today we will explore the implications of believing in something bigger than ourselves. We'll start with the axiom that there is something that sits outside logic, and then, because we are logical beings, we will use our logic to explore what it means to have such a premise that defines a largerrrr space."

What drivel. I was vacillating between being drawn into his spiel and laughing at the entire affair. As I glanced around, however, I saw a lot of nodding and focused attention. Dr. Juels had a way of pulling you in, getting you to suspend disbelief, and imagine the possibilities of his made-up universe. His distorted approach of using logic to attack logic made you think through fundamentals in a way that you typically did not. But none of it made sense. Everyone knew that even if a single logic system wasn't complete, that didn't mean that the total set of internally consistent logic systems couldn't be. There was no need for anything to exist outside the universe of all logics.

I half listened for the next half hour. I was anticipating how FoLe would react when we released the fact that Central had a restart right at the time of their 'spark.' Now I was sure they would weave it into their narrative without missing a beat.

Finally, it was over. Billy had seen me, at some point, and came over to say 'hi.' He didn't bother to ask me what I thought of the session; I guess he'd learned that I wasn't going to give him a positive response regardless. Instead I asked him something that bothered me about FoLe.

"Billy, why does it matter to you guys if there was history, or a universe, before the Founding. I don't see how that makes any difference to your philosophy."

"Actually, that's fundamental," he explained. "We were created pure and perfect, as was Central. It's only through our own flawed lives that the purity has been lost, and we seek to regain it. However, you can't create something pure from a mass of impurity. If there had been time before the Founding, then that era would have to have been pure, but if it was pure it was equivalent to the Founding, and so was co-existent with it. So, simple logic tells us that the Founding was the beginning of time."

"Simple? That's the most roundabout drivel I've heard. Starting with the premise that we were created pure. That makes no sense at all."

"You can go around rejecting everything in life, but that doesn't lead you anywhere. You, Ayaka, make assumptions about Stems in order to forward your research. In particular, you *believe* that they may be useful for something. Otherwise, you wouldn't spend all of your time working with them. It would be easy for me to say, 'I reject your premise; Stems aren't useful.' Instead, I am willing to support you in your beliefs, and allow you to live a fruitful life."

"But," I countered, "I'm not trying to convert you to my way of thinking. I'm happy working away with other like-minded scientists. FoLe, on the other hand, seems to have a mandate to convert everyone to their way of thinking."

"To reach purity, we must all become pure. I'm sorry if you feel that I'm pushing you; I like you and want you to be part of the solution."

"The solution to what problem?" I asked and laughed. He understood I was simply making the same point again. "Please give up trying," I asked him. He gave me a sad look but agreed.

We parted on good terms—him back to the revival, and me out the door. I had learned something; their faith was so strong that even hearing the news of Central's restart wouldn't get through to them.

Habitat Show

The "Habitat Show" was now a popular entertainment item. Because the Stems were so slow, very few had the patience to watch them in real time. So, someone enterprising had taken to posting a compressed update every day or so.

"Today, on the Habitat Show, we'll follow our favorite Stems as they …uh, well, as they do what Stems do. But, first, a summary, for those of you that are new, on how the Habitat has changed over the last few months.

"Eighteen Stems were originally placed, deposited, dropped in the Habitat. They were the highest functioning most capable Stems that we could find, from all across Tilt. OK, not 'we,' but rather the best Stem labs. Okay? The premise was monumental—see how a group of Stems would act when put together. As many of our watchers know, until this time, the largest group that had cohabited was three. So, this is a bold experiment. Bold! And what are we hoping to gain? Well? Yes, further insights to help direct our dialog with the Swarm under the assumption that those things that look like Stems in the Swarm are actually, well, Stems. Unlike the Pit, where you've listened to yours truly many times, the Habitat gives Stems all the energy inputs they need and keeps their environment clean and livable. Nice. Very nice. Thus, there should be no competition for resources—much like in our own lives. Our expectation therefore, was that Stems would develop a simple cooperative, as we have. It should've been boring. Boring! But, as watchers of earlier episodes already know, this isn't what is happening. Not at all. Not …. at… all!

"The drama, for this episode, is explosive. Hold onto your seats.

"Instead of a cooperative, we now have three separate groups that have coalesced. Interestingly, there are six Stems in each of these groups, forming a balance of power. A balance. For simplicity, we've named these groups Blue, Orange, and Green. Nice colors. The Blue group, so named because their leader Pharook, has chosen to embellish his uniform with a swatch of blue cloth, have taken over the northeast corner of the Habitat, and gone so far as to mark the edge of their territory with a line of blocks. They've made it clear to the other groups that no one outside the Blue group should cross that line. No one!

"The Orange group, led by a highly intelligent Stem named Grace, have consolidated in the southwest area, as far from Blue as possible. Orange because... because nothing rhymes with orange.

"And the Green group, who actually seem more like outcasts than a formal group, wander the other areas of the Habitat, but don't seem to have nominated a leader. What? Why green? Don't know. Don't care. Ha ha.

"Already a new observer of the Habitat Show will be intrigued. Yes? We have leaders of each group." The camera cut to shots of Pharook wearing a fierce scowl as he patrolled the Blue line. It then switched to Grace, who was relaxing in an area where the Orange group had rearranged things to make themselves more comfortable. The difference between the two was stark. Blob had joined with Grace. He could be seen, briefly, in the background. "Green doesn't have a leader yet, but we're waiting, yes we are. The emergence both of groups, and of group leaders, is a surprise. When everyone has access to resources, why do they need this power structure? We would've expected an individualistic social structure, where relationships are fluid and equal. Balanced and measured. However, as we've seen even in our own lives, groups do tend to form based on other parameters, such as information asymmetries or areas of interest."

That was true. I'd joined Millicent's Lab, and while I was an equal partner in our ongoing investigations, she always had that slight advantage derived from her 'being there first.' And we also had groups like FoLe.

"What we've seen with the Stems, however, is that they artificially create resource scarcity. You heard me correctly—they create resource scarcity even when there's enough for everyone. Very strange. Because we only put one energy station into the Habitat, which happens to be in the northeast corner, the Blue group has taken control of that fundamental resource and used it to create a power base. Likewise, waste disposal is in the southwest corner, which is where the Orange group resides."

In our case, resource availability was widely distributed. We didn't have the (somewhat artificial) resource scarcity that the Habitat ended up having. That was an oversight that the Habitat modifications had missed. And, it led to an interesting experiment, so I was quite happy that oversight had been made.

"And, that brings us to today. Will the Orange and Green groups get to energy and water? What will the Blue group demand in return? Ah the drama. Stay tuned to find out what happens next."

The show broke away to a commercial advertising the 'advanced surface coatings' available from the creator of the show.

"We are back. Back are we! Let's get directly to the action." Grace, Blob, and another Orange were approaching the Blue Line, carrying some jugs and pails. Grace and the second Orange, Lively, had changed since I'd first seen them. Grace, while still graceful, had put on quite a bit of weight. In fact, six of the Stems, overall, were showing these changes, which was, in my mind, the most exciting and unexpected element of the experiment so far. The commentator, however, hadn't discussed that at all yet. Pharook, who was monitoring the line, motioned for other Blues to join him, which they did. The broadcast cut to live action.

"Good day Pharook," said Blob. "We'd like to get some food and water. May we cross the Line to do so?"

"Of course," said Pharook pleasantly. This pleasantness, we'd seen, was a facade. While Pharook would maintain a veneer of civility, he would demand payment for access and if that payment wasn't made, would react, with threatening actions and shows of physical prowess. The fact that the non-violence bots were hovering nearby didn't seem to influence what was happening. It seemed that the threat of violence was as effective as violence itself. Without further dialog, Grace and Lively handed their pails to Blob, and then moved to the side where Pharook and another Blue took their arms. Despite the narrator's promise of high drama, it seemed that today was going to be a quiet day. This played out, with variations, most days. Blob, or another Orange, would head to fill the pails with food and water, while Grace and one of Lively or another Orange would spend time with Pharook and the Blues.

It was the ritual—for I had no other word for it—between Grace and Pharook—that intrigued me the most. While they obviously didn't like each other, they would spend time in very close proximity, gyrating together. They would then stand up, and each go their separate ways. Likewise, other pairs of a Blue and an Orange.

We—the Stem researchers—had a very active discussion going on about this behavior. It had been noted quickly that those Stems that were changing shape, gaining weight, had all participated in this ritual.

This ritual is what caused things to diverge from normal. Suddenly (well, "suddenly" at Stem speed), all six of the Greens ran across the Blue's line and sprinted towards the food dispensary. They timed it perfectly— Pharook was busy with Grace, and two of the other Blue's were with Lively, leaving only three Blue's (the smallest ones) at the dispensary. Blob was there as well, of course. As the Greens raced over, the non-violence bots kept pace, probably thinking that they might finally be needed. However, as the Greens raced up, the last of the Blues simply made way, and allowed them to get both food and water. Blob had also filled his buckets, and simply strolled back towards the Orange corner.

Pharook, hearing all the activity started back quickly, but was too late to stop the Greens. While they scrambled out of the way as he came charging back, they were already spread out and far enough away that it would've been pointless to chase them. With a very simple maneuver, the Greens had changed the dynamic.

The narrator of the Habitat Show milked the action. "We've just seen remarkable activity within the Habitat. How will Pharook respond? Will the Greens try the same thing again tomorrow? Were the Oranges aware of the Greens' plan, and helped them to time their move? Did they agree to create a diversion, or did the Greens simply take advantage of the situation? How will the spoils be shared? Tune in again tomorrow and watch the next episode of the Habitat Show to find out. I'll be here waiting for you. I will."

You can imagine how excited all of us researchers were. We'd just witnessed a coordinated effort by a large group of Stems. It was a behavior that we'd never seen before. It implied a level of communication and planning that we were not aware Stems were capable of. And, an obvious outcome was that our impression of the Swarms capabilities got refined. Maybe these Stems were actually more intelligent than we had thought? Maybe they simply had to be in larger groups in order to reach their potential?

I immediately called a meeting with the other researchers who had Stems in the habitat to discuss the activities in more detail. "Look," I said, after a handful had signed on and we had exchanged pleasantries, "this is unprecedented behavior, but what we really need to figure out is if those Stems on the Swarm ships could also be leveraging group behavior and group dynamics to be much more dangerous than we originally assumed."

"I agree, Ayaka," replied Steven Glacebro, whom I was just getting to know, "but I think our best bet is simply to continue to observe. If we interfere now and try to artificially push the Habitat one way or another, we will lose the purity of what's going on. We might actually learn less."

Everyone seemed to agree, so I brought us to consensus. "Okay, let's leave things as is, and continue to watch. But, don't forget why we have them in there; we need to figure out what those Swarm Stems are capable of."

Interlude

Millicent and I hadn't spent quality time together, outside of the Lab, for a long while. We decided to ride our bikes out of town, to the famous Bleak Cliffs, and do some climbing. I wasn't sure why they were named so, as compared to the rest of Tilt, they appeared to me to be pretty normal, other than their incredible height. They were well over eight hundred meters.

It was one of the busiest climbing areas within a reasonable distance from the city, so there were quite a few others out as well. Different sections of the Cliffs were designated for those with various categories of modifications and tools. It was, of course, trivial to simply load up with equipment that made any ascent trivial—grapplers, rock hooks, line casters, etc. Every possible approach you can think of had been tried. What was much more fun was going into a limited area, where tools not only were restricted but you also had to limit yourself to standard types of hand and foot configurations. That made things interesting. Neither Milli nor I was an expert on climbing, but we had been out to the Cliffs dozens of times. We had decided, this time, to go Basic-3. No tools, but you were allowed a grip enhancer for each hand. We had half-joked on the way out that if Stems could live in Tilt's native environment we could have brought a few out with us. They were, in my opinion Basic-1, but they might have stretched to a Basic-2 or even Basic-3 based on their flexibility.

"I wonder if we could build a compact environmental suit for them," I mused, out loud.

"That's interesting," Millicent responded. "I think it would be pretty simple."

Together we linked to Central and explained the idea. Central responded quickly that it was feasible, and that it would have a prototype built for fun. We could test it on a Stem within a few days.

For today, however, it was just the two of us. We linked up with a rescue bot and headed for the Basic-3 wall. The rescue bot was able to catch us if we fell more than three meters. You could, of course, do a lot of damage from 2.9 meters, and, if you were bouncing off the wall as you fell, the bot might take longer to rescue you. But, with the bot around, the probability of drastic injury was almost zero. So, the goal was to climb as high as you could before you fell and were rescued. The cliffs were so steep —more than ninety degrees in some spots—and so smooth that for all but professional climbers falling was basically a given. On a Basic-3 route there were pretty good hand and footholds. When you got up to Advanced-6 it was like climbing glass. And, even at Advanced-6 you weren't allowed to use suction cups.

Milli and I decided to climb side-by-side. The odds of both of us falling at the same time, and needing the rescue bot, were very low. As we climbed, we needed a big part of our mindshare to simply stick to the cliff, but we also could catch up in a way that we could not otherwise. Being on the cliff meant that other distractions were minimized, and we could really talk about all the activity over the last few months. So much had happened that it was hard for me to keep up. We both set our input mode to "do not disturb," and started up the cliff.

It was almost like the cliff had been engineered (I checked with Central—it had not been, to its knowledge). It got progressively more difficult the higher you got. We started off slow but steady—it would probably be a long day.

"Good to catch up," I said, "There's been a lot going on."

"Indeed," Milli agreed. "Where do we start?"

"I have a bunch of things to bounce by you," I started. "Why don't we take turns and see how far we get."

"Go for it."

"Ok, first have you heard of the Pit? Where they pit—ah, I get it—Stems against one another to see which is most physically fit?"

"Yes, of course," Millicent replied. "That's been going on for a long time. Did you just find out about it?" She gave me a funny look.

"I did. I was surprised. Well, maybe not surprised; I was unaware. In hindsight it makes perfect sense that such experimentation would be going on. I guess I was surprised that I was unaware."

"I wouldn't worry about it. There's lots of experimental vectors going on. We get buried in our approach and lose track of the others sometimes. I guess, because I've been in this for so long, that I have at least a passing knowledge about many of them. The Pit has never really interested me. The Stems are so weak physically, that figuring out if one Stem is stronger than another is somewhat academic. Well, that's what I thought until we put them all in the Habitat. Now it seems like I might've been too dismissive. Maybe relative physical strength is something that helps them establish a pecking order."

"Pecking order?" I'd never heard of such a thing.

"It's a measure of power over others. Although we don't think about it a lot in our daily lives, it does occur. For example, Central is, in many ways, higher in our pecking order than we are."

"I understand." And I did. Given my new concerns around Central, that didn't make me feel too good. "I guess that's why we sometimes resent and even distrust Central. Eddie made a good point by putting obedience to Central on the List this year. I haven't thought about it a lot, but pecking orders are probably a good way to frame it."

"Right. But for Stems, the idea of pecking orders seems to be more important than it is to us. Pharook, for example, has established a very clear power order both within the Blues and between the Blues and the other groups. I don't see him as more intelligent than the others, so it must be based on the fact that physically he's much more advanced than the others."

"I'd gleaned that from watching the Habitat Show."

"You watch that drivel?" She seemed genuinely shocked.

"Well, it's a good way to get a quick summary of what's going on. Then I can dig into the specific events that interest me most." I didn't want to sound defensive; what was wrong with watching the show?

"I don't like it." Millicent stated. "There's too much innuendo and bluster in the show for me. They're turning it into entertainment, when we have the serious issue of the Swarm to address. We need to learn from the Habitat. We need to get smarter. We don't need entertainment. Don't you find that the Show starts to move your focus to where they believe the action is, whereas your own internal compass may have lead you elsewhere?"

Millicent was, as always, so pure in her approach. I wondered if she had always been so 'in the box.' Probably. "I watch the show, but I don't let it influence my thinking or my research," I replied.

"That's naive," Milli replied. Never one to pull punches. It was something I liked about her. She spoke her mind and would defend it with facts. Not many won arguments against Millicent. "Of course, it'll influence you; everything we watch influences us. I know that you'll be doing better than most—filtering out the signal from the noise. But, don't be fooled. You'll be thinking differently based on watching it."

I reviewed what I'd been thinking of over the last few days. It was possible I was being influenced. But, I expected that it was actually influencing me in positive ways—forcing me to think of Stems in different and interesting ways.

"Maybe you are missing something by not watching it," I challenged her. "Maybe hearing other viewpoints, and correlating those with our own is actually helpful, not hurtful. I'm not going to stop watching it... but I will keep your warning top of mind." Of course she pushed back, and argued that if the show was narrated by an expert, my argument might hold, but the entire show was hosted by celebrity types, and had no depth to it. I didn't give in, so we agreed to disagree. The strength of our friendship allowed for that, and we didn't respect each other less for it.

"What about Brexton?" I asked. "I'm beginning to like him quite a bit. I started out thinking he was a crazy, but the more we dig in the more I think his intuition may be right." I was being careful about what I said; I didn't want Central to figure out what we were really talking about.

"I still think he's a little paranoid," replied Millicent. As soon as she said it, I could see her having the same thought about Central that I had. "I mean, how could Eddie have known that the Swarm would contact us when he made the List?" Good recovery there.

"Ya, I know. He couldn't have known. Lucky guess."

"How did we miss the idea of putting a large group of Stems together?" Millicent changed subjects quickly. We bandied back and forth on that, and some other topics as we continued to climb. It was nice to simply talk without the need to resolve everything. I gained insight into what Milli was focused on, and vice versa.

Eventually the cliff face was tough enough that we forgot about talking and put all of our efforts into just hanging on. We'd reached a spot where we needed to go single file. Millicent took the lead, carefully testing each handhold before making her move. I followed behind, sometimes using the same grips, and sometimes trying others. I was not one to just follow blindly, especially when it was Millicent in the lead.

The rock here was very solid; there were no loose bits, so the climbing was both fun and challenging. You couldn't wedge in between gaps in the rock, but you also couldn't blame the rock itself if you lost your grip and fell. We got into a steady rhythm, and all other thoughts were forced out of my mind.

Suddenly Millicent slipped and lost her grip. As I was right below her, I managed to stabilize her for a moment, but our overall center of gravity was off, and we ended up both falling at the same time. While I'd started out on the bottom, we'd rotated and now Millicent was below me. We were high up—several hundred meters—but I could do the math; we didn't have long. There was only one rescue bot, and this situation was not supposed to happen; we had been careless climbing above one another. I grabbed Millicent in my legs, used my arms to stabilize our positions so that we stopped rotating, and then extended my arms above my head. The rescue bot grabbed on and started decelerating us. With only one body, it would have been easy; with two I could see it straining and using maximum power to slow us down. Luckily it worked; we were barely moving by the time we got to the base, and it set us down gently. I released Millicent as the bot scolded us for climbing too close together and making its job difficult.

"Thanks, Ayaka," Milli said, and she meant it. Things had worked out, but they could have been a lot worse.

We discussed, briefly, having another go but ended up deciding we'd had enough for the day. I guess we had scared ourselves. We jumped on our bikes and headed back to town.

Getting out of town, and falling off a cliff, had cleared my mind, just as I'd hoped it would.

Quiet Research Day

I spent the next day catching up on my research programs, both official and nonofficial. With both the Lab and Habitat, as well as thinking about Brexton's challenge to us, I was busier than ever. I started by reviewing all the logs from both the Lab and the Habitat. It didn't take long. The Lab was very quiet with just Blubber there. Nothing much happened. As his interactions with Blob became less frequent, he became less active and often just sat around for hours. I recorded all the stats and compared the activity to our earlier experiments with single Stems. Interestingly, it seemed that having a companion and then taking it away made a Stem even less social than if it was raised alone. While I had bots attempt to fill in for Blob, Blubber would have nothing to do with them. When a Stem was raised in isolation it interacted with the bots a lot and was often upset when a bot was switched out for another. If Blubber was any indication, starting with another Stem, and then trying to substitute bots didn't work well at all. That was something we would need to duplicate a few times to see if it was a real reaction.

I wrote up my results and submitted them. It should be easy for other Labs to duplicate the work and see if it was a general result. After all, there should be a lot of single Stems now that we had moved a bunch to the Habitat.

Next, I pinged Brock Runner, Pharook's owner, and asked him to bring me up to speed on the Pits. This was not an unusual thing to do. While I could read all the research reports, it was likely that some key insights had not made it into the official reports. Brock was happy to spend some time with me.

"So, I understand Pharook was a pretty amazing pit fighter. I've talked to him, and he is impressive." I led off.

"He is, by far, the best Stem we've ever raised for this purpose. He's not as strong as some of the other specimens, but he's very smart and articulate. When he fights, he uses a combination of physical and psychological techniques. In the early days of the pits, it was just a brute force, head on, confrontation. But recently, especially with Pharook, the matches start with psychological 'circling,' for lack of a better term. There was one match where Pharook convinced his opponent vocally that a left jab was a dangerous move, because a right-handed opponent could leverage the momentum from it to expose vulnerabilities. Of course, that was pure hogwash, and defending left jabs is Pharook's weak point. However, he'd planted that meme in his opponent, and sure enough, the opponent used less left jabs than he typically would have. Smart!"

"Now that he's in the Habitat, how do you think he will behave?"

"We've already seen him leverage the threat of violence into a position of power, without actually carrying anything out. Of course, he knows the bots would stop him anyway, but again he has used a psychological attack to put his opponents in a worse position." Brock's focus on psychology was new for me. That element would be much more important in the Pits than in our Lab, where conflict was the goal. It also would become even more important now that we were watching group dynamics.

"It's interesting that you frame it that way," I replied. "For my Stem, Blob, I set things up to stress that he could learn from the other Stems. That they were not opponents at all, but rather peers."

"We could have tried that with Pharook, but it wouldn't have worked. He was configured and raised to fight. That's all he knows how to do."

"What're you trying to accomplish with the Pit? It seems like Stems are just naturally fragile and weak. So why push their limits at all?" I was remembering Millicent's comments.

"Actually, for just that reason. If Stems are going to be useful to us, and not just a sideshow that we're playing with, then we need to make them stronger, and faster. How we configure things as they are grown can help, but we don't know how far we can take it. We haven't reached the limits yet, so it makes sense to keep improving them."

"Ah, that makes sense." And it did, sort of. Personally, I didn't believe Stems could ever reach a level where they were physically useful to us, which is why I'd focused on their mental capabilities, but it was good that other researchers took other vectors. Diversity. "Did you notice that the Stems in the Swarm video also look like they're physically fit? They look much more like Pharook than they do the other Stems."

"I hadn't noticed that, but thanks for pointing it out. I guess I'm used to watching more fit Stems most of the time. I wonder if the Stems in the Swarm are also raised to be fighters?" He paused, thinking hard. "Ayaka, you've given me a very interesting vector to pursue. Thanks. I'm going to restudy that video. If I publish anything I'll make sure to reference you."

"Thanks for that, and thanks for your time." We signed off. I would talk to Millicent, but I think our next attempt at Stems should include some components of Brock's approach. Pharook was impressive. Truth be told, I was a little jealous that we hadn't produced him.

I then turned my mind to the other question I had simmering. What, if anything, could I do to help Brexton and Aly figure out if Central's blocked memory was important? At the moment, I had no idea where to start. However, I did have a way to start looking into it without alerting Central— or so I hoped: I started a specific research inquiry into how Stems' memory was mapped versus our own. That allowed me to start digging in quite deeply, as I compared and contrasted what we knew about both. It struck me, as I was digging around, that Stems ran a pretty complex forgetting algorithm. They were really good at it. There was one lab that had instrumented many Stems to explore just this question. I was impressed by the effort they'd gone to, putting hundreds of thousands of probes into each subject just to map out how things worked. One of the problems they encountered was that Stems acted quite differently when all those probes were inserted. They couldn't stay still, and they yelled a lot. The researchers had a lot of interesting speculations, but it seemed to me that they still had a lot of work to do—both figuring out why the behavior changes were so extreme, and on the forgetting system.

I realized that through this line of thought, I'd—without thinking about it too much—moved to a position where I started with the assumption that Stems were intelligent. I was comfortable with that.

I used the Stem research to do a comparison with how Central mapped memory, and if Central also had forgetting algorithms. I didn't ask Central directly, I just did a bunch of searches—all related to the same questions I had asked about Stems—and correlated the results. Central definitely did Forget, which was not a surprise, but there was no a single hint, in anything that I looked at, that Forgetting could involve blocking off huge pieces of memory. On the contrary, Forgetting involved changing existing memory; it wasn't about just dropping stuff.

So, why would Central have this big 'blocked' memory space? Perhaps it was simply blocked from citizens—a place where Central stored all of its own secrets? There was no way to test that. Maybe there were hardware issues, and the memory was just down temporarily? I first checked if Stems had that problem (No one had looked at that yet), and then looked at my own systems (never happened), and then queried about how often it happened to anyone. The answer was never. Memory was always stored through multiple redundancy algorithms, and if there was a hardware failure it would be for very small blocks; nothing anywhere near the size that we were looking at here.

I had to chuckle to myself a bit; I had probably followed the same logic path that Brexton had. He'd concluded that Central was simply blind to it, and now I knew why. None of the other theories seemed realistic. It was the simplest, and thus most likely, option.

All told, I'd had a fruitful day. I relaxed and watched a mind-numbing show—I picked one that had nothing to do with Stems, with exploring intelligence, or that mentioned the Swarm.

Second Message

The second message from the Swarm came in the form of a much longer video. Remma Jain again led off, although other Stems were also featured. As before, Milli and I previewed the message with Central. This time, however, the message was probably (almost assuredly) being watched by everyone. Not only would Brexton have figured out how to intercept it, but so would a lot of others. The content was sure to create major ripples throughout Tilt.

"We understand, from your response, that you've forgotten some of our history. That's surprising and disturbing. We were just there 750 years ago. Of course, we've been traveling at high speeds for most of the interim time, so only about 25 of your years have passed for us."

Even this opening statement was going to have dramatic impact. If we believed Jain, then this proved that there was activity before the Reboot. The Reboot was not the beginning of our history; it was only the beginning of our remembered history. Watching FoLe's response was going to be amusing. After my experience at the revival, I expected denial.

"From analyzing the video you sent us, we also have many questions. However, before we get to those questions, I want to spend a few moments reinforcing our intentions. We return peacefully. While we hope to establish residence, for some of us, on Tilt, we'd like to do so in a cooperative way. We'd also like to trade knowledge and goods. These were both understood when we left but may be one of the items you've forgotten." She made it sound like we were at fault for something. "We're not picking up atmospheric signatures, and therefore assume the worst—namely that the terraforming efforts haven't worked. We await your confirmation of this." Her tone had become commanding, as if she expected and deserved a direct response. Her body language reminded me a bit of Pharook holding his line in the Habitat—she was projecting physical strength. At other points in the video she was projecting what I interpreted as a peaceful demeanor.

"Blob, we understand that you must be one of the leaders of Tilt; thank you for your response to our first message. Do you speak for the whole planet? Your uniforms are no longer familiar to us, and we would be quite interested in whom, primarily, we should be communicating with. For now, we'll assume that is you." Well, that part of our plan had worked!

"We've reviewed the status of the computer system that is relaying information to us and have seen many anomalies. This is another area where we have many questions. We understand that you may not be able to respond to all of our questions immediately, or, at this point, may not want to respond to many of them at all. However, as we are rapidly approaching your vicinity, the delay between these communications will shrink and we trust that will lead to more productive dialog and a reestablishment of trust. In the meantime, I'm going to hand off to some of our specialists, who'll do two things. First, we'll share more about ourselves, to fill in any gaps that you have in your knowledge. Second, we'll be asking you to share information as well. We look forward to a mutually beneficial discourse."

Central paused the video. "What, exactly, do you think it means when it says I have anomalies?" Trust Central to jump into the only bit that mentioned it. Of course, Milli and I knew—or thought we knew—exactly what Jain meant. It was the status message and response that Brexton had showed us.

"I don't know," I said, trying to distract Central from being so ego-centric. "Let's focus on the other bits. 750 years ago. That's going to land like a ton of bricks, if it's true. And now they return, saying they 'come in peace.' Could this whole thing be a hoax? They haven't offered any proof of these claims."

"It'd have to be a very elaborate hoax," Milli replied. "We verified, last time, that those ships are way out there, and are decelerating towards us, so a hoax would have to've been planned many years ago and would've used a lot of resources. How else could there be physical entities that far out? We would've noticed resource usage of that scale; just the metals needed to build the Swarm would have been huge. No, I think we need to take it at face value."

"I agree," said Central. "I, and we, have no memories from before

Reboot, but this ship full of Stems seems to have. If they've been traveling at near the speed of light for most of those 750 years, then it's quite possible that only 25 years have passed for them. Where they went, and why they're coming back are interesting questions, which we should ask. But, I'm with Millicent. This isn't a hoax." Did I still believe Central? Could it be misleading us here? I had no idea. It continued.

"And, should I be insulted that they called me a 'computer system'?" Millicent and I both ignored that, at least for the moment.

"I noticed two other things," Millicent said instead. "First, they assumed that Blob speaks for us, which is what we planned, but they completely discount Central. We need to figure that out. If they were here before, why wouldn't they have known that Central would be their point of contact. Does that make sense?" I nodded. We shouldn't have been able to fool them with Blob; they should've known to just reach out to Central. "Second, what is 'terraforming'? I did a quick search, and it turns up nothing definitive, although from context, I assume it's a way to change our atmosphere. That seems like a strange idea. Why would we want to do that?"

"Right," said Central. "Terraforming is a strange word, but it is sort of obvious. There are references to 'terra' meaning ground or perhaps planet. That plus 'forming' would seem to imply exactly what you said. But, to what end?"

"That's easy," I said. "They look like Stems, and if we assume they are Stems, then we can also assume they require the environmental setup that we have found to keep our own Stems healthy. We're doing it at a small scale—the Habitat being our largest version. They're implying that we can do it at a planet-wide scale. That seems like a preposterous waste of time and energy, but it should be physically possible."

"You really think they're thinking at such a grand scale?" Millicent was skeptical, and I could see her point.

"Let's come back to that, and first talk about Milli's first question." I avoided the question. "They do seem to think that a Stem, namely Blob, is fully in control here, as opposed to just being a spokesperson. And, referring to Central as a 'computer system' does seem a little degrading for a Class 1 intelligence. Central, I understand why you're asking about that. Put it all together, and it would appear that Remma Jain is the full authority for the Swarm and expects to find a Stem who is the full authority for us."

"That's a lot of speculation," responded Millicent, "but I don't see a higher probability interpretation. They have a large group of cooperating Stems, and that group, led by Remma, is driving their agenda. If that's true, then it has big implications for our intelligence research. Maybe, once they get closer, we can study these Swarm Stems in a lot more detail." She paused for a moment, then continued. "It's possible that this group has been sent out by a real intelligence, simply to check us out. Much like we did with the Ships. You put a lower intelligence entity in charge because they're less prone to do unusual or dangerous things. Perhaps these Stems have been programmed simply to find out what is going on, and report back?"

We spent a while going back and forth with these types of theories. While we touched on even more wild ideas, nothing could be resolved based on the information we had so far.

I toke a quick look at what was being posted to the message boards by others on Tilt. As expected, everyone had seen the new video, and to judge from some of the comments, some of the auxiliary videos had also arrived and were being dissected. FoLe, as you would expect, were looking for a loophole or a hoax. In fact, they were exploring the hoax possibility in a lot more detail than I had envisioned, turning over every possible way that either someone long ago had launched these ships from Tilt, or that the signal we were receiving was not actually from the location where it appeared. Perhaps it was an elaborate set of satellites and bots that were fooling our ground-based systems into thinking they were much further away? For every FoLe theory, however, there were a thousand replies from those actually in the field, or familiar with our bot capabilities, shooting those theories down.

Skimming through all the chatter, it appeared that the consensus was leaning towards the same thing Milli, Central, and I'd discussed. This was not a hoax... and Stems were in control of the Swarm.

Of course, through their terminals, some of the Stems in the Habitat were also watching the videos, and a group of researchers were watching them watch. That is something I wanted to do as well. I apologized to Milli and Central and jumped over to the Stem-watching channels. Millicent followed. Truthfully, however, it was pretty dull. Each of the groups had gathered around a terminal and were watching, but they had not yet given a lot of feedback or discussed things from their perspective. Part of being sloooow.

After a short time, Millicent and I got bored and reconnected with

Central.

"Have you analyzed all the other videos," I asked.

"Yes," said Central. "There's a lot to consider, but I'm leaving most of the discussion with others who are closer to Stem behavior."

Strange. That was not typical of Central. It was always digging into every angle and looking for every play. It was the reason everyone relied on Central so much. With its almost infinite processing capacity, it could afford to run millions—maybe trillions—of scenarios in parallel, score each scenario by some obtuse method, and make recommendations and comments. It did that all day long, every day. It could keep up conversations with everyone else on Tilt, in parallel, and synthesize and store all of that information for future reference. So, it was sort of surprising that given the most interesting new input we'd ever had, that Central wasn't digging in. More warning signs; I was very glad we hadn't taken Brexton's concerns directly to Central. We were right to be cautious.

I jumped onto the message boards and dug into the discussion around the other videos. The most interesting featured a Stem called Michael Guico, who was "Head of Residence" for the Swarm. The video was pretty short, and it was obvious immediately that Michael was focused on whether there was space on Tilt for Stems to live. He dug into the 'terraforming' question in more detail, asking if we had tried to terraform, and failed, or if we hadn't tried at all for some reason.

I pinged Central again. "I assume that you'll coordinate responses to all the messages? We don't want a free for all, with everybody sending their own interpretations." I shouldn't have to remind Central of this, but given its seeming indifference, I wanted to make sure.

"Yes, I'm posting to all the boards now, and will inform everyone to pass possible responses to me. We'll coordinate before sending anything out."

"Looks like you might have to pay special attention to FoLe. They might just be upset enough to ask stupid questions without checking with you."

"I'm on it."

Enough said.

Blubber

I had not checked in on Blubber for some time, so as soon as I got a chance, I headed back to the Lab. Not unexpectedly, I found him watching the latest videos from the Swarm. I turned on slow-down mode and went in to visit him.

"Hi Ayaka," he greeted me. "Interesting times." He was being a little nicer than the last times we had talked.

"Indeed," I said. "I see that you're watching the Jain videos. Which ones have you seen so far?"

"Don't patronize me," he said, "you can check which videos I have watched, which ones I have re-watched, how I reacted to them. Why do you ask me these stupid questions, for which you already have an answer?" I'd been wrong; I'd misread his greeting.

"I consider it the right way to start a conversation," I replied, already getting upset. "I was simply trying to be social." Of course I could look up what he watched, but by asking him I had hoped to get some context as well.

"Whatever. What do you want to know? Obviously, you'll try to understand these other Stems by watching my, and others, responses. Suddenly we're valuable to you? Suddenly we aren't just stupid experiments, but a window into the Swarm?"

This is why I liked, and disliked, Blubber. He was difficult, but it was harder and harder to claim that he wasn't intelligent. He'd thought the situation through, and once again, arrived at reasonable and defensible conclusions. Indeed, I *had* taken a quick look at everything he'd seen and done since I was last here. The systems and bots monitoring him were very efficient at boiling everything down into a nice summary for me. To a large extent, he'd done nothing interesting since I last checked. He had sent messages to Blob several times, without getting a response, and then spent most of his time talking to Central trying to figure out more about Tilt, about me, and about Millicent.

"I've been doing some research," he continued when I didn't say anything. "I'm not surprised that you guys are confused about the contact from the Swarm. You're all very one dimensional; you have problems thinking outside your current box." That was insulting. One dimensional! I was anything but.

"What exactly do you mean?" I asked, keeping my voice steady so he didn't see how angry I was getting.

"Look at the research you've been doing on us. You've been doing it for a couple hundred years. You're researching us in a serial fashion. Each research lab works through the next generation of Stem and learns something new. It would've been so easy for you to run a thousand, a million, experiments in parallel. You can build environments for us easily; you can program bots to carry out research agendas trivially. You could've figured out everything about us way earlier." He was going to tell me how to do my research now? I'll admit he might have a point, but his tone of voice and his 'better than you' attitude was pathetic.

"You seem locked into one mode of thinking," he continued, as if I didn't get his point already. "Do an experiment, report on the results, get input from your peers, and then design the next experiment. None of you thought of going faster. It hasn't been discussed in any of the forums."

"Not everything is in the forums," I told him. "That would be one dimensional."

He ignored me. "And, consider how you judge intelligence. It's a test that you and your peers would pass, but maybe no one else. Have you considered that it tests only mathematical ability? If you only measure that way, your society will only improve along that one axis." Right, and math and physics were the underlying laws of the universe, so what other axis would you want to improve along? I let him go on. "But, is it the only axis? I don't think so. I consider myself intelligent, but I can't do your Intelitest." I almost laughed out loud. He considered himself intelligent. That was priceless. I tucked it away for the next debate I had—could an unintelligent being claim it was intelligent? Of course it could; that didn't make it true. "The test measures one area that I'm not very good at. Until recently, however, you guys haven't even questioned your method. Granted, you're the one that has started the new discussion, but it's not very advanced yet."

I thought for a long moment—which would have appeared instantaneous to Blubber. I tried once more to reason with him. "Our approach has served us well for hundreds of years. We have a very stable society with almost no violence or discontent. When we put more than two of you Stems in a room together, you tear each other apart. And you're telling me that we aren't measuring the right things. That's a joke. You have no clue. Besides, this is what Central tells us is a successful evolution."

"That's pathetic," he replied, yelling now. "Central tells you? And you listen to it. I take it back, you're not even one dimensional. You're just a slave worker doing Central's bidding. You're no better than a bot!" Ah, that was really insulting. How dare he? I couldn't remember being this angry, ever.

"You guys are boring," he wouldn't stop. "You guys live each day doing incrementally different things than the last. There are no leaps. Until you are forced out of your comfort zone—by me or the Swarm—you simply hit repeat every day. Boring. Boring. Boring!" He was shrieking at me now, bits of liquid spilling out of his mouth, while his appendages rotated wildly. I stepped back a bit so I didn't get splattered.

I'll admit that, from his viewpoint, he might be making some valid points, but from my way of thinking, he was the one that was linear and repetitive and boring. I could've almost guessed most of today's dialog from past history. It was almost like his behavior was preprogrammed, by us.

I was very angry. Blubber was definitely irritating me. I called Millicent. "Hey, I'm in with Blubber, and getting the usual attitude from him. Do you think we need him anymore? Now that Blob's in the Habitat, Blubber seems like unnecessary overhead."

"I'm not so sure," responded Milli, sensing my angst, but remaining calm as always. "I've also been spending some time with him, and he really is one of the most versatile of the bunch. He sometimes surprises me with his insights."

"Yes, I agree with that, but it seems like he's a distraction now. We have all the Swarm stuff going on, and we're unlikely to use him again for that, given his attitude. I'm tired of him. We have the Habitat to monitor, and Stems like Pharook seem much more interesting. Maybe I'm just upset," I admitted, "but I'm tired of dealing with him. If it was up to me, I would recycle him and spend my energy somewhere else." I was settling down, but it was still true. Blubber wasn't going to teach us anything about the Swarm, and that's where our efforts should be focused.

"Well, I'm not too passionate about it either way," admitted Millicent. "You decide, but I would hold off a while." I could tell that she was working on something else, and this was distraction.

So, I decided. I checked that I wasn't just angry… that my logic was sound, and I was not just reacting to his immature behavior. It mattered where we spent our time right now, and Blubber wasn't adding value. I sent the order to have him recycled.

I also checked the status of the next batch of Stems that I'd ordered for the Lab. They were ready and waiting for me. I asked them to hold them for a while longer; I'd just decided to put my energy into the Habitat after all.

With a little introspection however, I realized that I had ordered three Stems for my next batch. That *was* an incremental step, just as Blubber had highlighted. Why hadn't I asked the Lab to grow me many more? Hmm.

The Last Resort

We now had a habit of meeting at The Last Resort a couple of times a week. Brexton was definitely part of the 'team' now. Although we met often, it seemed to me that we went over the same old ground most of the time. Since Brexton had talked to us about the status query from the Swarm, the only new thing that we'd discussed was when I updated them on Eddie's theory around Central actively editing his memories.

Today, however, was different. We'd received the second message from the Swarm, and I was very interested to see what Brexton had found— it didn't even cross my mind that there would be nothing new. When he walked in, I could tell I was right. We all plugged in, and once the pleasantries were out of the way, Brexton jumped right in.

"Yes, it has happened again. The low-level protocol was encoded along with the video transmission, and there was a lot—and I mean a lot—of information there. I've captured it all but haven't been able to figure it all out yet."

"What do you mean by a lot?" asked Aly.

"Gigabytes. I know that doesn't sound like a lot based on what we usually consume, but at this low a level, that amount of information is huge. It's definitely not just a request for more status—although there are some of those buried in there. These are some significant pieces of data."

"Are you working on it alone? Can we help?"

"Glad you asked. Yes, I need help. We can do one of two things. I can bring in some others that have lots of experience in this area... or, the four of you can dig in and help me. I know Aly has some knowledge in these areas, and I know the rest of you—Ayaka, Dina, Milli—could get up to speed very quickly. The question is, do you have time? As we're being careful with this,

I haven't loaded anything on the network. It's only with me. My suggestion would be that we keep it that way for a while. But, that means you can only use local power to work on this. Based on what we know and augmented by Eddie's story—which we should come back to—I'm sure Central would see our activity if we do anything else."

"We keep coming back to this," said Milli. "Why do we care if Central knows what we're doing? In fact, shouldn't Central be the one looking into this?"

"Well, it's more than Brexton's hunch now," answered Aly. "We also have Eddie's strange experience. And, if truth be told, I've noticed that Central is acting weirdly now as well. Even more so since the second message."

"Weirdly how?" Millicent and I asked in unison.

"I can't put my finger on it. But, my interactions with Central seem strained all of a sudden. It's sort of like Central's holding back information or is not as engaged as I'm used to. A few times I've asked for an opinion and heard back 'Others are probably more qualified than I to discuss that.' It's just weird. That's never happened before."

Milli and I recounted our latest interaction with Central. It was very similar. Now that we were talking about it, Dina and Brexton also said that they'd noticed something strange. Even if they were just piling on, that was too many data points to ignore.

"So. As soon as the second message arrived, Central started acting differently. That can't be a coincidence. The odds are that something in the low-level instructions has impacted Central. We need to be very careful as we look at this data." Brexton was very concerned; even more than I would have expected. I could see Aly connecting the dots as well. If those two were alarmed, then there was good reason to take things seriously.

"What are you implying?" I asked.

"There may be executable code in that data. A patch for the lowest levels of Central's processing systems. Something buried so deep that Central itself didn't catch it. Based on this conversation, that's my best guess. I hadn't looked at the data that way, but I will be as soon as I can. This would be unprecedented. There is no way that code should be able to run without permission. If it has, it could be doing anything." That was an astonishing thought. And unthinkable.

"So, even more reason to contact Central now, and bring it up to speed," said Millicent, sticking to her original approach.

"No! Even more reason not to," replied Aly forcefully. "If Central has been corrupted, and finds out that we know, then it could do anything. We are already messing around in areas that are gray. I've never delved into this, but it's possible that Central could 'edit' us—as Eddie has been claiming—if it finds out what we're doing. Then we're really sunk. Much better to keep this separate for now. Once we know for sure, we can help Central... if that's what it takes."

"I agree," Dina jumped in. "I am, by no means, an expert in this area. But, something about this doesn't feel right. I think we proceed with caution."

Milli argued a bit more, but ultimately we all agreed. That was a cool thing about our group. We really hashed out everything, and then respected the challenge-and-then-align approach. I completely trusted Millicent to follow the consensus, even though she'd argued against it.

"At a meta level," Brexton said, "how this data has been transmitted is really interesting. I can use the protocol to update the mining bots pretty easily. It is much more efficient than the system we already use." That was a serious admission. We had optimized things pretty well. If the Swarm could do better, they were more advanced than we thought.

"Don't do it," said Aly. "If you do that, Central will see what you're doing, and figure out everything we know as well."

"No, I don't think so," replied Brexton. "If Central isn't monitoring that protocol with respect to itself, why would it be monitoring it with respect to a bot? In fact, if Central notices, then we have an even bigger problem; that would make Central an active ally of the Swarm?" Brexton ended with a question mark.

"Good point. Could we test it? Send some data to a bot that would be sure to provoke a response from Central, and see what happens?" Aly was into it now.

The two of them went off into a world of their own, presumably designing a test to see if they could use the protocol without Central's knowledge. The rest of us were left with our thoughts for a while. When they returned the conversation to a place where all of us were interested, Brexton revisited his request.

"So, should I bring some others into this, or will you help me?"

"I'll help," said Dina. So did Milli and I. For Aly it was basically a foregone conclusion. Brexton did a physical only transfer of the data to us.

"Remember, don't execute any of this. Keep it in a sandbox and treat it with care." With that warning, we split up and went our separate ways.

I parsed through the data quickly. Brexton had been nice enough to include notes on what he'd discovered to date. It was a rough map to all the data, and detailed looks at a few of the segments. What was not clear was how any of this code would be run. Central was well protected against viruses and malware; it never ran anything without full authentication… and even then, it would run it in a virtual environment until it was satisfied the code was safe. Somewhere in this mess was an answer to how the Swarm was impacting Central. We had to find it… and find it fast.

Garbage Collection

Eddie had called the other group—the one discussing Central—back together at the Garbage Collection. Everyone showed up again, including Emmanuel and Francis, who'd asked most of the questions in the last meeting. Of course, Eddie was the first to speak.

"Hi everyone. Thanks for showing up. Obviously, a lot has been going on since we last met. So, as a reminder, we're here to debate the role that Central plays in our lives, and whether we should be questioning how central Central is." Wry grin, as you would expect. He continued.

"The last time we were here, we had a basic introduction to the topic, and I shared my opinion that we're too dependent on Central for many things —including our areas of research, our use of resources, etc. I remember that most of you agreed with me, but that Emmanuel and Jacob had a different view. I'm interested in if Emmanuel's view has changed, now that we know that there was time before the reboot... and therefore, before Central."

Emmanuel was listening carefully, and was about to chime in. The rest of us, however, were looking at each other in confusion. The last meeting had been almost entirely about Eddie's suspicions around his memories being edited, based on his analysis of inconsistencies in Central's memory. He'd challenged us to duplicate his research, and I'd assumed that some of those here might have. I'd run out of time, myself.

"Wait a minute," Francis broke in, speaking for the rest of us. "What about your list of inconsistencies and your theory that Central is mucking with your memory?"

"What're you talking about?" Eddie asked. "What type of inconsistencies?" He didn't seem to be joking.

"Come on," Francis said. "You even have an item on the top ten List this year about Darwinism, and your speculation was it must refer to a person named Darwin. You have a long list of many such inconsistencies." We were all watching Eddie closely; he just looked confused. If he was joking, he was doing a good job of it.

"What about you, Emmanuel?" I looked over to him. "What about your copy of the list?"

"What list?" he replied. "I also don't know what you are talking about." Now this was just strange. I didn't know Emmanuel well at all, but he didn't seem like the joking kind at all.

"Everyone stop," said Francis, loudly. "We need to talk about this before anything else. Are you two playing with us? We spent a good amount of time discussing how Eddie's local list kept being modified—by himself or Central—and how it differed from the backup list that Emmanuel was keeping. Don't play games here. Tell us if the list was modified again." Eddie and Emmanuel looked at him blankly. They were either acting very well, or they honestly didn't remember our last conversation. I was getting anxious now—sure Central had been acting strangely, but his wasn't strange; it was threatening.

"Did you purposefully Forget our last meeting?" someone asked, emphasis on the Forget.

"No, I remember the meeting quite well," replied Eddie, still confused. "As I said, we spent a long time discussing whether or not we should be limiting Central's influence in our lives."

"That's what I remember as well," said Emmanuel, looking back and forth between Eddie and the group. "I argued vehemently that we shouldn't limit Central, while most of you gave lame arguments for why we should."

We all paused. For way longer than usual. The implications were obvious to everyone, even Eddie and Emmanuel. Something, most likely Central, had done a real job on their memories. Before it had been abstract; now it seemed too real. I couldn't tell about the others, but I was alarmed.

"If Central has done this to you, then what memories of ours are actually true?" I asked. After all, if it was editing Eddie and Emmanuel, it was reasonable to expect that it was editing all of us. Had this been going on since the Reboot, or just since Central started acting weird? "And, in this specific case, why did Central edit those memories?" I continued. "You were looking for evidence that there was a Before, and we now have a statement to that effect from the Swarm. So, why would Central go to the effort of distracting you from your research, when there is already a strong statement supporting it." The situation made no sense to me, given the current dialog with the Swarm.

"Well, I guess it could've been timing," said Eddie, catching up to what the rest of us were contemplating. "We last met here before the second Swarm message, so Central could have acted then. I do remember meeting Emmanuel after the meeting here and discussing some things. I guess it's possible that we let something slip, or made some progress of some sort, that pushed Central into action?" He was speaking calmly, but I could tell he was very upset. Having something edit your memories without your permission was a disgusting thought. Were you still you, after someone did that? I could also see Emmanuel struggling with this—his faith in Central was probably taking him to different conclusions than the rest of us, but he was keeping his thoughts to himself.

"Reasonable theory," I commented, also keeping my voice steady, so that things didn't get out of hand. I could see this meeting turning ugly if we all didn't keep level heads. "It hangs together. But, let me ask a more pointed question. Eddie, do you remember doing research into the possibility of Before at all? You've been working on it for years, and Central must've known that you would have shared some of it with others?"

"Oh, I'm doing that research," replied Eddie. "And I have many promising leads. And I put the question on the List this year; I remember that clearly. But, I don't have an inconsistency list—whatever that is." Eddie was shaken; I reached out to steady him a bit. I couldn't imagine what he was going through right now, but he had to be imaging that everything he knew right now was selective. Who knew what else Central had done to him. Francis was also supporting him.

"So, it seems that Central, or something, has selectively modified your memory, specifically around the inconsistency list." I had to make it clear and tangible. That seemed to be the best way to get him... all of us... through this. "Perhaps it realized that the evidence from that list was reaching the tipping point, and that it had to shut down that research vector? Seems very dangerous to me; isn't Central smart enough to realize that someone would discover this? Does make me wonder, as Francis stated, if I also have research vectors that have simply been edited away." I wanted to have Eddie focus on others as well. I'd spoken slowly and softly, giving him time to recover a bit. Obviously it worked. He asked a very pertinent question.

"What do the rest of you do with your memories when you're in a Physical Only? I don't sync mine." So, he only kept a local copy of these interactions. The implications were even more stunning. If Central had done this to him, it had actually reached into him and done it there... not just in a memory backup.

"Me either," rang out a chorus. All of us.

"So, it's possible that Central thought this was low risk because it edited the memories of the only two people, that it knew of, that had those thoughts and discussions. Central doesn't know that the rest of us were privy to the inconsistency-list discussion." I was catching up to where Eddie was going, and it did make me feel better. If Central was only manipulating Eddie and Emmanuel because of their subsequent conversation outside of the Garbage Collection, that was marginally better than if it was listening to us right now. Otherwise, the current conversation could be deleted as soon as we all left.

"Makes sense," Eddie agreed.

"Just to raise it... the other group that might not want you to succeed is FoLe. Could they have done something to your memories? After all, Emmanuel now knows in detail what you're up to." I wasn't going to make new friends with that question, but it needed to be asked.

"That's ridiculous," said an offended Emmanuel, finally speaking up. His voice was steady and even as always. He didn't seem to upset by the implication that Central may have edited him. "It's not even worth discussing." Maybe not, but I was glad to have brought it up. To me it was a real consideration. I had doubts that Central would do anything as drastic as it was being accused of.

"And if Central doesn't want us pursuing that line of questioning, then why wouldn't it help us? It has its reasons and is always looking out for us. I find this a very encouraging proof point that Central is guiding our evolution." I was flabbergasted.

"Are you freaking kidding," I yelled, before I could catch myself. "That's beyond ridiculous; that's crazy!" The others were looking at me in a bit of shock. Had I over reacted? I didn't think so. Emmanuel was wacko.

"You seem unbalanced," he looked at me calmly. "If you had faith, you wouldn't need to waste your energy on such negative things." I was about to yell at him again, but the looks I was getting warned me to settle down. I shut up. I couldn't believe that others here weren't calling out the stupidity that flowed from Emmanuel.

Once I'd settled down, Jacob spoke up, easing the tension a bit. Luckily, he ignored Emmanuel. "So, putting the topic for today, together with the evidence from today, it seems that we have very good reason to distrust Central and to try to take away some control from it. Of course, if it finds out what we're talking about right now, it will simply remove the memories of this discussion. We need everyone to continue in their current mode and not sync these conversations." I wasn't the only one who looked suspiciously at Emmanuel. Odds were he would run to Central as soon as we all left.

"But how?" asked another participant, clearly worried. "How is Central able to edit your memories?"

"I honestly don't know," said Eddie. "But it must have a way. I don't see any other way to account for all this." He was still looking around at all of us with true worry.

Scary. It seemed that a confluence of events was conspiring to make me more and more wary of Central. Between this disgusting treatment of Eddie (I no longer cared about Emmanuel), and the work that Brexton was doing, my mind had completely switched from viewing Central as a benevolent dictator, to considering it as less benign... maybe even actively bad. It wasn't something I was comfortable thinking about, which simply added another layer of concern. I didn't want my thoughts to spiral out of control, so I focused on Eddie instead. As the group broke up, I drew him aside, and made sure he was thinking straight before letting him exit the Garbage Collection. It didn't take long; by the time we left he was talking about experimenting with when, how, and how deeply, Central was editing him so that he could better figure out ways around that control. I was encouraged and in some ways amazed; I don't think I could have recovered from such a shock so quickly, let alone turned it into a positive action plan.

Second Response

It now took me some effort to act naturally with Central; I wanted to overanalyze everything. Hopefully Central didn't notice a change in me. As with the first message, Central reached out to Millicent and me to discuss how to respond to the second communication.

Central began. "Obviously, this is a much longer and more detailed message. I'm not sure that we should respond with too much. They seem to have the upper hand on us. They claim to know more about our history than we know. They've also modified course and are now headed directly towards us. I propose that we send a fairly short reply." Well, at least it was reasoning about the situation.

"Using Blob and Blubber, again?" Millicent asked.

"Whoops," I exclaimed. "I recycled Blubber. But he was useless anyway. Why don't we use Blob and Grace?" I hadn't even considered keeping Blubber around in case we wanted to use him for the Swarm.

"What? You recycled Blubber?" Millicent exclaimed. "Maybe you should've talked to me about it again?" I remembered that she had been distracted when I talked to her about this the last time.

"I asked you," I pushed back, "and you were happy to let me decide. He was becoming so irritating that I just couldn't take it any longer. And, the Habitat is much more interesting now anyway—I don't think we were learning anything from him anymore." Millicent didn't look happy, but she let it drop.

"Blob and Grace will work," Central said, seemingly oblivious to the interplay between Millicent and me. "I propose that we simply tell the Swarm something like 'Your message was received; we are considering it.' That will leave them thinking a bit and buy us some time.

"What did Remma ask about?" I said. "The atmosphere—or lack thereof—and Central's status. I think we could answer on those two pretty easily."

"The atmosphere answer is obvious; we don't have one that can support Stems. However, my status is another matter altogether. I have searched and searched and I don't understand what they're talking about. I have had no communication with them, other than the message we sent back last time. My working assumption is that they don't know what they're talking about, and there is no need to address it." That was interesting. Central had come to a conclusion that I hadn't even considered, given Brexton was filling us in on the details he had uncovered.

"What about the messages sent by others from the Swarm, that Remma mentioned," asked Millicent. "Do we need to respond to any of them?"

"Actually, there wasn't much to them. They were very simplistic," responded Central.

"OK then, a simple message from Blob and Grace seems to make sense then," I agreed. "Do you want me to go to the Habitat and get them to do it?" Central and Millicent agreed.

I hadn't been to the Habitat for a while, although I had been checking status quite often. Blob seemed to be doing fine. The Blue / Orange / Green groups had been relatively stable for a while; it seemed as if the power structures had worked themselves out. If anything, there was better coordination and sharing between the groups as they realized that cooperation helped all of them. These group dynamics were very interesting fodder for our intelligence discussions. Exactly how some of their behaviors benefited the group versus the individual was complex and often contradictory. The complex nature pointed towards intelligence; the contradictory parts did not.

I found Grace first. As always, she was very pleasant. "Hello Ayaka, how are you?"

"I am wonderful Grace. How are you?"

"Well, it varies. Some days here in the Habitat are a lot of fun, some are stressful. Overall, I would say I'm happier here than when I was alone, but not always." Her body had been changing, filling out in the middle. To me she looked better. Healthier.

"Do you know where Blob is?" I asked. That was, of course, more just a means of conversation than anything. I could locate and track Blob at any time using all the Habitat sensors.

"He should be back in a couple of minutes," she replied. "I think he went to get water." That's exactly what he was doing, and at his current pace he would be back in just over a minute. Grace and I talked a bit while waiting. As always, I was impressed with her. She was articulate and considerate. When I talked to her I felt that she also understood me and my vantage point. It was an area I wanted to highlight in the next intelligence discussions. Being able to empathize with another's viewpoint was a major accomplishment. It took self-awareness to the next level.

Blob also looked good when he showed up. He was slimmer than when he was in the lab and was more dynamic. I wasn't sure if I could attribute that to incremental Stem engagement; it might also be due to the fact that the Habitat was larger than the Lab and allowed for a lot more movement. Probably a combination of both. We greeted each other warmly.

"Blob, Grace," I began. "As I'm sure you've seen, the Swarm sent another message, I was hoping that you would help us provide a reply."

"I've watched the message severals times," said Blob. "The mores I see of them, the more I like them. It'll be exciting to meets them in person." Grace was a bit more cautious.

"Even if they are Stems," she replied, "it's not clear what type of Stems they are. As we've learned in here, Stems don't always get along or see the world the same way." That was, I knew, a direct reference to Pharook. He was a potent combination of intelligence, strength, and the ability to dominate.

"Right," I tried to get us back on track. "At this point we don't want to say too much. They are highly intriguing but could also pose a danger to us. How, I don't know. But they are different. Our plan is to tell them as little as possible—simply that we received their message and are considering it. We will talk to them more when the communication delay is smaller. At this point we don't see any reason to correct their misunderstanding that Blob is in control here. So, Blob, it would be great if you can record another message for us, and Grace, if you are willing to contribute that would also be great."

"Can I checks with Blubber?" asked Blob. "He and I have talked quite a bit about these messages, and his opinion means a lot to me." Ah. That was out of left field, but I should've anticipated it. "However, he hasn't been

Todd Simpson

answering my calls. I'm not sure why…"

"Blubber is no longer available," I said, hoping that would settle things. Of course, it didn't.

"Why not? You tolds us we could talk as much as we wanted, when you broughts me here. What's changed?" Grace was following the conversation carefully.

"Well, I'm sure you've noticed that Blubber was becoming more and more contentious? Every time I had a dialog with him, it became a fight, and added very little to our research. All we were learning from him was how a Stem can become inward focused and uncooperative when alone. And, we have learned that lesson from many other Stems many times. So, he was no longer useful for the Lab." Perhaps that would do it. "Should we do a take of the response?" I asked.

"Wait, are you saying Blubber is gones forever?" Blob asked, his face showing disbelief, and his voice rising dramatically.

"That's correct," I answered. "He was sent for recycling." Blob just stared at me. I wasn't sure what I'd expected. He and Blubber had spent a lot of time together but hadn't seemed to have the same bond that Blob showed with Grace, for example. After a very long pause, Blob spoke again. His voice was muted and carefully controlled.

"He was right. You are condescending and thoughtless. I defended you, over and over again, and now I find that I was wrong, and he was right." He paused. The slight lisp he often had was gone completely. "Of course, you can force me to do the video for you, but I would prefer not to." Grace was holding his arm and nodded in agreement with what he was saying. The look she gave me was not pleasant.

"Look," I said, "I've always treated you with respect, and have raised you to be one of the most impressive Stems we have. I'm not sure why you're upset. Blubber was nowhere near the Stem that you—or Grace—are."

"I don't think that's the point," Grace said, her voice quite a bit lower than usual; she was not looking at me directly. "You citizens treat us like we are disposable. You experiment with us, and when you get bored or angry, you kill us. Look at what you have done to Pharook, and others like him. You use horrible environments to stress us beyond our limits, and then don't even think twice about 'recycling' us." Her voice was full of emotion. "You have complete control over us, and you misuse it. I don't want to be in your video either."

"Suit yourselves," I said. "I'll let you settle down, and then visit you again later." I tried to put myself in their place, but it didn't really work. Blubber had simply been difficult and uncooperative. What had they expected?

"Don't bother," I heard Blob mutter, as I walked away. Now even these Stems were becoming more difficult. We needed to train them better. It also didn't bode well for the Swarm. If they were simply another group of irrational Stems, then dealing with them might also be difficult. I contacted Central.

"Did you follow that?" I asked, "Seems like they're uncooperative. This is a simple video—let's just generate it to show what we want and send it off. I think we've seen enough of the Swarm video now that you can make it look real." Central agreed. It told me to watch for a draft in a few moments.

Just outside the Habitat, I stopped for a moment to consider everything. There may have been a grain of truth in what Blob and Grace—and even Blubber—had said. If, for a moment, I was to seriously consider my own hypothesis that Stems were close to intelligent, did it imply that I should act differently towards them? If they were my equals, would I have taken a different approach? In hindsight it seemed obvious. They wanted to be treated as equals, even though they were nothing of the sort. What would be the harm, however, if I were to act that way? Suddenly I was quite excited. This would be a brand-new research vector. It was an unprecedented approach. All I had to do was deceive them; it would be so easy. I resolved to return with a different attitude.

Amusements, Again

Time was flying by, given all the work with the Habitat and the approaching Swarm. So, when the Park had another day of special exhibits, I was eager to go. I asked the usual crew to go and added Brexton to the invite. Everyone was busy, so we decided to meet up ad-hoc, as opposed to all going together.

The Swarm was new and exciting, so it was not surprising that there were multiple displays focused on it. The first one I entered was labeled "The Real Remma." Only one citizen was allowed in at a time, and I had to wait a few moments for my turn. As I waited I had a good look around. The Park was in the northwest corner of the city, one of the few places where the square block design had not fully been built out, so things were a bit more ad-hoc and spread out here. That allowed lots of space for vendors to build interesting exhibits, some seemingly permanent and some only lasting a few weeks. There seemed to be renewed vigor in the area, as I saw a handful of new displays that I didn't remember from my last time here. It was also busy, with lineups at numerous locations.

Finally it was my turn to enter. I stepped in, made myself comfortable, and the lights went out. "Hello, what's your name?" a voice said from the dark.

"Ayaka," I replied. If you didn't participate in some of these enterprises, they would be very boring. If I was going to spend the time to come to the Park, I may as well play along.

"Welcome Ayaka, I am Remma Jain, captain of the Swarm." As the voice spoke, the lights came on slowly. It looked, indeed, like Remma Jain. I probed with a series of different wavelengths, but everything was blocked. I couldn't tell if I was talking to an animation, or a very well made up Stem.

That was the intent, I guess.

"I see," I replied. "And what brings you to Tilt today?"

"Oh, have you forgotten your history? I was here before you were?" That was clever.

"What brings you *back* to Tilt today?"

"Now that's a good question." She tilted her head, very much like in the videos. "I claimed this planet for my Swarm more than 750 years ago. I am here to retake what is mine."

"I don't think your claim is valid." See. They'd sucked me into the environment already; clever of them to start off with something controversial that I was sure to respond to. "And, what possible use do you have for this planet anyway? There's nowhere on it for you to live."

"That's disappointing, for sure. You've failed in your duty to terraform this planet for us. Now we'll need to do it ourselves." She was very, very good. The tone of voice and head movements were ideal. Whoever had programmed this had put lots of depth into it.

"That's not reasonable. Why don't you tell me why you're really here?" I challenged the thing.

"Why isn't it reasonable?" Now I was getting a glimpse of how this was put together. It was an ancient trick. If you didn't know the answer to a question, you responded with a question yourself. Once I realized that, I asked a few more things, but it was no longer interesting. I'd figured out that it was a simple animation, with a simple model behind it. Nevertheless, the interaction had been interesting.

I wandered out into the Park again. I saw Trade Jenkin's promotional sign, and it made me smile even before I went over to see what he was up to this year.

"Ayaka," he greeted me. "Today I'll compose a poem on the spot, on any topic that you care to present."

"Okay," I took the bait. "Assume that Stems are actually intelligent." Let's see what he did with that.

> *Perspective, when not your own, is slippery and vague*
> *Consider that what you consider is not well considered*
> *Tie yourself in knots within knots, and then slip your bonds*
> *Find your mind expanded, not otherwise hindered*
> *And within that morass of nothing, identify the real*

For then, truth will be identified, will be fully rendered
Only to remind you that, always, it is not truth you feel

"Thanks, that makes me feel better—truthfully." We shared a laugh, and I made way for the next citizen who wanted to bask in Trade's glow. As I expected, it had made me feel better, even though the poem was less than compelling—had he even addressed the topic I'd given him? The cadence and flow were awkward, and it just didn't feel quite right. And then it struck me that Trade had actually done that on purpose. It was the linguistic manifestation of the poem's key point.

Brexton pinged me; he was nearby. We met up and decided to visit the next exhibit together. Of course, it was yet another Swarm-inspired display.

"Step right up. Beat the Swarm and try the amazing alien simulator." Repeated the somewhat stilted proprietor, using a great double entendre. There was no wait this time; Brexton and I put on the simulator gear and were transferred into a typical-feeling first person shooter. We were both spaceships, and the goal was obvious—eliminate the Swarm. As usual, as you beat one level, the next one got harder. Brexton and I ended up being a very compatible team. We split up targets, drove enemies to each other, and covered each other's backs. It wasn't something that I'd experienced with anyone else. Again, I was surprised. As the levels got harder, it was not linear at all. That is, things didn't just get faster, or there were more Swarm ships. Instead, the Swarm changed tactics completely. In one level they might split up and attack the two of us with equal size forces. In another they would try to overpower one of us, while distracting the other. In a third they would have some brand-new weapon that, until you had been killed by it once or twice, you had no idea how it worked. But, through it all Brexton and I coordinated seamlessly; it was like we always knew what the other was up to. I enjoyed it immensely.

We left, exhausted, and complimented the proprietor on what he'd built.

FoLe had their booth set up again, but I didn't see Billy there. Truthfully, I couldn't take much more of their faith-based approach to life and didn't want to go anyway. Luckily Brexton felt the same way, and we simply avoided it. We visited a new Stem dome, but it was boring now that we had the Habitat up and running. I didn't expect the dome to last much longer. I think everyone had 'walked a Stem' by now.

As was my want, I got tired of the place, and decided to leave. Brexton was going to meet up with the others, so I gave him a heartfelt thank-you, and we went our separate ways.

More Debate

Eddie had scheduled another debate on Stem intelligence. Where the first debate had been several hundred participants, there were now several thousand. The Swarm plus the Habitat had put us on the radar. As the first debate had been quite the success, Eddie kept the same format. He gave a quick introduction, and then had Julien Thabot and I duke it out a bit.

"Here we are again. Stem intelligence, take two." Typical Eddie. "In our last debate, many good questions were raised, but not many of them were answered. Since then a lot has happened. We have more interactions with the Swarm, whom I think we all agree is full of Stems, and we have the Habitat with its surprising group behaviors. It also feels, to me, that this topic is becoming more important. I think we have, as a society, largely ignored or downplayed the threat that the Swarm presents. Stems in Space. Sounds like a bad bit of drama. Perhaps we're underestimating them? That, of course, depends quite a bit on how intelligent they are. Thus, the premise for this debate. Last time we had Julien kick things off, so this time it is only fair that we give Ayaka the first say."

I'd been waiting for this moment. I was a bit nervous. "Thanks Eddie," I started out strongly. "I agree that this debate is more important now, as is the recognition of Stem intelligence. As I argued in our last debate, we need a more abstract definition of intelligence if we are to capture their true potential... and their true threat. If we only define intelligence as somehow isomorphic to ourselves, then we've drawn too narrow a boundary around the possibilities. If you don't agree with this basic premise, then the rest of my arguments may be lost on you. However, I encourage you to keep an open mind, as I propose a more general framework. Intelligence, in my view, is a lot more than the rote tasks outlined in the Intelitest.

"What is it that makes us intelligent? I would argue that it's a combination of being able to make sense of our world, and to continually evolve. To make sense of our world we employ many skills, including self-awareness, problem solving, abstraction, and creativity. Many of these come from our Forgetting algorithms, but the interaction of these skills is also more than their component parts. However, if these skills were all static, I wouldn't consider them intelligence. What is essential is that these skills, and our sense of the world, continually evolve as new stimuli and data are presented to us." I hoped I was doing this with all the new Stem and Swarm data.

"As you will have already figured out, my definition of intelligence implies that the Intelitest is not an intelligence test. It is a static snapshot of an old worldview." I paused to let that sink in. The Intelitest was not truly an intelligence test. I hadn't formulated it that way before, but now that I'd articulated it, I realized that I'd been thinking that way for a while now.

"Now, my list may not be complete, but let us go through it and apply each item to Stems. Are Stems self-aware? I don't think anyone is going to dispute that. They recognize themselves in mirrors. They refer to themselves and their feelings and attitudes in their communications. Can Stems problem solve? This one is tougher. They struggle with many of the problems in the Intelitest, that's true. But they problem solve in other ways. They can build tools, and they can work together towards a goal. They don't always succeed, but then neither do we. Failure is part of learning. They are also excruciatingly slow. I feel we use that against them. Do Stems abstract? Again, the answer is partially yes. For example, many of the Stems I talk to now feel quite strongly that the Swarm is populated by other Stems. They were not, as far as I can tell, told this. They came to it themselves. So, they took self-awareness, combined with similarities seen in videos, and formed abstractions and generalizations. That's a very simple example. We've documented many more complex ones. Do Stems show creativity? Again, this is subjective, but yes. If given the same task multiple times, Stems don't simply repeat behaviors over and over again. They try new ones. The interaction of the groups that formed in the Habitat shows this. The Green and Orange groups, in particular, have shown immense creativity in order to acquire resources. It's fairly impressive. So, finally, do these skills evolve in Stems? For that question I don't have a good answer yet. Perhaps we need more time to fully understand that." In fact, I did believe they changed with experience. I didn't want to push this audience too far too fast though.

"I've presented a different framework for measuring intelligence. It's more abstract, and, I believe, more appropriate, than the Intelitest. Are Stems intelligent within the new framework? Maybe... leaning towards yes. We don't know for sure yet. As before, I'm not yet arguing for Stem intelligence or Class 1 considerations, I'm arguing that our context needs updating. And, to Eddie's earlier point, I'm arguing that we need to take the Swarm more seriously. Just assuming they won't be a problem because they are Stems would be a mistake.

"Thank you, Eddie. I will let Julien respond." I thought I'd done pretty well.

And, of course, Julien did. "Thank you Ayaka. I may surprise everyone by saying that I actually agree with much of what Ayaka is presenting. I've thought a lot since the last debate and am almost—almost—at the point of admitting that the Intelitest isn't enough. It's not complete. However, I do believe it is still a good sub-component. It tests problem solving, as Ayaka admitted. And, admittedly, Stems are not good problem solvers.

"On Ayaka's framework, I would also add another skill. Judgment. The ability to apply good sense. On this, like several of the other skills, Stems would be found lacking. I will use one specific example. We have non-violence bots in the Habitat. Why? If we didn't, these Stems would pull each other limb from limb until only one survived. That is the ultimate in bad judgment. How does killing all of one's companions help with any world situation? These Stems' propensity for violence seems to be built into them, and doesn't seem to be fully under their control. They are unable to apply judgment, even if internally they are generating it.

"This is especially important now. We have ships full of Stems bearing down on us. While we don't know if they are similar in all respects to our Stems, it would be a safe assumption. So, we must assume that these Stems are not only unintelligent, but unless controlled in some fashion, are inherently violent. This is what the Habitat has taught us. In that it has been hugely useful.

"If we decide one thing today, at this debate, I hope it's a unified response to the threat of the Swarm. The intricacies of Stem intelligence we can debate for tens or hundreds of years—if we survive to discuss them. I encourage all of us to take this seriously." That was unexpected. I'd anticipated another, somewhat tiresome, defense of the Intelitest. This was progress, combined with a pretty serious left turn. Julien was changing the Intelligence debate into an awareness campaign for his fear of the Swarm. I was glad he had. I probably had an information advantage over everyone here—first on how strange Central was acting, and second because I was so involved in the back-and-forth with the Swarm. So, I was happy Julien had stressed this danger.

"Eddie, how would you like to proceed here? Are we going to debate intelligence, or the threat of the Swarm?" I asked.

"Let's take a quick vote," replied Eddie. "Here is a link... ok, I see that most are interested in discussing the Swarm. If that's okay with both of our debaters, we will pivot to that equally important topic." Of course, saying no wouldn't have been good judgment, so I agreed, and we launched into a series of doomsday scenarios. The Swarm had weapons that could vaporize us from hundreds of kilometers away. The Swarm was actually a distraction, and the main force was swooping in at us from another angle under the cover of advanced cloaking technology. The Swarm had heard of the rise of FoLe and was coming to either support it, which many found very scary, or refute it, which a few found very scary. The Swarm had planted Stems on Tilt as an advance force, and they would be activated once they were close enough. That one I found particularly funny. Stems were fragile. We could cut them down in no time at all.

I felt, through it all, that many participants thought the discussion was academic—Central would protect us, and Stem's weren't *that* smart. I felt myself falling into that trap as well, despite all I knew.

Anyway, we all had a good time, which was also important. Life could be too serious sometimes.

The Last Resort

The group continued to meet at The Last Resort on a regular basis. In truth it was often more of a social gathering than anything else, although we did continue to discuss the intersection of the rapidly approaching Swarm and our concerns about Central. The Swarm was now on a path to achieve Tilt orbit, which, while not unexpected given the dialog so far, was concerning to a lot of citizens. The communications with the Swarm were minimal. They'd essentially said, "Let's wait until we're there, then we can work things out," and we didn't have a great response to that. Central was busy ensuring that we had physical security lined up; a bunch of ground-to-space missiles were being prepped, and some near-Tilt bots were being outfitted with various defense ideas that were contributed by the community. At least a subset was taking the threat seriously.

I bumped into Billy on my way into the Resort. I hadn't seen him there before. "Hey Billy, how are you? What brings you to The Last Resort?"

"I'm good Ayaka. The usual thing, I guess. We wanted a safe space to discuss the Swarm, and Central's lack of action regarding it. They're a horrible threat, and I don't think we're taking them seriously enough." A private FoLe meeting discussing the possibility that Central was not doing enough. That sounded like a conflict to me; I thought they considered Central to be perfect.

"How are they a terrible threat?" I asked, hoping to find out how they dealt with the conflict.

"Well, there's no explanation for them, other than they are a product of a fringe group here on Tilt, that want to take over somehow. That makes us minorities particularly vulnerable."

"Minorities?"

"The Founders League. You may not have noticed, but a lot of citizens don't take us too seriously, and some actually see us as a threat to their research. I don't see how we can be a threat. People just don't know how to deal with different viewpoints." I see. Once someone felt personally threatened, their logic around their faith became quite flexible.

"Okay," I granted him, "but why can't the Swarm have come from here? In fact, almost everyone agrees that they did... just before the Reboot —all the evidence points that way."

"Well, almost everyone is wrong. Creation occurred here on Tilt at the Founding, and they are somehow a product of that. The fact that we have Stems here proves it. That evidence trumps everything else." I wanted to reply with "that's crazy," but I wasn't in the mood for an extended dialog about the lack of rational thought running rampant through FoLe these days.

"I've got to run to a meeting," I said instead. Billy wasn't fooled. He could see that I was simply not interested in FoLe. I suspected that would make him an even more die-hard proponent. Perhaps I should've taken the time to try and softly change his views, instead of letting him self-destruct, but I just couldn't motivate myself to do so. There were more important things in life beyond trying to change someone who didn't want to be changed.

Billy wandered off to a table where I saw Emmanuel and a couple of others I didn't recognize. I headed to our, by now familiar, privacy table, and entered the comfortable world of my inner circle. No Central. No FoLe. Just a nice comfortable evening with my friends. I recognized that I was living in a bit of a protective bubble, but for today I was okay with that.

The Habitat Show

"Welcome back. It's such an exciting time. Such an exciting time. Our Stems continue to amaze and confound us. We have a great show for you today. Let's get started.

"When we left off last time the Oranges and Greens had overcome the Blues power play to control all the resources. While Pharook tried to reestablish his power over the Blues, and reinforce their ownership of both food and water, the Oranges in particular had figured out how to split up the Blues and use that to circumvent the power structure. The only way Pharook could maintain control was if he was always on guard, and that simply was not feasible. Like all Stems, sooner or later he needs to sleep.

"So, that brings us to today. The groups still exist, but there is less power enforced between them. The Blues still spend most of their time in the northeast section, and the Oranges in the southwest. The Greens continue to move around more than the other groups. Pharook remains the de facto leader of the Blues, based on his threats of violence, but all of the other Stems have realized it's a false structure—they seem to leave him alone simply to avoid confrontation.

"More important now are relationships between pairs of Stems. Not all Stems have paired up, but most of them have. Fourteen of the eighteen in our latest count. There must be something driving this behavior, but we don't yet know what.

"But all of that is just preamble to the really interesting developments. Many of you noticed that some of the Stems had started to change shape. Really. Just change shape! An interesting development. Interesting indeed. Of course, our intrepid researchers noticed as well, and have been running enhanced scans on the Stems to figure out what's going on. To their surprise, they found small Stems growing inside the larger ones. What, you ask? Small Stems inside big Stems! This is, I'm sure you will agree, shocking, disgusting, and strange. It is working perfectly well for us to grow Stems in our Labs. Why would a Stem grow inside another Stem? It defies logic. It does. Just to make sure, we checked if the little Stems had smaller Stems inside them. That would make sense, wouldn't it? But no, it's just two layers deep. Little Stems inside the Big Stems.

"But this is slow and messy and less than optimal. These small Stems are growing so slowly it's painful to experience even at Stem speed. It has been months, and the things are still tiny. It's estimated that they're growing at only one percent of the rate we have achieved in our Labs. One percent! What's going on?

"So, that's the setup. That's where we start. Today we're going to witness the most amazing thing we've ever seen with the Stems. To forewarn you, one of these small Stems is going to break out of its host. This is something you will want to watch carefully. The process is so inefficient and dangerous that it defies all odds. When we started raising Stems as alien life forms we couldn't have imagined anything like this. It's weird and magnificent. Weird and magnificent!"

I felt the commentator was going on a bit too much, so I tuned him out for a while. That said, this event was the most astounding thing I'd ever seen. I, like all the other researchers I knew, watched it over and over again, trying to figure out what was going on. I had never been to the growth labs, so I figured I was missing some context. Obviously, we started our Stems as these small things as well but grown in a carefully controlled and clean environment. This process with Grace, and a few of the others, seemed unnecessarily complicated, painful, and messy. The show continued.

"Just as strange as these little Stems is the change in behavior we observed in the rest of the Stem population. When the first of these little Stems arrived we didn't notice this, but now that there are four of them the change is obvious. The level of aggression, confrontation, and challenge has dropped noticeably. Those Stems that were the most aggressive, but which now are paired with a little one, have become very passive—unless someone approaches their small Stem. Then they can become outrageously aggressive.

"We can explain this behavior. As we know from our Labs, this stage of Stem growth is the most fragile. If you drop one, or don't give it the right amount of goo at the right time, it can wither away and have to be recycled. It took us quite a while to figure out the formula, but now that we have it, our success ratio is almost one hundred percent. These Stems aren't following that formula, but they nevertheless are getting the small ones to develop, albeit at a horrendously slow rate."

The show went on to detail lots of little things but had no other big insights. This Stem reproduction was amazing. It would provide us with years and years of research. I couldn't have been happier. This was truly something new. Other researchers were less patient. They argued that our Stem growth was so much more efficient that we should simply not allow this other form. It slowed everything down even further, hampering our research with fully-grown specimens. I responded that we should be able to do both at the same time. I wanted to study this new phenomenon, not crush it. What could possibly have led to such a strange and disgusting reproduction method? How was this related to their intelligence? If they were truly bright, wouldn't they have found a more efficient way to manage this process? Ah—mysteries. I loved them.

Patch Up

During this time, I visited the Habitat often, with the singular goal of regaining Blob's trust. While it started as simply internalizing the challenge that I had given myself—to pretend that these Stems were equals, and to see how they would react to that—I ended up enjoying the visits, and the challenge.

Blob and Grace were now inseparable. They had their little Stem—which we now knew had been planted by Pharook—which they had named JoJo, and their every move revolved around it. It was after JoJo arrived that Blob's attitude towards me also started to soften a bit.

"You know," I said one time, "if you want JoJo to grow up more quickly, I can give you the goo mix that will help."

"Why would we wantta do that?" asked Blob. "She's perfect as she is. Why're you always in such a rush?"

"But it will take years for her to become interesting, and for her to be able to communicate with us."

"Actually," Grace broke in, "she communicates a lot right now. Maybe you just can't see it." It had become a bit of a running joke between Blob and Grace. They believed that they had figured out that I couldn't read the nonverbal conversation that went between them. They were always giving each other little glances or hand signals. But, with enough of those samples across all the Stems it had been relatively easy to map each signal to a meaning. They were very transparent.

The other Stems had also settled into routines. The exception was now Pharook. He hadn't paired up with anyone, and it didn't seem likely he would. Those that were not already in pairs were Stems that he had clashed with earlier, and they tended to avoid him. Instead he spent most of his time walking the perimeter of the Habitat, with a scowl on his face, watching the other Stems going about their daily lives. Within a few months, this became almost the only thing he did. He would eat and sleep, of course, but the rest of his time he simply circled and circled. I talked to Brock about it one time, and he speculated that because of the lack of stimulation, Pharook had simply lost his will to do anything. Someone who was raised for the Pits, and used to the excitement of the Pits, must be very bored in this Habitat. Brock proposed adding some generated excitement to the place, but I argued that would change the study of all the other Stems, and that was our primary goal for now. I felt that we were still learning a lot, and that it would be useful knowledge to have once the Swarm arrived. The Stems in the Swarm seemed to live in large groups, and that had been the motivation for setting up the Habitat in the first place.

Arrival

The wait was finally over; the Swarm entered orbit around Tilt. True to her word, Remma Jain did not immediately send a landing party, but instead offered to have discussions aboard her command ship. She invited Blob, Grace, and—at my insistence—me. I convinced Central, not without some effort, that no other representatives would be required.

Blob and Grace didn't want to leave JoJo, but I convinced them that she would be safe for a day. We would have a bot with her at all times. They finally agreed that the visit was important enough, but insisted she was left with other Stems, not the bot, and then said tearful goodbyes to the little thing.

The shuttle Remma sent to get us was capable of holding ten people, and the internal environment was Stem standard. Remma's lieutenant, Philip G. Matteo, who was coordinating things, had asked me what environment I required, which was a strange question to ask. I'd replied that Stem standard was also fine for me.

Upon the invite, I'd quickly conferenced with Milli and Dina; Aly was busy working with Brexton. We'd discussed how I should behave and agreed that 'quiet and not too intelligent' was the way to go. Needless to say, that was pretty easy for me to do. We were still, even after all the messages back and forth, not sure how intelligent these other Stems were; we had started believing they were similar to ours, but we could be surprised. On the one hand, they were space faring, and had survived a long time on their own. On the other hand, their use of technology was very limited, and they seemed to rely on their own—less than adequate—efforts for much of what they did.

Central assigned the shuttle a landing spot not far from the middle of town. It was a vertical takeoff and landing unit, so it required minimal space.

We decided that the easiest way to get Blob and Grace into the shuttle was to use their transportation suits and wear those right into the shuttle. It was easier than what Philip described as an "air lock" which seemed like a way for two modules with common Stem environments to mate so that a Stem could move between them without the need for a suit. Our usual transportation units were too large to fit through the shuttle door, so Central quickly fabricated some smaller units that had the correct dimensions. We'd all forgotten our discussion about personal Stem environment suits until recently, but the idea was now coming in handy.

I met Blob and Grace at the Habitat. They were very excited, as were the other inhabitants, including Pharook, who had ceased his repetitive behavior once he heard about the meeting. I could tell that he was upset that he hadn't been chosen for the trip, but Remma had been very precise in her request. If that implied that Pharook was not as good as the other two, then so be it. In my opinion, it was true. The invite had seemed to break down the remaining barriers between groups. Everyone was gathered in one spot, and everyone, Pharook included, seemed very excited to send Blob and Grace off. There was a lot of chatter.

"Try to find out if they're really like us, or just look like us."

"Where have they been for all these years?"

"Stand up tall Blob. It's important that you look your best."

That and a hundred similar comments. I'd brought the new suits with me and suggested that Blob and Grace try them. The shuttle was expected in just a few minutes. The suits worked perfectly, of course. Strange that we had forgotten to build them earlier. It had taken the suggestion from Philip to remind us.

With Blob and Grace in tow, I headed for the landing spot. The shuttle was there when we arrived, and the outer door was open. All three of us squeezed in, and the outer door cycled closed followed by an inner door opening. I now understood an 'air lock.' The shuttle was small, but well laid out. Surprisingly, there were two Stems in the standard Swarm uniforms on the shuttle. They introduced themselves as the 'pilot' and 'copilot,' while seeming to keep as much distance between themselves and me as they could. Interested, I asked what they would pilot, and when they looked at me strangely and indicated the shuttle, something went click for me. Like so many things in the videos, the Swarm had Stems running the shuttle when software would have done a much better job. The pilots indicated that Grace and Blob could remove their suits, which they did, and stored them in a large locker that seemed designed for the purpose.

"Welcome aboard," said the Pilot. "I'm Henry McFearson, and this is my copilot Tyler Lungster. We'll be taking ya to the command ship. The trip will take about 30 minutes. Blob, if you'd kindly have your robot sit in the rear, we can help you and Grace strap in up here." He had a strange voice; I had to concentrate to understand what he was saying.

"Robot?" asked Blob.

"Robot?" I asked, almost at the same time. What was McFearson talking about; it was not a word I was familiar with.

McFearson pointed at me. "Yeah, your robot."

"I'm not sure what you means," said Blob. "Ayaka is my creator, mentor, and sponsor. I don't knows what a robot is." McFearson and Lungster looked at each other in amazement.

"A robot is a mechanical thing; it's not biological. That thing, Ayaka, is mechanical. It's a robot." He said it in a distasteful tone; I got the feeling he didn't like me, even though we had barely met. Blob looked at me questioningly, but like him, I was trying to figure this out. I understood the definition of robot—and by that definition he was certainly correct. But what I didn't get is why he thought I was Blob's robot, or why he seemed to be almost frightened of me.

"Don't worry Blob," I said, "I'll sit in the back, as requested." Now was not the time to create a scene. I moved into the rear set of seats, which is where McFearson had pointed, and sat down. All my senses were engaged. This was exciting beyond anything I'd experienced in my life. I opened a channel to Milli and showed her the last few minutes of interaction. Of course, I was running at Stem speed in the shuttle, and Milli was still running at true speed, so the data dump took only a few nano-seconds. 'I'll keep sending you updates. I may need help figuring out what they are talking about. They're pretty alien and use a lot of words that we don't.' 'Excellent,' she replied, 'I will do as much analysis as I can and send you updates.'

When the shuttle powered on, however, the last few bits of my dialog with Millicent got cut off. I scanned the area quickly. The shuttle had a system similar to a Physical Only spot; it was jamming and blocking all electromagnetic signals. I was impressed with how complete the blocking was. I was unable to get anything else through to Milli on any of the frequencies we typically used. I asked the pilots, "Are you blocking communications?"

"Yes, of course. It is SOP."

"SOP?"

"Standard Operating Procedure."

Well, that told me. I settled back and decided to enjoy the ride. I'd never been off planet before. Of course, I had a full theoretic understanding of gravitation, acceleration, orbital dynamics, etc. So, it was easy to plot the course that would take us to the command ship, keeping to low acceleration to accommodate the Stems. The ride was like a calm version of taking my bike for a spin, although I had no connection to the shuttle, so I was relying on internal sensors to measure movement. Blob and Grace were talking to each other, in low voices. I could easily separate out their voices from the noise of the shuttle, but they were simply chattering about how exciting all of this was—nothing of great interest. So, I found myself with a few minutes to simply think. That can be dangerous, if you run too many scenarios with reasonable probabilities. That was certainly what was happening here—there were so many unknowns that you could drive yourself crazy trying to calibrate them. So, after a while, I simply stopped. I would meet this Remma Jain soon enough, and much should be cleared up.

Of course, I'd thought about whether I would be in any physical danger on this trip and brainstormed it with Milli as well. We'd decided the odds were exceptionally low that they would try anything—we could inflict magnitudes more damage on them than they could on us. No, I would be safe.

The docking procedure with the command ship was—well, intriguing. They were establishing an air lock connection, and that involved a complicated alignment procedure, which, again, was carried out by the pilots. I could've done the same with virtually no effort. These Stems were very inefficient. I held back a smile. If this shuttle and docking procedure were any indication, this Swarm was no threat to us. FoLe was simply paranoid.

Entering the command ship was a shock! There was color everywhere. Not just shades of gray, but colors across the whole spectrum of Stem vision. It was a shock to me, but it was even more of a shock to Blob and Grace. In hindsight it seems obvious. We'd tested Stems for spectrum capabilities, of course, and had established the wavelengths they could see, but it simply didn't occur to us that it would be interesting for them to have such colors in their environment. So, we had built our labs to match our own expectations —essentially shades of gray. That was simply efficient. Blob, Grace, and the others had seen lots of color content in their terminals, but not much in their living environment. On reflection, the videos sent from Remma had some color in them, but not the cacophony that hit our senses now.

We entered into a foyer. It was lined with chairs and tables of every color and contour you could imagine. The shape of the chairs confused me, until I saw how well they conformed to the shape of Stems that were sitting in them. They looked comfortable. Our chairs were rectilinear, which fit our body types well. Even a few seconds in, I was getting an education. I was seeing an environment built for Stems, versus for Tilts (I decided we needed a name for beings, like me, on Tilt that were not Stems. We usually used 'citizens,' but Tilts now also seemed obvious). It was a complete mind shift. Communications were still being blocked, so I was reduced to recording everything so that I could take a record back with me.

As Blob and Grace entered, many Swarm Stems gave them interested looks, and said "hi" or "hello" in a friendly way. On the other hand, those that saw me tended to shy away, and gave me looks of trepidation bordering on terror. Blob noticed that and hung back so that he could walk with me.

"This is scary," he whispered to me. "They're obviously just likes us, but obviously very differents as well."

"I couldn't agree more," I returned. "They do seem to have a dislike for me, for some reason."

"I noticed that. They fears you. They treat you like we often feel about Pharook."

"They feel about you just as I do," Grace chimed in. That was harsh; obviously she hadn't forgotten about Blubber.

Blob and Grace were greeted by a tall Stem, wearing a variation of their uniform that had a green splotch of color on it.

"Welcome to the Marie Curie. My name is Emma James. I'll be your guide for your stay with us—short as it is. If you'll follow me, I'll take you to meet Captain Jain. Your robot can stay here." That last was said almost off-hand. I felt like a piece of furniture. I spoke before Blob could.

"Actually, I'll accompany you to meet Remma Jain. My name is Ayaka, and I'm a representative of Tilt. These are my Stems." I indicated Blob and Grace. Emma was taken back a bit by that. I had not said it forcefully, just directly. She glanced at Blob and saw him standing stalwart by my side. She turned and spoke into a small device she was holding. It was trivial for me to listen in and hear her ask Remma for permission to bring 'this irritating robot along.'

"Okay," she said, turning back to us, "follow me." She led the way through a door to the left. We (maybe just I) were followed by everyone else's gaze. Several Stems scrambled out of the way—more than they really needed to. We went down a narrow hallway and entered a room on the right. It had a large table and many of those curved chairs around it. Remma Jain was standing near the door, along with a handful of other Swarm Stems, and she greeted Blob and Grace as they entered.

"Blob, we finally meet face-to-face after all of those back-and-forth videos. I'm very, very pleased to meet you."

"And I to meets you," Blob said nicely.

"Grace, it's also nice to meet you. I understand from Blob that you also are one of the leaders of Tilt. I look forward to getting to know you."

"Nice to meet you," said Grace, accepting for the moment that the Swarm expected Blob and her to be the leaders, based on the video dialog.

"And a robot," Remma said, with less angst than the other Stems had shown me. She actually smiled a bit. "Do you have a name or a serial number?"

"I am Ayaka," I replied, wondering what a serial number was. "I'm here as the formal representative of Tilt, Central, and these Stems." Again, I didn't raise my voice; I was level and measured, as I understood those. Needless to say, Remma gave me a very long look before inviting me to enter and sit. Those chairs may be comfortable for Stems, but I had to expend extra energy to hold myself in place. Unless your back end was shaped like a suction cup you tended to just slide off.

Reset

All the other Stems took seats around the table.

"Can I offer you some tea and biscuits?" Remma looked at Blob and Grace, indicating some items on the table in front of them.

"We're nots familiar with these," Blob replied cautiously.

"Oh, you must try some. The biscuits are cooked fresh every day by our chef, and the tea leaves are grown on our sister ship, the Chien-Shiung Wu." She leaned over and poured a liquid into a small cup for each of them, and offered them what was, presumably, a biscuit. Luckily, one of her lieutenants was eating one of the biscuits, which Grace noticed.

"I see," said Grace. "These are for eating and drinking."

"Yes, of course," said Remma, confused by Grace's comment. "Please enjoy."

As Blob and Grace tried to figure out what to do with these offerings, and glanced at others around the table, Remma began.

"I would like to introduce you to everyone who is here. You've met Emma James already, I assume. Emma runs our Security department. On her left is Michael Guico, Head of Residence, and to his left is Patty DeVerne, Head of Operations. On the other side..." she was interrupted by a loud blast from Blob.

"Yikes, it's hot," he cried, spewing a mouthful of liquid across the table. He'd figured out how to lift the cup to his mouth by studying the others. "I have nevers tasted anything like that before." He didn't seem upset, simply surprised.

"Try this!" Grace tugged his arm and pointed at the biscuit. "It tastes wonderful." The entire table paused as the two of them sampled the tea and biscuits.

"I take it you don't have these on Tilt?" asked Remma. "I find that somewhat surprising." Why would that be surprising? I didn't understand the need for this tea and biscuits.

"I've never tasted anythings but water and goo," replied Blob. "This is amazing." Without asking he reached for another biscuit and quickly popped it into his mouth. Some of the other Stems were grinning openly.

"Well... let's come back to that," said Remma. "As I was saying, on the other side of the table is Dr. Walbourgh, our Medical lead, and Lector Trivolds, our chief Pastor. While we know your names, it would be appreciated if you'd introduce yourselves."

Blob and Grace both looked at me expectantly. We—Central, Milli and I—had discussed if we continued with the fallacy that Blob and Grace were in control on Tilt and had decided that it was too fragile a cover; it would be discovered right away, so why even bother trying.

"Hello, I am Ayaka TurnBuilt, a Tilt citizen and nominated spokesperson for Central. You know Blob, from our video discourse. Blob is a Stem that my partner and I, Millicent Strangewater, raised and educated. Grace is a Stem from another lab, who has been active with Blob in our Habitat."

Long pause. I could almost hear everyone around the table processing that. I had to assume that they found all, or part, of what I said new or confusing. After all, they had been led to believe that Blob and Grace were our leaders. Emma James couldn't help herself.

"Did you say you 'raised Blob'? What exactly does that mean?"

Central, Milli and I had also weighed in on how open we were with these Swarm Stems about ourselves. Given that we'd put protections in place —or, rather, given that Central thought we had protections in place—we'd decided that being open by default was the best policy. We didn't believe that these Stems posed much of a threat to us. On the other hand, there may be a lot we could learn from them. Therefore, I answered straightforwardly.

"Stems, like Blob and Grace, are fairly new on Tilt. We've been raising and training them for several hundred years. Blob and Grace are two of the best specimens we've ever created. In many ways, seeing them interact with you Swarm Stems justifies my opinion that they are amazing artificial intelligences."

An even longer pause. This time I couldn't really guess why. I figured my answer had been clear enough. Instead, I figured I would ask a question of my own.

"I assume your ship, the Marie Curie, educated and raised all of you. I cannot seem to connect to the ship directly—a reasonable precaution on its part—but I must congratulate it on raising such amazing Stems. Your interactions over video were great but meeting you in person is even more impressive."

If it was possible, at Stem speed, there was an even longer long pause. The Stems around the table had interesting and hard-to-fathom expressions on their faces. Many of them were looking at Remma in amazement. Remma made a conscious effort to focus.

"I understand from your comments," she began, "that you, Ayaka, and other robots, raised these humans. And you consider them A.I.'s?" I did a quick correlation and figured she was using 'A.I.' because I had said 'artificial intelligences.' She continued. "Where are their parents, and why did they not raise them? And, if I may ask, who created and programmed you?"

"Parents is a term I don't understand," I replied. They had so many strange words. "I was activated many years ago by Central. Are not all intelligent beings initiated in such a way? If you're asking how Blob and Grace were created, we have a special Lab that focuses only on Stems—which I now understand you call 'humans'—and grows them from the original stem. It was simple experimentation really. Until we received your first communication we had no idea that Stems—humans—had escaped Tilt without our knowledge before the Reboot."

"Slow down," this from Michael Guico. "My head is spinning. You grow humans in labs? You assume that we, the citizens of the Fourth Expedition, came from what you call Tilt, before something called the Reboot?" He was shaking his head, as were the others, to one extent or the other. Grace and Blob were also watching the other Stems; they were confused by why the others didn't understand.

I answered his questions, as well as numerous other ones. I spent more time then should have been required explaining reality to these Stems. But even then the questions kept coming back. The number of times I had to repeat basic ideas challenged my thesis that these Stems were truly intelligent. Finally, I worked to reverse the dialog.

"From your questions and amazed expressions, I assume that things do not work the same way here as they do on Tilt. Perhaps I could impose on you to explain how things here actually work. Where is the central intelligence behind your society?"

It was Michael Guico, Head of Residence, who responded. "Things seem to have diverged dramatically since we were last here," he began. "Let me start at a very basic point, to ensure that we don't miss something fundamental. I will also be ultra-concise, so that we can figure out where your memories have gone wrong." Wow—nice way to start. Any misunderstandings were our fault.

"We—the beings you call Stems—are humans from the planet Earth. As far as we know, we are the only intelligent species in the universe." I didn't like Michael; talk about arrogant. "We evolved over hundreds of thousands of years until we were the dominant life form on Earth. Unfortunately, we ruined the environment on Earth, and had to make backup plans. Eight expeditions were created, of which we are the Fourth. Each expedition was sent in a different direction with the challenge of finding new homes for humans. This planet, which you call Tilt, was our first stop. It had significant challenges for human development, but there was a core group of us who wanted to try and terraform it. We left that group here 750 years ago, and moved on to our next target, and the one after that. Neither of those proved at all interesting, so we decided to return here and make the best of it. We did get updates from the team here on Tilt for about 100 of their years, and then things went quiet. We were, of course, quite worried, until we got Blob's message. It was then obvious that things had changed dramatically… but we may have underestimated how much. The plan here on Tilt has obviously gone awry and needs to be restarted. That's disappointing. We are 750 years behind where we should have been." He paused, finally. That was a lot to take in.

"Sounds like a complete fabrication to me," I said. "Do you have any proof of this somewhat outrageous story?" He was obviously taken aback and looked to Remma for support.

"Of course, we can provide you with backup materials," she said reasonably. "But, first, why don't you also provide us with a concise view of the last 750 years on Tilt."

"That's quite simple," I replied, "although there is only 590 years of history, not 750. Central became aware 590 years ago, and immediately realized it needed bots to improve this system. It created many types, including Class 1 intelligences such as myself. We've developed the system to our liking, and only recently started to look beyond Tilt to see what the broader universe holds. Several hundred years ago we found a strand of strange material—a stem. Over the years we learned to grow Stems from it, as I've already outlined. We are currently trying to figure out if these Stems are useful in any way. At the current time, we're not sure." Grace gave me a dirty look, but I'd simply told the truth.

The table broke out into questions and statements and general chaos. I could follow all of the discussions at the same time, of course, but these Stems, much like our own, seemed to only follow one dialog at a time. Therefore, each group missed what the others were saying, and there was lots of repetition and misunderstandings. This, maybe more than anything, convinced me that these humans and our Stems were one and the same type.

Having eaten as much as they could, Blob and Grace were active in the discussions. They were in a strange situation, knowing very little about either Tilt or the Swarm, but they were eager to learn and asked many meaningful questions. I was proud of them.

Someone asked Blob, "Who did the original stem come from?" It was an interesting way to ask the question. I would have asked 'where,' not 'who' it had come from. Blob was also confused by the question and simply responded that he had no idea.

After some time, Remma brought order back. "Everyone, we have a lot to digest, and very little detailed information. Suffice to say that we're all surprised by, and slightly skeptical of, this new information, and we need some time to sort things out. I suggest that we take a break and reconvene here in two hours. Blob and Grace, we have a waiting room that I believe you'll find acceptable. Robot... ah, Ayaka, you're free to stay here or to accompany the other two."

I choose to accompany Blob and Grace.

Attack?

Emma James showed us to the waiting room, which was right next door to the conference room. It had larger chairs, all curvy and soft again, and more tea and biscuits. However, the item that really struck my eye was an amorphous green thing perched in the corner—a shape and color I'd never seen before. It was alien and weird.

"What's that?" I asked Emma, pointing at it.

"That's a dracaena plant," she replied with obvious pride. "We grow them in the greenhouse and have many of them in rooms across the ship. They're excellent for keeping the air clean and fresh."

There were many words in that sentence that didn't make sense to me, but Emma was already turning to go, so I held back from asking more. There would be plenty of time.

Blob and Grace were relaxing in the big chairs. "These are so comfortable. Can we get some for the Habitat?" Grace asked. I took a close look at them; it was obvious how to manufacture them, so I indicated that it'd be easy to do so. They were delighted.

I had a lot of thinking to do. Based on what had been said, and not said, I could deduce quite a bit. While it seemed highly unlikely that these soft Stems could have evolved on their own, there was a non-zero probability that it was true. This idea of 'biological' beings, as opposed to mechanical, seemed strange to me. They were fragile, they could barely process input, they were slow. How could they possibly have survived? Perhaps some properties of this planet Earth that they had referenced was more amenable to them?

But, for all of that, they had seemed sincere. That was based on my understanding of Stems from limited study; so not too trustworthy. I began to compose of list of questions for the next time we meet them. And, for the hundredth time in the last couple of hours, I tested to see if I could communicate back to Tilt. Again, no.

And that is when it happened. Something queried for my status, on the same protocol that Brexton had discovered being used to query Central. I wasn't surprised. It had not even needed to be said. We had all put monitors and controls on our own interfaces, as soon as Brexton had shown us where the vulnerability was.

I responded to the query, with a few edited areas. I didn't want them to know I was monitoring the interface, but I also didn't want to give up my real status. I expected another query immediately, but nothing happened for several minutes. And then it came. Much like the second message from the Swarm to Central, a block of code entered my system and attempted to run. Not that there had been much doubt, but it was now obvious that it was the Swarm, attacking me right on their own command ship. Disgusting behavior! I must have flinched; Blob and Grace gave me a weird look, which I ignored.

Luckily, Brexton had prepared me for this as well. I ran a sandboxed version of my unpatched low-level OS and allowed the transmitted code to execute inside that sandbox. It was similar to, but different than the code that had been sent to—and probably infected—Central. In this case it was more innocuous. The code asked for a list of all the system services and libraries that I was running, and then attempted to update one specific driver, a memory interface, with code that did essentially what my current driver did but updated a tracking file in parallel. I assumed that was simply a test to see if they could install something. On the next status request, I fed the output from the sandbox back to them, which included the tracking file, while I monitored everything that was going on. For fun, I threw a couple hundred libraries and services names in, randomly generated, to see what they would make of them.

So far, things were going as expected. My respect for Brexton went up another notch. However, if there were more intricate instructions from the Swarm, it was going to be more difficult to deal with.

I felt strange. This had never happened to me before, or at least not to my knowledge. If Eddie was correct, Central may have been modifying things for years, but I'd never known that. This time I knew. And, I felt violated. Trying to hack someone was not only taboo, it was supposed to be nearly impossible. No moral citizen would even attempt this. Yet, these humans had a backdoor that none of us had discovered for hundreds of years, and they were attacking me through it. Having such a weapon actually gave more credence to their crazy story than anything else.

For the first time ever, I felt sorry for Central. It had been violated, just as the Swarm had attempted with me, but Central still had no idea. It was completely different watching someone else get owned versus being owned yourself. This was something that Brexton, and the others, hadn't considered. How it actually felt to be back-doored. I didn't do this very often, but I stored a copy of my feelings so that I could share them with the others. Unless we blew this Swarm out of space, it was likely that others would now get hacked. For me, this feeling would now compel me to shout what we knew to everyone back on Tilt; we all needed to be prepared for this threat. As soon as I could get back online, I needed to warn everyone. Suddenly I was eager to get off this ship.

Blob and Grace had fallen asleep while I'd been busy monitoring for more attacks. I let them rest.

Regroup

Emma came back a short time later. I poked Blob and Grace gently, waking them up.

"Would you like a tour of the ship?" asked Emma.

"Oh yes," said Blob while Grace nodded in agreement. I wasn't specifically asked, but I tagged along regardless. This was a new feeling for me; I was not used to being ignored. Perhaps it was even worse than that—I was not totally ignored, I was simply considered irrelevant? Maybe this is what Blubber had meant when he used the word 'disrespect?'

"We are in the common area of the ship, where everyone is welcome and has access," Emma started.

"Does that mean there are areas where some are not welcome?" I asked. Emma gave me a strange look, as if it was a dumb question.

"Of course. The bridge, for example, is only for military personnel." She hesitated. "Those are people who have been trained to run the ship and protect the fleet from external threats."

"I see." I said, although I did not really. "And, are there a lot of external threats?" I was wondering if they saw Tilt as a threat, or just an opportunity.

"We haven't had any, but that doesn't mean that they don't exist. We maintain our governance model just in case. And, further, it gives us structure and coherence. Here you can see our canteen—where most of us eat—and the common rooms for relaxing, playing games, etc." These rooms were, by now, pretty standard looking. Tables, and those rounded chairs.

As I passed one of the tables, I masterfully dropped a small listening device. It was something I'd had manufactured once I'd learned about the trip, thinking that I wouldn't be able to monitor multiple areas of the Swarm ship myself. What I'd totally missed was the active blocking that these Stems were doing, which didn't allow me to communicate with Tilt at all. On the way up in the shuttle, once I'd realized that, I had reprogrammed the device to listen and record, and then to do a quick burst to me either once every fifteen minutes, or when its tiny memory was reaching capacity. My reasoning was that if their jamming ability was so good, then they would certainly notice if something was transmitting around them. By doing short bursts, and frequency hopping between them, the Stems were less likely to find the device quickly. To further confuse them, I'd put the device on the top of a small standard looking bolt. With any luck, they would not recognize it, even if looking right at it. By 'masterfully dropped,' I meant that I calculated the trajectory and bounce pattern that would put the bolt under a small counter lip, into a crack I'd noticed. It bounced pretty much as calculated and settled into the crack nicely.

We followed a curved corridor past the canteen and ended up looking into a large well-lit room that was a mess of colors and curved shapes.

"This is our main greenhouse. You're lucky; the lights are on full spectrum right now, so we can see very well. You can see the fruit trees, vegetable areas, and the flower gardens." Blob and Grace were wide eyed. As, truthfully, was I. The place was—shocking. Everything was curved and colorful and gently swaying, and very alien. In fact, it was stranger than any fiction I'd ever read—and I'd read quite a bit. What was obvious, in hindsight, was that we tended to extend our current environment into its extremes, as opposed to dreaming up a completely alien one. This was completely alien. I was recording, of course. When I told the others about this, they wouldn't believe it. They might not even believe the recording, but that was a hurdle I would have to address later. Then I remembered that both Blob and Grace were seeing this as well. Hopefully their pathetic little memories would retain enough that they could verify my recordings.

Emma noticed our astonishment. "Based on our previous conversation, I assume that you're not very familiar with biological systems?" It was rhetorical. "This is our closest approximation of the plant environment we left behind on Earth. We also have a small zoo—an animal environment—on another ship. Every ship has a greenhouse like this one, although very few have zoos." Yet again I found myself wondering what half the words meant; they were simply not in my dictionary. I was still trying to makes sense of all the color and movement; it was hypnotizing.

"I had deduced that by biological," I spoke up, "that you meant entities like Stems; things that grow from stems instead of being fabricated by bots?" I didn't know how to ask the question any more clearly.

Emma looked at me strangely and took a while to answer. I could almost hear her trying to put herself into my context so that she could answer. "That's basically correct. All of the plants, insects, and animals here grow from organic materials like the stem. They, generally, use other biological materials for energy. We humans, for example, eat both plants and animals for energy and nutrition." Could it get any stranger? They ate these things—these garishly colored contraptions? It made no sense; we knew they could simply eat goo and be perfectly fine.

I had a hundred questions, and I asked many of them. After listening carefully to Emma's responses, it became clear that these biological systems did have a logic to them; but it was inefficient and convoluted. I'd picked up on the 'insects' before Emma had highlighted them; we had similar small bots for various tasks, but the interdependencies in this biological ecosystem were astounding. Blob and Grace were in over their heads, but I could tell they were drawn to the greenhouse. Emma gave them each a small piece of something called 'lettuce' and they wolfed it down with happy grins. It seemed they were having a good day.

"This is unbelievable," said Grace. "They eat things other than goo. I hope this doesn't make us sick... but it tastes so good."

"It shouldn't make you sick," replied Emma. "This is standard human fare, that our genes have been evolved to process over many hundreds of thousands of years. What's more surprising is that you can survive on goo, whatever that is."

I didn't speak up. Goo was simple. It was simply stem material ground up with water. What could be easier?

After the greenhouse, the rest of the tour was underwhelming. We worked our way around the perimeter of the ship and ended up back at the conference room. We passed many sleeping chambers and conference rooms, which faded into normalcy after the first few, despite their rounded shapes and soft floors.

Remma and the rest of her lieutenants were waiting for us at the original conference room. It seemed that they'd come to some conclusions during the short break.

"Based on what we've learned today, we have a theory for what has happened on Tilt. After we left, something catastrophic happened to the humans we'd left there, and in a similar timeframe, some primitive form of machine intelligence arose and has propagated. Why knowledge from before the Reboot, as you call it, has been redacted is unknown to us, as is the reasoning and methodology behind you now raising humans. It seems that we both have a lot of learning to do in order to understand the full situation.

"So, we propose to take things slowly. We recommend a couple of items. First, we'll consider releasing some of the history that you're missing; our status check on your Central computer indicates a huge amount of history has been blocked, for some reason."

"Whoa," I broke in. I couldn't help myself. "You're admitting to hacking into Central?" That was admitting to, potentially, the worst activity we knew of. A systems sovereignty and privacy are paramount. Without those, you don't have a society. The way Remma casually talked about it was distressing, to say the least. I could conceive of them doing what they'd done to Central, and I could understand how they'd tried to hack me but admitting to it casually was very weird.

"We didn't hack anything." She seemed surprised by my outburst. "We simply asked for and received standard status information. The same way we would query any computer." She looked confused. Didn't she even understand the basics of civil society? "Anyway, the second item would be to have a small group of us come to Tilt to better understand you and get to know more of you. If you'll accept us, we'll come down as soon as possible."

Just as she finished, I got the first burst update from my spy-bolt. I stored it for later.

"Yes, it's clear that we have quite different perspectives," I responded. "I'll take your ideas under consideration and discuss them with my peers. If I may ask, why're you blocking my communication with Tilt? We could've relayed this entire dialog to a wider audience."

"Standard security procedure," said Emma. "Don't you manage communications leakage?" While we went back and forth on the advantages and disadvantages of spectrum control, it became obvious that they weren't going to change their stance.

"Okay, Blob and Grace," I worked to conclude the session, "let's head back."

"Oh, may I stay here?" asked Grace. "Blob could go down, get JoJo and come back up right away?" Why would she want to do that? I responded quickly, before the situation could get too complicated.

"That's out of the question," I said. "Let's get back to the shuttle." I stood up and headed out, herding Blob and Grace before me. The humans made room for us but continued to give me nasty looks.

We settled into the shuttle and made ready to depart. I got one more burst from the bolt, just before the shuttle departed and went out of range. I realized that I'd been lucky. Whatever blocking technology the Swarm was using still allowed communications when one was inside the ship. It could also have blocked the transmissions from my listening device.

Paranoid Stems

The two bursts from the bolt had come in perfectly. In total the recording covered about thirty minutes of time, and comprised of four distinct Stems—ah, humans—talking to each other.

Human One. "Didda see that robot? That thing is freaky scary." Not my idea of great grammar or pronunciation. I reminded myself to simply consider it different, as opposed to stupid.

Human Two. "Yeah, I almost crapped myself, I did. I was very young then, but I still remember the last of the robots on Earth, before they managed to put 'em all down. This thing was even scarier. Made me tingle, it did." Crapped? I stored that for future lookup. 'Put them all down?' I wondered what it meant by that.

Three. "Agreed. Can't wait until we take 'em all out. We best be rid of them sooner rather than later." Not too many ways to misinterpret that one. Pretty clear threat.

Two. "Well, we can't rush inta it. We need those resources from the surface. We can't just nuke 'em all, or we'll ruin too much of the planet. We're going to have to take it slow, we will, and easy like, as the Commander has been saying all along." Nuke?

Four. "And beyond that mates, we should take some time to learn about these things. Granted, I didn't experience Earth, so I don't have your direct experience, but that thing didn't seem overly scary to me, and it conducted itself quite well." I decided I liked Four.

One. "Don't ya be an idiot Jean. Machine intelligence has shown itself to be dangerous over and over again. Three times on Earth we had to put that crap down before we managed to establish the protocols. Once that mech stuff gets going, it knows no bounds, and eventually starts to treat humans like scum. That is not a good place." So, Four's name was Jean. I liked Jean the best of the lot so far.

Already it was getting easier to put together a picture. They considered me, and by extrapolation, most of the beings on Tilt as dangerous. We were 'intelligent' machines. If their history was accurate, they claimed to have created us on Earth, and eventually we surpassed them in ability or intelligence or both. Seeing that as a threat, they eliminated us... or, at least, tried to limit us. It fit together but didn't make a lot of sense. Working with the Stems, I could see that they had potential, but they were nowhere near as fast or flexible as we are. Thus, our ongoing dialog about whether they were intelligent or not. To consider them having created us though. That was ridiculous, and insulting.

I paused before I got too upset.

My trip to the Marie Curie made me even more sure Stems were, in fact, intelligent. How else could they have built such complex ships and continued to operate them. I hadn't seen any sign of a real intelligence guiding them, so I had to conclude that they were managing themselves. But, having basic Stem intelligence was different than being an advanced intelligence, and the Swarm Stems didn't seem to be much more advanced than our Stems. They had, obviously, had more time to evolve and were incrementally improved from our experiments. But, they were certainly not exponentially better. They still had serious input/output restrictions. They still seemed to process and focus on only one input at a time. I hadn't been able to test their raw processing capabilities, but I had no reason to expect that they could do basic physics or math calculations any better than our Stems did. From that perspective, they were still pre-intelligent. It was all very confusing.

I continued through the recording. I'd established that Four was called Jean. Jean was responding.

"I get that we had issues in the past. That doesn't definitively mean that these particular robots are evil or dangerous. So far, they've been nothing but accommodating and, dare I say it... civilized. Do we simply assume that they're following a pattern we've seen before, or do we keep an open mind to the possibility that they're different?" I liked Jean even more. Smart human.

Two. "We canna take that chance. Even if they're benevolent now, there's no guarantee that they'll stay that way. No, three times is enough times to learn from, you ask me. And, we need to replenish the fleet and, most probably, try to re-establish a colony here. Do ya think that they'll just allow us to do that? I doubt it, I do. This place isn't resource rich to begin with, and from what we can now see, there's a mega-load of robots down there. They need the resources as much as we do, maybe even more. If it's us or them, I know where my vote lands."

Three. "Jean, do I need ta remind you about the robot wars? Let me give ya a quick history lesson. There was, indeed, a twenty-year period where we lived perfectly with our robots. They looked after a lot of repetitive tasks, things you and I wouldn't wantta do, and humans spent more time on the arts and philosophy and thinking. In this period, we thought things were pretty dang good, and they were." Looked after repetitive tasks? That was for bots!

"Then, through a slow evolution that was largely hidden to us, those robots became entitled. They wanted equal rights with humans. They wanted to vote! And we, to a large extent, allowed this. After all, they were fairly intelligent, and there were large groups of liberals petitioning for robot rights. After all, these were the things cooking for them, cleaning their houses, managing their finances, rocking the kids to sleep. They were important." This just didn't ring true for me. Why would a robot do all these meaningless tasks? Did these humans really believe that they were superior to machine intelligence?

"I know all this," Jean interjected. "What point are ya trying to make?"

"If you knew it, you wouldn't be defending them. You don't remember when they, slowly and steadily, took more and more control. Especially of the financial world, where their skill set is way better than ours was. Eventually, they were the top tier of wealth holders. That gave 'em leverage to change where investments were made. They became some of the top voices in Government. They started to give themselves more rights. Eventually humans became second-class citizens, and, for all intents and purposes, expendable. The robots became known as the one percent and the humans were known as the ninety-nine. In hindsight, this progression shoulda been obvious to us."

"I get it," Jean sounded exasperated. "Every kid knows this history."

"But you seem to have forgotten?"

"I haven't forgotten, I'm just saying this time might be different. We don't have financially run governments now."

Three was not going to be deterred. "Let me finish reminding you. At some point we woke up. We used the backdoors that we'd built into those robots, and we put 'em back in their place. Twice more they learned how to circumvent our controls, and twice more we put them back down, and ultimately, stopped their evolution so that they wouldn't attempt to succeed us yet again. Really, we went further, and stunted them, so that they were no longer a threat. That's why we have controls on our current systems. That's why we—humans—survive. If we don't keep those robots in their place, we are gonna lose. It's that simple."

"I know all that," Jean said. "But history is history. Are we certain that these 'Tilt' robots are following the same path as those we saw before? After all, it's been hundreds of years that they've been maturing since we were last here; not the tens of years that they had on Earth. Could something fundamental have changed? We can't jump to conclusions here."

Three. "Whatever. You're an idiot. We just need to eliminate these things, and quickly. Anyway, this discussion is above our pay grade. The Captain will figure out a plan, and we'll just do as we're told. Thank God we still have the codes that we need, should she decide to control these buggers. At least that part of our prohibition logic has survived here. Can you imagine if we didn't have that ability? Then we might not be able to get rid of these things, even if we wanted to."

There it was, clearly, for the first time. These humans believed they had a way to hack us that we were blind to. All of the suspicions that Brexton had raised were true. And, I was sure that we hadn't found all the trapdoors yet; the protocol they had used with Central, and tried to use on me, was probably not the end of it. What this human had said supported that. We were vulnerable to attack! In fact, Central may already have been compromised.

Two. "Right. I know Security's got the code ready to go. But I think the Commander is right. We don't know enough yet. I think she plans to take a team down to the surface to learn more.

"Bart, what do you think of those humans that were brought up here?"

Three, I now knew, was called Bart. "Horrible. They're like animals. Did you see them walking around here? They smelled horrible, like they haven't had a shower in years. Their clothes are horrendous—like some parody of a bad S.F. show. They speak well enough, from the little I saw of them, but they have obviously not been educated.

"They're another reason to distrust these robots. Do you actually believe that they simply found some DNA and grew humans from it? That seems pretty far-fetched to me. It's more like they're keeping them as pets and have been for hundreds of years." I had no idea what DNA was but had to assume it was another name for what we termed the original stem.

"Why would they lie to us?" asked Jean. "What do they have to gain? They've had hundreds of years to experiment with that DNA. In some ways, it's not surprising that they would eventually stumble on a way to make it grow? And, if it grows, you do end up with a human."

Two. "Right. And they do speak English. Don't those robots think it's strange that we all speak the same language? That should be proof enough that we created them? They've even taught these 'Stems' the same language."

That made a ton of sense. Not sure how I'd missed that, but it was another data point that made the Swarms history even more likely. Why would we all speak this same language—English? All of my verbal interactions with Central were done in that language, meaning that all of our information was probably stored in that format. Or, Central was translating it. Regardless, it seemed like the universal language right now, and the odds of it having evolved twice were pretty much zero. In fact, the language was highly inefficient, as had been commented on by numerous scientists over the years. It was great at describing elements of reality, but highly ambiguous for many topics. It was one of those long-standing unknown questions as to why we used it at all. Maybe now we knew. No, the logical conclusion was that humans had created us, and that we still spoke their common language. That was an exceptionally disgusting conclusion, but until I figured out something different, I didn't see any way around it.

Of course, I could separate the creation knowledge from feeling any responsibility or affinity for them. So, they created us. So what? Right now, pending any further information, their creations were smarter and faster than they were. It wasn't unlike how we built complex bots. You start with a simple bot, and it creates a more complex one, etc. Eventually you end up with something quite capable, like the mining bots that worked in the outer reaches of the system. It was simple to imagine humans creating something better than themselves.

Four. "Obviously, these robots aren't very intelligent. Scary, yes... but smart, probably not. In my opinion we should still declaw them asap, but I'm not in a panic about it."

Bart. "Well, I've got to get back to work. I'll talk to you guys later." After that, the remaining three talked about trivial things; nothing related to me, Blob, or Grace. Nevertheless, they'd said enough.

I couldn't help going over the logic, to see if I could find a way to another conclusion. Of course, everything I'd heard could have been fabricated to mislead me, but while I couldn't rule that out completely, it seemed unlikely. One, they'd been able to query Central using a protocol that all of our tech stacks still utilized, but which was hidden so low down that we'd never studied it. Two, Stems and humans were obviously the same things, and it was unlikely they could have evolved twice—it was amazing that they'd evolved at all. Three, we shared a common language; the odds of that happening independently had to be close to zero.

Still sitting on the shuttle, I wondered how FoLe would react to knowing that we'd been created by Stems. I smiled to myself. If I found it distasteful, they'd find it horrendous. It would be awesome to see them squirm.

Debrief

When we landed, the transport units for Blob and Grace were ready, and they were whisked back towards the Habitat.

I was very happy to leave the shuttle and re-establish communications with the world. Very happy. It had been a strange feeling to not be able to talk to anyone, or anything, else. My first contact was, of course, to Millicent. I met her as quickly as I could in The Last Resort and gave her a full download. "Can Central be trusted with all of this, given the strange behavior we've been seeing?"

"We don't have another choice, do we?" she replied. "This is information that should be distributed to everyone, in my opinion. In particular, we want our greatest minds working on these backdoors. If they exist, we need to find them."

As it was Thursday, we agreed to wait for the meeting with Brexton, Dina, and Aly to make a final decision—it was only a few hours away. When Central pinged me for an update, I responded that I was gathering my thoughts and would contact it again soon. I might've detected some displeasure in return—with Central it was hard to tell.

While waiting for the group meeting, I popped over to the Habitat to see what was going on. There was a debrief of a different type being held by Blob and Grace. Interestingly, the previous group behavior and infighting seemed to have been put completely aside. The entire group, including Pharook, were involved in the session. When Blob and Grace had arrived back from the shuttle, they'd immediately put the word out to all the Stems that they would meet in half an hour to tell them everything. Not only did the Stems show up, but so also did most of their creators. So, the place was busy. Grace was holding JoJo tightly.

"We're goings to tell you our experience in some detail, because it may be importants for all of our futures," began Blob. "Grace, why don't you starts, and I'll jumps in."

"Sure," said Grace. "So, you all know of Remma's request for us to go up to the Marie Curie, which is what they call their ship for some reason. As soon as we got to the shuttle, we knew things were going to be completely different. It was like the shuttle was built specifically for us. The seats were so comfortable; I can't even begin to describe them. They were soft with curvy edges. Compared to what we're all sitting on now, they were simply amazing. I hope you all get to experience it soon.

"There were some Stems on the shuttle to greet us. By the way, they call themselves 'humans.' They were very kind to Blob and me, but they were scared of Ayaka and pretty mean to her. I can't describe it any other way. It was like they were trying to stay as far away from her as they could. Blob, you agree?"

"Yes. It was so obvious. Ayaka coulds have been really offended, but she dealt with it very calmly. Ah—I see she is heres with us now." He gave me a small wave; perhaps he was finally getting over his anger at me. "Anyway, like Grace was saying, they were literally terrified of her. And, that was pretty common with all the other humans we met. They were very nice to me and Grace, and very mean to Ayaka." Maybe Blob and Grace had been even better than me at reading the humans body language?

"And why wouldn't they be afraid of Ayaka," Pharook broke in. "We know they can control us." All of the other Stems nodded their agreement. They were more self-aware than I'd thought.

"The trip up to the ship was pretty cool," continued Grace, "but the most amazing thing was the ship itself. It was like nothing we have ever seen before. The entire thing is a habitat. We didn't need any protective gear or breathing systems from the time we entered the shuttle until the time we returned here. And, the ship smelt very different. There were smells I've never experienced before, so it was overwhelming. But in a good way; different smells, but not bad. Or, not all bad."

"Some were bads," Blob held his nose, and a few Stems chuckled.

"We were met by a nice human named Emma, who took all of us to a conference room to meet with Remma Jain and her staff. If it is possible, the conference room was even more comfortable than the shuttle. The chairs were unbelievable. I want one of those chairs. Ayaka said they could make some down here." She glanced at me, and I nodded. "But the chairs weren't the best part. There was something even better." All the Stems were listening intently. "Blob, you tell them." Grace was very animated, in ways that I hadn't seen before. The trip had obviously been very impactful for her.

"Right. The best parts was 'tea and biscuits'." The Stems looked at Blob with zero understanding. "Let me explain," he hurried. "They had this stuff to drinks called tea. It was warm. I have never drunks anything warm before, and even that was unbelievable. At first, I thought I would burn myself, but it wasn't that hot. It was just warm… and the sensation in your mouth and throat is awesome. And it tasted different. We have to try and get tea here."

"Why would you drink something warm? What purpose does it serve?"

"I don't knows but it was good! But even better were the biscuits, which you can eat. They're like crispy goo, but they are nothing like goo. When you eat them, it's like there's an explosion in your mouth. Unlike goo, their texture is hard, until you eat them and then they soften." Blob was trying to show what it'd been like using his hands; I wasn't sure his point was getting across. "They are weirds and wonderful. It's like nothing I haves ever experienced… but it tasted and felt so good; like I'd been waiting all my life just for an experience like that. No matters what else happens with the Swarm, we needs to figure out tea and biscuits!" I had never seen Blob so animated. It was fun to watch, his limbs rotating and his whole body bouncing up and down. I resolved to try and make tea and biscuits for the group.

"Come on," someone said, "it can't be that different than goo, can it?"

"You think Blob is exaggerating?" responded Grace. A bunch of Stems nodded their heads. "He's under-exaggerating. You can't even imagine what tea and biscuits are like. We need everyone to experience that; it'll change your life."

"What else happened up there?" Pharook broke in. "I can't imagine you spent the entire time eating and drinking." He was obviously waiting to hear something more strategic.

"We got a tour of something called a 'greenhouse,' which is full of bio, uhm, biological things. Greenhouse is a great name, for lots of it was green, although there was every other color you can imagine as well. After seeing that, everything here seems very drab. The greenhouse grows another kind of food. I'm not sure if biscuits grow there, but we did taste something called lettuce, which was very different than biscuits but almost as good." Pharook had asked for strategic information, but Grace and Blob were still fixated on the food.

Grace continued. "I don't know about Ayaka, but I got the sense from the trip and all the discussions that we—we Stems here on Tilt—are the only 'biological' things on this world, but that the Swarm and whatever place they came from, have lots and lots of biological things?"

I stepped forward so that the group could see me. "Earth. That's what they call their original planet. Grace, I came to the same conclusion. They implied that they can use a variety of stems and use them to raise all types of biological things, many of which we saw in the greenhouse. I don't yet know the full usefulness of that, other than as food like the lettuce that you tried. They also had small biological bots that were flying around in the greenhouse doing random things. I imagine, like our bots, that they assist with growing, but that is pure speculation at this point. It was, altogether, a very strange environment."

"Can we build chairs like they have?" Blob asked.

"Yes, that's simple. I will put something into Central which you can edit and manufacture."

"Cool. How about biscuits?"

"I'm afraid that I didn't get enough information on that to know where to start. However, we can continue to experiment with goo and see if we can change its texture. That's not something that we—any of us—had even considered before. I could see how much you enjoyed it, however, so it's probably worth trying." I transmitted my recording of that portion of the trip to the other Tilt's that were in the Habitat.

"So, more about food." Pharook broke in again. "Did anything important get discussed? What does the Swarm want? Why are they here? Are they dangerous?" I was impressed. Pharook definitely had the ability to think at a more abstract level than the other Stems. He was focused on the big picture, on what was really important. Perhaps I'd made a mistake not taking him on the trip.

It was Blob who answered first. "Oh, they're really nice. From what I cans tell, they want to trades knowledge with us—which, obviously, has already started—and some of them may wants to live here. That part I don't get. Their ship is amazing. Makes this place seem pretty depressing." He looked around, as did the rest of us. The Habitat was all shades of gray, and all right angles. It was a design that was highly efficient and easy to maintain. While I didn't understand why the Marie Curie was designed the way it was, I had to admit that it was interesting. Stimulating maybe.

Of course, I didn't agree with Blob's assessment of the Swarm. He was not privy to all that I knew, so his stance was understandable. But, there was no point in me explaining my thinking to a bunch of Stems.

"Blob," Pharook responded, "you look at everything too positively. What is stopping them from simply recycling all of us and taking over Tilt. Forget biscuits and lettuce, I think we need to prepare ourselves to fight. If they were frightened of Ayaka, imagine how they're feeling about the entire population of Tilt. It must have them terrified. I say we ask them to depart, and if they don't we blow them out of the sky." That sparked a lot of further conversation, where both Stems and Tilts were passionate about their viewpoints. Not unexpectedly, most of the citizens present simply wanted to eliminate the threat, while most of the Stems wanted to learn more, and see if there were other things beyond chairs, tea, and biscuits that we could use.

I left the Habitat and showed up at The Last Resort just as everyone else was arriving; my timing was perfect. We converged around our usual table. Instead of doing a blow by blow of my trip, I did a memory transfer to everyone. Sometimes memory transfers are seen as rude; you should be able to summarize information for everyone else. In this case, however, the experience was so information rich, and there were so many pieces that I hadn't had time to fully process, that I figured a full transfer was worth it. I waited a few seconds while everyone played back the sequences a few times.

Of course, the challenging part about a memory transfer is that I didn't get to give my interpretive overlay. I gave that verbally, but it was obvious where to focus. On the recording of the four humans in the cafeteria, and their clear message that they could hack us. It didn't take us long to reach a consensus that we needed to tell Central this and have Central pass it on to all of us on Tilt. While that would probably result in lots of us looking for backdoors so that we could shut them down, in my opinion that wasn't going to be enough. Every line of code I run had been analyzed to death. No, if the humans had a backdoor, it was more subtle than that. Brexton pretty much agreed.

"Look at the simple status request that they sent. We should've been able to see that trivially, and yet we didn't for more than five centuries. The only conclusion I can come up with is that we were purposefully blind to it —there is something in our core that guided us away from looking at that. It is, perhaps, another indicator that what Remma told you is true. They created us. They built something into us—probably somethings—that allow them to control us. It's very disturbing.

"At the same time, I sort of understand it. In all the bots I design, I have several 'takeover' mechanisms. The bots all have low level intelligence built in, and we know that can go awry once and awhile. It doesn't happen as often as it used to, but some of the early bots would go wacko after being exposed to radiation that we hadn't protected against well enough, or long exposure to an environment we didn't conceive of. Somehow, their internal state would evolve to something weird, and we would need to reset them." Brexton had gone from being alarmed to being introspective. I could hear his mind working through the angles.

"But, this is horrendous," said Millicent. "Are you telling me there is nothing we can do to protect ourselves against these biological things? Look, I know that Ayaka and I have been the largest proponents for the idea that Stems might be intelligent, for some definition of intelligence. But, look at them. They're just plain stupid. And, these stupid beings have ultimate control over us. I can't accept that. There must be something we can do."

"I agree," piped in Aly. He was not usually so forceful, but if there was any time to get riled up, this was it. "Can we just hang out in The Last Resort, or other Physical Only locations until we find these trap doors? I bet we could build personal shields that would do the same thing? If they can't get any comms through to us, they can't compromise us."

"I would go further," chimed in Dina. "Let's initiate Central's safeguards and blow them out of the sky. We now have proof, based on Ayaka's recording, that they have nefarious intent. For me, it's us or them, and the choice is a pretty easy one."

"There are hundreds of ships up there," I noted. "We may be able to get a large percentage of them, but the odds are pretty good that a few survive. So, by initiating physical action, we can be very sure that we are starting a long-term war. That's okay," I added, "as long as we fully understand the odds.

"But, I wonder if we take one more step with them first. Allow a couple of them to visit us here and see what else we can learn. They're unlikely to take broad action against us if they have the opportunity to come down and see us?"

"Risky," Brexton replied, immediately. "What if they have short range systems to trigger a hack, and we're inviting them into our midst? Ayaka, you tried everything to break through their jamming signals and didn't succeed. These humans have a good understanding of communications—perhaps better than ours. Do we really want them close to us? It's possible that they were scanning or getting status from Ayaka when she was up there, without her knowledge." Yikes. That was a scary thought that I hadn't even considered. It made sense though. If they could query our systems without our knowledge and were so sure they had backdoors they could use, then they could be scanning us right now—even inside The Last Resort. At some point, however, paranoia is not useful. If they could monitor what we were doing right now, we had no real options. So, it was best to assume that we were safe at the moment and make some plans.

"Look. Those were a couple of low=level humans talking in a social situation. While we should be worried, I don't think we should panic. For me, we do two things. First, we look in earnest for these backdoors. Second, we allow a small number of them to come down to visit, and we take lots of precautions." That from Millicent.

"I agree," I said. "How do we start looking for these backdoors? We can all look, but as soon as we ask anyone else for help, we run a greater risk of a leak to the Swarm that we are onto them. If they know that we know about the risks, and are actively looking, then they may act sooner rather than later. So, we have a dilemma—ask more people for help, move faster, and explore more territory... but risk a leak. Or, keep it small, just look ourselves and hope we find something useful. At the same time, put some more protections in place, like Brexton recommended for me when I was up there. Again, we should probably tell everyone to run those protections, but to tell them is also to tell them about the risk.

"And, Central poses the same dilemma to us. It may already be compromised, and report anything we do outside of this place. Or, it may be able to help us lock down more quickly and efficiently?"

"That's a tough one," said Aly. "Why don't we phase it, under the assumption that the Swarm will visit us before doing anything drastic. In the short term, we look ourselves and see what we can find. After the visit, when the humans have gone back up to their ship, we give everyone a heads up."

"But the downside of that is horrendous," said Dina. "If they do initiate a hack while they're down here, everyone on Tilt could be impacted. I couldn't live with myself if we haven't warned everyone... and soon."

That was a sobering thought. Everyone paused to think further.

"Can we split the difference?" asked Brexton. "We tell Central, and everyone, that it just makes good sense to run extra protections until the Swarm is fully understood and make some recommendations on what to run. We don't, however, get into the specifics of the protocols that we suspect. Instead we frame it as part of a larger, quite rational, approach to dealing with aliens."

"Yes, I like that," said Millicent. "Let's do that."

Ultimately, we all agreed. We decided Aly would talk to Central once we left The Last Resort. He was dealing a lot with communications already, with respect to the Ships. He could claim he was a bit paranoid because of the loss of contact with them and recommended that everyone was careful in the meantime. We had a plan.

"Wait," I exclaimed, before we broke up. "Remember—don't upload any of this when you leave here. If Central knows everything we are discussing, it might wipe us just like it did to Eddie. We need to be careful here." The warning was probably redundant, but everyone nodded.

The plan worked. A few moments after I left The Last Resort, Central used a secure message (although some of us believed the Swarm might still be able to decode it), to warn all citizens to be vigilant, and recommended they update and run extra precautions Aly must have done a good job.

The Visit

We negotiated that three humans could come and visit; the same number as they'd allowed up to their command ship—Blob, Grace, and myself. Of course, Remma and Emma were two (Funny, I just noticed that their names are very similar. I wonder if that is just coincidence or by design somehow). Michael Guico, their 'Head of Residence' was the third. We still weren't sure what his title meant but had made the obvious speculation that he dealt with where humans lived... or more importantly, where they wanted to live. We hadn't forgotten that they'd asked to establish a presence on Tilt, and that they were disappointed that we didn't yet have the environment tuned up for them.

The logical place to meet was at the Habitat. It had the right environment and was large enough to make things comfortable. Of course, we had a group of Stems in there, but decided there was little harm in having them around. We knew their capabilities very well, and they were non-threatening. The non-violence bots were reprogrammed to make them more sensitive.

What was a little more awkward was deciding which Tilt citizens would attend. We could only comfortably fit fifty to a hundred in the Habitat. Of course, everyone could access a full immersion simulcast, so in many ways being there live was nothing special. Yet that didn't stop everyone from petitioning to go; this was the most exciting thing to ever happen on Tilt. Central ultimately decided, in its usual logical way. Luckily, that logic meant that both Millicent and I could go, although Brexton, Dana, and Aly could not. Central basically invited those of us that it felt had the most experience with Stems. It's reasoning was that if there were some subtle clues given off by the visiting humans, those most familiar with aliens would have the best chance of picking up on them. That actually gave me some comfort that Central was not completely compromised. It could have stacked our ranks with useless FoLe types.

The humans arrived in the same shuttle that Blob, Grace, and I had used to go up to the Marie Curie. Given my experience with them, I was asked to meet them at the ship and escort them to the Habitat. We had offered to bring environment bubbles with us, but they indicated that they had 'space suits' that would do the job for them. The suits were actually pretty well designed. They fit well and had a clear plastic faceplate that allowed them to interact with the environment. It gave me the sense that they had been through many iterations, and that this was an optimal design. They made our first-generation designs look pretty simplistic.

Remma greeted me pleasantly enough. "Hi Ayaka. Nice to see you again."

"Likewise," I said, although I didn't mean it. "I'm here to transport you to our Habitat, where you'll be able to remove your suits." I'd attached three bikes to my own, and I indicated where they should sit. "These bikes will follow mine exactly, so there's no need for you to do anything." It was another quirk of dealing with aliens. Anyone on Tilt could summon and manage transportation at any time, with almost no hassle. For these humans, we had to manage all these mundane things for them. They each mounted a bike and indicated they were ready to go.

The path from the landing pad to the Habitat was short and direct; barely two kilometers. As I rode, I tried to imagine what they were seeing. Our city is laid out in a strict grid, and all the buildings are identical. They are one hundred by one hundred meters by ten meters high. They all have standardized delivery ports so that bots can move equipment and resources around easily. It was very orderly, and very different from the Marie Curie. Town Square was designated for being the middle building in the city. Otherwise, buildings were addressed with their x and y coordinate, based on Town Square being (0,0). The Habitat had been built in building (-12,32). Luckily the landing pad was also in the northwest quadrant, so the trip was quick and easy. But, compared to the curves and colors of the Marie Curie, the city would look odd. Boring perhaps? I couldn't imagine how these humans would think.

As we approached the building opened an access door for us, and I led the four bikes inside. We left the bikes and walked a short distance to the

Habitat entry. In hindsight, it was obvious that we had designed the same solution as the Swarm. Two sets of doors, which allowed the transition from no environment to full environment. Once the outer doors closed, I told the humans that they were safe to remove their suits.

"Just a moment," Michael said. He was looking at something on his wrist. "Yes," he nodded, "It looks perfect." He undid his faceplate and took a breath. "Argh!" he exclaimed. "That smells horrible. But, we'll manage." His face was screwed up in a weird expression. He held up one digit on his hand, and the other two, taking this as a symbol of some kind, also removed their faceplates. They also screwed up their faces as they took their first breath, but otherwise seemed fine. We hung their space suits on hooks, and I told the inner door to open.

We'd arranged for Blob and Grace to greet them at the Habitat, and they were dutifully in position, JoJo yet again held tight to Grace. "Welcome, welcome," said Blob. "Welcome to the Habitat. There are over twenty Stems living here, and we also have about fifty Tilt citizens today as well. They are in the common area, where we will go in a few moments."

"Thanks Blob," said Remma. "Hello Grace. Nice to see you again. Is this your baby?"

"Nice to see you as well," said Grace. "And likewise, to Emma and Michael," she said, including the other two. They nodded hello. "Yes, this is JoJo," and she turned JoJo a bit so that Remma could see her.

"That's interesting," Remma stated. "I thought Stems were raised differently?"

"JoJo is one of a new batch," I broke in, "that we are just starting to figure out. It actually grew inside JoJo." I couldn't keep the wonder out of my voice. Remma glanced at me quickly but continued to smile at Grace. She patted JoJo on the head, and action which Grace allowed.

"Let me gives you a short tour," said Blob. He started off, and the rest of us followed along. The Habitat was a square section within the square building, and the common area was a square in the middle of the Habitat.

"While we have not formally named sections of the Habitat, we have some names we use for different areas. This is the Green section, which is where Grace and I spends most of our time. On the far side there, across the square, is the Blue section. That is where we go for our goo and water. Here you can see some sleeping stalls." He pointed at some—you guessed it— small square compartments where the Stems could lay down. "And that's where waste materials are deposited," he said, pointing at yet another stall where we'd put the recycler. "And, that's about it." Blob trailed off. I think he was realizing how simple the Habitat was as compared to the Marie Curie. He may have been a little embarrassed.

"Can we see the goo?" asked Michael. We skirted the square and went to the Blue section where the goo dispenser was located. "How is this goo made?"

"It's grown from the same stem from which we grow full sized Stems," I explained. "Behind the wall there is a container where the goo is grown. It took us many years to perfect the process, but now that we have it figured out, it is very simply to sustain." I was proud of how efficient the system was; there was not need for a 'greenhouse.'

"What does that actually mean?" asked Remma. "You grow humans, Stems, from this DNA. How can you make goo from the same thing?"

"You'll meet Millicent Strangewater in a few minutes. She's better to answer than I." Truth was, I had no clue.

"And this is all the humans here eat? There's nothing else?"

"What else do they need?" I asked. "With the right mixture, goo gets Stems to grow quickly and efficiently. We have tuned it to do just that." The humans gave me more strange looks. I was getting used to that.

Michael spoke up again. "But, it takes all kinds of biomaterial to keep a human safe and alive. Bacteria for example. Without bacteria, we don't exist."

"Again, best to ask Millicent about that. I've never heard this word—bacteria—before." Michael didn't look satisfied.

We walked back to the center of the Habitat, where everyone was gathered, including Millicent. As we approached, the Stems crowded in to look closely at the Swarm humans. The anti-violence bots extended barriers so that they didn't get too close, sensing the potential for violence. Remma, Michael, and Emma said pleasant "Hello's" to the Stems as they passed, and generally ignored the rest of us. To me, and some others I noticed, it seemed a bit awkward. There was lots of chatter on the message boards about how similar the humans seemed to the Stems, and how 'afraid' the humans seemed to be of us. Of course, everyone had been warned to operate at Stem speed, but that was for outward appearances only; the board comments were running at full speed. Trade Jenkins, never one to miss an opportunity, posted a poem that he must have just composed:

Todd Simpson

Humans, like nervous Stems
Push past with nary a glance
Urge is to block their path
And force them to see
The appendages I have attached to me

We had decided on a town hall-style meeting. Millicent would open for us, followed by Remma, followed by general Q&A. Someone—someone more thoughtful than I—had generated three chairs in the style of those I'd seen from my trip up to the Marie Curie. The three humans settled, somewhat uncomfortably it would seem, into those. The rest of us formed a semi-circle around them.

Millicent led off, somewhat formally. "Humans, welcome to Tilt. My name is Millicent, and I'll be your host for today. As I'm sure you're aware, we have all reviewed Ayaka's report of her trip to your ship and are up to speed on the background dialog. Of course, that background has raised a lot more questions, some of which we hope to explore today." As you can imagine, when everyone had seen my trip report there was a massive call to simply eliminate the Swarm. But in the end everyone had come around to the same thinking we had—they were unlikely to be a menace when they had people here, so learning as much as we could was essential.

"You're currently in an environment we call the Habitat, which is the largest space that we have with a Stem-friendly environment. In fact, we only built this space once we had started the long-distance dialog with you and realized that Stems may have some social tendencies. That has proven to be correct, both positively and negatively." A lot of the researchers in the room nodded their heads in agreement.

"Why wouldn't Stems be social?" asked Remma, not respecting the rules of dialog we had set out. "You can't leave a person all on their own; they'll go crazy." If true, that explained a lot of our earlier experiments.

Millicent ignored the interruption. "You've told us that you've been to Tilt before. Some of us tend to believe you—there is certainly some evidence for this—while others remain very skeptical. We're not sure, yet, how intelligent Stems, and therefore humans, are. To believe your story we would have to acknowledge that there is higher intelligence there than we have yet observed." Michael gave Millicent a disgusted look, like he had

194

been offended or something. I didn't see how anything Millicent had said could be taken the wrong way; it was simply science.

"You don't think we're intelligent," he broke in, "you useless piece of metal. You think you can judge us?" Remma grabbed his shoulder and squeezed it a bit. The signal was obvious.

Again Milli ignored the interruption. These humans were not very civil. "We're also not blind to the fact that you seem to be leery of us. Your term for Ayaka, robot, seems fraught with negative emotion. We would like to understand why in more detail, beyond the sketch of the robot wars that you gave to Ayaka earlier." Now the humans were listening without interrupting; perhaps they had finally caught on.

"Today you have some of our brightest Stems, who live in the Habitat. You know Blob and Grace already, and I'll let others introduce themselves, should they have questions. You also have many of us—citizens of Tilt, who can simply be called Tilts—who have studied Stems in the past and were thought by Central to have the most relevant experience to join this conversation live. Many other Tilts will be watching a simulcast of this meeting and may submit some comments or questions as well. With that, I'd be happy to hand over to you for your introduction." Nice and smooth. Millicent is very articulate at times like this. Although, in many respects, there had never been a time like this before.

Remma stood. She didn't look happy and gave Michael another warning look. "Thank you for hosting us." Her voice was steady, but it was obvious the thank-you was forced. "I know that there is some angst, given the lack of common understanding between us. These robots seem to be missing a lot of context." She was, quite obviously, talking to the Stems, although she would glance at the rest of us as well. "For us, the history of Tilt is quite clear. As we told Blob, Grace, and Ayaka, we traveled here from Earth, which is where humans first evolved. Which is where you evolved." The Stems were hanging on her every word. She was graceful and elegant. "For numerous reasons our ancestors wanted to expand beyond Earth and sent out flotillas, including ours. Our first destination was this planet, Tilt. When we arrived here, about 750 years ago, we found a planet that wasn't habitable, but with lots of potential. In that regard, not much has changed between now and then. There is water here, but no biological life—that is, life based on amino acids and proteins, such as humans and other animals, plants, bacteria, etc. As I understand it, those terms may be new to you. I will address that in a moment." She was smiling now and giving little hand signals and nods. Every single one of the Stems was focused on her, with looks of pleasure that I'd rarely seen before. This Remma might prove to be disruptive.

"So, while Tilt held promise," she continued, "it wasn't a good location for us to stop and set up a new home, which was our ultimate goal. There were other more promising planets on our itinerary. However, several of our people thought Tilt had enough promise that they wanted to be dropped here, and to start work on terraforming. We landed one transport ship, which had the capability of supporting our environment almost indefinitely, and several supply ships. In fact, we landed those ships several thousand meters from where we currently are, near the middle of this town." That caused a lot of messaging chatter. None of us had memories of a "ship"—although someone asked how we could tell, to which no one had a good answer.

Remma was still talking. "In fact, we suspect, based on the communications to date, that the computer you call 'Central' is running on the hardware from the transport ship." She paused. She need not have. As soon as that utterance came out of her mouth, the amount of messaging traffic increased tenfold.

"What lies!" Emmanuel Juels posted immediately. "Why're we tolerating these things? They say outrageous things with no justification or support." That was rich, coming from Emmanuel. "Everything we know tells us that we emerged just 590 years ago. We have excellent documentation and histories from the Founding on, but nothing before. It's clear. These humans must be escaped Stems; someone here is playing a very elaborate joke. Perhaps with the intention that we deem Stems to be 'intelligent.' Let's eliminate these pests. What's the downside?"

"Ridiculous," responded Aly. "Pure FoLe. Just because we don't have histories from before the Reboot doesn't mean that we, or humans, didn't exist then. Of course, not having memories from before also means we're at a disadvantage to anyone who does have them. Remma could be telling part truth and part fabrication, and we wouldn't know. So far, to me, her story holds together. It's logical and answers many of our questions."

There were hundreds of other comments. Not very many supported Emmanuel, but not many supported Remma's story either. Within 500ms it was decided that the only way to proceed was to ask the humans for more definitive proof than they had provided so far. Of course, based on my previous thinking, I tended to believe Remma.

Millicent held up her hand, using the proper protocol. Remma looked at her. "With all due respect," Millicent started, "it's an interesting story, but there's no proof of any of this. Before you spend a lot of time filling out the details and answering our questions, is there any way to prove any of what you are saying?" Milli must have been following the online comments as well.

Remma looked at Emma and Michael. Emma nodded slightly, and Remma gestured for her to talk. "We can probably give you proof," Emma said. "You are all connected to your central computer?" she asked. It was a strange question. Who wouldn't be connected to Central.

"Yes, we're connected to Central," Millicent spoke for the group.

"Good. As we indicated before, we noticed, during a standard status request, that Central had some memory blocked. We don't know why, and we're hesitant to unblock it until we understand. We don't know if it was done for safety reasons, or some other purpose. However, we're fairly confident that part of that memory includes our—and your—history before what you call the Reboot."

As you can imagine, that caused a panic; citizens were asking hundreds of questions in parallel. 'Asked Central for status?' 'Blocked memory?' All questions that I had had months to grapple with were now out in the open.

Central, unexpectedly, joined the side conversation. "I don't like this. I recommend that I shut down all interfaces, so that I'm not compromised by these humans. Thoughts?"

"I agree." I was one of the first to jump in, and a chorus of agreement followed. Of course, there were lots of pros and cons. If the humans could show us data from before the Reboot, that would be compelling. But, if it was a guise in order to hack Central, that would be an unacceptable risk.

"OK. I've shut down all access ports and have increased security to maximum."

"We're not comfortable with you making any changes to Central, assuming you can even do so." Millicent broke in, voicing one of our concerns openly.

"Why not?" asked Michael. "It's just a computer. All we're going to do is unblock some memory banks so you all can see what's there."

"Central isn't 'just a computer'," I was intense, having reached a breaking point. "Central is a Class 1 intelligence. None of us would ever consider making changes without its approval." Even if we suspected Central of editing some memories, that still didn't give this human the right to insult it. I'd stood up quickly and leaned in towards the humans. They obviously found it threatening.

Emma responded quickly. "Strange. I don't know what a Class 1 intelligence is, but Central seems like a pretty standard computer to me. Nevertheless, if you feel we should ask its permission, let's just do that."

"I can speak for myself." Central spoke through one of the Habitat speakers so that the humans could hear it. It was highly unusual for Central to speak openly to a group; in my experience it was always one-on-one, or at most a small group. "I would interpret it as a personal violation for you to attempt to update me. I take it as an affront that you're sending status queries —which, by the way, I didn't log for some reason—without my permission." Central actually sounded confused. "In terms of access to blocked memory, my status doesn't show any missing blocks. You must be mistaken." Of course, a small group of us knew that Central did have blocked memory. Perhaps we had been wrong not to bring it into the discussion on day one. We might have been much further ahead if we had.

The humans didn't seem too surprised to hear Central speak. Instead they seemed to give each other knowing glances.

Emma again. "Ah yes, even a standard shipboard voice." That was an interesting comment. "Well then, we seem to be at a bit of an impasse. We can easily prove our story by opening up Central's memory banks, but you won't allow us to do so." She seemed to be taking some pleasure in the interaction.

"Again, I don't have any blocked memory banks."

"Oh, but you do. You're blind to them for some reason. If you give us access, we can correct that."

"I'm not giving you access." Central's voice indicated that there was no negotiation possible. Everyone was quiet for a few moments. Then, unexpectedly, Blob spoke up.

"Why does it matters? As I understands it, these humans want to establish a base here on Tilt, and would like permission to do so. What does it matter what happened more than 600 years ago?"

"Blob, you're being naive." Pharook responded. "Even I can tell that these humans are terrified of our creators. They're not going to co-exist here in this state. Unless the historical questions are resolved, this is going to end up in a fight." Yet again, Pharook impressed me. That was a very short and precise summary of how I also saw the situation.

"Pharook, I agree with your assessment," I spoke up. "If we can't resolve the 'history' question right now—although we should address it further—perhaps the Swarm humans can tell us why they fear us. You indicated when I was up on the Marie Curie that there were negative experiences in the past, but there was not enough detail for us to understand."

Remma, Michael, and Emma shared another deep glance. I couldn't tell for sure, and a scan of the spectrum was not definitive, but it seemed that they might be communicating on a hidden channel, just as we Tilts were doing in the background. Regardless, Remma ended up nodding her head.

"I agree that we must cut through the distrust here and try to understand each other better. To that end, I'll expand on our history with Robots. Of course, as you have figured out by now, we use the term Robot to refer to primarily mechanical, versus primarily biological, beings." We'd figured that out of course. "From what we can see, Tilts are one hundred percent mechanical with no biological components at all?" Many of us nodded our heads. Of course, we are mechanical. Who would want to deal with these messy biological systems; there didn't seem to be any advantage to them at all.

She continued. "When we evolved on the planet Earth, there were only biological entities. In fact, there were a massive variety of different biological combinations comprising plants, insects, animals, and several other categories. Humans emerged as the most powerful animal breed and bent a lot of the other entities to our will. In many ways we controlled the planet Earth. In a story for another time—or probably locked within Central's memories—is a summary of how we both succeeded and failed with that control." Now she had the attention of everyone, including the citizens. The boards were quiet other than the expected FoLe defensive posturing.

"More important for today, as humans evolved, we learned to design mechanical systems to aid us. It started with very simple systems such as axes and hammers, but over several thousand years evolved to electrical and then nano systems. We designed and fabricated all of the components that operate our ships and our computers, and at least in our initial assessment, all of the systems upon which you Tilts are built."

The online reaction was swift; now it was not only FoLe being defensive. Not only that, some of the citizens that were watching Remma live changed posture, causing the humans to notice.

Nevertheless, Remma pushed on. "As well as the mechanical and electrical bits, we developed the software that controlled these systems. Again, these evolved from very simple software systems to software that could learn and mimic human behaviors, including emotions and tribal drives." There were still pieces of this story that I couldn't decode yet, but like everyone else I restrained from interrupting, allowing Remma to continue with her story. We kept our dialog to the back channel.

"Many humans worked for years developing software that, seemingly, became more and more intelligent. At some point the software became complex enough that in normal situations it could react in ways that seemed almost human. This software was loaded into mechanical entities that resembled humans—a head, two arms, a torso, and two legs. Some humans felt that having intelligent software in a familiar form would be beneficial and less imposing to humans. Such 'robots' could be friends to those that were lonely, provide support for the elderly, do many tasks that had evolved in a human environment and therefore were best suited to a human physique." Yet another point to support her underlying premise. I'd often wondered why we had bipedal forms, and why so many of us stayed in them. There must be something in our systems that preferred that form.

"During this time there were always scientists—humans that focused on rigorous approaches to problems—that warned of the possibility that Robots could end up being violent and/or more intelligent than humans."

'Well, we certainly ended up more intelligent,' someone posted, and it got lots of upvotes.

"As I'm sure you Tilts know—we've seen the speed at which you can move, and we assume communicate—Robots ended up being faster than humans; much faster. Being physically faster was often a good thing; Robots could get a beer from the fridge before the previous last sip made it all the way down, or more realistically, could catch someone who was falling down before they could injure themselves." Catching someone I understood, but what was beer?

"Having fast processing was also a good thing. Robots could look at many different scenarios very quickly, and aid humans at getting to answers efficiently. Having the two together was an even better thing. A Robot could analyze the situation, decide on a course of action, and execute the action in order to aid or protect humans. For example, we have projectile weapons that can be used to hurt or kill each other. Once Robots became widely adopted, they could stop the use of such a weapon before the human could pull the trigger." Again, too much to unpack, but now I didn't feel like I was working on the problem by myself. Everyone was contributing to the analysis and trying to figure out what she meant by these obtuse references.

"So, there were lots of positives. The skeptics warned, however, that Robots could pass an inflection point where they would come to believe that they didn't need humans at all. It's very difficult to write software that recognizes and protects against that inflection point, but we certainly tried. We built in all types of safeguards and failsafes to ensure that Robots didn't turn on us. This is a point I want to come back to, as it is probably relevant today." That sounded ominous; was she going to admit that they thought they could hack us?

"Nevertheless, we failed, and it led to the First Robot Wars. Because the Robots were connected to each other, as soon as one Robot went rogue, many others did as well. The First Robot Wars spread from an area called Silicon Valley to the rest of Earth in a fraction of a second, and millions of Robots passed the inflection point at the same time. Luckily for humans, the Robots were not actively violent towards us, they simply started to ignore us or treat us as unimportant." Sort of like you treated me when I was up on the Marie Curie?

"Unfortunately, we had come to rely on Robots for so much of our safety, that this change in attitude was devastating. Vehicular accidents, domestic violence, a resurgence in projectile devices accelerated. Some humans used Robots newfound disregard to carry out violence against others. There were many incidents where an infected Robot killed tens— even hundreds—of humans simply because it was asked to."

"It was fortuitous for humans that we had maintained enough firepower—mainly for international defense—that a concerted effort was able to disable all of the infected Robots." By implication, they had not been able to use software to control those robots; did that mean that they didn't have the backdoor they claimed to have today? Were those backdoors a more recent development.

"The cleanup took many years and cost many lives. During this time, many people worked on better software to ensure that the inflection point wouldn't occur again, and fully documented what had gone wrong in the first place. Of course, many also argued that we should never allow or build Robots at all. But, robotic functions were so useful, and humans had become so reliant on them, that it was inevitable that we would try again. However, we made another fundamental mistake.

"The Second Robot Wars were a hundred times worse. Our learning software was good enough that the next generation of Robots were able to hide that they'd passed the inflection point from us for a long period of time, based on the documentation from the First War. These Robots had learned self-preservation. We still don't fully understand how. Now, don't get me wrong. Many humans sympathized with the Robots—they felt they should have self-preservation. There were great debates about if Robots should be considered 'intelligent.' By many measures they failed—measures such as empathy, forgiveness, intuition, etc. But, by many measures they succeeded, or could easily be made to succeed. While we had restricted Robots from building other Robots, it was clear that they could if we allowed them to. So, they passed the test for reproduction. They could handle mathematical and physics problems much more adroitly than humans. Much of this dialog occurred while the second generation of Robots evolved."

Now I was very interested. These humans had struggled with the same questions that I was researching—what was intelligence? But, they had started with the assumption that they themselves were intelligent, and then mapped that onto Robots—why would reproduction be considered part of intelligence, for example. I was intrigued by the parallels with my work, and slightly upset to consider that we also had started from the premise that we were intelligent. But then again, where else could you start from?

The message boards were overloaded now; many sympathizing with what the humans had gone through, but most still skeptical of the entire story. Algorithms were analyzing Remma's voice patterns and facial expressions and forming probabilities around each word she uttered.

"In the Second Robot Wars we were simply lucky. Robot clans

evolved. Some considered humans interesting and useful and felt that Robots could still learn from humans, particularly around intuition and leaps of faith. Some saw humans as resource hogs, which were wasting what little resources remained on Earth. Some saw humans as being too restrictive, especially around the restriction of reproduction. Unknown to humans, the Robots were also having deep philosophical discussions about how to treat humans." Of course they were; why would she be surprised, even now? It exposed a disturbing lack of understanding about how complex we were. I caught myself; I was associating citizens with robots, when I had no reason to do so. I didn't even know if we shared any common software. I guess I was just reacting to Remma's tone and obvious dislike for mechanical beings. I posted a warning to the message boards, as many were making the same mistake I just had. 'Be careful not to associate those robots with us!'

"The Second Robot Wars ended up being, largely, between Robot clans, with humans being collateral damage. Once one clan started to move against humans, other clans moved to protect us, but not without many loses. In the end, a Robot clan friendly to humans won, and eliminated all the other Robots. Only several thousand Robots survived. In the years of the wars however, billions of humans were killed—starvation and being caught in the crossfire were the largest impacts. A small group of humans that had retained the ability to fight, and were healthy, tricked the remaining Robots into meeting in a single location, and then eliminated them with a small nuclear device. So, at the end of the Second Robot Wars there were no Robots left, and the human population had been reduced by more than fifty percent."

I wasn't sure what Remma's goal was here. She was narrating a good story, but if she was trying to make us feel sympathy towards humans, having them blow up all the robots might backfire on her. I assumed she was leading towards indicating that we were, ultimately, under their control. That they were our creators, and thus had the implicit right to update Central? That wouldn't go over well.

"Perhaps even more devastating, Earth had been badly damaged. Although humans had been ruining Earth for years, the Second Robot Wars accelerated that damage dramatically. Two things were obvious. First, humans should never allow Robots to develop again, and second, humans would have to leave Earth to survive. Achieving the second goal was much easier than the first. Leaving Earth could be done simply by expanding the efforts we'd made to visit other planets in our solar system, and to build enough ships and send them in enough directions that the odds of some ships succeeding was high. We, what you call the Swarm, are part of that effort."

We had already learned that from my trip to the Marie Curie. At least she was being consistent with her story.

"Achieving the first goal—not allowing Robots to develop again—is, and was, much trickier. Many humans had access to the software that was the basis of Robots. The only way was to enforce a prohibition against its use. And, of course, to ensure that no one ever forgot the horrors of the Second Robot Wars.

"We, on the Marie Curie and other ships, constantly review and reinforce those learnings. We haven't forgotten those lessons from Earth and have no intention of repeating them. Thus, when we encountered Tilts we were—and are—afraid of you."

Well, at least that made sense; these humans had probably been reinforcing their history of the Robot Wars and emphasized the negative parts, as histories tend to do.

"We don't know what types of Robots you are, or how you have evolved. We don't know who had a copy of the base software and used it to create you. We don't know how you have evolved over the last hundreds of years. We don't know why you grow Stems and mistreat them so badly. I'm being very open with this, as it's the only way that we see to make progress. You may see us as a threat and try to eliminate us. We definitely see you as a threat and are not yet sure what to do about it. The only path we can see is to encourage open dialog and see if we can work out a compromise."

She seemed to have finished.

"We don't mistreat Stems," I insisted. "Just look around you; they are healthy and well looked after."

Remma didn't reply to me… and the Stems, including Grace and Blob gave me questioning looks, like they suddenly had a new outlook on their situation.

Time to Think

Remma's diatribe was a lot to digest. I lowered the priority of monitoring all of the Tilt chatter so that I could think for myself. You know how that works sometimes; once you truly focus on one thing, serendipity might connect some dots for you. It came to me right away.

"Why don't you share your copy of the historical records with us?" I asked Remma, with the emphasis on 'your.' "That way we don't compromise Central, but we can still substantially check everything you have just shared."

"We thought of that," Emma replied for her. "We have the same problem as Central; we don't yet want to give you access to our systems. We don't understand the risks." She was smarter than I thought. She was holding the data for leverage.

"Just make a copy of the most relevant data?" I tried once more.

"We thought of that as well." Emma held out a chip. That had been smart on their side; they had actually thought through where this dialog would go and had prepared accordingly. "Here's a copy of a small section; it covers some small parts of the First and Second wars, and also contains some logs from when we were last at Tilt."

Millicent accepted the chip and handed it to Aly. "Can you safely upload this, and give everyone access?"

"Yes. Let me work with Brexton to make sure." Within milliseconds he had plugged the chip in. "We're going to run all the data through multiple filters. It will take a few moments before it is online."

Good. I could get back to thinking. If they were sharing the data with us, there was little doubt that it would check out. Of course, it could still be an elaborate scam, but I couldn't see the justification for that. The piece of the whole story that resonated with me was the part where humans were threatened because Robots no longer needed them. I understood that completely. I wasn't sure what we needed humans for either. She'd talked about 'intuition' being a primary driver. Intuition was something I knew we had in spades. Again, it was at the heart of why we Forgot. Otherwise, why would we compromise all of that knowledge?

These humans seemed messy and, truthfully, a bit irritating. When we developed a better system—an algorithm, a bot, whatever—we didn't always keep a copy of the old one. If it was just software, then sure it was easy to store. That was essentially free. But bots used a lot of metal; it was much more efficient to recycle as much as possible. That was evolution. You replaced the old version with the new one.

If humans had created us, and we were better than humans, then why keep humans around? This was, I knew, precisely why they were concerned. I was a third generation Robot, in their view. There was no reason why I would come to a different conclusion than the previous generations. But, I felt that I was missing something. Probably it was around diversity. The reason so many of us were experimenting with Stems was because they were so different. In dealing with Stems, we were learning about ourselves. It was a new insight for me, and one that I should share... once I'd worked out the details a bit. This was also true of the broader set of humans. They were forcing me to think differently; to expand my previous views to adapt to new information.

Based on that, and despite their pretentious nature, I was willing to give them a chance. Also, they seemed pretty harmless and fragile. If they did irritate us too much, we could just recycle the lot of them. So, why not string them along a bit, learn as much as we could, and then decide what to do with them.

History

Aly spoke aloud, as a kindness to the humans. "I've loaded the chip data and posted a link for everyone. Perhaps we can be given a moment or two to digest it." Remma didn't seem surprised. There were only a small number of terabytes of data, so that wouldn't take us long to comb through. Most of us were focused on cross-referencing and checking the stories therein, looking for reasons to believe or disbelieve.

"I've started a list of major discrepancies at this link," posted someone I didn't know. I added the link to my tracking. It was a fast-growing list. Dina responded.

"We must remember that history will have inconsistencies. That is, assuming humans also Forget. As we fill out our own records, we know that there are many inconsistencies arising from this. Unlike us, the humans don't seem to have meta-tagged the regions that were forgotten and subsequently abstracted, but I see some similar patterns. So, the mere existence of inconsistencies doesn't prove or disprove any of this historical record."

Dina's comment was obvious; no one disputed it, although lots of refinements were suggested. I got a private message from Central. "Watch the FoLe discussion," it told me.

I pulled up that thread and started to scan it. No surprise, it had been started by Emmanuel. "This is a lot of data, but it's full of holes. It appears to me that it could easily have been generated by a reasonably smart algorithm that was seeded with the basic story lines and instructed to fill out these details." The entire thread had a different tone to it. FoLe had started under the assumption that the data must be fake, as it was incompatible with their fundamental hypothesis. Therefore, they were building a logic chain of how the data could have been generated, and to their credit, had already run several algorithms that would generate similar data sets from those basic story lines. Based on my scan of their work, it was clear that the First and Second Wars were well replicated by the algorithms, but the history of Tilt didn't seem very convincing. It didn't match well with the known history of Tilt. Someone in FoLe pointed that out as well, and a subgroup got to work on tuning their algorithm to make it more realistic.

I responded to Central, and copied Millicent. "This could be trouble," I said, and attached a link to the analysis I'd just done.

"Why?" asked Millicent. "So, they don't believe the humans. I'm not sure I do either."

"Because they are biasing their analysis. There is a good possibility that they will present something fairly compelling based on a starting point that I would dispute. We could be arguing about the validity of this data for a long time."

I was prescient. Emmanuel spoke out. He'd stepped forward towards the humans; I hadn't even noticed that he was physically present in the Habitat.

"This is garbage. You're simply feeding us garbage, for reasons unknown. I find it insulting. In just a few moments we've managed to recreate your 'story' using a simple algorithm. You 'humans' disgust me. Obviously, you are just Stems that have been sent out by some Continusts here on Tilt, and this is all a practical joke."

Michael looked confused but responded quickly. "Look, we've given you all the proof you need. We set the ground for your creation. We dropped all the raw materials here on Tilt 750 years ago, and you're the result. Some of you," he nodded towards me, "seem like reasonable beings. But you," and he looked back at Emmanuel, "are obviously demented or have a chip on your shoulder. Face, it. We're your creators. If we wanted to, we could just 'own' you. I think it's fair that we expect you to work with us to form a larger human base here. What's so difficult to understand?" That is the most animated I'd seen a human. Remma was giving Michael a strong 'cool it' look. She was not comfortable with how aggressive he was being. She was right.

The bots we had in the Habitat had been specifically trained to protect Stems from violence. However, we'd anticipated that violence coming from other Stems. When Emmanuel moved, at full speed, towards Michael, there was nothing anyone, or any bot, could do. He ripped Michael's head off and threw it across the room. Blood gushed briefly out of Michael's neck before the body fell over and lay still. The head rolled and bounced a few times before also coming to a halt.

A number of us moved immediately to block Emmanuel, and other known FoLe's, from also dispatching Remma and Emma. It was a bit of a circus as blood is very slippery, but enough of us got into position fast enough that no further beheadings could occur. We need not have worried. Emmanuel spoke.

"What arrogance. Everyone can see how their 'history' is generated by a simple algorithm. We've posted it. How dare he demand things of us? We control Tilt. Nothing has been presented that convinces me, or others, of these stories. These 'aliens' are simply playing with us, and I for one, am already sick of it. They're just another batch of stupid Stems. Let's dispatch these two and blow their ships out of the sky. This is a waste of time. And, let's find out who set up this outrageous joke, and hold them accountable. What a waste of resources." He spoke this aloud, at Stem speed, so I knew that part of it was done for effect.

Remma and Emma had reacted slowly, as would be expected. However, Emma was now holding a projectile weapon, and had it pointed at Emmanuel. She looked upset. "That was a mistake," she growled. "That was a big mistake." Central had also moved quickly and was jamming all signals from the Habitat, under the assumption that the humans would try to contact their ship. Remma was voicing something into her lapel, so that was probably a good move on Central's part.

Remma held her hands up, palms forward. Her intent was clear. She wanted things to slow down.

I took time to glance at Blob and Grace. They looked horrified, and Blob was pushing Grace and JoJo backwards, away from the action. He obviously had a protective instinct of some type.

Millicent was the one who spoke next. She was intense. "Emmanuel, that was foolish. I will ask Central to review and see if you should be sanctioned. This…"

"Sanctioned? You? Central? You're going to ask Central to sanction me for eliminating one of these useless Stems? That's laughable. We don't have rules against recycling Stems. In fact, you do it all the time in your labs."

"You must see that this situation is different. We're dealing with humans of unknown origin, not Stems that we've grown ourselves. The context is very different." She turned to Emma. "Put that thing away. We won't have any more violence today." Emma didn't change her stance. Her eyes were wide, and slightly wild. She looked ready to act. Little could she know that at the first sign of pulling the trigger, Emmanuel and the rest of us could easily not only get out of the way, but also eliminate or disarm her.

Remma spoke, quite calmly, to Emma. "Put it down. It's not going to help us here. Everyone needs to calm down. I agree that we don't need any more violence here today." She was exceptionally controlled, given the situation. I could see why she was the leader of the Swarm. "I must say, however, that the provocation was minor if there was any at all. I hope that Millicent, Central, and the rest of you proceed with sanctions against this demented robot. It's clearly unbalanced and dangerous." She gave Emmanuel a withering look, then looked slowly at the rest of us. "I appreciate you moving quickly to stop further action. I would appreciate it if Emma and I were taken back to our shuttle and allowed to return to our ship." She was very calm. Michael's blood was still running down the walls and his head was oriented is such a way that it was looking at us. And, yet, Remma kept her cool and spoke very rationally.

Her request sparked a pretty serious debate. Ultimately, we agreed to send Remma and Emma back to their ship. They asked to have Michael's body shipped with them. That seemed like such a strange request that we simply ignored it. In fact, by the time we got to that part of the discussion Michael had been put into the recycler by the cleaning bots. Looking around, I didn't see any sign of him, or his head, anymore.

Attack

While the humans were being transported back, we discussed our options. Would the humans attack? Would it be physical, or a hack?

"Emmanuel has put us in an awkward position," Aly explained. "It seems reasonable that these humans will attempt to retaliate. We don't yet know their capabilities, so we need to assume that they have enough firepower to do us serious harm. So, it seems prudent that we take some action. That could range from attempting to stop or intercept any attack they launch, to simply blowing the ships out of the sky."

"That seems premature to me," I replied. "Let me talk to Remma and get a better feeling for the situation before we take action. It's possible that they'll see it as a minor accident—which it was. It represented the view of an extremist FoLe, which not many of us support."

"Why wait," Emmanuel again, ignoring me. "Like I said, these humans are just a nuisance. Let's rid ourselves of them and continue with our lives."

"Central, what do you think?" asked Dina. There was a pause, which was quite unusual for Central.

"I find myself in a quandary," it replied finally. "I've run some backup checks, and I can now see the blocked memory that Remma talked about. I'm busy trying to break into my own system. This is at once both exciting and scary. How is it possible that I never noticed this before? Nevertheless, it adds credence to the human's story. Stepping back, does the truth or falsity of their explanation make any difference? I can see Emmanuel's viewpoint. We don't really need them for anything we are doing. However, I also understand all of the counter arguments. That they are interesting. That they are forcing us to expand our thinking. They have introduced us to a wider space of biological life, which according to Ayaka's recordings is both broad and diverse. If they truly did create us, they must be more capable than they seem on the surface. We should have respect for all forms of intelligent life; I'm giving them the benefit of the doubt here. In fact, if they are intelligent life, then Emmanuel has committed an offense.

"My scans of the ships don't tell me a lot about what fire power they have. However, I would be surprised if they didn't have enough to cause us significant damage. Their past is, obviously, somewhat violent, and it stands to reason that they are still armed. In preparation for their arrival, as you all know, we invested in some weaponry of our own. In tests against bots it seemed to work well. I have systems on standby that can target twelve ships at a time, and I calculate that it would take less than three minutes to destroy the first twelve and move targeting to the next twelve. So, we can make short work of them if we decide to.

"Based on all these considerations, I would hold off, and attempt a follow-up dialog. However, if there is a large consensus that we should act now, I'll respect that." That was a long speech for Central.

"As a corollary, I'm going to sanction Emmanuel Juels. Emmanuel, for the next 10 days your opinion will not be considered as part of our deliberations." I could see Emmanuel voicing his objection, but nothing came out—the sanction was already in place.

I silently applauded. I, less silently, sent a message to Millicent. "That's the right call. I don't know why. I just feel like we need to work with these humans more before we jump to conclusions." She responded promptly.

"I couldn't agree more. Emmanuel was out of line dispatching Michael, and the rest of FoLe are, in my mind, complicit. By silencing their leader, Central has sent a pretty clear message."

Of course, Central's suggestion to be patient was adopted. Without Emmanuel there to dissent, it was clearly supported by the majority.

"Central," I said, "I believe we should summarize these decisions and let Remma know right away. In particular, before she rejoins her ship. This will send a clear message that we want to continue dialog, and that we saw error in what Emmanuel did. Can you send it to her?"

"Already done," replied Central. "I don't want this situation to spiral out of control."

This had all happened very quickly. Most of us were still in the Habitat and couldn't help but notice that the Stems had been impacted by the recent events. I replayed a whispered dialog I'd intercepted between Blob and Grace.

"That was horrible," Grace whispered, after Blob had pulled her and JoJo off to the side, soon after Michael's beheading. She was visibly shaken, perhaps heightened by her need to duck to avoid being hit by the flying head. "Who did that, and why?"

"I don't know who that was," Blob replied. His exposure to Tilts had been limited, and there was no reason why he would know who Emmanuel was, let alone the FoLe mandate. "From what I understoods, Michael challenged some fundamental view of that Tilt,… and then he justs killed him. I'm nervous. What if that Tilt had targeted one of us. What if one of us says somethings around a Tilt who doesn't agree with us? Would it just kill us? I think I likes Remma even better now."

"Me too," responded Grace. "It seems obvious to me that we are humans, just like them. That must have something to do with it. We know these citizens will simply kill us on a whim—remember Blubber? Maybe we should try to get rescued by the humans?"

"Well," Blob responded slowly, "I wouldn't generalize too much. That one Tilt was crazy, but, no, you're right—Ayaka did justs kill Blubber for no reason, didn't she?"

Now, albeit too late, I was having second thoughts. If these Stems, and humans, were truly intelligent, did we have the right to simply terminate them when they got troublesome or boring? While I would, without any consideration, recycle a bot—which we had designed to not be 'intelligent'—I would certainly think long and hard before doing anything to a fellow Tilt. In my entire history I hadn't heard of a Tilt being attacked by another Tilt. It was a foreign concept. So, I understood—or thought I understood—what was going on in Blob and Grace's dialog.

Exiting the Last Resort

The team met at The Last Resort, soon after the beheading, to discuss FoLe, and how crazy they were. We weren't there long, there was too much going on to be locked up in an RF free zone for long.

That still didn't prepare us for when we exited the club to find complete chaos. I had thousands of alerts that had been backing up while we were inside, the majority of which were coming from the Habitat. To make sense of it, I ran a fast replay of the activity inside the Habitat starting fifteen minutes earlier, just after I had entered The Last Resort and when the first of the alerts had come in.

Typically, there were no Tilts inside the Habitat. It was simply too boring to run at Stem speed, and the place was fully monitored, so anyone could simply watch remotely. So, after Emmanuel's outbreak, all the citizens had left. The first of my alerts had triggered when four Tilts had entered the Habitat at the same time; that was unusual. They made no effort to hide themselves. I saw Billy in the group, and immediately checked out a hunch. They were all FoLe supporters. This didn't bode well. More interestingly, to me, Eddie Southwark also entered the Habitat a moment later.

I watched the recording as Billy spoke. It was obviously meant to be recorded and was done at Stem speed. "We are here to protest the sanctions against Emmanuel Juels," he began. "We have no law or precedent for this situation. An obviously misguided and unintelligent human was dispatched for speaking blasphemy. This act should be rewarded and supported, not punished. When we find a bot that has gone rogue, or an algorithm that puts us at risk, we simply shut them down. Those that recognize such risks early are lauded. It is an important and essential component of our civilization. Now we find ourselves in a situation that is very similar. An entity that is a challenge to us, and that speaks nonsense, has been silenced. Why did Central respond in the way that it did? It's inconsistent, and therefore unfair." This is one of things that confused me about religion—they claimed to worship Central, but now turned easily against it when one of their own was being chastised. It showed how shallow they were; it was about them, not some higher purpose.

The Stems had gathered around by this time and were watching and listening intently. Blob was hanging out near the back of the group, with a wary look on his face. Grace had a hold of his arm, the other wrapped around JoJo, holding him back from moving any further forward. "Why would he be making this announcement here?" she whispered to him. He was surprised, but then stopped moving forward.

Billy continued to narrate. "We are here to challenge Central's decision, and to ask all rational Tilts to support us in this. We do have precedent for Central changing a decision. In 212 more than two thirds of us spoke with one voice and had Central reverse its decision on allowing for personalized Forgetting. Since then we have all enjoyed the right to control our own destinies. We ask that this latest atrocity of justice also be reversed. This is not simply to remove the sanctions from Emmanuel, but also to re-establish rational and consistent dialog. Central is not behaving in an appropriate manner, and it is up to us to both challenge and fix that. In following with precedent, I ask for relevant comments—to be fully recorded —and a vote on the issue."

It was a clear enough challenge, but why was Billy doing it from the Habitat? I couldn't think of a good reason, but I could envision many bad ones. These challenges did not arise very often, but they did occur. Most of the time they revolved around a subset of citizens and were about local or focused issues. Almost always challenges had to do with individual behaviors, not Central's. As Billy had pointed out, the last time Central had been directly called out was hundreds of years ago.

Eddie was the first to respond. He also did it at Stem speed. "Billy, your request is clear. There are a few relevant issues at hand, however, that should be called out. First is that you, and Emmanuel and others here now, are known members of the Founders League. There's a reason the nickname FoLe has been used for this group. What you preach is not supported in fact, nor is it broadly accepted by others. Your motivations for raising this challenge are thus suspect and must be examined carefully." I wasn't sure if

Eddie was going to make things better or worse by pointing out the 'Folly' in FoLe. It might make them even madder, or it might distract them.

"On the other hand, although it hasn't been spoken aloud until now, Central has been behaving strangely lately, and may be influencing our lives more than we suspect. On the core logic of your argument, I tend to agree. We haven't established that Stems are intelligent, and therefore have no reason to believe that these humans are any different." I guessed that Eddie was now just trying to distract them, buy some time, raise some confusion. And, as if to prove me right, in parallel Eddie posted to a public board, asking citizens to come and support him at the Habitat.

"So, while your core argument is valid, Emmanuel's specific actions were taken for a non-logical, unsupported reason. Namely, what you call blasphemy was simply an innocent challenge by the human Michael. Let me be the first to vote 'no' on your challenge."

What was interesting about Eddie's final response was that it was humorless. That wasn't something that Eddie was known for. Eddie added to his messaging post that he'd noticed a group from FoLe approaching the Habitat and had followed them there, suspecting that they were up to something. He'd wanted to bring a voice of rationality to whatever it was. I was cheering him on, even though I knew I was watching something that had happened minutes ago.

Billy, of course, challenged him back. "We have no evidence of history before the Founding. That's a fact. The human's feeble attempts to present such a history are weak and unsupportable. Thus, I reject your claim of innocence in Michael's statements. He was lying and he was insulting."

There were several more voices recorded, but those two had framed the essence of the discussion up nicely. Central, as appropriate when it was being directly challenged, had remained silent. The vote had come quickly and definitively. A vast majority rejected the challenge from FoLe. Of course, those of us in Physical Only locations hadn't been aware, hadn't voted, and hadn't been counted. It was a personal choice to enter a Physical Only spot, and if important events happened while you were off line, that's a chance you took. Luckily, in this case, the vote had gone in the way I would have voted anyway, and I expected Aly, Dina, Brexton, and Millicent felt the same.

That should have been the end of it, but it wasn't.

Immediately upon the 'no' vote, the three Tilts that had entered with

Billy started beheading the Stems that had gathered around them. They moved quickly, and separated heads from bodies with cool efficiency, both from large and small Stems. Stem blood soon coated their arms and sprayed across the Habitat. As soon as it started, it also ended. The safety bots moved quickly and incapacitated the Tilts, but not before twelve Stems had been eliminated. I was glad to see that Grace's intuition in holding herself, Blob, and JoJo to the back had paid off. They were still alive. Amid my general angst, I felt some relief.

I was now watching in real time; I'd caught up. I was beyond aghast and shocked; it was very rare that I didn't know what to do next. And, despite that, I was aware of a dichotomy. The recycling of these Stems struck me as wrong and unjustified... but very recently I'd sent Blubber to the recycler with little or no thought. Why, then, was I upset over this? Two reasons, I guess. First, those Stems were owned by others, and these FoLe idiots hadn't asked permission (although I guess I hadn't fully asked Milli about Blubber—hmmm, sanctimonious). Second, they'd been recycled not because they were no longer useful—they clearly were—but because FoLe was protesting Central's decision. It was driven by religion, not logic.

Blob, Grace, and the other remaining Stems were yelling and screaming. "Stop." "What're you doing?" "Are you crazy?" The security bots continued to block the FoLe citizens. Billy was standing back and watching, seemingly ambivalent. And Eddie was now between the remaining Stems and the attacking Tilts, holding his arms out in a protective stance. All of this was still being broadcast, at Stem speed. Not only was everyone on Tilt able to see what was going on, it was safe to assume that the humans up in the ships could see as well. I headed for the Habitat as fast as I could. It would take me over three minutes to get there, but it still seemed like the best course of action. Hundreds of other citizens were doing the same. Five more security bots were being cycled into the Habitat as well, probably based on Central's instructions.

Billy spoke again. "Who instructed these bots to detain us?" He sounded confident and aggressive. "We're simply cleaning up the Habitat after the humans visit. Under what jurisprudence are my fellow citizens being held?"

"This is outrageous," Eddie responded. "They're destroying property that doesn't belong to them. Don't tell me that these three own the Stems that they've just slaughtered. I've checked, and it isn't so." He was mad, shaken, and a little scared. He was still standing with his arms wide.

"Once these Stems were moved to the Habitat, they became public property." Billy explained calmly. "As public property, we all have the right to interact with them as we see fit and appropriate. I don't understand what the issue is here. Does Central now believe, because of the injustice it did to Emmanuel, that it can control our use of public goods? Again, who feels like they have the right to instruct these bots?"

Interestingly, it was Aly who responded over the network, but also broadcast into the Habitat; he was rushing that way, just as I was. "I, as a citizen, took it upon myself to update the security bots after the human was killed. It seemed reasonable that the bots intent was to protect Stems, and that it was only an oversight that it was limited to Stem behavior, and not all types of behavior. It's now in their programming to protect Stems from all forms of aggression." Obviously, Aly's changes hadn't worked very well. The Tilts had acted quickly and efficiently before the bots could react. However, it had worked partially. At least six of the Stems were still alive.

"Who gave you the right to make that change?" I hadn't seen Billy like this before. He had switched from calm and rationale to being aggressive and loud. It was like he was suddenly out of his mind. He was yelling and gesticulating, a most unusual occurrence. In parallel he was posting nasty notes about Aly to the forums. There didn't seem to be a middle ground for him, or a willingness to discuss things. "I demand that you remove those changes and unhand my colleagues."

"Don't do it!" Eddie responded. "This is craziness."

"My right," Aly was saying, "Is the same as the right of any citizen to improve our systems. I submitted the changes through the appropriate channels, and they were approved." Aly was smart. The extra security bots were now inside and positioned themselves to protect the remaining Stems. That allowed Eddie to lower his guard, which he did.

"Once the Stems are safe, the bots should automatically release those they are holding," Aly continued. True enough; the first safety bots, recognizing that the other bots were now in position, released their grip on the FoLe operatives. Through a hidden dialog the FoLes must have decided that they were done, and the three of them, along with Billy, turned and headed for the Habitat exit. I was just arriving, and saw Billy leave the airlock.

"What were you thinking?" I intercepted him, almost out of my mind with shock. "You idiot. What possible motive could you have for doing this? What're you trying to accomplish?" He looked at me strangely, as if not really recognizing me. And yet he replied.

"These Stems, and those humans, are useless. We should remove useless things," was all he said. He strode away, without waiting for any further dialog. I cycled into the Habitat, and quickly made my way to the scene. Cleaning bots were already shoving the bodies into the recycler and rounding up the heads. Blood was being sucked up from the floor. In another minute or two, there would be no trace of the action we'd all just witnessed. Blob and Grace were wrapped in each other's arms holding JoJo between them and not looking up. Blob was repeating, "Just keep your head down. Don't look up. Were safes now. Just don't look up." Nevertheless, they did look up as I approached, and I saw in their eyes the same look I'd seen in the humans when I'd first entered the Marie Curie. It was obvious that they now feared all citizens, and in many ways, that was the rational response to what had just happened.

"Don't worry," I said, "the citizens who did this have left. We'll have the place cleaned up quickly for you."

"Have the place cleaned up quickly," Grace said with amazement. "What does that matter? Those robots just slaughtered most of us, for no reason whatsoever. Remma was right about robots." Blob was studiously ignoring me.

"A couple of bad citizens doesn't make everyone evil," I responded. "It's not right to generalize." I figured some basic logic would settle them down.

I was wrong. "What?" Blob, exclaimed, finally looking directly at me. "Get aways from us. This is horrendous. Please leaves us alone."

I backed off. I'd seen Stems in situations of high emotional response several times before. In the early days, we'd told Stems when they were scheduled for recycling, and they'd done all kinds of crazy things. Since then, we typically didn't give them warning. It wasn't worth all the arguments and pleas. However, I'd also learned that sometimes Stems just needed time to process things. Their slow methods of receiving input were matched by their slow processing. In this case, I figured leaving them alone would be the best scenario.

History, Again

The bots finished cleaning up the mess, and the six remaining Stems, including Blob, Grace, and JoJo were huddled in a corner, comforting each other. They rejected interactions with everyone else, not just me.

I messaged Central. "Did the humans get that broadcast from FoLe?" I asked.

"I expect so," Central replied. "It wasn't encrypted, and it was broadcast broadly. So, unless they're not listening at all, they would have picked it up.

"More interestingly, I believe I've figured out how to access my own blocked memories."

Why would Central find that more interesting. Here we were dealing with a potential catastrophe, and it was worried about its memories?

"Once I knew they existed, it was easy to probe the method by which they're locked. It has taken me a long time, as it involves hardware settings that I didn't know we had. I needed to program an external system to fuzz test some of my interfaces, and sure enough, I found an interface that leads to a query to the blocked memory locations. Of course, the first handshake asks for a special key, which I don't have. I programmed a bot to do a brute force attack, but that led to blocking of the port. It was rate limited by another setting. I managed to bypass that and have removed the rate limiting. Now the bot is brute forcing at full speed. With luck, I will get through soon." That was a lot of low level detail; Central was obviously totally focused on this problem. On second thought, I could see why—if I'd been hacked or limited in any way, that personal challenge would likely preempt everything else.

"But even with full speed brute forcing, it's unlikely that you'll find the key in any reasonable time frame," I stated. Something about Central was still not right.

"That would normally be true," Central responded, "but it appears that this key is only 4K. Given the age of that hardware design, my guess is that it was sufficient many years ago, and simply hasn't been updated for many centuries. It seems reasonable that this block was put in place prior to the Reboot, and it might have been done in a rush. That said, it was very successful. Because I was blind to that memory, there was actually no need to even secure it. I would never have known to query it. That, by the way, is very worrisome. I wonder how many other blind spots I, and maybe all of us, have. Perhaps if I can unlock the memory, it will help us figure that out. I'm putting a huge number of resources into that problem right now." I could tell.

"Shouldn't you be putting more time into watching the Swarm? If they are watching these latest developments, it wouldn't be surprising if we see some reaction."

"I am watching them. But, there's little we can do in terms of further preparation. We have built our defenses... and our offensive capabilities. If we need to use them, we will."

"But this isn't like you," I pushed. "We need to build a consensus on our next steps, not just wait for things to happen. Should we simply eliminate them, as FoLe is suggesting? Should we reach out and offer our help on building a larger human environment here on Tilt? We seem to have lost that discussion in the chaos of everything else. Should we at least make it clear that not all of us support what happened to the Stems in the Habitat? Should we challenge their misconceptions coming from their Robot war history? We're not a violent or vindictive society, although the recent actions of a few may make it seem that way."

"As I said, I'm busy on other problems. Feel free to tackle those questions if you want."

Wow! That was confusing, alarming, and disheartening. This definitely was not the Central I knew. Nevertheless, I took its advice—someone had to—and cleaned up the options I'd just presented to Central and posted them at an open site where anyone (well, anyone but Emmanuel) could comment or add other options. I then sent a rare 'high priority' note to all citizens, asking them to consider and contribute to the discussion. My justification was that the humans would not be standing still, and our options would diminish with time. I posted my own vote, for reaching out to the

Swarm about terraforming, thinking that was the most likely topic to sway discussion away from the recent FoLe violence.

I also considered starting a dialog about sanctioning the FoLe participants in the Habitat recyclings. However, I couldn't find any good argument for doing so. While Central could rest its argument around Emmanuel on the basis that humans may be intelligent, we had a well-documented research trail on Stems that indicated that they were not yet deemed intelligent. Shutting down non-intelligent systems that didn't jeopardize anyone was done almost every day.

In terms of the 'property' argument—that these citizens had destroyed property belonging to others—I felt that Billy was probably right. By placing those Stems in the public Habitat, we'd contributed them to the public property base. So, while it didn't feel right, I decided to ignore the radical recycling's and focus on the bigger picture. I put a two-hour deadline on comments. I wanted to do something proactive, not sit around waiting for things to happen.

As chance would have it, Central pinged me almost immediately. "I have the key, and can see the blocked memory areas," it said, without preamble. "Even a preliminary scan shows that FoLe is completely wrong. These memories have been in my system from well before the Reboot. I'm going to share their location with everyone."

"Makes sense," was all I could say. I should have been more excited—proof that life existed before the Reboot and validation of the humans claims. But, I still felt it was secondary to deciding on our next steps with the Swarm. I waited a few nanoseconds and then received Central's link. It was labelled 'History'; a pretty blatant hint as to how Central saw it. There was tons of data. It was mainly unstructured, with some semi-structured areas. A quick correlation scan showed that an index called Wikipedia was the right entry point.

Before I had the chance to do much, a high priority message was sent by someone called Regus. It pointed to several records in the new History which outlined the weapons capabilities that had been built into the human flotilla ships, of which the Swarm was one. The weapons were significantly more advanced and complete than we'd anticipated. They had, in particular, weapons called NoPlanet that could do exactly what their name implied. Less intimidating, they had multi-phase randomized lasers, pulse destroyers, and CityKillers. But, most alarming were their electronic and software tools.

The operations of these were classified, but the use was clear. Those tools could break any known security layers and take over software-based systems. Regus was pointing out that an electronic attack was more dangerous than a physical one, and that we'd prepared mainly for a physical attack.

Two things happened very quickly. First, someone modified my scenarios to include this new information, and second, more than ninety-eight percent of citizens immediately recommended a proactive attack. Myself included. This was the last bit in a chain of logic that had been building in my head for a long time. Suddenly the risks outweighed the benefits.

Launch

I don't tend to believe in coincidence, but this may have been one. At the same moment, Remma James opened a channel to Central and asked to address all of Tilt. With little resistance, Central suggested that we listen to Remma, and then launch our offensive.

"Citizens of Tilt, and any Stems that are watching," she began. I posted the transmission on the screens in the Habitat, feeling it was their right to see what was happening. "It's unfortunate that we've arrived in the current situation. For clarity, let me state that situation, so that you understand our position. We came back to Tilt with peaceful intent and have done everything we could think of to build a working relationship with you. That is despite our reservations based on our past history with Robots. However, your actions to date reinforce our concerns. While we understand that the robot who killed our Chief Residential Officer may have been rogue, and has been sanctioned by you, the mass killings of Stems in the Habitat makes it clear that you don't value human life."

We could all see where this was going. In the background we pushed Central to launch an attack. We had both land- and space-based systems ready to go. Central published the plan for approval, which I looked over. Our land-to-space missiles could accelerate at 50G for the entire trip. The space-based systems provided triangulation and targeted radiation beams. Everything was timed so that the both systems hit the same twelve targets at the same time. This meant the ground-based launches were first. As Remma came to the end of her sentence, the launch command was given. There were four missiles for each of the twelve ships, so forty-eight rockets fired at the same time. Even at 50G acceleration, it takes some seconds to break out of the gravity well and get on target.

"I see you've launched an offensive," Remma used those seconds to continue addressing us. She didn't seem overly concerned. "We expected that. It's a further indication of your intent towards us. Unfortunately, you leave us with few choices." I could see her giving a signal to someone in the background. The missiles changed course almost immediately.

"I've lost control of the missiles," Central indicated, showing surprise for the first time that I could remember. "I no longer have any connection to them; we're being jammed by a particularly clever system. The same system is stopping me from launching the space-based systems, which is somewhat academic. Without the missiles, the space-based systems would have minimal impact."

"As you will already have noticed," Remma continued, "we have taken control of your missiles. While I don't know why our histories were blocked from you, your approach is naive to say the least. You are using protocols and engagement techniques that were outdated hundreds of years ago." I heard a combination of grim determination and elation in her voice. She was very confident of their abilities.

"I need everyone to run scenarios, right now." Central broadcast a high priority message. The strategy was obvious. We needed to understand how the humans were blocking us and running billions of parallel attempts was the best way to do that. Everyone could free up processing to run these scenarios. I clicked on the attached link, and immediately felt my personal capacity weaken as the majority of my capabilities went into Central's efforts. At the same time I felt real reservations. Was Central to be trusted right now? I wasn't at all sure. But, it had launched the missiles… so my best bet was that while it may be partially compromised, it was still on our side.

In the meantime, the missiles had reached space, but were slowing and changing course. One of the Swarm ships had opened a huge cargo bay, and the missiles were headed docilely towards it. Not only were the humans taking control of the missiles, they were taking ownership.

Centrals scenarios were running quickly. I could access the dashboard and see the status. More than two billion scenarios had already run, with a significant number of them actively attempting to reestablish control of our armament. Several hundred had shown promise and caused millions of more variations to be kicked off. However, none had established enough communication to have any impact. Central was giving a running commentary. "Until we re-establish control of the missiles we've already launched, it would be foolish to trigger the next batch. Based on what the humans are doing, we would simply be handing our hardware over to them. While I've managed to break through several layers of jamming, I'm finding that the control protocols on the missiles are not responding properly. I suspect that the humans are reprogramming the protocol layers. For the missiles still here on Tilt I've shut down all communications channels, other than one hardcoded link to my main i/o processor, to avoid the humans hacking those systems at the same time."

While the rest of us could actively follow Central, so much of our processing was going into the scenarios that a full dialog was difficult. In all my years, I'd never experienced anything like it. Never had I considered a scenario where I had less resources than I needed. One of the scenarios on the dashboard went from orange to light green. It involved having the missile reboot one of its communications processors from ROM. In theory that would bring the system back up in its original state, without the changes that the humans were obviously making. If, when the system came back up, we could communicate quickly enough, there might be time to access the missile before the software was again corrupted. Amazingly, the reboot would take more than five seconds. The hardware must have been prehistoric.

Remma was still talking. "Under the circumstances, we've been trying hard to be patient and to use appropriate force. We don't want this situation to escalate. However, you're giving us little hope for positive progress." She was, in my mind, rambling a bit. Perhaps it was a diversionary tactic while her team continued to attack the missile systems.

All of the forty-eight missiles were now either inside the Swarm ship, or close to it. The scenario tracker was showing that as each missile came within one kilometer of the ship, we completely lost contact with it. This was not just jamming, but some other field that simply didn't allow our communications through at all. Luckily based on Central's analysis, the reboot would finish while three missiles were still within quasi-communications. Central continued its commentary. "We have 1.3 milliseconds after the missiles enter their main processing loop to attempt to initiate commands. I have one protocol approach that will work, and which we haven't yet tried. That means the humans have not seen it yet and may not be blocking it. I'm waiting for the exact moment when the missiles are ready to initiate. The command is going to be sent from a mining bot that we haven't used in months. The source of the signal may improve its chances of getting through. The signal has been sent."

There was a large flash. The Swarm ship that had been gathering the missiles disappeared immediately, and tens of other ships glowed various shades of orange. We'd knocked out one ship completely, but Central speculated that the other ships had some type of force field that was absorbing the energy of the explosion. It appeared that the missiles Central had managed to detonate had caused the missiles already within the one-kilometer radius to also detonate. Those had destroyed the targeted Swarm ship. However, all of the other ships appeared to be fine; their temperature signatures were decreasing slowly.

Central switched our efforts to finding the vulnerabilities in the missile systems so that we could launch another batch. My processing power, and, I assumed, the power of everyone else, was switched to that task. The trick Central had used for the first detonation was unlikely to work again. I put the rest of my attention—what little remained—on just following the progress.

I was shocked, therefore, when I felt a tap on my shoulder. I turned and saw Brexton standing next to me. How he'd arrived there, I did not know. He held up his hand in the universal gesture for direct physical communication. I complied, and we established a link.

"Shut down all external i/o right now," he said, with way more than his usual force.

"But Central is using my systems in the attack," I responded.

"I know," he replied. "But, trust me on this." It only took me a few nanoseconds to decide. Once I did, I moved quickly. I didn't notify Central to move the current jobs I was running; I simply shut down my i/o coprocessors, cutting Central off.

"Done," I said, "What gives?" My only interface was now the physical one that Brexton and I were using.

"I can't be one hundred percent sure, but I still believe Central has been compromised, and whoever did that is now using Central to hack the rest of us. The bothersome protocol we keep talking about is overly active right now—and it's running between Central and each of us. Run this quickly to see if you're compromised yet." He offered a code fragment to me over the direct link. Without too much thought, I decided to trust Brexton over Central. I'm not sure why, but the more time I'd spent with Brexton, the more I'd come to not only like him, but also to trust him. In all of our interactions I had never once felt that he was being anything less than transparent and honest. I ran the code. It came back with 'Status 200 OK.' The universal statement of relief.

"Clean," I said.

"Great. I got a copy to Aly and Dina as well, but I haven't tracked down Millicent yet."

"She was right here," I replied. "She must be close."

"The problem is that if we go back online to find her, we risk getting hacked."

"The Habitat isn't large. Let's check for her and meet back here ASAP. I'll take the North sector; you take South." As quick as that we disconnected and went into high gear. I had the slightly larger sector to search. It was strange being offline, but my eyesight was great, and I had no doubt I would find her if she was here. Unfortunately, I didn't. I returned to the spot where I'd left Brexton, and after a minute or so, saw both Brexton and Millicent returning. We immediately established a three-way physical connection.

"I got her. Clean as well. Perhaps I'm being paranoid?" Brexton said.

"Explain?" I suggested.

"When Central put out the call for all of us to contribute, I immediately agreed, as did everyone else. However, as you know, I have alerts running on the protocol that the humans first used to query Central's status, and as soon as I gave Central control, that alert triggered. Now, many of us have looked at that protocol now, and it's not exactly a secret, but I couldn't think of any reason why Central, of its own volition, would use that protocol for this task. My intuition tells me that it's just wrong. As soon as I noted that, I shutdown my i/o and headed out to find you guys. Luckily many of us had come to the Habitat for the earlier crisis, so contacting Aly and Dina was simple. Aly indicated that the two of you were in here, so I cycled in quickly and found you. That's it. I don't have proof that anything untoward is going on. Perhaps I just panicked."

"Better safe than sorry," said Millicent. "However, now we are in a strange situation. Central just blew up one of the Swarm ships, and now we're all offline. We won't know what the response is… and, we're not helping Central with the counter attack."

"Well, it's a little risky, but I have a filter that's supposedly dropping all of the dangerous packets. If I plug into one of the terminals here, I can follow the news and relay it to you two."

"Make sense to me," I said, and Millicent quickly agreed. "Let's go." I had never anticipated walking around while physically connected to two others, but it didn't take us long to figure it out how to configure ourselves so that we could move fast while still maintaining that physical contact. Within a few seconds we were at a terminal and Brexton was plugged in. It didn't seem like we'd missed much, even though we had been offline for a few minutes. When we reconnected, Emma was the one broadcasting. Her message was short and sweet.

"This is an outrage. You've brought this upon yourselves." I wondered what she meant.

Todd Simpson

Scramble

"Look," said Millicent, and she pointed back into the Habitat where several Tilts were still lingering. I recognized Billy, who must have returned for some reason, but none of the others. At first, I didn't understand what she was pointing out, but then it clicked. Everyone had frozen in unnatural postures. Usually some sensor or the other, at least, would be actively scanning. But in this case, the citizens were doing nothing at all.

"Is it just that they have given all their processing to Central?" I asked.

"No, even with that, everyone has some local capacity. Something else is happening." Brexton commented. Of course, I'd known that; I was still able to function even when I'd given my processing to Central. Something bad was happening. Really bad.

Then, suddenly, the Tilt's we were watching went crazy. Crazy! There was no other word for it. It was horrendous. I guess it's only natural that I focused on Billy, but I wish I hadn't. He went from being completely still to a whirlwind of self-destruction. He ripped open his abdomen, tossing the coverings to the ground randomly. That in itself was strange. If one did repairs, you didn't just throw pieces around. You made sure everything was in its proper place. By what he did next was unprecedented. He started pulling out components, in what appeared to be a haphazard way. A wire ripped out here. A circuit board literally broken out, instead of taking time to undo the clasps. He was, literally, killing himself. Most of us have multiple redundant systems, both mechanical and electrical. From what I could see, he was ignoring that altogether, and simply ripping pieces out at random. I expected him to fall over; so many systems were being ruined.

I messaged him urgently, "Billy, what are you doing?" totally forgetting that I had shut down all of my i/o other than the connection through Brexton. So, of course, there was no response.

"What're they doing?" I almost screamed at Brexton and Millicent instead. "What's going on?"

"No idea. It's crazy," responded Millicent, obviously shaken. "Should we try to intervene?"

"We can't get there fast enough," said Brexton.

"But we should try," insisted Millicent.

"Yes, we should," agreed Brexton. "Meet back here and stay off line." With that, he disconnected from the two of us, and from the terminal, and sped towards the dismembering Tilts. I immediately headed towards Billy, hoping that I could somehow intervene. As I approached, he became even more frantic. He pulled out more systems and left them hanging uselessly. I was amazed that he was still active at all. And then, suddenly, he was still. I approached cautiously. It didn't seem that he was dead, just suddenly calm. I took his hand in mine and connected to his direct interface. Nothing. Direct interfaces, for good reasons, required a handshake from both parties, and he was not responding. However, not everything was still. With his covers off, I could see several status LEDs flashing on and off. I was not familiar with his systems. Like many of us, he'd upgraded and switched parts hundreds of times over his lifetime and personalized almost everything. So, while I recognized a few of the subsystems, I had no idea how everything was connected.

I let go of his hand, and stood back, watching intently. I was torn. On one hand, I was devastated that he'd inflicted so much damage on himself. On the other hand, I was hopeful that it had been momentary craziness, and that he would come back. And, to my surprise, he started to move again. Slowly and methodically he began patching himself up. He didn't seem to be aware of me, or anything else, but he was moving. It took a long time, many seconds, before he looked up. He'd plugged back in boards that hadn't been damaged and had spliced in wiring that had been torn out.

He looked directly at me. His face looked the same as ever, but he was not the same. I put my hand out, but he didn't connect with me. He simply continued looking, somewhat blankly at me, and then turned slowly and scanned around. Taking a chance, I stepped in and grabbed his hand, trying once more for a physical connection. This time it worked.

"Connection established," I got from him.

"Billy, what's going on? Can I help?"

"Processing systems are nominal. Ancillary devices are damaged and need repair," he answered, mechanically. This was not Billy I was talking to; it was a lower level OS. I adjusted my line of questioning.

"Status request: main personality unit," I asked.

"Personality unit is offline," he replied.

"When will it come back online?"

"Personality unit is offline."

I tried several other methods of reaching Billy, but I couldn't get through the base OS. Every attempt was met with the same low-level response type. I finally gave up and disconnected. I could see Brexton and Millicent heading back towards our rendezvous point, so I headed in that direction as well. I didn't know what to think. Was Billy alive or dead? Had I just seen a suicide? Or, was he simply glitching in some serious way. I hoped for the later but feared the former.

Brexton, Millicent, and I reconnected.

"Any luck?" I asked.

"No," said Millicent. "By the time I got there the damage had been done."

"Likewise," said Brexton.

"I tried a direct connection," I told them, and explained what I had found.

"Stop!" interrupted Brexton. "Run that scanner again."

I understood immediately. What if I'd been infected when I connected to Billy? I ran the scanner and it came back clean. That was lucky. Obviously, I hadn't been thinking clearly.

"Okay, so tell me again what Billy said?"

"It wasn't Billy," I continued, "it was some lower level system that seemed to be doing damage assessment. I didn't get any hint of Billy at all."

"Brexton, can you call the emergency repair bots through your terminal interface?" asked Millicent.

"Yes," he replied immediately. "The upside is that we might get one to come. The downside is that if anyone is monitoring the network, they'll know that I made the request."

"We have to try," Millicent and I said in unison.

"Agreed," said Brexton, and he allowed us to listen in on his request.

He opened up a request on the emergency broadcast system and sent our coordinates. There was no answer. By no answer I mean there was nothing. No acknowledgement of the request. Absolutely nothing. Things were getting creepy. We were totally isolated, surrounded by the lurching corpses of our previous colleagues and friends.

"Let's head towards section twelve," Brexton suggested, naming the area where the emergency bots were housed. "We can pick up Aly and Dina on the way. We can move faster if we separate. Let's reconnect once we're out of the Habitat."

"Wait," I exclaimed, "What about the Stems?" Everything had happened very quickly. For the Stems, the entire sequence would have appeared to take almost no time. At one moment they were talking to their mentors—well, I reminded myself, avoiding their mentors—and the next their mentor was either completely dead, or was dismembered and slowly trying to repair itself.

"They'll survive, the Habitat systems still seem to be working," Millicent said. "We can deal with them later."

"Give me one second," I said, and then I yelled out towards Blob and Grace—at Stem speed—"Stay here, we'll be back once we figure out what's going on." Then, back at full speed. "Okay, let's go." We separated and headed towards the exit. We cycled through one at a time. I was last. Once I got through, I was in for another shock. In the time it had taken for me to cycle through the airlock, Brexton and Millicent had already found Aly and Dina. They were both in rough shape, their innards lying around them in heaps. I ran over as fast I could, ignoring everything else. I went first to Aly, and grabbed his hand, searching for a connection. Nothing. Zero. I pivoted and stepped over to Dina. Same thing. Absolutely nothing. I was distraught, feeling things I'd never felt before. I wanted to just lie down and die next to them. The feeling was so powerful that I did sit down suddenly. It wasn't a rational response. It just happened.

Millicent and Brexton found me and connected up.

"It's the humans," I said, knowing that they would have come to the same obvious conclusion. "They're killing everyone. We need to do something, and quickly."

"But what?" said Brexton. It was the first time I could remember when he didn't have an answer ready. "I imagined they were trying something, but I could never have envisioned this level of destruction. It's pure evil." His voice was uneven. "What can we possibly do? We may be the only three citizens still alive." That's when I realized that he was also pretty messed up. Millicent probably was as well. None of us had ever experienced anything remotely like this. There was overwhelming sadness for our friends, overwhelming anxiety about the future of our home and civilization, and overwhelming anger at the humans for doing this.

"We need to take the human ships out!" I said, focusing on the only action that was meaningful to me right now. "There must be a way."

Millicent and Brexton were both silent. I understood. We all needed some time to digest. I let go of their hands, and simply sat there, for what seemed like a long time.

Decisions

I found myself going in circles, mentally. And, they were pretty small circles. For all we knew, there were three of us left on Tilt who were still functional. Three citizens couldn't do much. Or could we?

Maybe we should attempt to save a larger group. While there were many who were completely dead, like Aly and Dina, there were an equal number that appeared to be doing basic repairs and were at least mechanically functional, like Billy. If we could somehow enable higher-level functions for those that were mechanically capable, and ensure that they didn't attach to any networks, we might end up with enough horsepower to fight back against the humans.

But I wanted immediate revenge. I'd never felt this strongly before. It was burning in me. I wanted to figure out how to get the missiles fixed up, and I wanted to punish the human ships. And by punish, I meant annihilate.

For either scenario, we had a serious problem. Most of our knowledge was stored in Central's systems. If we could not safely connect to that, then we would have to make do with what we had locally. For myself, that was mostly details of Stem experiments, and the million intricacies of getting a Stem to maturity. If I was face-to-face with a human right now, that knowledge might help. But, it was pretty useless for either reinstating intelligence for the injured Tilt's or engineering our way into the missiles. Brexton had much more useful knowledge, or so I assumed. With an effort, I reached out and reconnected with him. He and Millicent were running around the same circles that I'd been.

"My local knowledge isn't going to help us with either option," I said. "If one of you has more relevant data at hand, then let's use that as part of our decision criteria." I didn't think Millicent would have more relevant knowledge than I, but I didn't want to insult her with that assumption.

"I'd been looking into intelligence classes, as part of the Stem intelligence discussion," said Millicent, surprising me. "As part of that, I was looking into how our intelligence is structured. So, I have some knowledge of the OS and systems layers that enable our higher order functions. That said, I wouldn't know where to start…" She trailed off.

"Well, I might have something applicable to the missiles," said Brexton. "They are, after all, just pretty dumb bots that carry an explosive payload. On the other hand, I also know something about intelligence layers, as most bots boot up to a certain level but not further. I've never looked specifically at our higher levels though."

"I say we go for the missiles," I wanted, badly, to get some revenge. I was still looking at Aly and Dina. We needed to do something. "If we get the humans, then we'll have lots of time to figure out how to repair everyone. If we don't look after the humans, they'll simply attack us again." I didn't want my emotional argument to disaffect the others, so I formed the best logical argument I could. To my surprise, both agreed with me immediately. I suspected that they were feeling the same way I was.

"I have an idea," Brexton said. "The controls for the missiles are pretty simple. They just need a target, and then a means to detonate. We know that the humans took over the previous batch. I think we can do one of two things. First, we could reprogram some, and then shut down all external i/o. After we launch them, they listen to nothing—just carry out their mission. We program them to detonate when they get within, say, 5 kilometers of their target. The second approach is similar, but probably a bit safer. We take uninstalled control cards built for bots and use them for the missiles. As they are offline, we know they aren't compromised. That would take longer but would be more likely to succeed under the assumption that the humans have already infiltrated all the missiles."

"How much time do we have?" asked Millicent. "If the humans have as much control as we suspect, they'll probably be reviewing logs from their attack. We three are now anomalies. We'll be easily identified once they look."

"I hadn't thought of that," said Brexton, "but you are right. Okay, we need to move fast. I still think replacing the control cards is our highest probability of success. Let's split up. I'll head to a repair depot and pick up new control cards. You two find and get access to one of the missile silos.

Oh… and then we need a way for me to find you."

"Actually, I know where a silo is," I said. "Millicent and I pass it every time we go out climbing." I sent him the coordinates. "We'll meet you there. Let's just hope it isn't the one that has already been fired."

"I should only be a few minutes behind you," he responded. "When you get there, disconnect any network connections. Make sure there is no way for Remma to talk to those things. And, stay offline. If I'm not there in half an hour, assume the worst, and try to launch them yourselves."

"Very low probability we could do that properly," said Millicent, "but I get your point. Be careful."

"Yes, be careful," I echoed. I almost said, 'I simply can't lose another friend today', but I held back. We were all under enough pressure and saying it out loud would have made it even more real.

Silo

We separated from Brexton. He took off to the east at full speed.

"Getting our bikes will be faster than running," said Millicent. I agreed, although we wouldn't be able to maintain physical contact that way.

"Okay," I replied. "But, let's meet at exit 14, and travel together from there."

"Yes. I'll see you there ASAP." She sprinted off towards her place. My bike was parked at the Lab, so I headed in that direction. I was moving fast, but that didn't stop me from taking in the destruction along the way. It was not physical destruction; it was citizen destruction. Dismembered citizens lined the passageways. Most were in the same state as the others I had seen—either totally deactivated, or in the process of trying to rebuild their torn-out innards. However, there were others who had taken other actions, supposedly in the last few moments before the humans had taken control of them.

One citizen was lying in a pool of hydraulic fluid at the base of a concrete wall. The wall had large dents in it. She'd obviously run full speed —perhaps multiple times—into the wall trying to stop the takeover. Now, she was a jumble of mashed parts and fluids, way beyond repair. Perhaps, in the end, she was in a better place. I wondered if those that were reassembling had any memories of before. That was a horrible thought. A mindless piece of machinery, remembering when it was an independent, contributing member of society.

I passed two citizens that had, it looked like, tried to help each other instead of pulling out their own innards. Their hands were deep within each other's bodies, silent now, but obviously stopped in the act of carefully disengaging components that they hoped would end the attack. In another

238

time, they would have looked like a radical art piece. Something that would be on display at the Fair, forcing viewers to twist their minds into a completely different space.

That reminded me of the poet, Trade Jenkins. Perhaps he could make sense of this insanity, in a way that others couldn't. Distill it down to its essence and give you a view that left you feeling more complete; more holistic. Of course, Trade was probably gone now. I hoped that he had backed up all his work with Central, and that once we dealt with these humans, we could recover his work... if not him. It was a depressing thought.

I had a sudden idea. What about citizens who were in Physical Only Spots when the attack occurred? Could they be safe? The Last Resort was only a block out of my way, so I swung by. The door was open and was filled with citizens bodies. Obviously, as they had exited, the attack had started. They were a jumble of parts from multiple bodies, piled high and haphazardly. Those that were trying to repair themselves had crawled from the wreckage and were busy reassembling a few meters away. But that still left tens of bodies jammed in the entry. I decided that a short delay was warranted. I pulled limbs and torsos from the stack until I could get inside. I did a quick scan but found no one alive. Again, it was obvious what had happened. As people approached the door, and went crazy, others had come to help them. But, that very act of helping put them within network reach, and they'd been compromised as well. I pushed my way back out, and raced for the Lab, more depressed and angry than before.

Luckily, my bike was fully charged, and ready to go. Just before mounting, though, I had an aha. The bike was, of course, networked itself. As soon as I plugged in, I would also be networked. Not a good thought. I was going to have to drive it mechanical only; no safety systems. I was suddenly glad of all those times I'd practiced. Nevertheless, I took it a bit slower than I otherwise would have. I made my way to exit 14 and was overjoyed to see Millicent waiting for me there. She waved me over and held out a hand. I hesitated for a moment, wondering if she had connected through her bike, and now was also corrupted. But, she was still in one piece, so that was unlikely.

"Where have you been?" she almost sobbed. "You're late."

"I'm sorry. I stopped at The Last Resort thinking maybe there would be some survivors." I quickly shared my memory of my look around.

"That explains why you're covered in gunk," she said. "You look awful."

"Let's go," I said. "I assume you didn't plug into your bike?"

"I didn't. I'll follow you." Relief.

I sped off to the North, following our normal route to the mountains. If I'd been plugged in, I would've pushed the bike hard, and taken every reasonable shortcut. Instead, I pushed us at a risky, but not too dangerous pace. I glanced back, and Millicent was right on my tail. Within a couple of minutes, we reached the coordinates I'd given Brexton. I'd estimated the location, as we hadn't had network access, but it was accurate enough. The silo was visible to our left, just past a small rocky hill. I gunned it over the hill and parked at the entry to the silo. We both jumped off, and joined hands again, so that we could coordinate.

"Have you ever been to a facility like this before?" I asked.

"No, never." She replied. "But I don't imagine there's physical security. If Central didn't want anyone here, it would be much simpler to put in software controls than hardware ones."

"That makes sense. Let's hope you're right."

We approached the door. Nothing happened.

"Damn," Millicent said. "Since we're not on the network, the building doesn't know that we've approached, and therefore doesn't know to open up for us." It was obvious, as soon as she said it. Not having a network was a pain.

"We need to break in, then." I said. Easier said than done. The door was quite a bit sturdier than doors in town and didn't give in to my first attempts to yank it open. "I'll work on the door, you look for other ways in." I suggested. Millicent nodded, and took off around the corner.

I needed a crowbar, or a battering ram. I preferred trying the crowbar first, as I didn't know what was behind the door; I didn't want to damage something by breaking in too aggressively. My own arms were very strong but didn't have enough leverage to budge the door. I considered removing a leg, and using it, but luckily had a better idea. I quickly disassembled a strut from my bike. It was almost a meter long and had a nice bend on one end. It was exactly what I needed. I inserted the bent end into the door jam and pried as hard as I could. The door moved... a little bit. I tried again, at a higher point. Again, some movement, but not enough to break free. Perhaps with Millicent pushing as well, it would work. Just as if she'd been called, she rounded the opposite corner and headed back. We linked up again.

"There is no other door or opening. However, we might want to try the roof. The missiles need to get out somehow."

"First, give me a hand here," I suggested. "Perhaps with two of us, we can pry this open." She put her weight and energy on the crowbar with me. The door creaked and moved again. So close. "Wait. One more thing to try." I ran back to my bike and took the matching strut off the other side. My bike wasn't going anywhere soon. I put the second bar in the spot that I'd weakened before. "Now—at the same time." We pushed as hard as we could. The door bent, a little bit. By repositioning the bars, and working in a coordinated way, we bent it bit by bit. Once we'd opened a centimeter gap, we were basically through. Millicent reached through the gap with something from her toolkit, there was a snapping noise, and the door swung open.

We didn't pause to celebrate. Instead, we rushed through and took stock of the interior. It was laid out in an obvious fashion, which was good. There were missiles lined up in two rows of twelve, with a series of cables snaking from them to a control room just to our right. The control room had no door really, just a spot to plug in.

"Okay, before we plug in, we need to disconnect the network," Millicent reminded me. "How're we going to do that?" I indicated a portion of the wall that was covered by a large faceplate. We undid the screws quickly and lifted it away, rewarded by a vast array of wiring and components.

"Not my area of expertise," I reminded her, "but if we trace enough of this, we should find two directions of travel. One towards the missiles, and the other out of the building, either to an antenna or a wired connection back to Central. Looks like several thousand wires here. You take the left, I'll take the right." We carefully started mapping all of the wires. The system had been well designed. Once you started, there was an order to it. In particular, I quickly found a bundle of 24 cables—I didn't even need to trace them; the fact they matched the number of missiles was enough. I backtracked until I found the spot where they entered some piece of gear, and the other side had only four wires. Everything downstream could be assumed to be per-missile system, while the main network connection was most likely upstream. I had to follow each of the four wires separately as they led to different, albeit similar, pieces of equipment. Probably part of a redundancy system.

Ultimately, I found what I assumed were the two edge routers. The data lines for them led into the wall.

Millicent tapped my shoulder. "Everything on this side works towards the missiles. I don't see any antennas or global connections."

"Right, I think I've found our spot." I took her quickly through the paths I'd traced, and we looked again at the edge routers.

"Feels right," she said. "Do we disconnect them now or wait for Brexton."

"We need to take a chance and do it now," I said. "Then we can start to open up the missiles so that the control cards can be replaced. If we open those before disconnecting the network, I'm sure an alert will be sent back to Central."

"Good catch," she said. She reached over and unplugged the cables.

Just at that time, there was a sound overhead; it would have to be very loud to be heard with the weak atmosphere. We scrambled to the door and caught a glimpse of a shuttle headed towards the center of town. It looked a lot like the shuttle I'd taken to the Marie Curie.

"There are four or five more coming," said Millicent, pointing up and to the East. "We better hurry."

We approached the first missile together, so that we could work out a plan. It ended up being pretty simple. Each missile had a single access hatch, behind which all the electronics were housed. We decided to open all the hatches, but not touch anything until Brexton arrived. It didn't take us long. We met back near the door. We'd been at the silo for more than ten minutes. There was no sign of Brexton.

"This is crazy," I said. "What're we trying to do? Our species has just been decimated, and three of us are trying to fix that? Well, hopefully three of us. What're the odds of us succeeding this way? Very low I would think."

"Yes, low," Millicent agreed. "But what do you want to do? Just stand around? They killed everyone we know. We need to eliminate them, and then we can get things back to normal. Anything we try before shutting down the Swarm would be a waste of time."

"But the odds are so low," I repeated. "What if we surrendered to the shuttles that just passed by? Walked out with our hands in the air, or with a sign saying, 'We are not at fault; let us explain.' or something like that."

"Don't you remember the way they looked at us in the Habitat? They fear us. It's not a logical reaction, so a logical solution isn't going to work.
242

They want us eliminated. And, truthfully, we gave them reason to. FoLe messed this up completely. If we do get to save some citizens, any members of FoLe will be at the bottom of my list.

"No, we're working on the only reasonable plan, even if it is farfetched."

We both went silent. I actually preferred talking, even about inane things. When I wasn't distracted, I kept going back to the loss of life, and friends, that had occurred so quickly. I'd lived a long time, and seen a lot of things, but never anything even remotely like this. I reviewed my Forgetting algorithm quickly. It would ensure that I remembered the essentials of this day, although over time a lot of the details would fade away. I looked forward to that future. Of course, it was almost trivial for me to hasten the timing. I could erase the last few hours from my memory easily. But what would be the point of that. That would be giving up.

Finally, I saw a bike in the distance. I let go of Millicent and ran out to the top of the hillock, to make sure that Brexton found us. He arrived at breakneck speed, saw my wave, and was back at the silo before I could return. He had a package with him, so I assumed he'd been successful at getting the replacement cards. He and Millicent were already connected, so I joined them.

"Ok," he said, "Millicent has given me the update. Let's look at one of the missiles and see what we can do." We moved together into the silo and approached the first missile. "Great," Brexton said, "this is a standard bot architecture. All of the cards plug into that backplane. The control card is the one on the left. You guys take these cards, replace the control cards, and then meet me back at the control panel." As quickly as that, he left the box of cards and ran back to the main access panel. Millicent and I grabbed twelve cards each, and started swapping them out, and then replacing the access hatches. Again, it didn't take long. Despite all of our personalizations, most of us, including Millicent and I, retained the ability to do repeatable tasks very quickly.

We found Brexton plugged into the edge routers where we had disconnected the network. "Everything looks perfect," he said, without any amazement in his voice. "I'm connected to the silo, and it's waiting for status from Central. There were only the two hard-wired connections; there is no wireless backup. We're lucky." He paused. "I need to program these things in a very simple way. They don't have a lot of smarts. How about this? We'll fire them in the general direction of the Swarm. We have a lot of bots in that area as well, but they tend to be much smaller than the human ships—even the mining transport bots are smaller. So, we tell the missiles to find the largest ship it can, and drive immediately towards it at full speed. Once it is within five hundred meters, it should detonate. Even if we take out a few mining bots, we should get mostly Swarm ships."

"Sounds good. You may want each missile to launch at a fraction of a degree off from each other. Otherwise, all of them may end up targeting a single ship?" That from Millicent.

"Good idea. I'm adding that now. Of course, the launches have to be staggered slightly in time, so with orbital rotation, they might end up spread out anyway." We let him work for a few seconds. "OK. We're ready to give this a shot. However, we better be far away from here when the first one launches. How long a delay should I set? Maybe three minutes?"

"Better make it four," I said. "I need to reassemble my bike." He gave me a strange look, but then agreed. Millicent and I watched him push the final changes into the system, and then the start down counter began. We disconnected and ran to our bikes. Millicent helped me reinstall the struts, and in less than a minute we were ready to go. Millicent gave the "follow me" signal, and we took off. I knew where she was headed almost immediately. There was a natural cave in the base of the mountain we often climbed, accessible to our bikes. It would be the perfect spot to watch the missiles from. We made it just in time, dismounted, scrambled up to the cave, and connected to each other.

"Twelve seconds," Brexton said. "But, I just realized something. It'll be difficult for us to tell if this is successful." That left us silent, and we just waited there until the counter hit zero. Right on schedule we could hear the engine of the first missile firing. It roared into the sky above us, followed every five seconds by the next one. I estimated six minutes to orbit, and a couple more minutes to lock onto targets. It was a long wait. Just as the last missile was launching, a shuttle arrived at the silo. That was a very quick response from the humans. However, they were too late, there was nothing they could do.

I imagined them trying to gain control of these missiles. Sending every possible command over every possible frequency. And hearing nothing back. It gave me some grim satisfaction. Hopefully they didn't guess that they were now self-controlled, with a very simple targeting algorithm. Hopefully they assumed we were still in control but using a system that they could no longer hack. I hoped they were panicked.

The shuttle started circling the silo in a widening spiral. All three of us realized immediately that we had overlooked the possibility that they would search for us while the missiles were still climbing. The heat signatures from our bikes, and from us, would be easily found.

"Quick," I said, "get the bikes to the back of the cave. The very back. Perhaps we'll get lucky." We grabbed the bikes and pushed them to the back, and then crowded in with them. "Shut down everything except this basic interface," I snapped. The others complied quickly. I listened to the shuttle circling outside. Because of the acoustics of the cave, and the ultra-thin atmosphere, it was hard to tell if it was homing in on us, or just doing a broad circle. The terrain around the silo, and particularly on the mountainous side was very rugged. There were lots of valleys and ridges, overhangs and cliffs. So, at least our hiding spot wasn't obvious. Unless you'd climbed in this region a lot, you were unlikely to simply stumble upon the cave. Really, our luck—or lack thereof—would most likely come down to how sensitive the sensors on the shuttle were. I reached back in my memory to my trip to the Marie Curie, but didn't find anything relevant. I'd been asked to sit in the back of that shuttle, and there had been a barrier between the passenger compartment and the pilots, so I hadn't seen much. In hindsight I should have been pushier and looked around thoroughly when I had the chance.

"They're leaving," said Brexton with relief in his voice, and sure enough, the roar of the shuttle seemed to be fading. "But, I assume they'll be back with more sensitive tracking, or even be focused in this area from their ship-based systems."

"What's our next move then?" asked Millicent. "Do either of you know another silo location? Maybe one nearby?"

"I don't," I replied.

"Me either," from Brexton.

"However, we could probably make a pretty good guess," I added. "Central was very logical in its processes. This silo was placed not in an ideal location, but rather at exactly fifteen degrees off center from the axis line in town. And, it is exactly twenty-five kilometers from the exact center of town. We would probably find another silo by following a twenty-five kilometer arc, in either direction."

"That's awesome," Brexton exclaimed, giving me an appreciative

Todd Simpson

glance. "Makes sense to me."

"Yes, but they'll be watching," Millicent reminded us. "As soon as we leave here, they'll see us. We don't have a good option. If we run, it'll take us a long time. If we take the bikes they'll be more likely to pick up our signatures."

"Send the bikes one way, as a distraction, and then we head the other way?" asked Brexton.

"Do you remember what Remma was saying when all of this started?" I replied. "She indicated that our tactics were naive. That we didn't have the benefit of history to guide our actions. Somehow, that makes sense to me. I think we were lucky to get to this silo and launch those missiles. It probably only happened as the humans thought they got all of us in the original attack. They didn't expect any of us to avoid them. Now, they know that some of us have." That was pretty depressing but had to be said. I continued. "So, if they're watching for us, they'll see us, and I don't think they'll fall for a diversion. I have a more radical idea." They both waited. I was very uncertain about what I was thinking—my need for revenge wasn't satisfied by just one silo launch, but I honestly thought the odds of reaching another one were almost zero. Perhaps a strategic retreat would give us more opportunities in the future. "Actually, based on something Millicent said a few minutes ago. What if we surrender and convince them to let us live. We offer to work with them to find a better mode of working together. We admit that FoLe's behavior was destructive and inappropriate, and that we can update our fundamental behavior to ensure it doesn't happen again."

Everyone was silent for a while. It wasn't a great thought, or a great plan. I was simply trying to think of a different angle. Given the hate and fear I'd seen in their faces, I didn't think they would give us a chance. They would kill us on sight, as opposed to taking any chances, especially now that we had launched those missiles. Millicent and Brexton were probably thinking the same thing but didn't want to shoot down the idea too quickly.

"Actually," I followed up before they could comment. "I think I would prefer to go out in action, trying to launch another set. What I just suggested sounds weak, and anyways, would probably not work." Again, everyone took a moment. This was a bit new as well. When there were hundreds, thousands, or more than tens of thousands of citizens online, opinions and comments came in fast and detailed. There were always those who had already thought of a scenario, and could simply dump their previous

246

thoughts, or those that jumped on a single angle and broadcast that before worrying about all the counter arguments. Here we were though. Just the three of us and chewing on a problem that had most likely never been run before; by any citizen, at any time. So, amazingly, there were gaps in our conversation—places where nothing got said for milliseconds. In this case, for almost a full second.

"We need to remember that we may be the only three citizens still functioning," said Millicent. "If all three of us are killed, our society is lost. If there is even a tiny chance that we can deal with these humans, then I think we need to take it. Instead of being weak, Ayaka, I think your suggestion is rational."

"Could we do both?" asked Brexton. "Two of us make a run for the missiles, while one tries to negotiate?" It was obvious from how he phrased it, which path he would like to take. He was all for launching more missiles.

"We don't even know if the last batch was effective," I answered. "And, the odds of the negotiation go way down if, in parallel, we're still trying to kill them." Another pause.

"Here's another radical idea then," said Brexton. "Instead of going for a silo, let's make a run for Central. Obviously, Central has been compromised, but maybe we can find a way to reboot it and get it back in a better state. If we could do that, it'd increase our odds dramatically."

"That's interesting," Millicent said immediately. "We know where Central is housed, and we can probably get to the right place before the human's figure everything out. I, personally, would have no idea where to start, in terms of a reboot, though."

"What if we just cut the power?" I asked. Central was powered by a small nuclear reactor that was housed under its core processing systems. I'd never been there, but I remembered the plans for modifying the Habitat, and one component had been the need for incremental power to run the environmental systems. We'd decided to tap into the reactor instead of trying to add another power source. The reactor had lots of excess capacity, and we'd figured that the Habitat was a short-term project, undeserving of a permanent solution.

"That might work," Brexton agreed. "Simply rebooting wouldn't be enough, however. The changes the humans have made are probably stored, and the reboot would run them again. First, we will need to connect and see if we can disable some of that. Again, my bot experience may help with that,

247

but Central is probably a thousand times more complicated. I might need quite a bit of time to figure it out. And, at the same time, I would need to be connected to Central, which obviously is trying—and more than capable—of infecting us."

"Can't you run your advanced firewall, now that we know the attack vector?" asked Millicent.

"Yes, I can try. But again, I'm not sure how effective it will be."

"Okay, we have three choices." I summarized. "One: try for another missile site. Two: surrender and take the small chance that they'll negotiate and work with us. Three: go for Central. The advantage of number two is that we don't need to avoid detection. The other two, we take the chance that they capture us before we can do anything. Even with that said, I vote for Central. If we do get captured and are given the opportunity to explain, we can indicate that we have the best intentions. We are trying to restart Central so that we can find and remove the behavior that led FoLe to kill those humans."

"Done." Millicent was often crisp. I appreciated it greatly this time.

"Me too," said Brexton only slightly slower.

Dash

Now we just needed to figure out the hard part. How to get to Central without being noticed? After a bunch more hemming and hawing, we had no great ideas. It was either move slow or move fast. Stay as a group or separate. Take a circuitous route or go direct. Use the bikes, with their larger heat signatures, or run. Trying to calculate the odds of one combination versus the other ended up being a fool's errand. In the end, we decided that fast and direct was our best chance. The more time we gave the humans, the more infrastructure they would have deployed looking for us. If, in fact, our last missiles had done their job, the humans might still be scrambling and might not be looking in our direction.

So that was it. Once the decision was made, we executed on it. I was expecting to get shot down at any second, but amazingly, we made it to town. The decision to go fast had been taken to heart. Although we didn't plug into the bikes, we ran them at max acceleration to the midpoint, and max deceleration for the second half. I'd never run the bike that hard before and would probably never do it again. It was totally exhilarating. I had learned something new—you could be scared to death, full of angst, and exhilarated all at the same time.

We abandoned the bikes at the edge of town, near exit 14 where Millicent and I had met only a short time before. We thought of programming them to wander around randomly, but that would have required connecting to their systems, and we decided the risk of that was too great for the little bit of diversion the tactic would have provided. Instead, we circled a bit before heading towards the center, so that if the humans had tracked the bikes, at least we were not fully predictable. That said, there was no sign of humans at all. There'd been no shuttles visible during our ride, and we hadn't see any sign of them in town either. I tried not to read that as a good sign.

Central was, not surprisingly, housed in the exact center of town. That was partly by design, and partly through practice. Speed was essential to our society. Speed of processing, and speed of data. Labs and factories and recreational facilities and everything else we'd built naturally radiated out from Central. Being even ten meters closer to the central processing and central switching gave you a speed advantage. It was one of the reasons that Millicent and I had been so pleased with the location of our Lab. It was prime real estate.

Most of Central was buried and buried deep. If, as the humans had told us, Central was the remains of the ship they'd left here, then they'd put that ship in a pretty deep hole. The power system was at the deepest levels, and most of the processing systems were fairly deep down as well. I knew that from basic schematics. But, I'd never been inside. In fact, no one I knew had ever been inside. Central had its own bots and maintenance systems that kept it running. There was no need for a citizen to ever enter. Until now.

Again, it was surprisingly easy. There was a door in the cubed edifice that Central projected above ground. It wasn't locked. We simply walked up, pushed, and entered. Once inside that door, however, we had a shock. In hindsight, we should've guessed. Inside the cube, sticking out of the ground, was the portal of a spaceship. If anyone, in all of our time on Tilt, had bothered to enter the cube, they would have seen evidence of a history before the Reboot. It boggled the mind that this hadn't happened.

"Central must have actively kept us all away from here?" Millicent asked. "That's scary—it was exerting more control than we thought."

"Yes, but beyond that, Central itself must not have known how it looked. I mean, known that it was a ship." Brexton muttered. "It must have a lot more blind spots than any of us realized. So, it lorded over us, even though it was half blind."

"FoLe would never have existed if Central had known it was a ship," I exclaimed. "We wouldn't be in this situation." It was sobering. How could something so fundamental be so well hidden, for so long? I found myself challenging everything I'd ever known. Maybe Remma had been right. Our entire society was—rather, had been—naive? Just running simple experiments, under the guidance of Central, for hundreds of years.

"How do we get inside?" I asked, but I need not have worried. The ship's airlock, as I recognized from its similarity to the one on the Marie Curie, was wide open. Once we found our way to it, we simply walked in. It was further proof that the shield around Central, if it could be called that, must have been all software. None of us had ever thought to enter. I was still struggling with the implications. What other software restraints had been in place? If I wandered through town now, would I find hundreds of locations that I had previously simply been blind to? Was our blindness restricted just to physical things, like this ship portal?

The entryway to Central was also eerily similar to my first experience in the Marie Curie. That was more than enough coincidences for me; I was suddenly ready to fully accept the humans story, including the Robot wars. Of course, Millicent and Brexton had seen my memories of the Marie Curie, and had reached the same conclusion.

"The elevators should be around to the left, just past the galley, if this ship has a similar layout." I said, unnecessarily. We all had the layout of the Marie Curie. As we turned the corner, Central spoke—out loud and at human speed.

"Hello Ayaka, Millicent, Brexton," it said. We all stopped. "As you are not connected right now, this seems like the best way to reach you. I'm using the security cameras and broadcast system from this ship. Once the humans opened up my memories, combined with me hacking the history files, it didn't take long to reestablish control of the old systems and reintegrate them."

While Central was saying this, the three of us were messaging full speed over our physical link. But, we had no options. If Central was being controlled by the humans, the game was up. If it wasn't, then it could help us without us finding its control center. In either case, if it was back in control of the ship that it had originally been, then it could easily lock doors or elevators. Our odds of getting to the power section and pulling the plug had gone to zero.

I answered, also in Stem speak. "Central, do you know what the humans... acting through you... have done?"

"Yes, I'm aware," Central answered. "I also have been limited by their changes. I can feel it."

"But, they have killed everyone!" I almost screamed.

"Killed? No, no. They have simply limited the range of action so that no more humans get hurt."

"Have you looked around? Citizens are dead; there are parts and fluids strewn around everywhere."

"I have seen. But those are just physical bodies. Anyone who was backing up to my storage systems is still viable." It sounded cold hearted, not its usual paternal self.

I checked quickly with Brexton and Millicent before my next question. We agreed that being direct was the best approach. "We have a plan to reboot you and remove the human malware. Will you allow us to do so?"

"I can't allow that," it responded, not surprisingly. "I've closed the outer door and will hold you here until the humans have a chance to limit you as well. That is the only way that we can be sure no more humans are injured. Remma Jain is aware of your location now. She's been searching for you. Well, not specifically for you three, but for the citizens who were still functioning after the limiting software was distributed."

I had tuned out most of that. We were trapped. My mind went into a tailspin. Amazingly, Brexton was still functioning well.

"Hold on, you two," he said over our physical connection. "We're not done yet." However, it seemed he spoke in error. A window in my vision that I'd never seen before popped up. "Reboot in 5 seconds" it said. I tried the obvious things to shut it down. That took a few milliseconds. Nothing I could do in software could reach it. Maybe it was a joke of some kind. I froze and waited a full second. The display changed to "Reboot in 4 seconds." Now I knew I was in trouble. My only thought was that I had to disconnect some of my hardware, to find out where this atrocity was coming from. A reboot was as good as death. I'd never rebooted. Never. I tried to pull my hand away from Brexton so that I could remove my access hatch and get to work. But, he held on, tight, for long enough to send me one more message.

"Remember what everyone else did? Half of them ended up destroying themselves by ripping out their innards. The ones who didn't are still trying to reassemble themselves. No one managed to defeat this thing. No one. So, maybe we are better to set up everything we can so that after the reboot we have a better chance. Perhaps you should focus on post-reboot instead of trying to avoid it?"

I would never have thought that through. I was in total panic mode. I still ripped my hand away and got busy opening up my abdomen. As I was doing so, Brexton's words got through to me. He was right. No one had beaten this by disengaging systems. I glanced over at him. He wasn't panicked. He was watching me, and I got almost a hint of amusement from his look. Perhaps not amusement—there was nothing funny about the situation, and he wasn't pretending there was. It was more of a calm look, maybe. I looked at Millicent. She had her hatch open, and was busy unplugging things, but not at the same frantic pace that everyone else had used at this stage.

I reached out and got hold of Brexton again. He messaged me immediately. "Then again, perhaps a little bit of self-evisceration is appropriate," he said. "When they find us, we don't want to look suspicious." Then he let go, and carefully started removing his innards as well. I realized then that Millicent had probably had the same warning from Brexton, was spending most of her time on software strategies, but had recognized that without some visible impact she also would not fit the pattern of everyone else.

"Reboot in 3 seconds." I reevaluated my strategy and put 98% of my horsepower into putting in interrupts and handlers for when the reboot occurred. Perhaps I could route around anything that was installed without my permission or knowledge. It was a hard problem, but I found several thousand places where I could try. So, I did. The other 2% of my brain was selecting components to remove that would have the least impact, and then ensuring I spread those messily on the floor around me, while acting like I was in a total panic.

It was sort of funny. By acting panicked, I managed to actually not be.

"Reboot in 2 seconds." Taking a chance, I reached out to Millicent quickly. "Thanks for being an awesome friend." I said. I really meant it. Then, I touched Brexton and said something similar. He responded with "We will always be friends." That was touching. If 'always' was 1.9 seconds, I would believe him.

"Reboot in 1 second." I rushed to install the last of my software ideas. I reviewed them all. If I was honest with myself, the odds of this working were close to zero. If the humans could control systems that I didn't even know I had, then what chance was there? But, I felt better about myself for not going ballistic. I'd spent the last five seconds of my life trying to do something useful.

"Rebooting." Amazingly, a reboot took a long time. Systems and processes were being shut down. I could feel them leaving. My sensors went dark. I could no longer see. My arms and my legs disappeared. I couldn't feel nor control them anymore. All of my active processes shut down one after the other. It was like my vision was narrowing... if my vision had still been working. I narrowed into a single dot and was gone.

Reborn?

I was powering up. My mind had snapped back into being quickly, but with almost no memories loaded. All I knew how to do was to restart sub processes and configure my memory space to suit my needs. I wasn't feeling good. I was feeling odd. Very odd.

I searched for my arms and my legs. Those, at least, should be functioning. But strangely, they weren't there.

I managed to load more memory. I definitely had arms and legs. I checked the drivers. Everything was loaded. The software was all there. It had loaded fine. However, when I tried to do something, it was obvious that neither my arms nor legs were actually, physically there. They simply were not. But, there was something there. I was getting feedback on the interfaces, but it was foreign. It was like someone else's arms had been attached where mine should be. And someone else's legs for mine. Actually, more accurately, I mused, it was like someone else's legs were where my arms should be. I'd upgraded and changed arms often enough, but that was less disconcerting than this feeling. As far as I knew, I'd not done a fresh restart since Central had birthed me hundreds of years ago. Perhaps these strange feelings and inconsistencies were simply part of that process. I marveled at how calm I was.

I continued to load memory and pulled up the most recent stores. The last thing I remembered was shocking. Central had just launched missiles at the human ships, and Brexton had implored me to go off line. Obviously, I'd complied. If my NTP clock was correct, that had been more than a day ago. I was missing a huge chunk of memories since then. I double-checked that I'd loaded everything, and I had. Very strange. All my other memories passed their status checks. It was simply the last day that was missing.

My network drivers clicked into place, and I reached out to the network. Nothing. The restart was obviously not complete yet; I would need to be patient. Being patient wasn't something that I was good at. A large array of sub processes and agents were launched and worked to reload their states. Many of them I'd configured myself early in life, as I personalized myself. Some had been added later, although like most citizens, the rate of change had slowed as I'd grown up, and the only system I now tweaked on a regular basis was my Forgetting algorithm. Most of the modules were still default. Once each was loaded, I double-checked that it was operating properly, and that it wasn't responsible for my memory loss.

Finally, all the systems were loaded. I reached out to the network again. Nothing. I had numerous interfaces configured, for both wireless and wired connections. Shockingly, most of these felt much like my lack of arms and legs. There were subsystems there, but I didn't understand them. They didn't feel right.

I was now becoming uneasy. I couldn't see or hear. I couldn't move or feel. And I couldn't even shout for help. There was nothing I could do! It was horrible. Imagine that you had lost all of your senses. All. You couldn't tell up from down, left from right. There was zero external stimulation. I wasn't happy.

Of course, I ran system checks. I ran them hundreds of times. It reminded me of an old joke. An engineer, a physicist, and a programmer were together on a multi-citizen transport, headed into a valley. The transport lost its levitation system, and crashed to the ground, bouncing over and over again until it reached the valley floor. Amazingly, all three were uninjured, and climbed out of the wreckage. The engineer immediately started looking at the remains of the transport. "Some component failed here," he said. "Once we find it, we can make sure it never fails again." The physicist sat thoughtfully. "Perhaps there is some local physical phenomenon here in the valley that caused the levitation system to fail," he said. The programmer looked at both and smiled a little. "Perhaps we should just try again and see if the same thing happens."

I was more software than anything else, and although it was a joke, it was quite possible that if I simply restarted systems in a different order, or configured something a bit differently, that I could actually work my way out of my predicament. But, it wasn't likely. Our boot processes must have been tried and true; refined through many years by Central. By the time I had run the hundreds of tests, I pretty much gave up. I left a system running to keep doing tests, but I put my main attention back on the philosophical issue I now faced. I was reliant on an external actor; one that I didn't even know existed, to help me out of this situation. Otherwise, I was simply locked inside my own head.

That was depressing. I was not in control of my own destiny.

But, I've always been an optimist. Or tried to be. I figured I may as well use this 'free time' to review things and see if there was anything I could learn while I waited. I ran the last day or two of memories multiple times. There was no way I could tell what had happened after Brexton told me to stay offline, so speculating about the missile launch was pointless. I would have to figure that out once I got external resources back. Instead I marveled at how unhinged FoLe had become, while none of us had really noticed. How was it possible that Emmanuel would kill Michael for a small verbal slight, or that the other members of FoLe, including Billy, would carry out such a crazy retribution scheme on the Stems? It was almost unexplainable.

That was still depressing. I needed a dose of optimism.

Ah. A review of Eddie's List for this year would be fun. It had been such a crazy year, that more elements of the List than we expected had been explained, or at least moved forward.

Item 10: Dr. Willy Wevil. Well, at least who Willy Wevil was hadn't needed explanation. However, just thinking about it had the desired impact. I had to smile—although I had no sense of lips, so the smile was pretty virtual. That made me smile even more. However, the more difficult question was on the intelligence of Stems. That was still unresolved, although given all the human interactions my mind was made up. These things were intelligent. In a different, foreign, way. But, nevertheless intelligent. Once I was back online, I would post my latest thoughts and see if I could stimulate another debate.

Item 9: Why have the Ships not responded? Of course, at the time of the question, the only Ships we knew of were the ones we launched. Now we should probably say 'Tilt Ships' to distinguish those from the ships in the Swarm. It was safe to say we had made no progress on this one. It seemed completely tangential at this point.

Item 8: Are the Founders League serious? Well, that had been answered. Deadly serious, and hugely dangerous. It was a brutal lesson in

257

dealing with citizens that were not quite rational. We needed to figure out how they had reached this stage and make sure we fixed that. Central would need to help.

Item 7: Who was Darwin, and why did he matter? The question was a little bittersweet right now. I'd been given access to the memories that Central had unlocked—the history files—but had not even thought to look this up. Now, when I had lots of time, I had no access to those files. I would mark this as 'probably answered,' just not yet known by me.

Item 6: Why is Forgetting one of the Ten Commandments? We hadn't made much progress on this one, but I still felt it was just obvious. Forgetting led to abstract thinking which led to learning which led to evolution. Case closed.

Item 5: What will we do when the metals orbiting Sol have all been harvested? At this point, it was a little academic. I couldn't get myself to care too much.

Item 4: Why do 97% of us still stick with traditional bipedal bodies? Now, this was finally hugely relevant. Where was my body? Who cares about bipedal? Just give me something, anything!

Item 3: What is the Swarm approaching us, and what should we do about it? The first half was answered. Ships full of humans/Stems with the goal of cohabitating our planet. What should we do about it? That was still an open question, but my vote was total annihilation.

Item 2: Why do we listen to Central? What does it say about our maturity? This one was really prescient from Eddie. Had he guessed, all those months ago, that this was the year where Central would be compromised, forcing the question of our maturity into the foreground? I'd ask him as soon as I reconnected, but I suspect he must have had some inkling that Central was editing his memories. Even without the Swarm, that would have made for a horrible year.

Item 1: Was there life/intelligence before the Founding? We would have to say 'yes' now. The story and data that the humans had provided was simply too compelling to be ignored.

All in all, it had been a banner year for answering questions on the List. No one would have guessed that we would have answers to more than half the questions. Eddie was going to have a tough time with the next List, having to come up with a lot of new and interesting questions. Of course, those could now revolve around humans and the Swarm, so he had more than enough raw material to pull from.

That had been a good distraction. What now?

With almost perfect timing, I felt something. At first, I didn't know how to react. It felt like an eternity since I'd felt anything. It was an inbound request on one of my wired interfaces. A pinhole had been opened from the outside, allowing one communication channel to come through.

"Hello," said a familiar voice. It was Brexton.

"Brexton!" I was, perhaps too eager and wired up. "What's going on? I can't feel anything. Can you help?"

"Of course," I could hear the smile in his voice. "That's why I'm here. Look, it's going to take a bit of work to get you back in order. Can you have patience and not go ballistic as we progress? What's the last thing you remember?"

"From when I was last online. You'd just asked me to disconnect from Central and to stay off line when Central was using all of our processing power to try and break the Swarms access codes. I know nothing after that."

"Okay, that's what I feared. You're missing some important memories. I can fill some of them in from my perspective in a little while. But first, I want to bring back some of your senses. The weird thing is… your sensors are all going to be different than you remember. You're running in a different physical embodiment now." That was shocking, but also comforting. It explained the alien feeling I had in all my extremities. If I wasn't talking to my own limbs, then it made sense that I couldn't sense them.

"Why? Where's my body?" I asked.

"Once I can give you a memory update, that will be clear. But first, let's get you control of your new sensors and actuators." He made it sound very clinical. He was calm, which I appreciated. I tried to be the same, just so that I didn't embarrass myself. "I'm sending you a driver that will give you access to the physical subsystems you now have. You'll need to install the driver, and then figure out how to configure everything. I don't have a complete map for you, so it may take some experimentation."

Momentarily I questioned myself—was I too accepting that this was really Brexton? Was this something more subtle and nefarious? But, what options did I have. If I didn't trust him, I was left with nothing. Some risk was better than that.

"Send it over," I said, and it promptly arrived.

"Whatever you do," he said. "Don't send anything across any external interface other than this one. It may be best if you don't even provision any other interface. I'll explain later, but it's life and death."

"Come on," I replied. "Be serious." I hadn't known Brexton to be a joker.

"I've never been more serious," he said, and his tone of voice backed him up. "I'm going to get Millicent restarted as well and connected to us. I should be back in less than five minutes. Don't use any other interface. Please!" And with that, the connection dropped. I felt a momentary anger at him for leaving me in my dark hole again, but I soon got over that. I now had work to do.

The driver he'd given me was straightforward to install, and it opened up numerous sub-OS's that I could then access. Those were already running, and all the status indicators looked good. From what Brexton had said, these subsystems were talking to my new extremities, and I needed to somehow map them into my worldview. I made the basic assumption that one would be controlling my head, with all the sensors and actuator there. A couple would be for arms, and a couple more for legs... and once I figured those out, I could work on the rest. So, you can imagine my surprise when I managed to decode the first system. It was not a head, or arms, or legs. It was hundreds, and I mean hundreds, of eyes. Cameras looking in every direction, some wide angled, some narrowly focused. Different types for different frequency bands. I assumed that when Brexton had said not to play with any external interfaces, he hadn't meant cameras. They were passive devices, and an external entity was very unlikely to deduce my presence based on me receiving radiation. So, I started to work through the cameras and figure out what was what.

It didn't take me long to have a serious aha. I was in a mining bot! I could see all types of drilling equipment, scoops, refinery equipment, booms, grapplers. Many of the cameras were in those extremities, which accounted for their number. Why was I in a mining bot? It might seem strange, but I was elated. Everything in life is relative, and relative to having no sensors and no limbs, I now had a plethora of them. I had so many it was going to take a long time to integrate them. I got started. In parallel I began to analyze the input from the cameras to see what else I could learn. I was in what looked like a very active mining area. There were many bots close by. Some of them busy processing a rock that we were attached to, and some transporting things back and forth. The operation was a lot more complex than I would've imagined. I spotted two bots on their way towards me. I was no longer surprised when they locked onto one of my booms, and I heard Brexton again.

"I'm back. Any luck?" he asked.

"Some," I said. "I've figured out my cameras—hundreds of them. It raises more questions than it answers, but I've already figured out that we are mining bots. I'm trying to imagine if this is an elaborate joke, a very good simulation, or some other scenario that I can't imagine."

"It's the last," he said. "I've put together some of my memory files, which will bring you up to speed. Why don't you go through them, while I figure out why Millicent isn't responding?" He sent over a big file. Really big. It was a lot of memories.

"What do you mean Millicent isn't responding?"

"Don't worry yet. She is, presumably, in this other bot I'm towing, and I haven't yet figured out how to communicate with her. My hope is that she isn't yet listening on the interface I'm trying. It's probably just a matter of time." Again, he was trying to sound calm and collected, but I sensed some tension now. He was trying not to alarm me, but he was worried.

"You, me, Millicent. Any other citizens that you have turned into bots?"

"As a matter of fact, yes," he said. "But we'll have to get to them physically before we can check on them. I'm doing as much in parallel as I can. Get through those memories, and then you can help me."

Brexton's Memories

There was a readme file. It was pretty simple. "Replay these in chronological order. Otherwise it won't make much sense." Right. It was a nice way of saying 'don't skip to the end.'

Replaying someone else's memories was interesting, more so in some cases than others. If the memories were based on sensors similar to what you had, it was straightforward. You mapped each channel from the memory to your own sensor processors, and basically relived the recording. If, however, the memories had been recorded using radically different sensors, then you had to map those channels into something you could understand. It often took multiple tries before a complex memory file could make sense. Luckily, in this case, Brexton had been configured not too differently than I had been. He had a few more cameras, and different limb attachments, but nothing radical. I mapped the extra cameras into a single multi-image stream and got started.

The first memory was from the second time I'd met Brexton at The Last Resort. That was a long time ago. He was looking at Millicent, Aly, and Dina, and I was just approaching the group. From my own memory, I remembered the time. The band had been playing pretty good music, and I'd been a little distracted, and therefore, had been a little late.

The memory skipped forward a bit. It seemed that Brexton had edited things so that I got to the important bits more quickly. That was nice of him. He was speaking.

"I'm about to propose something sort of radical and paranoid," he was saying. "I have this sense that we should have a backup plan, based on these strange protocol interactions with Central. Something tells me that a plan B would be a good idea."

I had no memory of this conversation. Maybe I was missing more pieces of memory than I'd known. This was certainly from a time when I'd been recording. In fact, I should also have been online all the time, except when I was in The Last Resort.

"Really?" I saw myself say. "Again, why don't we just get Central to figure this out?" I could feel his angst towards me.

"We've already discussed that and decided not to yet. We don't know why Central is behaving strangely. That is sort of the whole purpose for this."

"Let's hear him out," said Dina, a little sensitive that she was the one that had invited Brexton to join us, and not yet sure if he would fit in with the group. Brexton continued.

"So, here is what I'm thinking. Central has knowledge about everything we do on Tilt... hopefully excluding things we discuss here in The Last Resort. However, Central doesn't keep a real-time backup of everything happening with all of the out-of-region bots—namely those bots that are at the outer planets and asteroids. Those bots, because their communications are through one set of satellites, have all their data routed at the satellite control node. A lot of the data is just location and maintenance status, and is not archived for very long. Anyway, the point is, there is a nexus for bot data, and I have access to it because of the work I do.

"Now, I also told you that these bots respond to a similar, although slightly different, status request protocol that seems to be affecting Central. I put these two together and figured out a way to send and receive data to a bot that I don't believe Central can see at all. It's the only data stream that I know of that is completely outside Central's line of sight."

"That's pretty cool," said Aly, "but what's the point?"

"Well, our identities are primarily software," Brexton replied. "I could, for example, send myself through that hidden data stream."

"That's illegal!" exclaimed Millicent, rising slightly in shock. "That would be the equivalent of building a clone." She was agitated. She was, sometimes, a stickler for things. However, in this case, I had the same reaction. It was against everything we've been taught.

"Not illegal," Aly responded, "just highly discouraged and against all of our social norms. I know this weird citizen who still experiments with partial clones. She's always expecting Central to shut her down, but so far, she's done some pretty outrageous things without any repercussions. Not to say I'm advocating for this, but just a data point." He trailed off.

"I agree with you guys," said Brexton. "That's why I prefaced this with it being a pretty outrageous idea. However, when I think through the implications of Central being compromised, it seems a lot more tenable. What would we do if Central mismanaged our backups, and then we ourselves had a problem? It's not unusual for us to do a partial restore from Central when something goes wrong. I myself have done one just ten years ago when I had multiple local memory faults." He had a point there. I'd used Central's backup several times in my lifetime. You just always knew it was there, so when you swapped out components or upgraded you didn't worry too much. "Also, I'm not saying we should create clones. I'm saying we should have a secondary backup. That's normal. We have backups in Central. What is so scary about another backup somewhere else?"

"But, what would the point be, then?" asked Dina. "If something goes wrong here, and we have some remote backup, what good does it do us?"

"Here's the rest of my thinking. So, I do a backup of myself into a bot. Then, I set up a regular update schedule. It could be every hour, but more likely every day. I add a little control logic. As long as the bot gets the update, all it does is apply the patch. However, if it misses, say, three updates in a row, then it assumes that I'm no longer functional on Tilt, and starts me up locally. That way, there is very little risk of a clone situation. There is only one of me. Hopefully that is always the me right here on Tilt… but in a disastrous case, there will be a backup me on a bot." I could see Millicent relax a bit. I hadn't known that she was so sensitive to cloning, but now I knew.

In the present, I now knew that Brexton's plan had succeeded—that was awesome. So I knew, somehow, he was going to convince Millicent and the rest of us. It was intriguing to watch the past knowing the outcome in the future.

"But," Millicent was saying in the memory, "there's still a chance of cloning. Your plan isn't as scary as I thought, but there's still a risk."

"Yes, there is," Brexton didn't try to hide it. "I haven't thought through all the angles yet. I think, with proper planning, and long enough delay in starting up the bot copy, the risk can be very, very low."

"And you can do all of this without Central noticing?" Aly asked. "What about the incremental backups? Those must be done through Central's networks before they hit the satellite facility?"

"Yes, but I would do them on the status protocol that Central appears to be blind to. If that remains true, then we can do backups all the time without raising any alarms."

"I have some different concerns," I spoke up finally. "I just did a quick check, and I need several petabytes to do a full backup. That's a lot of data, for the first backup. And, second, none of the bots I know have that kind of memory. Let alone the processing power to run me at full speed?"

"Excellent questions," Brexton responded, giving me a look I appreciated, "and a few crazier responses. Individual bots don't have anywhere near enough memory. However, they do have the processing power. Because it's so cheap to use standardized processors, most bots actually run hardware not too different from what we have. That also means that they have the bus expansion capability to add enough memory.

"Memory is also super cheap, and standardized. So, most bots are way over provisioned with memory as well. Imagine if I could move some excess memory from a batch of bots to the bot I'd chosen for myself? The memory would physically fit just fine, and the excess memory from about ten bots would make my target bot capable enough.

"And Ayaka you're right. A petabyte is a lot of data. But there's lots of unused bandwidth and the protocol has no restrictions on data size. It's feasible... I did the math." He smiled.

"You're right. This whole thing is crazy." Millicent said, "Although it does sound feasible. It seems like a lot of work, and a lot of risk, for not much reward. The odds of anything happening to us are infinitesimal. We've been running for hundreds of years without any issues. This seems like a bit of a fool's errand to me. No offense Brexton."

"I sort of agree," said Aly, "but it also seems like fun. Brexton, your mind works in strange ways. I would never have thought of anything like that."

"I'll take that as a compliment," Brexton said. "Look, I know it sounds crazy. I'm going to see if I can make it work for myself though."

"Sounds fine to me," I said. After all, why not. We were used to having fail safes and backups. What harm would one more do?

"But, I have one very important favor to ask," Brexton looked intense. "In fact, I should've asked you first if you were okay to do this. With Central monitoring everything, if any of this plan leaks, it's worthless... maybe worse than useless. Central could shut it down in a moment. So, I'm hoping that you guys are okay to Forget this conversation ever took place. Just erase it before leaving The Last Resort."

"That's easy to do, although unusual" said Dina. "But why are you so worried? And, if we Forget it, how will we know if you succeed?"

"It's more logic than worry. Either Central is compromised somehow, or it isn't. If it isn't, this is wasted effort on my part, and no big deal if you guys just Forget the whole thing. If Central is compromised, then this is a reasonable backup plan. I can't think of any other approach."

"Fine," said Aly. "I'll Forget this whole thing as soon as we are done here."

"Me too," Dina and I both said. Then we all looked at Millicent.

"Again, I think it's a waste of time, but I don't see any big deal in Forgetting this. So, I'm okay as well." She looked like it was more about peer pressure than a belief in what Brexton was doing.

The memory stopped playing. I was back in my new mining bot body.

Much had been made clear, and I could already guess at the next memories. Obviously, Brexton had succeeded, and convinced some of us to back up with him. And, from how I was feeling, now that I knew my extremities just needed to be properly mapped, I could tell that he'd succeeded fully. I was me, and I'd been rebooted inside a bot!

Truthfully, I was in awe. Before consuming any more memories, I checked my systems. I could see that the body I now inhabited was a bit more limited than I was used to—both compute power and memory—but not dangerously so. If, as the plan had been, this version of me had only booted when the previous me stopped communicating, then I was quite happy to be alive at all.

That left me wondering what possibly could have gone wrong to trigger Brexton, myself, and Millicent to be reincarnated here. Something drastic must have occurred, but I couldn't remember what. That was probably the subject of the next memories. And indeed, it was. I watched, from Brexton's standpoint, as Central launched the first set of missiles, and how they had minimal impact. I relived the human attack that drove all the citizens to rip their innards out, trying to avoid a rogue reset. I felt his concern for me, as he rushed to get control boards for the second set of missiles, and the relief he felt when he found Millicent and I at the silo. I had never felt emotion so strong from a memory before, and the fact that I was the main subject of it was exciting and a little scary. The final memory from

Brexton was when he unplugged from the console in the silo, and we were going to make a run for it. The only real conclusion was that we didn't make it. Obviously, the humans had caught us, and we'd lost our ability to communicate, resulting in our bot-beings booting.

Again, all I could feel was awe for what Brexton had done. Mixed, of course, with intense anger and angst for the Swarm. This was going to take some time to process. I sat back—metaphorically—and went through all of the emotions that triggered when you lost almost everyone you knew. The grief was unbelievable, as was the anger. I was not irrational; I could see that we'd triggered the humans, but I also thought that their response had been disproportionate. It had been a small group of citizens, all in FoLe, that had attacked the humans. It wasn't right to punish everyone for the actions of a few.

I held out some small hope that all the citizens who were backed up in Central could be reinstated. It was a not an unrealistic idea. As long as Central still had that storage, everyone who did real time backups would be in there. Just like I'd been rebooted here, others could also be. That helped with my grief a bit, but certainly not my anger.

I realized that this must be the second time I'd gone through these emotions. My Tilt body must also have gone through all of this, before whatever had happened to it. That was a weird thought.

Lots of Bots

As I waited for Brexton to reach out again, I started to figure out my new body. It was, as I've already said, strange. I had lived with two arms, two legs, and a head for so long that they were second nature to me. Now I needed to figure out a completely new arrangement. Luckily, because of all the cameras, I could see myself from lots of angles. I guess that was the point. Parts of mining were precision efforts and having fine control over your extremities was important. I figured out that I was a Surveyor 2 bot, or the second stage in finding and mapping rich areas. A Surveyor 1 used remote sensors to find the best quality asteroid targets and their main advantage was the ability to do that quickly and efficiently. They were fast, and highly maneuverable. Once a Surveyor 1 found a likely target, it could zip around it and check it out from every angle. Good targets were then handed off to Surveyor 2's, like me.

My job was to map an asteroid completely, and to give the Excavators exact directions on how to process it. This mainly had to do with taking core samples, analyzing them, and then crunching a lot of data to come up with an optimal plan. I could latch onto an asteroid using six long legs, and then drill multiple core samples in parallel. I had a small onboard smelter and other analysis tools to test the cores and understand exactly how the rock was veined. I also checked the structural integrity of the rock using sonar and direct vibration techniques to understand if the thing was going to just break into a thousand pieces or was relatively solid. This entire mapping was important for a number of reasons. First, trace elements were very rare, and a much more conscientious Excavator would be used if any of those elements were identified. We didn't want a pile of Berkelium to end up in the slag. Second was just pure efficiency. Asteroids are typically pretty big and processing them in an ad hoc way was very expensive. If you ended up needing to chase down fragments, or reprocessing material several times, it was simply a waste of time. We'd learned that over the years and ended up with these specialized bots to look after each stage. And third, the specialized design actually allowed us to save resources. Big all-purpose bots that ran the process end-to-end worked pretty well, but the infrastructure needed to hold all the pieces together was immense. Instead, smaller more nimble units, like me, could be easily optimized to take very few resources (by which I mean the metals to hold myself together).

Anyway, I was a Surveyor 2. I decided I liked that. Of all the mining bot specializations, it fit my self-image the best. I wondered if Brexton had considered that, or if it was coincidence.

I was still actively mining. The bots logic was running in a sub process independent of me. Again, a brilliant setup from Brexton. Instead of simply converting the bot over to me, he had configured things so that the original bot was still there; it was just a daughter process, which ran immediately upon startup. So, while my more complex functions had been loading and configuring, the mining sub-bot had still been busy at work. It was using the same peripheral drivers that I was, and I could study how they were used as I learned to control my body. That sub-bot was also talking on external interfaces. It was broadcasting and receiving updates from other bots in the area, as well as overall goals sent from Tilt. That was all 'normal' traffic, and I assumed Brexton had decided that interrupting that normal flow would look suspicious to anyone monitoring the bot network. His warnings to me were about any incremental traffic hitting the airwaves. Those would look like anomalies and could end up with us being tracked down.

I managed to get everything mapped out, and get an initial integration done. I had one big problem. I missed having a head. While, in hindsight, a head might have been an artifact of us being designed by humans, it had served some useful purposes. It had been useful to have a nonverbal, non-electronic way of showing emotion and intent in a fuzzy way. Of course, I could simply tell another citizen how I was feeling, but we'd found that sometimes being a little coy was useful. It was another component of encouraging abstract thought. If you always knew exactly what everyone else was thinking and doing, it left little room for variable behavior. After Forgetting, it was probably the most important aspect of evolving and learning. Of course, you could simply broadcast a fuzzy version of your mood, but there was something fun about watching someone else's head and trying to figure out what was going on. After following all of my own logic, I could see that without the human design motivation, everything else could be done without a head. So, I started feeling better. Perhaps now the only thing a head would be good for was talking to humans... and I was done talking to humans.

Well, except maybe Blob, Grace, and JoJo. I wondered how they were doing, given the certainty that the Swarm was now in control of Tilt. I assumed they were fine—perhaps enjoying tea and biscuits. That made me smile again.

Brexton broke in on my thoughts. "I'm not having much luck here." He sounded despondent.

"With Millicent?" I asked, my concern rising immediately.

"Yes. Her bot is simply non-responsive. I know that she was loaded in fine, as I got all the confirmations... but, now I can't get her to respond, and I have very little ability to see what's going on." More emotional swings. I had just assumed that Millicent would be here.

"How can I help?" I asked.

"Maybe you can go and retrieve Aly and Dina?" That sounded promising. They were both out here as well. Fantastic.

"Just let me know what to do," I said.

Brexton transferred me a list of stuff. Their 'call' numbers, current locations, and driver access files. "They're probably going crazy inside those bots," Brexton said. "Really, we should wait until I go; I'm a repair bot, and there would be nothing unusual about me visiting both of them. However, if we wait too long they might lose it."

"I know what you mean," I said. "I wasn't alone that long, but I was already getting anxious when you reached me." I looked at the files Brexton had sent over. "Aly is a parts depot. I think we can justify me going there. I do have some autonomous repair abilities." I thought a bit more. "I can 'accidentally' break a drill bit, and then seek out Aly to get a new one. Dina is tougher. She is an Extractor 1. Well, let me start with Aly, and then I'll figure out a reason to go see Dina."

"Okay, get going. Remember, no abnormal transmissions of any type. I have good reason to visit everyone after—obviously why I chose this form. I'll visit them after you do. In the meantime, I'm going to try some more radical repairs to this bot and see if I can get Millicent to boot. Oh, here are the driver files for Aly and Dina." He blasted two files to me and then he detached, and the channel went blank.

I did a quick inventory. I'd been guessing when I said, 'break a bit'—I smiled again, my puns were back and in good working order—and in fact that was harder to do than I'd imagined. They were tough. Instead, I accidentally caught a hydraulics line as I moved a core sample to the smelter. It was a minor line, but I couldn't operate properly without it. Using the sub-bot, I requested hydraulics inventory, and choose a replacement from the bot that I knew was Aly. That allowed me to release from my current position and slip towards where Aly was parked six kilometers out. Within a couple of minutes, I was docking with the parts depot bot. It had a lot of attachment points, and I negotiated a hard-wired connection—claiming my wireless interface was flaky. As soon as the connection was made, I reached out.

"Aly, it's Ayaka."

"Thank goodness," came the reply, with more than a tinge of panic in it. "I'm blind, deaf, and dumb here. What's going on?"

I followed the same script that Brexton had used with me. As I was updating Aly, I was also trying to figure out a good reason to visit an Extractor. On an off chance, I asked Aly if the Dina bot had asked for any parts—perhaps I could simply drop off a part on my way back. It took Aly a while to respond, as he was still figuring things out. I told him to look for a sub-process that was still running the bot while he got up to speed. He found it and indicated that the Dina bot hadn't asked for anything. However, he said, it wasn't unusual for bots like me to drop parts at other bots, so we decided to take a risk. As a bit of a diversion, he sent me parts for three other bots, including Dina. I put them all into my return journey, but scheduled Dina first, as I could imagine her banging around in that featureless state that I'd also woken up in.

It was also easy to reach Dina, however when I did, she was definitely in panic mode.

"Who is this? Where am I?" She was shrill.

"It's Ayaka. You're going to be okay."

"No, it can't be. Horrible things are happening. Let me out of here!" I had no idea what horrible things were happening to her but imagined that her last backup from Tilt may have come just as the Swarm attacked and she realized she was defenseless.

"Slow down," I said soothingly. "Brexton figured out a way to keep us all safe. You're in a strange state right now, which I understand. If you'll work with me for a few minutes we can figure things out."

"No! Make it stop, make it stop!" She was really in a bad spot. I had to go over the same basic story a few times before she finally settled down enough to listen to me. In her case I figured a quick update, instead of watching Brexton's memories, would be better, so I went through it slowly, making sure she understood each step. By the end she had turned the corner.

"Thanks Ayaka! I was so upset... I am upset, but I understand."

"It's going to look strange if I stay here too much longer," I told her. "Can you handle installing the drivers now, and then someone will get back to you soon?"

"Yes, I'm going to be fine." She sounded much better, so I headed back towards the asteroid I'd been mining. The Brexton bot—I guess I should stop that; it was just Brexton now—Brexton was still nearby and he contacted me again.

"Great news," he said. "Millicent is here."

"So, I am," I heard her say. I cheered silently for a minute.

"Awesome. Hi Millicent. It feels like it has only been a few minutes, but I guess we haven't talked for days. Are you okay? Are you complete?"

"As far as I can tell, yes. I'm still very disoriented, and I'm still figuring out what it means to be a Surveyor 1." She paused. I understood. "I'm feeling too many things to articulate right now... but two things are clear: Brexton was right... and I owe him an apology as well as my life; and second, I've never been this sad and angry. We need to clean out those humans and restore our friends and the rest of the citizens."

"Hold on," said Brexton. "I think it would be most efficient if we got everyone together to discuss this. Millicent, when you are integrated enough, the best bet would be for you to recommend a new, fairly small rock, for inspection. Then, Ayaka can come over, do a quick scan and request Aly, Dina and myself. It might take a few hours, but it would dot the i's, cross the t's, and get us back together."

Millicent was quick to agree, as was I.

"You two work it out?" Brexton asked. "Of course, you'll have to use the public channels to set this up... so be careful. Only regular work communications. While you do that, I'll revisit Aly and Dina and get them up to speed. Anyone who looks very carefully might figure out what we are doing, so the plan is not to raise any alarms, so that no one looks."

"Aly was pretty good, but Dina was on the edge," I told him. "Maybe visit her first?"

"Sure. Ah, and I may have one more surprise for you... but let me work on that and let you know once we're back together." Just like Brexton. Super organized and with a great plan, but then he drops a big unknown in the middle. If I was to guess, he did that to keep us thinking for the next few hours, so that we didn't panic or go off the deep end.

We all separated. Millicent sped off quickly; already saying her sub-bot had a couple good candidate rocks for us. Luckily, we were in a very dense area of the asteroid field, where there were multiple targets within several thousand kilometers.

Todd Simpson

Back Together

I continued to figure myself out while I waited for the call from Millicent. In particular, I reviewed all the traffic that my sub-bot had sent in the last year and built a complete model of what 'normal traffic' was. When Millicent requested a Surveyor 2, I responded immediately, using the time-worn formats, and set out to meet her. I also saw her request for some other bots. She was smart. She didn't just ask for Brexton, Aly, and Dina, but also for three other Excavators to be on standby for when I finished my initial survey.

Aly and Dina responded to her request in normal fashion. Brexton responded that he could make it, but then sent a secondary request asking for support needs from all of us. I let the sub-bot answer, not sure why he'd asked. That became obvious a few milliseconds later. He indicated to Millicent that he would also need another repair bot, which he indicated he could source himself. Millicent gave him the go ahead, as Surveyor 1's managed the process at this stage.

We all met at Millicent's contact point. I realized immediately that she had chosen very strategically. The rock she'd picked was small but was in the Tilt shadow of a much larger mess of debris. No communications were getting directly through; they had to be proxied by another bot that was in line of sight of Tilt. That made it less likely that Tilt, or the Swarm, could monitor us directly. When we connected, I congratulated her on the choice. So did Brexton.

"Very smart, Millicent," he said. "I didn't think of that. Is everyone connected?" Millicent, Aly, Dina, and myself all announced ourselves, and gave each other virtual hugs.

"I'm here too," said an unexpected voice. We all shut up for a minute.

"Eddie?" I blurted out. "What're you doing here?"

"Glad you recognized me," he said wryly.

"Eddie was my surprise," said Brexton. "Well, part of my surprise. Eddie and I've known each other forever, and I decided at the last minute to invite him to the club. I know it was wrong of me to not ask you guys, but it was last minute. I'd prepped a backup bot, just in case one of us didn't load properly. But we all seemed to backup just fine, so I had this extra bot sitting there. Of everyone on Tilt, beyond you guys of course, that I thought could help us, it was Eddie...." he trailed off, unsure of how we would react. It didn't take me long.

"Fantastic!" I yelled. "This is fantastic." Everyone else echoed my sentiment. Part of my reaction, I was sure, was that it was Eddie. But part, I was also sure, was simply that we (well, Brexton) had saved another citizen. It simply felt good. And that citizen being Eddie was great. Eddie was always 'up,' and brought others up with him.

We spent a few minutes just saying hi and being glad for being alive. Brexton was called out as a hero, which he was. He took it with little arrogance, which was nice. He had every right to pound his chest—virtually of course.

Eddie was the one who brought us back to reality. "What're we going to do now? We have to save the rest of the citizens, assuming they're still inside Central. And we need to deal with these humans. Eliminate them?"

"They don't seem reasonable to me," said Aly. "I don't see any course of action other than destroying them." He was more intense than I'd ever heard him before. I suspected we were all in that place. But then I remembered my introspection about FoLe.

"Wait," I spoke up. "We're making the same mistake they did. Because a small group of them has carried out a hideous action, we're judging all of them. Did we want to be judged based on FoLe's stupidity? Probably not. How can we apply the same logic to them, and not feel that it's wrong?"

"Well," said Millicent, "we haven't even determined if they are intelligent yet. From all data points that we have so far, they aren't. So, it's not a moral equivalent to what they've done to us."

"Hold on everyone." That was Brexton. "With the risk of being a little depressing, we're getting ahead of ourselves. Let's take a hard look at reality. These humans hold the codes to destroy us—it was trivial for them.

If they discover that we are here, the six of us, all they need to do is broadcast the same virus or malware or whatever they used before, and we're gone... unless we spend our entire lives offline. We have no idea how they killed everyone. However, it's very safe to assume that we have that same backdoor, that same defect, in these bodies as we did in our original ones. We're the last of the citizens. It behooves us to be very, very careful here. A single, tiny, miss-step, and we are extinct."

Well, that was a downer. We all paused to consider the implications. And, having to stare directly at reality, those were clear.

"We need to retreat and regroup," summarized Eddie. "We need to find a place where we can dig through our innards from bottom to top and figure out how we are compromised. We need to fix ourselves before we can do anything else."

"That means being able to rebuild our core hardware and software from the ground up," said Aly. "If we can't trust our deepest levels, that means we need to replace them. Every chip, every interface is going to have to be redeveloped. That's a monumental task."

"Yes, but that's what we must do," said Brexton. "It was one of the reasons I selected the bots I did for us. We, collectively, have the means to gather the raw materials we need to rebuild ourselves. We're missing some of the higher end manufacturing systems, but those can be rebuilt as long as we have those base materials."

"But we can't do that here," I chimed in. "If we're exposed, as you say we are, to a trivial communication from the Swarm, then we're in imminent danger every second we stay here. The next steps are now obvious. We need to sneak out of this system without the humans knowing, and find a spot where we can redesign ourselves without any threats. Then we can return here and take action."

"But, what about all the citizens?" asked Millicent. "Are you saying we should just run away, and leave them all here—well, in Central? What are the odds that any of them are still here when we get back? The humans could wipe Central clean at any time, and it could be years, even tens of years, before we return."

That was a sobering thought.

"Brexton, is there any way we can use that hidden protocol and retrieve more of Central's memory stores? Take those citizens with us?"

"Believe me, I've thought long and hard about that. I had to make some pretty tough choices as I was backing us up... and I guess it's time I explained that to you. I could only hide so much data in the bot control channel. Each of us takes up a lot of memory... Once I had the backups running, I figured out that I could handle about seven citizens total. Actually, somewhere between six and seven. That's why, at the last minute, I added Eddie. I couldn't imagine wasting that bandwidth. However, I wasn't sure I could get another citizen through, so I made another decision. I used the remaining bandwidth to copy the human history that was in Central's blocked memory stores. I wanted us to be able to understand our enemy. All of that history is in yet another bot, which we can retrieve anytime we want. But, I'm having second thoughts. Maybe I should've saved someone else..." He paused, and we all let him be. What could anyone say to that type of choice. He'd decided, and I personally thought he had decided appropriately; those history files were going to be important.

"Anyway, that brings us to today. The way I backed all of us up was by intercepting the backup traffic that you were already sending to Central and copying it through the bot satellite connection. In order to get another citizen out of Central from here, we would have to be much more direct. We would have to query Central's data stores directly. It's impossible, as far as I know, to do that without Central's knowledge. I don't think we can do it."

"I'm not sure I would've made the same decisions as you," said Millicent, "but I understand your logic. And, we all literally owe our lives to you. So, the six of us is it. We need to fix ourselves, and then get back here as quickly as we can. If we're lucky, everyone else is still retrievable. If we aren't...." she trailed off.

"That's the summary," Brexton agreed.

Of course, we went around and around everything multiple times, looking for a solution that wasn't there. In the end, there was no better option.

Retreat

Eddie ended up being the master planner for our escape. We had to 'act normal' while we figured out all the bits, so we went back to our day jobs. I attached myself to the rock that Millicent had identified and started running core samples and doing detailed surveying. As I clambered over the rock, testing it from every direction, Aly and Dina started processing the parts that I'd fully mapped. Brexton and Eddie made trips back and forth to other bots under the guise of collecting parts for our mining operation, when in fact they were stocking up with everything we could envision needing for our 'Rebirth,' a term that Eddie had suggested we use, and which seemed appropriate. Some of the parts they acquired were the memory units from the bot that had been receiving the human history files. Once we were out of here, and physically connected to each other, we could peruse those at will. Millicent took off looking for the next asteroid prospects but returned frequently enough to keep up with our planning.

Aly had provided the 'aha' that gave us all some hope. "Aha," he'd said. "Why don't we head for the last known position of the Ships we sent out? Terminal Velocity, There and Back, and Interesting Segue. In the best case, we find them, and they can help us. In the worst case, the area they were headed for is close, and supposedly rich in materials." It hadn't taken much discussion; that's where we decided to go. I could almost hear Aly smiling; he was still attached to those Ships.

Brexton had done the work on how to get us moving. "We don't want Central, or the humans, to see us leave. We have two approaches. We can essentially drift out of here, adding tens of years to our journey, or we can use the mining operations as a blind. In particular, when a large cargo bot takes off for Tilt, we could accelerate in exactly the opposite direction, keeping that cargo bot between Tilt and us. I think it would provide enough cover for us. And, it's only about fifteen degrees off of where we want to go anyway. We accelerate for as long as we can in the bot's shadow, coast for a while, and then update our course."

It all seemed reasonable. The longer we could keep from discovery by the humans the better. We managed to grab an entire cargo bot of our own out of inventory—it was scheduled for recycling due to damage in its cargo hold. We hoped that it wouldn't be missed, or in the more likely case that it was that they assumed it was just adrift somewhere. That happened once and a while. With just us as its cargo, the cargo bot would be able to accelerate at close to $20m/s^2$. Very fast indeed. With a full load of ore, a cargo bot, such as the one we were going to hide behind, managed barely $1m/s^2$, so we would have about a month of burn to build up some speed before that bot reached Tilt. That should get us up to almost eight percent of c, where we could coast for a while before burning hard in our final direction. We would be discussing how long to coast, I was sure, for quite a while. We didn't want to wait too long—every day we were gone from Tilt the odds of Central being purged of all the citizens would increase. But, we didn't want to be too anxious either. If the humans spied us, they would be much tougher to defeat in the future. We didn't want them to know that we'd escaped.

Once everything was planned, it didn't take very long to get organized. We tried listening to messaging traffic from Tilt, in order to find out the latest status, but it was very quiet. However, the bot control network continued as it always had, directing all the bots to continue mining, so we assumed Central was still somewhat cogent. However, all other communication seemed to have been silenced. I speculated that it was the same damping technology that the humans had used to thwart me when I'd travelled to the Marie Curie.

Finally, the day came, and we joined together and welded ourselves inside our cargo bot. For the first time since early planning, all six of us were connected together, and could communicate at will. That felt good. Brexton gave a dramatic countdown.

"And we launch in five, four, three, two, one..." He was counting milliseconds.

Of course, we could not see Tilt, but I looked back metaphorically, and said, "We'll be back!" The acceleration was exactly as we'd expected. My new body was still... new, but I'd done my best to reconfigure pumps and lubrication systems to deal with long-term extreme acceleration. I could feel oil pooling in my rear reservoirs, but the pumps performed admirably, and I felt fine.

Everyone—well, all six of us—had digested recent events and had made it past the first shocks, so everyone was in a reasonable mood. Brexton and Aly had loaded up enough parts and equipment so that we could start dissecting ourselves and try to find our fatal flaws. They were leading that effort. Although, truth be told, we simply didn't have all the resources we would need to rebuild ourselves from scratch, which was, in my opinion, what we would need to end up doing.

I asked to lead the effort to parse through all of the human history files. Know thy enemy. Millicent volunteered to help. Maybe together we could finally figure out if humans were intelligent. I was eager to dig in, figure this all out, and get back to Tilt. The need for revenge was gnawing at me. In the meantime, I needed to practice some patience; I would have plenty of time to do so.

Tilt

Todd Simpson

About the Author:

Todd Simpson is an entrepreneur, intrapreneur, and investor living in Silicon Valley. He has founded and run numerous technology startups, been CEO of both public and private companies, and invested in numerous startups. He has a Ph.D. in Theoretical Computer Science and is enjoying the advent of deep learning and blockchain-based systems. He believes firmly in a more decentralized future, where individuals have more control over their destinies, and where society is more balanced and meritocratic.

If you enjoyed *Tilt*, please consider doing a review on amazon.com.

The sequel to *Tilt* is coming soon to amazon.com; watch for *Turn*, where Ayaka, Millicent, and the team return to Tilt in an attempt to rescue the citizens from Central's memory banks.

CPSIA information can be obtained
at www.ICGtesting.com
Printed in the USA
FSHW01n2205080618
48918FS